The Takeover

Book 1 of the

Occupy Earth Trilogy

Robert Charlton

This book is a work of fiction. Any references to historical events, real people, or real places are used fictitiously. Other names, characters, places, and events are products of the author's imagination, and any resemblance to actual events or places or persons, living or dead, is entirely coincidental.

The Takeover: Book 1 of the *Occupy Earth Trilogy*

First Edition (revised)

ISBN: 9798327502956

Author website: wherewebe.com

Manhattan Ovates

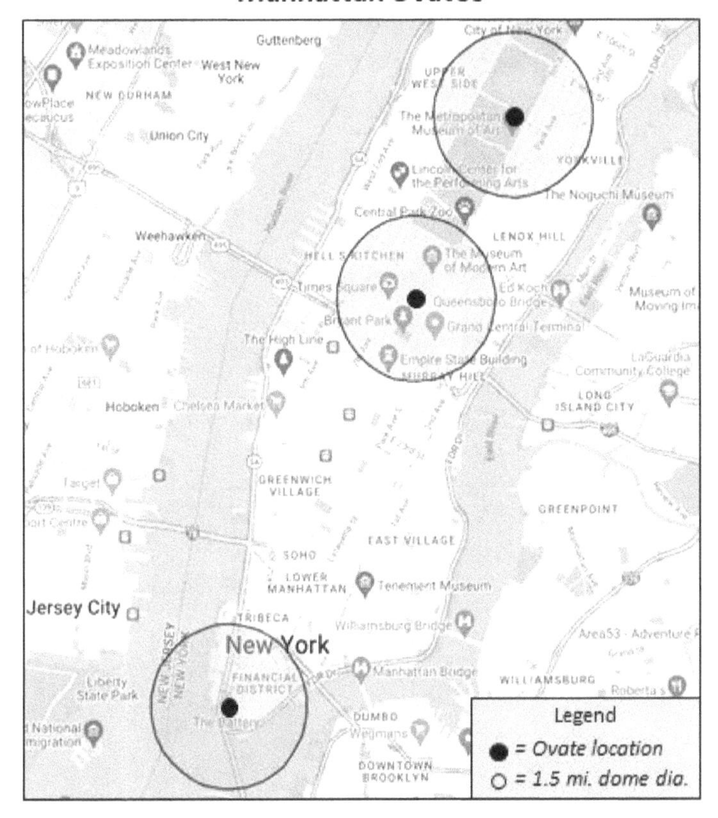

Washington D.C. Ovates

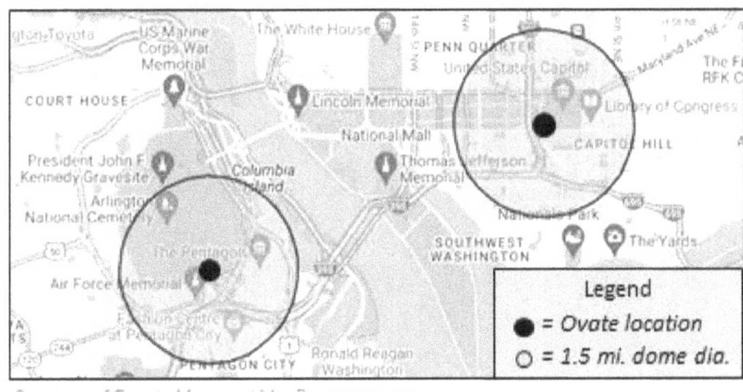

Courtesy of Google Maps and MapDevelopers.com

Prologue

July 5, 2041

The takeover of Earth began so discreetly, it went unnoticed by every human being on the planet.

In America, folks had just finished celebrating the second (and, as it turned out, last) Independence Day of the new decade. Long after the celebrations had ended, during the wee hours of the night, small bits of matter—"seeds" let's call them—began falling from the sky like pollen, drifting on the breeze and eventually planting themselves in the earth. Virtually invisible to the naked eye, they went wholly unremarked, even when falling in full daylight in other parts of the world.

Overnight the Earth's atmosphere was bathed in some fifty million seeds. Wherever they fell, they sprouted, tucked away in the soil or in tiny cracks of concrete. Not every one germinated, but enough did—some five million—to mark the beginning of the end of human supremacy on Earth.

*****

Few places on the planet escaped their reach. Over the next twenty-four hours they fell on all seven continents, every major island chain, and many minor ones too.

The terrain hardly mattered: whether jungle or desert, tundra or grassland, remote farm or busy metropolis, the seeds nestled into whatever bits of soil or sand or muck or gravel they could find and began to grow. Only the millions of seeds that fell into the Earth's oceans and lakes failed to take root and died.

In ten days' time the seeds had grown to the size of pearls. Looking at one, you might have thought it was a plastic bead discarded by a child—a bauble that had been bleached by the sun—but in fact it was now one of the hardest and heaviest materials on Earth.

Like all seeds, they represented *potential*. Tiny dead-looking lumps of matter can sometimes achieve great things. Acorns grow into oaks, cones fall to the ground and become redwoods, and winged maple seeds helicopter down from their parent tree with a full set of instructions on how to grow.

So it was with these seeds. Soon they would grow into something unimaginably big.

All they needed was time.

1

August 1, 2041

Every week they doubled in size, drinking in energy from some unknown source—the sun, perhaps, or the depths of the Earth. Before long they looked like round, translucent eggs.

Most sank down, burying themselves deeper in the soil, hiding there like unharvested potatoes. Those that fell on harder terrain—clay, gravel, cracked concrete, crumbled asphalt—grew half above and half below ground, forming what looked like miniature domes.

In less than a month they had grown to the size of ostrich eggs, and people were beginning to take notice. How could they not? Some had taken root on busy city streets. People were starting to walk around them, peering curiously at them and wondering what on earth they could be. Randomized speed bumps? An avant garde art installation of some sort? Some high-tech monitoring system installed in the ground to invade their privacy in new and creative ways? Who could say? It was still possible to drive over them in a car, but not for much longer.

A few people dug them up where the soil was loose and, with great effort—because they were much heavier than they looked—pried them out of the ground, lugging them back home to study or display as prized knickknacks on their shelves or coffee tables.

Much to their chagrin later on.

The first professional stirrings of interest, the first postings on the internet, the first scientists questioning what they were and where they had come from.

Just what were these things?

*****

In ten days' time the ostrich eggs had grown to the size of rounded watermelons and weighed some three hundred pounds apiece. Coffee tables and display cases exhibiting the prized possessions were beginning to sag and buckle. Those who could manage it lugged them back out of their homes, depositing them in their back yards or in nearby alleys or empty lots, relieved to be done with them once and for all (or so they thought).

Those who couldn't find a way to move a three-hundred-pound knickknack out of their abodes had little choice but to leave them in place. They started worrying they'd made a big mistake, like bringing home a cute little puppy only to discover it was a wolf.

If nothing else they were pretty. They had a deep inner luminosity that seemed to swirl and ripple—which was why they had so quickly became collectors' items in the first place. But they fell out of favor just as quickly due to their absurd weight—not to mention the disconcerting fact that they kept growing bigger.

*****

Ten days later they had grown to the size of prize pumpkins, the kind that win blue ribbons at state fairs—but these pumpkins weighed two tons apiece. They became impossible to move without heavy equipment.

The astounding growth curve of these objects had scientists baffled. Since they couldn't refer to them as "prize pumpkins" and keep their dignity intact, they began calling them *ovates*, but common folk kept calling them eggs—even though by now they were bigger than any egg ever laid by any dinosaur.

Each and every country around the world had ovates. China and Russia accused the U.S. of having unleashed a bizarre new form of biological weapon on the world, while the U.S. and Europe accused China and Russia of the same thing. At an emergency special session of the UN General Assembly, the accusations flew fast and furious. The word *alien* popped up for the first time at the higher echelons of government.

Meanwhile, the internet was abuzz with viral posts and conspiracy theories about the eggs' origins and purpose. Bloggers began to state with absolute certainty that tiny (or not so tiny) aliens were about to hatch out of them. Some claimed the aliens would be the world's salvation, others its downfall.

Scientists the world over hauled the ovates into secure labs and began examining them in detail. Most insisted they were constructs, not biological life forms. They pointed out that eggs don't grow on the outside, nor do they weigh thousands of pounds each. But that didn't stop pundits and bloggers alike from calling them eggs and describing in lurid detail the pterodactyl-sized nightmares that were about to pop out of these puppies at any moment.

2

August 25 – New York City

"Sorry I'm late," Aubrey Powell said with a sigh as she slid into the seat across from Royce Freeman. "Boy, what a day."

Royce had been waiting at the restaurant for some time now but it hardly mattered: Aubrey was worth the wait. Just seeing her made his heart sing. He pushed his drink towards her and said, "Here, maybe this will help."

"God yes." Aubrey took a big sip before pushing it back towards him. "Thanks, much better."

Royce signaled the waiter for another round. "So what's up?"

"Ugh, what's *down* is more like it. You know that luxury condo in Brooklyn Heights that I'm the listing agent for? The one on the eighth floor that's located right on the waterfront? Well, now it's toast. It seems the folks on the ninth floor brought one of those stupid eggs into their home as a souvenir back when it was still small. Now it's the size of a boulder, and last night it became so heavy it fell right through the floor—and kept on falling through all eight floors below it, all the way down to the basement."

"Yikes."

"Yikes is right. So now there's a gaping hole in the floor of every single condo unit in the building, and of course the entire building has been evacuated, and the egg or ovate or whatever you want to call it is still down there somewhere, embedded in the concrete floor."

"Holy shit. So what are you going to do?"

"What *can* I do? Wait for the floors to be repaired and the ovate to be removed from the basement—and how *that's* going to happen without destroying the entire building is beyond me. I spent my entire day consulting with lawyers and trying to talk my clients off the ledge. I'll tell you one thing: that poor couple on the ninth floor had better lawyer up fast; they're going to get absolutely hammered with lawsuits."

"Wow. No wonder you're stressed."

The waiter brought their drinks, and Aubrey wasted no time getting started on hers. Then she took her first real look around. "Hey, this place is nice. I've never been here before." She popped open the menu and whistled.

"The food's amazing and so are the prices," said Royce. "Nothing comes cheap in Manhattan."

"You can say that again. I thought Brooklyn had it bad."

"Get the lobster. It says market price, so it should be a bargain given how poorly the markets are performing these days. Isn't that how it works?"

"Yeah, right."

"Don't worry, it's my treat. We're celebrating, you know."

Aubrey looked at him and smiled. "Are we? And what are we celebrating?"

"Our fourteen-month anniversary," Royce said with mock indignation. "I can't believe you forgot!"

"Fourteen months, huh? That *is* a special one. What is that? Tin? Paper?"

"Paper clips. Here." He dug into his pocket and handed her a ring made out of a paper clip.

She laughed and put it on. "It's beautiful. And it goes so well with what I have on."

"Everything goes well with what you have on…or off."

"*Royce,*" she whispered, leaning into him, eyes shining.

"*There's* that smile."

She settled back in her seat. "So how was your day?"

It was Royce's turn to sigh. "Well, let's just say it's not the best time in the world to be a stockbroker. Lots of panicky investors out there. That's why I could only afford to get you the one-carat paper clip."

"One carat?" Aubrey pretended to take it off and throw it away. "After fourteen months? I'm appalled."

"I'm hoping the market-price lobster will help make up for it."

"It's a start, but you've got a long ways to go, mister."

They clinked glasses and sipped and then were silent for a minute as they looked over the menu. "Do you know what I'd really like?" Aubrey asked, looking up from her menu.

"What's that?"

"To forget all about these damn ovates for just one night and have some *fun.*"

"Well, you're in luck. I have the perfect evening planned. All you have to do is sit back, relax, and enjoy it."

"Mmm, now you're talking," said Aubrey, and her smile was so seductive it erased everything else from Royce's mind.

Longmont, Colorado

"*Finally* something exciting is happening around here," Kaley Reed exclaimed as she finished her last bite of cereal.

"You're awfully jaded for a girl of eight," her mother observed.

"What's jaded?"

"World-weary. Bored."

"But I *am* bored," Kaley replied, squirming all over the chair like she was strapped down and being held in place. Her mom had a strict no-leaving-the-table-until-everyone-is-finished-eating rule. "Nothing interesting *ever* happens around here. Until now, I mean."

"You're such a weirdo," her twelve-year-old sister Ashley replied around a mouthful of cereal. "There's nothing *interesting* about any of this. It's scary is what it is."

"Ashley, we're gonna be the first kids in history to meet *aliens*. Don't you know how cool that is? It's, like, the coolest thing ever."

"It's, like, so *not*," Ashley said, her voice dripping with sarcasm. "Those stupid eggs are going to make a mess of everything. You'll see."

"You're *sooo* smart," Kaley replied. "Well, *I* want to meet an alien. They're welcome to stay at *my* home anytime."

"Your home?" her mom asked with a smile. "Do you own some real estate I don't know about?"

"I mean *this* home, Mom." Kaley sounded disbelieving. "Mom, are you really saying you wouldn't share your home with an alien even if it asked really nice?"

"That's exactly what I'm saying."

"But there's plenty of room! It could stay up in the attic or down in the basement and we'd barely notice it. And Woof would be so happy to have a playmate, wouldn't you, Woof?"

"Woof and I will talk about it while you're at school. Now you two had better get going. The bus will be here any minute."

Kaley bolted out of her chair like she'd been freed from a torture chamber, while Ashley sulked off in one of her usual moods.

"Josh, get down here now," Cynthia called up the stairs.

A full minute passed with no sign of Josh. "Don't forget your lunches," Cynthia reminded the girls as they grabbed their daypacks and headed for the door. Kaley ran back and picked up both bags, calling out "Bye Mom!" as she skipped off to the bus stop.

"Josh, *now,*" Cynthia called up the stairs again. She shook her head. That boy was always late.

Josh came bounding down the steps in twos and threes. "I'm here Mom," he said, snatching the bagel she was holding out for him and taking a big bite while throwing on his daypack at the same time. He looked at the clock on the wall. "Jeez, I'm late."

"Like I didn't already know that. You're gonna miss your bus."

Josh gave Woof a quick pat on the head then grabbed his lunch bag and bolted for the door. "I'll make it," he said with confidence. "See ya later," he called out as the door slammed shut behind him.

"See ya," Cynthia said. She was smiling even though no one was left in the kitchen except Woof. Josh was a handful, to be sure, but his sunny disposition made him impossible not to like. At ten years old, he was the middle child, always trying (and usually failing) to play peacemaker between Ashley and Kaley.

Her husband Will came trotting down the stairs straightening his tie. Woof ran circles around his legs, hoping for a walk. "Sorry, buddy, I can't this morning. Mom will have to take you. I'm already late for work."

Cynthia rolled her eyes. "It's obvious who Josh takes after."

"You say that like it's a bad thing."

"I say it like he's late all the time and you're his role model."

"*I'm* his role model? Yikes, that boy's in trouble."

"Tell me about it."

"Jeez, you're not supposed to agree with me! What's gotten into you lately?"

"Sorry. It's these stupid eggs, or ovates, or whatever we're supposed to call them these days. They're stressing me out."

"Look, hon, I keep telling you, it's no big deal. Just relax. Whatever pops out of them, the authorities will take care of it. It's their problem, not yours."

"Mmm," Cynthia said, looking far from convinced. Or relaxed.

If Will noticed, he didn't let on. He gave her a quick peck on the cheek and said, "Well, I'm off," and then he was out the door and on his way to the office as if it were just another day, leaving her alone with her thoughts.

She tried to shake off the dark fears that gripped her these days. There was an ovate not far from their home—less than a quarter mile away—and that made it hard for Cynthia to *just relax*, no matter what Will said or how many times he said it.

The waiting was the worst part.

"Just hatch already," she muttered.

Oval Office, Washington D.C.

Mark Gardner, fiftieth President of the United States, paced back and forth in the Oval Office, looking calmer on the outside than he felt on the inside. Despite being in his sixties, he was fit and athletic, with the kind of serious good looks that got you elected President these days. It was a good thing his hair had already turned gray, or circumstances like these certainly would have done it for him.

"Any signs of life?" he asked for what felt like the umpteenth time that day.

"No, sir, not a peep," replied his Secretary of Defense, Bill Cohen. Cohen was the opposite of what one might expect of a military leader: bald, rotund, and short. The medals and insignias on his uniform looked in danger of popping off at any moment.

"Then why does everyone seem to think alien creatures are going to pop out of them at any minute?"

"Beats me, sir. You know how the press is these days. Once a story gets rolling, there's no stopping it."

"Anything...up there...that we can't account for?" The President's eyes wandered up towards the heavens.

"No, sir. We're getting plenty of calls from amateurs and professionals alike, and we're following up on every lead, no matter how outlandish, but so far nothing. We're also *transmitting* signals, as per your request—but if there's anyone or anything out there, they're not responding."

"So, we can't communicate with them, and they—if there is a they—aren't communicating with us."

"That about sums it up, sir."

The President turned to Gil Lametti, his Chief of Staff. Lametti was also in his sixties, with thinning white hair and wire-rimmed glasses and the kind of grandfatherly face you couldn't help but trust. He was also one of Mark Gardner's oldest friends. "What should we be doing that we're not doing, Gil?"

"I've already told you, Mark," Lametti said bluntly. "We should take a page from Europe's playbook and dump those eggs into the ocean just as fast as we can."

"I'm on board with that, Gil, you know I am. It's Congress that's the holdup." The President hated Congress and Congress hated him. It was a hallmark of his administration.

Lametti shrugged. "You asked. Europe's been at it for a week now."

"How far have they gotten?"

"Not very," admitted Lametti. "The scale of the undertaking is enormous. We're talking thousands upon thousands of ovates scattered all across Europe. So far only a couple hundred have been dug up, loaded onto transports, and transferred to barges for burial at sea."

"That's not very many."

"Agreed, but it's better than nothing. They're focusing on their biggest cities first, removing ovates from metropolitan areas like London, Paris, and Berlin. Smaller towns and cities are frankly on their own."

"What about Russia? What's their take on all this?"

"Oh, you know Russia, always daring to be different. They're calling it a typical overreaction from the West and opting to leave the ovates in place. They're saying people have jumped to the wrong conclusion—that there's absolutely no proof anything is living inside these ovates."

"They might just be right about that."

"No argument. But leaving them in place is risky, and lately their president has been spouting this theory that the ovates are some kind of homegrown pestilence due to the planet being under such constant stress."

"What? Like a bad case of acne? I don't buy that."

"Me either."

"And what about China? Are they still blaming us for all this?"

"Of course they are. They claim we got careless—that one of our weaponized biolabs unleashed this plague on the world, and now it's spreading through some sort of airborne mechanism."

"That's absurd."

"I know, but it's accepted as gospel by most Chinese because that's what they're being told by their media. Of course, we've denied it ad nauseam. Even if we *wanted* to create something like this, which obviously we don't, it's well beyond our abilities. These ovates have otherworldly origins, that much seems clear."

The President sighed. "So much for world unity in the face of an alien invasion."

Bill Cohen, Secretary of Defense, scoffed. "Like *that* was ever going to happen."

The President reflected for a moment. "All right, then, Congress be damned. Let's get started dumping as many of those ovates as we can into the sea. We'll focus first on the ones closest to the White House, the Capitol Building, and Wall Street. Even if we can't move all of them, we can at least make a beginning. What resources are we going to need, Gil?"

"All the heavy earth-moving equipment we can get our hands on," Lametti replied. "Bulldozers, excavators, backhoes, cranes, dump trucks. We're already at three tons per ovate, and by next week it could be four."

"Can you run with that?"

Gil nodded, scribbling a line in the notepad he always kept at hand.

"And Bill, let's get the ball rolling on bringing our troops back home. Our country is under attack, and we need them here, not halfway around the world."

"*All* of them, sir?"

"All of them."

"Yes sir, if you say so, sir," Cohen said. He sounded more than a little dubious about this decision, but it was the President's call.

"And I want to talk to NASA. Not tomorrow: tonight. I need to know what progress, if any, is being made on the scientific front. Gil, can you set that up with my secretary?"

Gil nodded and made another note.

"Okay, then, let's get moving, boys," the President said, clapping his hands together like a football coach. "I'm counting on you two to make this all come together."

The Gil & Bill team nodded their assent. It looked like it was going to be another long night.

NASA Jet Propulsion Laboratory, Pasadena, CA

Dr. Rachel Cavanaugh adjusted her glasses nervously as she videoconferenced with the President of the United States for the first time. As the first woman Director of JPL, she was used to being underestimated. Could she really be a woman and understand rocket science? Well, of course she could, but they didn't always know that. She wondered if the President would be one of the ones who didn't know that.

"So what progress have you made so far with regard to the ovate in your lab?" the President asked.

"Unfortunately, very little, Mr. President. Our instruments go haywire every time they get anywhere near the ovate. Picture a compass needle spinning crazily near a powerful magnet, and that's about what we've got going on here. We've run every kind of test imaginable across the full range of the electromagnetic spectrum, but so far we've been unable to decipher what's inside."

"That's disappointing, Dr. Cavanaugh. We really need that information."

"I know, sir, but unfortunately the ovate's shell is impenetrable. We can't bore through it, we can't shatter it, we can't force it open, and we can't see inside it. We've tried every possible kind of materials test you can imagine, but suffice it to say our equipment shatters before the shell does. It's almost as if the ovate is resistant to being probed."

"Resistant. That makes it sound sentient."

"I wouldn't say sentient, sir. *Designed* would be a better word. Designed to be impenetrable. To us, I mean."

"Everyone keeps calling them eggs. So are they eggs or aren't they?"

"Well, sir, *we* don't call them eggs. Virtually no one in the scientific community does. It's only an egg in the sense that it has an outer shell that appears to be incubating something inside. But what's going to 'hatch' out of it is anyone's guess."

The President looked frustrated. "Egg, incubation, hatch—these are all words used to describe a chick about to be born. Dr. Cavanaugh, tell me plainly, is there or isn't there life inside these things?"

"It's extremely unlikely, Mr. President. I'd say the ovate is a construct, not a biological life form."

The President's shoulders seemed to relax just a little. "Well, that's something, isn't it? Not a living entity. That's a good thing, right? Millions of alien babies running around seems like just about the worst possible scenario I can imagine. What would we *do* with all of them? Adopt them? Exterminate them? I don't want to be the one to have to make that call."

"I can't blame you, sir. But even if they're not life forms, I wouldn't underestimate the danger they may pose to us. Their energy levels are, quite literally, off the charts…you might even say out of this world. I'm, uh, not sure if I can say this to a sitting President or not, but these things frankly scare the shit out of me."

3

September 1 – Goodland, Kansas

Ken Stubbs had years of experience operating a combine harvester, but never in his life had he had to detour around so many obstacles. Six enormous ovates lay half-buried in his fields, hidden by tall stalks of wheat. He'd had to plant red flags atop poles to mark them. His cut lines, usually as true as if they'd been drawn with a straight-edge, bent like an old coat hanger as he worked his way around first one ovate and then another.

He was ruminating on his exceptionally bad luck (none of his neighbors had even one ovate) when he spied what looked like a shimmering up ahead. It looked like heat waves rising from asphalt on a hot summer's day. He knew one of the ovates was right up ahead, so he turned off the harvester and waited for the motor to grumble to a stop.

It felt almost too quiet as he opened the door and stood on the top rung of the ladder leading down from the harvester's cockpit. Usually he could hear a few birds chirping, but the only sound at the moment was the rustling of the wheat stalks as they rubbed against one another in the breeze.

He clambered down with some effort (his beer belly made everything harder—he should really do something about that), then stood there for a moment wondering if it was wise on his part to approach any closer. He took a few hesitant steps forward, then a few more, then he was parting the few remaining stalks of wheat that stood between him and the ovate and watching it...

What, hatch?

That must be it.

Well, golly. This was all anyone had been able to talk about for weeks now, and here he was with a front-row seat—not that he was sure he wanted one.

The ovate was half-sunk in the ground. Its top half formed a dome approximately six feet in diameter and two feet high (with the other two feet being underground). For weeks now it had been growing bigger and heavier, but the changes he was seeing now were even more dramatic. From what he could tell, the ovate seemed to be melting.

It looked sizzling-hot to the touch, if one were stupid enough to touch it. Waves of heat were rising up from it like a charcoal grill someone had forgotten to turn off. The stalks of wheat nearest it were beginning to smoke rather alarmingly, and the red flag atop its pole looked like it might catch fire at any moment.

"That can't be good," Ken murmured aloud.

What else wasn't good was the ovate's appearance. Instead of looking lustrous like an opal, cracks were beginning to show all over its surface. Ken's mind jumped to a ceramic pot his wife Marie had once cherished as a family heirloom. It had been knocked off the table (Ken blamed the dog) and had shattered into dozens of pieces. He'd painstakingly glued it back together, but it had never looked the same. That was what the shell looked like now, to his mind's eye, with its myriad cracks running every which way.

The cracks widened even as he watched, energy radiating through them with an almost blinding intensity. The shell blackened rapidly, thin layers flaking off like burnt onion skin.

The red flag caught fire and started to burn. It fluttered in the breeze like a warning sign. The stalks of wheat in the immediate vicinity began to smolder.

"Holy smokes," Ken whispered. He knew he should get out of there *now* but found it impossible to leave. It was like watching a snake slough off its dead skin to reveal the shiny new creature underneath.

The blackened layers of skin were piling up all around the egg now, mixing with the smoldering wheat and creating a steaming mess of goo that looked altogether unpleasant.

Somehow the egg transfixed him: he couldn't take his eyes off it as it finished its miraculous transformation into something wholly new.

In a matter of seconds the last smoking remnants of shell flaked off, falling to the ground like some awful afterbirth—and then the ovate, the actual ovate inside the shell, lay bare before him.

It looked naked, translucent, and disturbingly otherworldly. It was almost too bright to stare at, but stare he did, feasting his eyes on its unearthly brilliance.

He shook himself as if released from a spell and began stumbling backwards.

But the ovate was quicker than he was. In the blink of an eye it *flashed.*

And just like that, Ken found himself inside a dome of energy of some sort looking out.

Shit shit shit.

The physical ovate was still there, right where it had been before, but now it radiated a shield of energy—a force field of some kind. The shield *shimmered.* What the purpose of such a small force field could be he had no idea—but he knew he didn't like being on the inside of it, no, not one little bit.

The force field was dome-shaped and maybe sixteen feet in diameter. The top of the dome wasn't much taller than he was, maybe seven feet high at its apex. Good thing he'd been crouching down when it trapped him, or it might have cut his head right off! He continued crouching, terrified of touching that shimmering field. The dome's walls tapered down all around him like a physical dome's would, except these walls *pulsed* with energy.

He was trapped inside what amounted to an electrified yurt. Suddenly he felt very much afraid he might die in here. He felt like he couldn't breathe, but maybe that was just the fear talking. It didn't help that the red marker flag he had planted was still flickering with tiny tongues of flame inside the dome *he* was now in, or that smoke was still rising from the smoldering mess of blackened goo at the base of the ovate.

He could scarcely look at the egg it was so bright. He hoped he wasn't getting exposed to massive doses of radiation.

First things first. He reached for the flag pole and stamped out the fluttering flames with his boot. He considered stamping out the smoldering mess of goo at the base of the ovate but wisely thought better of it. Instead he dropped to all fours and moved as far away from the physical ovate as he could get, careful to watch his head where the dome curved lower. He wanted to stay low to avoid the worst of the smoke—although, now that he was paying attention, he could see that the smoke was rising straight up and out of the dome instead of accumulating inside.

Well, that was good. At least he wasn't going to asphyxiate to death.

He took some deep breaths and tried to calm himself. Panic wasn't going to help here.

The dome was transparent, sort of like a soap bubble. He could see out of it, but things looked distorted on the outside. The wheat field, for instance, looked all warped and wavy. It was like looking at your own legs in a swimming pool and seeing them all ripply and disconnected from the rest of your body. Soap-bubble colors swirled and whirled and slid up and down the dome walls, coruscating with an iridescent quality. Those walls looked beautiful but deadly.

He edged closer towards the center of the dome, still on his knees. He wasn't sure which frightened him more, the radiating ovate or the shimmering walls, but he was already beginning to feel claustrophobic.

From what he could tell, the walls of the dome continued straight into the ground. He was already surmising that the force field was actually a sphere, with its other half hidden beneath the surface. If the earth was disturbed in any way by the sudden appearance of a force field cutting through it, it showed no signs of being bothered in the least. But one thing was clear: he couldn't dig himself out of this mess.

Ken knew it was ridiculous to yell for help, stuck as he was in the middle of a Kansas wheat field, but he yelled anyway. The dome seemed to dampen his voice. He pulled out his cell phone and took a look. Not surprisingly, there was no signal. That was often true even *without* a dome of energy surrounding him. His farm was remote, but sometimes he got a weak signal from a cell tower out near I-70.

Face it: he was on his own. No one would miss him for hours and hours yet. It was harvest season, and that meant Ken often worked late into the evening, sometimes until eight or nine at night. His wife Marie wouldn't even bat an eye at his absence until after nine-thirty or ten, assuming she hadn't already gone to bed by then.

Which meant he could be in here all night.

He sat down on the ground and tried to zone out for awhile. It didn't look like anything was going to happen anytime soon, so he might as well take a breather.

As he was sitting there, Ken realized to his surprise that he wasn't alone. A tiny field mouse was looking around with a startled expression on its face.

So he had company after all. The mouse was near one of the curved walls. It seemed unharmed, but its senses were on high alert.

The mouse sniffed at the air as it stood on its hind legs. Ken watched, fascinated, waiting to see what would happen next. He figured he'd let the mouse go first.

Of course the mouse, being a mouse, took its own sweet time about it. But eventually it must have decided it was safe and got back to the business of foraging.

The mouse inched closer and closer to the curved wall. Any minute now, Ken expected to see it get zapped and keel over dead. Roast mouse. At least he wouldn't starve. But to his astonishment and endless relief (not so much for the mouse's sake as for his own), he watched the mouse pass *right through* the dome wall unharmed.

The mouse actually stopped for a few seconds halfway in and halfway out of the dome wall, its body effectively cut in two by the force field. It didn't seem to mind a bit. Then the mouse scampered the rest of the way out and stood there, as if to say, "See? I'm fine! Nothing to worry about here!"

Okay, Ken thought. Well, that's something. That's a very *big* something. He might just get out of this alive after all. Whatever the dome's purpose, it apparently wasn't designed to kill hapless idiots like himself.

Ken picked up a stalk of wheat and touched its tip to the inside of the dome wall. The stalk passed right through. As he drew it back, he half-expected to see the stalk shear off, but it remained intact. He threw the stalk to the ground and picked up a clod of dirt. Tossing it at the dome wall, he watched it, too, pass right through.

He decided it was time to try the same experiment with his left pinky finger. He could afford to lose his left pinky if it came to it. It wasn't easy to touch that shimmering wall of energy, but he forced himself to do it…

And felt nothing.

He drew his pinky back and found it intact. His heart rejoiced.

Courage now, Ken told himself. It was time to crawl right out of this dome. If a mouse could do it, so could he.

He steeled himself and decided his best bet was to lunge out of the dome so he didn't chicken out at the last moment. Okay: one, two, three.

He stood stock still, unable to move.

Dammit. Coward.

What are you, a man or a mouse? Try again.

Deep breath: one, two, three.

He tumbled through the wall in one fell swoop.

For a long time he just lay there on the ground, whooping and laughing and thanking the good Lord for his escape. He found himself feeling very generous towards that little mouse all of a sudden. Maybe he should adopt the little fella and feed it cheese wheels for the rest of its life. But unfortunately the mouse had already disappeared among the wheat stalks, never to be seen again.

From the outside, the dome looked like an enormous soap bubble ready to pop. The ovate still stood at its center, appearing ripply and bright from his new vantage point.

He clambered to his feet, broke off a stalk of wheat, and pushed it against the dome wall. The stalk bent instead of going in. Picking up a small pebble, he tossed it at the dome wall and watched as it bounced off. Hmm. It was time to risk his left pinky again. What was that finger really for, anyway?

He touched just the tip of it to the shimmering wall and got *zapped* for his troubles.

His hand sprang back, feeling all tingly and warm, but at least his pinky was still there. He'd gotten a similar jolt any number of times in the past when he'd inadvertently touched the electric fence surrounding the horses' paddock, except this jolt was more intense.

Things were becoming clearer to him. Obviously the force field was meant to keep things *out*. But if, through great stupidity or ill fortune, you somehow managed to find yourself stuck inside one, it was designed to let you back out—but not back in again.

"So you're a one-way portal," he said out loud to the dome. "And a human bug-zapper to boot."

He walked a little unsteadily back to his harvester, started the engine, and made an extra-wide detour around the dome. He still had a lot more harvesting to do, and that would give him time to ruminate over his and Marie's future, what with six of these monstrosities on his land. In other parts of his fields, he could see more shimmering going on, and he knew exactly what that meant.

How could he ever forget?

4

September 1 – JPL, Pasadena, California

"Dr. Cavanaugh, it's really not safe for us to be in here any longer."

Rachel Cavanaugh stood with her hands on her hips staring at the ovate just three feet in front of her. She could feel the heat emanating from it. What its purpose was she had no idea, but she thought she was about to find out.

"Dr. Cavanaugh..."

The ovate was physically suspended inside an enormous aerospace laboratory at JPL's facilities in Pasadena. The lab was as big as an airport hangar, and at its very center hung the ovate, suspended by means of a specially engineered metal truss. The incredible and still increasing weight of the ovate was such that the engineers at JPL fretted it might overwhelm the truss and fall to (or through) the floor despite their best efforts to keep it suspended, but so far the truss had held.

"Doctor..."

"Okay, let's clear out," she said reluctantly.

They exited the room, some with more urgency than others, sealed the doors behind them, climbed a set of stairs to a platform, and stood in front of an enormous viewing window looking down on the lab from above.

Waves of heat were now rising from the top of the ovate, and the metal bars on the truss were turning a dullish red. Even as they watched, fissures appeared in the ovate and the shell began to blacken and crack. The parts of the truss that were in direct contact with the ovate began to glow red-hot. The ovate's shell began to half-flake, half-ooze off, creating a steaming mess on the floor. Seconds later a sphere of energy flashed into being around the exposed and almost blindingly bright ovate at its center.

"Holy hell," one of the scientists breathed.

They all stared in rapt silence. The entire force field was visible above-ground. It formed an oblate spheroid—perfectly circular at the middle and somewhat squashed at the top and bottom. Its sixteen-foot diameter partially enclosed the metal truss holding the ovate in place. The field seemed to pass right through the truss without affecting it.

The scientists might have continued staring at it all day if Rachel hadn't broken the spell. "Okay, people," she said, clapping her hands, "let's get instruments on this."

The scientists hurried off, talking animatedly among themselves about what they'd just witnessed. Rachel heard numerous references to sci-fi movies, which didn't surprise her in the least: most scientists were geeks at heart, and this force field was about as geeky as you could get.

Nature, of course, had its own force field: the geomagnetic field that surrounded Earth, protecting the planet from cosmic rays and other harmful radiation; but that force field, while impressive, wouldn't stop a bullet—and Rachel suspected this one just might.

*****

"We've run some initial tests on the force field in our lab," Dr. Cavanaugh informed the President by way of videoconference a few hours later. "One thing we've learned is that the resistance varies. If you throw a rubber ball at it, the ball just bounces off. Same with a piece of paper: if you fold it up and push it against the wall, it just bends. But anything living—that is, anything human or animal—warrants a stronger reaction."

"Stronger how?"

"I've touched the force field myself and received quite the shock. One of my subordinates pressed the palm of his hand against it and had to be sent to the hospital with second-degree burns. I didn't sanction that, by the way. But what this suggests is that the force field is 'preprogrammed' to resist human entry in particular."

"So they knew we would try to get in and made sure we couldn't," said the President.

"Exactly. Whoever 'they' are."

"Yes, the mysterious 'they.' So in your opinion, there *is* a 'they'?"

"I would say so, sir. Or at least, there *was*. I suppose this could be an artifact of a long-dead civilization, still carrying out some automated function long after its creators had perished. But I would tend to believe the 'they' is out there right now, waiting and watching...for something. Maybe for the force fields to keep growing bigger and stronger."

"That's a scary thought."

Rachel nodded. "By the way, the force field is equally aggressive about resisting anything coming at it with speed—a bullet, for instance. We tried using a pure-lead bullet, figuring that since lead has no charge, it might pass right through the electromagnetic field, but no such luck. It's more sophisticated than that."

"Why doesn't that surprise me?"

"The force field also makes a notable exception for water. Any form of H_2O—rain, snow, freshwater, saltwater—it doesn't matter—it all passes right through the dome's membrane. It's another telling indication that the domes have been preprogrammed by beings who want the domes to behave in a certain fashion. They *want* water to pass through, so it passes through. They *don't want* other forms of matter to pass through, and so they don't."

"So if we could disguise ourselves as water, we could pass through," the President said dryly. "Get to work on that, will you, Dr. Cavanaugh?"

"Yes, of course, Mr. President. We've been able to take initial readings on the force field, and they're quite literally off the charts. The best tesla meters we have go up to five thousand teslas, and the magnetic energy of this force field measures well beyond that."

"Umm, not to sound ignorant," said the President, "but what exactly is a tesla...other than a car?"

"It's a unit of measure, Mr. President. It's used to measure the strength of magnetic fields."

"So five thousand teslas is a lot?"

"It's way more than a lot, sir. It's frankly incredible. The highest non-destructive magnetic field we've ever been able to create was at Los Alamos National Laboratory. Back in 2012, their MagLab facility broke the one hundred tesla barrier for the first time—and that was considered the holy grail of magnetism for decades. That's a magnetic field *two million* times stronger than the Earth's magnetic field. They used a pulsed magnet to do it. One hundred teslas is quite impressive—for a non-destructive field, that is.

"What do you mean, non-destructive?"

"I mean controlled or safe. The magnet at MagLab can be used over and over again; it can be pulsed for fifteen milliseconds once per hour. We've managed to create even stronger magnetic fields than the one at MagLab, but the hardware explodes right after the experiment for which it's used."

"It explodes. You mean that literally."

"I do."

"And why does it explode?"

"Because the hardware isn't structurally capable of withstanding the forces created by such a powerful magnetic field. Back in 2018, scientists at the University of Tokyo literally blew the metal doors off their own lab when they were running an electromagnetic experiment indoors. They used a specially designed coil and an electromagnetic flux-compression technique to produce a massive magnetic field that reached twelve hundred teslas. That experiment lasted all of forty *microseconds* before it blew the doors off their lab."

"What happened to the scientists?"

"Fortunately they were in a control room, protected from the blast."

"Smart scientists."

Rachel nodded. "Even larger magnetic fields have been generated outdoors using lasers in wide-open places like Siberia, but those experiments were incredibly short-lived and resulted in even larger explosions. We've never gotten above three thousand teslas under *any* conditions, explosive or otherwise."

"Which is why this force field is so amazing to you."

"Exactly. The fact that this alien force field is registering above five thousand teslas and is completely stable at room temperature and at such a size is nothing short of astonishing. I don't know what to make of it, except to say that it is most definitely alien technology. We can't understand it, or duplicate it, or reverse engineer it...not yet, anyway. But give us enough time, and we'll figure it out."

"Unfortunately time is the one thing we don't have in abundance, Dr. Cavanaugh. I want your scientists working on this around the clock—and I mean that literally."

"Yes, sir, of course. I understand the urgency."

5

September 2 – Oval Office, Washington D.C.

The President bustled into the Oval Office with his Secretary of State right behind him. "Sorry I'm late, fellas. Lorene, we'll have to finish this up later. In the meantime, I want you to get in touch with our allies overseas and see if they know anything about these domes that we don't." His Secretary of State nodded and left the room.

The President sat down in one of the chairs in the middle of the office and sighed. He looked exhausted. "Catch me up, Gil," he said to his Chief of Staff.

"Unfortunately, none of the news is good," said Lametti. "It looks like our efforts to make cities ovate-free were doomed from the start. There were just too many hidden ovates out there—ones no one could have found because they were buried deep in the soil or concealed within dense thickets. So far we've identified seven hidden ovates in New York City and two in the D.C. area, including one that's painfully close to the Capitol Building. Congress is already having conniptions about that one, as you can imagine. It was buried deep in a flower bed in the U.S. Botanic Garden of all places."

"Jesus, that's less than a quarter mile away from Capitol Hill. You can *see* the Capitol Dome from there."

"Well, now there's a smaller alien dome nestling beneath it," Lametti said. "And that's not all: the second D.C. ovate hatched this morning in Arlington National Cemetery, near a spot called Patton Circle. That's distressingly close to the Pentagon."

The President swore under his breath.

"We only just found out about that one an hour ago," Lametti said. "Plumes of steam rising from the ground gave the ovate away just before it hatched. Crews rushed in and tried to dig it out in time, but unfortunately the only result was severe burns to the crew. Three of them had to be taken to the hospital."

"So we have two of these new mini-domes to worry about in D.C.—and how many did you say in New York City?"

"Seven all told. That's across all five boroughs. Three of them are in Manhattan proper."

"Oh, for the love of—that's three too many!"

"Believe me, I know. On the plus side, crews did manage to remove seventeen *known* ovates from all five boroughs before the hatch, as they're calling it, but these seven remained undiscovered."

"Okay, walk me through where the three in Manhattan are located."

"The first is in Battery Park at the southern tip of Manhattan. It was concealed within a dense thicket near the Netherland Monument."

"The Netherland Monument? Never heard of it."

"It commemorates the original Dutch settlement of New Amsterdam. Anyway, the whole area has been cordoned off as if it were a crime scene. Apparently folks noticed plumes of steam rising from the ground early this morning and notified police, but the ovate hatched before anything could be done about it. It's located less than half a mile from Wall Street."

"Of course it is. And what about the other two?"

"One was discovered in Central Park, just south of Central Park Reservoir near the Metropolitan Museum of Art. It was hidden in dense undergrowth close to a popular jogging path. Contingency plans are already underway to relocate the art in the Met, should it become necessary."

"And the third?"

"Brace yourself. It was found in the crawlspace of a building near the corner of 48th and 6th, close to Rockefeller Center and Times Square."

The President stared at Lametti in disbelief. "You're kidding me. How in the hell did an ovate get into the crawlspace of a building in Midtown Manhattan? And how is it nobody found out about it until now?"

"Well, it's plenty visible now—now that the building that contained it has burned to the ground. But before that, the building was under renovation, and apparently the work had stopped due to lack of funds or some such. Our best guess is that gaps in the outer Tyvek wrapping allowed a seed to infiltrate and take root in the crawlspace. The ovate has remained hidden down there ever since. When it hatched last night, it started a fire down in the crawlspace. Old paper files stored down there made for excellent kindling, and the rest is history."

"My God." The President shook his head.

"Besides the three ovates in Manhattan, there's also one in Brooklyn, two in Queens, and one in Staten Island."

"You're right—that's all terrible news. But what are these force fields *for*? What's their purpose?"

"No idea," said Lametti. "Maybe they're advance bases for a race of aliens who have yet to arrive."

"Aren't the domes too small for that?" asked Bill Cohen, Secretary of Defense.

"Who knows? Maybe the aliens are small themselves. Or maybe the domes are going to get bigger over time. All we know for sure is, they're designed to keep *us* out. They're actually spheres—completely enclosed and safe for whoever or whatever happens to be inside."

"Can they be moved?" asked the President.

"I doubt it," said Lametti. "*Can* you move a sphere of energy? These aren't physical constructs anymore—they can't be picked up and transported like the ovates could."

The President swore softly again.

"And that's just the beginning of our problems," said Lametti, who was beginning to sound to the President like one of those doomsday prophets of old. "The domes are popping up *everywhere,* not just in D.C. and New York. We've got reports of them in small towns, big cities, rural farms, remote wilderness areas—literally every nook and cranny of this country. The same is true overseas. They're dealing with the same problems in London, Paris, Moscow, Delhi, Beijing, and beyond. Basically, everywhere. Not to mention, the ovates burned so intensely when they first hatched, they ended up sparking wildfires across our entire country—thousands all at once. Too bad they had to hatch at the beginning of September when things were already tinder-dry."

"All right, so hold on a minute," the President said, waving his hands as if he couldn't bear to hear another word. "Exactly how many of these domes do we have within our own borders?"

Lametti shook his head. "No idea."

Bill Cohen spoke up. "We're working on getting an accurate estimate even as we speak."

"I want one of those push-pin maps up in the Situation Room as soon as possible that shows every dome in every state in America."

"That map's gonna have an awful lot of pins in it, Mark," said Lametti. "Based on what we know so far, the number has to be over a hundred thousand at least."

"A *hundred thousand*? Good God, I hope not."

"Well, let's see." Lametti stared up at the ceiling for a moment. "The U.S. has some 3.8 million square miles of land, give or take." He jotted that number down on his notepad. "Now, we know there are seven domes in New York City, plus the seventeen ovates that were removed before they could hatch. That makes twenty-four ovates altogether. Pretty much every square inch of that city has been combed through at this point, so we can use it as a representative sampling. Bill, how many square miles are there in New York City—the five boroughs area?"

"Why don't you look it up on your smartphone?" Cohen asked. "Oh yeah, that's right, you don't have a smartphone."

"No, but I have a smart*ass*."

Cohen grinned. "Says here it's got 303 square miles," he said after a moment.

"Okay, so if we divide 3.8 million by 303 and multiply by the 24 domes in New York City, we get..." Lametti scribbled madly.

"Wait for it," said Cohen.

"We get roughly 301,000 domes in the U.S." Lametti said. He held up his notepad as if it were proof.

"God help us! That many?" exclaimed the President.

Cohen scoffed. "You can't believe a back-of-the-napkin estimate like that."

"It's better than nothing," Lametti replied.

"Three hundred thousand," the President intoned. "And that's just here in the U.S. What the *hell* are we gonna do with three hundred thousand domes?"

"Destroy them," said his Secretary of Defense. "Starting with the ones in D.C. and New York."

"Easier said than done," said the President. "But yes, let's do exactly that, if we can."

Fort Bliss, Texas

"General McMillan, I'm putting you in charge of the military effort to eliminate these domes," the President said by way of videoconference. "Are you up to the task?"

General Drew McMillan saluted and winked at the same time and said, "Yes sir, I am. I'm pleased as peaches to be of service. I won't let you down, sir."

"Good. I want you to get started right away. Throw everything you've got at these force fields. Start small and get bigger as you go. Hopefully something will work, or else it's going to be a bad year for all of us."

"They'll never know what hit 'em, sir. Just you wait."

"You're stationed down at Fort Bliss, isn't that right, General?"

"That's right, sir, just outside El Paso. But wherever you need me to be, that's where I'll be."

"Are there any domes out that way?"

"Oh, there sure are, sir. We've got more than a dozen of 'em right in the middle of our training range. I'd love nothing more than to throw some live fire at 'em and see what happens."

"I'm guessing it's pretty remote down there, isn't it?"

"Why, this is the biggest training area in these U-nited States. We're talking over a million acres of desert terrain stretching from Texas to New Mexico. The range area sits in permanently restricted airspace, too—the largest contiguous tract of it in the continental U.S. That means you can fire all the missiles you want and never have to worry about killin' civilians or shootin' down an airliner. And that's not even countin' White Sands Missile Range to the north; they got even more domes up thataways."

"What about troops and weaponry?"

"We've got near forty thousand military personnel stationed down here at Fort Bliss. You're looking at the home of the First Armored Division—Old Ironsides—the Army's oldest and most renowned armored division. We're talkin' every sort of combat capability you could wish for: tanks, artillery, attack helicopters, missiles, you name it. You couldn't do much better than Fort Bliss if you want to throw a whole lotta shit at these domes and see what sticks."

"The domes are made of energy, General, and that's what worries me: I'm not sure shit or anything else will stick to them."

"Well, we can certainly try, sir, we can certainly try."

The President nodded. "Then get started immediately, General, and keep me posted. I want to hear from you at least twice a week with updates."

"Yes sir, will do. You'll be hearin' from me plenty, maybe more than you'd like. Some people have accused me of being on the talkative side, if you can believe that."

*****

Fifteen minutes later, General McMillan met with the commanding officer at Fort Bliss. "Our orders from the President are to start small and work our way up," McMillan told him, "so that's exactly what we're gonna do. We'll start with small-arms fire, then move on up to grenades and rocket launchers. I expect all of 'em to fail, but we can at least report back and tell the President what bullets do when they hit a dome wall. Do they ricochet off? Hit and fall flat? Sink in? Whatever they do, we'll want to report it."

"Understood."

"Same for explosives. What damage do they do, if any? Where does the shrapnel fly, and how far? That sort of thing."

"Got it. When would you like us to start?"

"Well, the President said immediately, so there's your answer. Get some troops out there ASAP and let's see 'em light up one of those domes for target practice. Bring every kind of firearm you've got. And video drones too: we're gonna want to document all this."

Half an hour later, the soldiers of Bulldog Brigade were firing every type of assault rifle, sniper rifle, and machine gun they had at the dome, which was conveniently located in the middle of the firing range. The bullets all peppered off the dome walls, dancing a pirouette as they deflected and spun off sideways.

They graduated up to grenades and rocket launchers, which created dozens of splashy fireballs against the force field wall but had no effect otherwise. Next came plastic explosives. Soldiers piled enough C-4 around the base of the dome to blow several city blocks to kingdom come, but the dome emerged unscathed. Next, Abrams tanks came rumbling up from the First Armored Division, all firing simultaneously at the much-put-upon dome, but despite using armor-piercing rounds featuring depleted uranium penetrators and steel tips, they left no mark. Finally, soldiers from the 27th Field Artillery Regiment let loose with dozens of 155 mm howitzers, but the only damage they did was to the ground outside the dome, which began to resemble a cratered moonscape.

"Nuts," General McMillan said after each failed attempt. "Have we got any missiles lying around that pack a punch?"

They settled on a Precision Strike Missile, the replacement for the ATACMS surface-to-surface missile. Traveling at Mach 3, it hit the target dead-on, sending up a huge fireball, but the dome itself remained as undamaged as ever.

"Nuts. Time to get serious."

McMillan requisitioned an Air Force fighter jet to release a hypersonic cruise missile traveling faster than Mach 10. The entire base turned out to watch that strike. Even a relatively small object traveling at Mach 10 can produce devastating results, but while the troops were by no means disappointed by the tremendous fireball that resulted from the direct hit, they were as discouraged as ever by the outcome.

"Nuts."

Their last attempt of the day was a MOAB. "If this doesn't work, we'll call it a day and see what else we can come up with tomorrow," McMillan told the base's commanding officer.

MOAB was short for Massive Ordnance Air Blast, but most said it should stand for Mother Of All Bombs. It was one of the most powerful non-nuclear weapons in America's arsenal. Designed to be delivered by a C-130 Hercules, it wasn't a penetrator weapon, but rather a type of air burst ordnance intended to take out targets at or near the surface. Weighing twenty-two thousand pounds, it was filled with nearly nineteen thousand pounds of explosives. Its blast radius was one mile.

As soon as the C-130 flight was ready, the test range was cleared of all personnel. The bomb was satellite-guided directly onto the dome. With an explosive yield comparable to that of a small tactical nuclear weapon, the resulting explosion was nothing short of spectacular—enough so that every soldier watching from a distance cheered when it struck the dome head-on. But the cheers turned to groans once the smoke cleared and they saw what they always saw: the dome undamaged, despite the surrounding terrain having been blown to smithereens.

"Nuts," said General McMillan for the last time that day.

6

September 2 – Brooklyn, New York

"So I'm a reasonably smart guy, aren't I?" Royce asked as he lounged on Aubrey's couch, staring pensively out the window of her third-floor Brooklyn apartment.

"Sure you are," Aubrey replied from the kitchen. "I mean, for a guy."

"Right, thanks for that. So then why do I feel like I'm so far behind the eight ball on this one?"

"Because everyone's behind the eight ball on this one, Royce," Aubrey said as she poured red wine into two glasses. "It's not like any of us has been through an alien invasion before."

"Well, I can't argue with you there."

Aubrey padded back into the living room in her bare feet and set the two glasses down on the coffee table. She leaned over, giving him a view to remember, before awarding him with a condescending pat on the cheek. "You're smart, sweetie, but not *that* smart. That's why I'm here: to keep you out of trouble."

"You *are* trouble," Royce said, tackling her onto the couch. Aubrey shrieked and play-fought as he kissed her all over. "Your brains isn't even my favorite part of you."

"Mmm, do tell."

That was the end of the talking for awhile. When they came back up for air, their clothes were strewn all over the living room floor. Now they were lounging around in barely more than their birthday suits, drinking wine and feeling fine.

"Better?" Aubrey asked with a winning smile that almost had him tackling her again. "Still behind that eight ball?"

"Oh it's still there, but I feel like I just made a bank-shot around it and won the match anyway."

"Huh. I thought *I* won that match."

"Call it a tie. A very satisfying tie." He swirled the wine around in his glass and stared into it, lost in thought.

"So tell me about this eight ball of yours," Aubrey said after awhile, breaking into his reverie.

"Mmm? Well, it's these domes: they're throwing me off my game. Usually I'm pretty good at predicting the future, you know? It kind of comes with the territory of being a stockbroker. Reading the tea leaves and all that. But ever since these ovates hatched, it's like valuations don't matter anymore. Good companies, bad companies, it's all the same—their shares are plummeting."

"Because people are freaking out."

"Exactly. There's so much uncertainty out there, it's safer just to get out of stocks altogether."

"But *you* stayed put."

Royce looked up. "Yeah, I did. How'd you know?"

"Because you've told me before: you're a buy-and-hold investor.'"

"That's right. Buying stocks at good valuations and holding onto them for the long run is what makes investing different from gambling."

"If you say so. The only investing I do is in shoes."

"And your portfolio is looking mighty healthy, I must say. I've had a peek inside your closet. Anyway, when stock prices drop, I've always bought more shares because it's like buying them on sale."

"Except..."

"Except I'm not sure how wise that strategy is right now. I'm worried I might lose my shirt."

"You've already lost your shirt," Aubrey observed with a wiggle of her eyebrows.

Royce grinned. "I wish that were the only shirt I had to lose. I don't know, Aubrey. Ever since these ovates first made headlines, the markets have been tanking faster than I've ever seen before."

"People are panicking."

Royce nodded. "Everyone was expecting tiny aliens to pop out of them, and so they sold."

"But you didn't."

He stared moodily into his wine glass. "No, I didn't."

Aubrey was silent for a moment. "At least we don't have to worry about gremlins running around."

"True, but now we have these miniature force fields to reckon with."

"What do you make of them?"

"I don't know *what* to make of them—but I know one of them is far too close for comfort to Wall Street. I think the markets are going to be a bloodbath tomorrow. Labor Day weekend has given people plenty of time to think."

Aubrey spread her hands wide. "Then sell."

"I may do just that...but it already feels like I've missed the boat. The S&P 500 is already down fifty percent from its all-time high of just two weeks ago. If I hold on, maybe stocks will bounce back and I can recoup some of my losses. That's what I'd usually do. Heck, that's what I did during the last two recessions: I held on, and in time the markets bounced back."

"But you're worried they won't this time."

Royce nodded. "Those other recessions were serious, but neither involved an alien invasion. This might be—I can't believe I'm saying this—this might be a crisis the markets can't recover from."

"How much are you invested in stocks?"

"I'm one hundred percent invested in stocks, Aubrey. And it hasn't been pretty these past two weeks, let me tell you."

"Yeah? How bad is it?"

"Bad enough that I'm nowhere near being a millionaire anymore, I can tell you that much. I'm back to being a five-hundred-thousandaire."

"That's still a decent chunk of change."

"Yeah, but if I'd acted a little sooner…I'm starting to feel pretty exposed."

"You *are* pretty exposed," Aubrey observed.

Royce smiled. "I mean financially exposed."

"Well, what little money I've managed to save is in the bank, so I guess it's safe enough. I can always give you a loan if you need one. You can be my kept man."

"That's very generous of you. I'd love nothing more than to be kept by you, but hopefully it won't come to that. And hey, you never know; the markets may surprise on the upside."

"I love it when you talk business to me. Sooo sexy. You're the sexiest five-hundred-thousandaire I know."

"I prefer former millionaire."

"And still only in your twenties."

"Mmm. Five hundred thousand doesn't exactly make me a master of the universe though, does it?"

"A master of the what?"

"Master of the universe. It's a catchphrase from *Bonfire of the Vanities.* This guy, he's a big-time bond trader on Wall Street. He's also kind of a jerk, but he thinks of himself as a master of the universe because he's making so much money hand over fist."

"You work on Wall Street. Doesn't that make you at least a master's apprentice of the universe?"

"Hardly. I'm just your basic stockbroker. I'm nowhere near master of the universe level."

Aubrey placed her wine glass on the table and crawled towards him on the couch. "You're the master of *my* universe." She leaned into him and gave him a smoldering kiss.

"Jesus, let me put my glass down. I'm gonna spill it for sure."

"I don't care," she breathed.

"You'll care when there's a big red stain on that white carpet of yours." He set the glass down and kissed her back—and more time elapsed with no conversation needed, at least of the coherent kind.

*****

Eventually they returned to their wine, sipping quietly for several minutes and basking in the glow of shared time together. With him living in Jersey City and her in Brooklyn, they didn't get to see each other all that often, except on weekends—which helped explain all the fireworks when they did.

"This place is about a million times nicer than mine," Royce observed, looking around her apartment with an appreciative eye. They were in her brownstone bordering Fort Greene Park, and the place was decorated with obvious taste. "How do you afford it?"

"I just showed you how I afford it, silly."

"No, seriously."

"Well, I'm pretty good at what I do...the real estate business, I mean, not the other. People seem to enjoy working with me."

"And why wouldn't they? You're smart, you're sexy, and those eyes of yours could melt metal."

"All true," she said, preening. "But to be honest, I put a big chunk of my monthly income into this apartment. More than I probably should." She drained the last of her wine. "But I love living and working right here in Brooklyn, you know?"

"And not a dome in sight. That counts for a lot these days."

"You're right about that: no one wants to live near a dome. It's like having a nuclear power plant in your back yard." She sauntered into the kitchen with their two glasses and poured them full again before returning to the couch. Her hair was all tousled and his borrowed shirt barely covered her. "So what's your work week looking like?" she asked.

"Brutal. Last week I had to work crazy hours just to keep up with all the sell orders. This week's not going to be any better. You won't be seeing much of me, I'm afraid."

"That sucks. I'll have to hit up my other clients."

"Don't you dare. What's *your* week looking like? How's the real estate market?"

"Dead. Everything was on hold *before* because people were waiting for the eggs to hatch—and everything is on hold *now* because people can't figure out what to do about the domes. No one wants to buy property until they can get some clarity."

"Yeah, clarity would be nice." Royce took a sip of wine and stared at her appreciatively. "How is it my shirt looks so much better on you than it does on me?"

"What? This old thing?" She got up and twirled around. The bottom of the shirt rode up a little higher.

They kissed and groped like teenagers. He carried her into the bedroom, all conversation ceasing for a third time.

September 3 – Wall Street, New York

Royce showed up early for work the next day, as prepared as he could be for what was sure to be a long one.

He had no idea.

The opening bell rang and in less than ten minutes the S&P 500 plummeted seven percent from Friday's close. That triggered the first of three circuit breakers designed to halt trading and prevent market crashes due to panic selling. The first halt was known as Level 1.

After a fifteen-minute pause, the markets opened back up again and within minutes slumped another seven percent, past the thirteen percent mark from Friday's close, triggering the second trading halt, known as Level 2.

Another fifteen-minute halt, another chance for traders to catch their breath. During this second halt, news emerged of the government's plan to infuse massive amounts of cash into the economy. They were talking nearly *twenty trillion* dollars, an absurdly huge amount. The primary goal of the stimulus package, which reporters were referring to as the Safeguard Act, was to bolster the markets—and for awhile it seemed to work.

When the markets reopened, stocks shot upwards, then traded sideways through most of the afternoon. But half an hour before the closing bell, they fell sharply again, triggering the third and final halt to trading.

A Level 3 trading curb had never before been triggered during regular trading hours. It meant that markets had fallen twenty percent from the previous day's close—and when that happened, no matter what the time of day, trading was halted for the rest of the day market-wide.

Throughout this harrowing workday, Royce was on the phone nonstop with clients making trades on their behalf. Virtually none of them were buying, despite the massive stimulus package that had just been announced. Most wanted to unload stocks and convert to bonds, cash, or gold just as fast as they could.

As a financial consultant, Royce was obligated to put his clients' interests before his own, which meant executing their sell orders before initiating any of his own, so it wasn't until after trading hours that he could finally afford to take a look at his own portfolio.

He could scarcely bring himself to look. For several minutes he just sat there, then he hit the enter key—and hugged his head in both hands as he stared at the screen. It was filled with big, bloody red numbers with minus signs in front of them that made investors want to puke, or throw themselves off buildings. He had known it would be bad, but not this bad. His portfolio was down seventy percent from its all-time high of just two weeks before. Suddenly he was a three hundred thousandaire.

And it had all happened so fast.

For five years he had been living in a crappy basement studio apartment in Jersey City and commuting by train to New York City so he could invest every extra penny in the stock market. Now all that frugality was looking like a lost cause, and his tidy nest egg wasn't looking so tidy anymore.

He turned off his computer and staggered out of the office. The PATH ride home happened in a blur; he barely remembered getting on or off the train. His mind felt anesthetized. The next thing he knew, he was turning the key to the door of his basement studio apartment in Jersey City.

He shut the door, collapsed onto the couch, and slept for two hours in his work clothes before waking up feeling dazed.

*****

The clock said 10 pm. He'd missed dinner but didn't care. It felt like the last five years of his life had all been for nothing.

Pouring himself a glass of scotch, he downed it in one go, then poured another.

He opened his laptop and stared again at the horrific numbers.

He downed the second scotch and refilled again.

He was about to slam the laptop shut, but since he was dealing with his own great depression anyway, he decided to look up "Great Depression" online, figuring it was the closest historical comparison to the situation he found himself in now.

Reading the first few paragraphs of the Wikipedia entry, his sense was that even the Great Depression hadn't been *this* bad. First had come Black Monday: October 28, 1929. The Dow had lost 12.82%, which frankly didn't sound all that black to him by recent standards. "Should have named it 'Same-Old Same-Old Monday,'" he mumbled to himself as he poured himself another shot.

The next day, October 29, 1929, the Dow had lost another 11.73%, which still didn't seem that bad. "Par for the Course Tuesday," he said to the picture of the Charging Bull on his wall, raising his glass and drinking to the year 2041. The Great Depression had nothing on *him*: he had just experienced a 20% drop on a Tuesday. So there.

But the more he read, the more the "great" in Great Depression began to live up to its name. After a short-lived rally, the markets had begun a steady slide that lasted from April 1930 to July 1932. When the Dow closed on July 8, 1932, it stood at just 41.22, its lowest level of the 20th century. That represented an 89.2% loss for the index in less than three years.

"Okay, that *is* pretty bad," Royce said out loud to his shot glass as he poured himself another and drank.

And here was the kicker: it took twenty-five years—from September 3, 1929 to November 23, 1954—before the Dow got back to where it had been before Black Monday—

to its old high-water mark of 381.17. "Ouch," Royce mumbled into the hand that seemed to be holding up his head.

He had to admit those were some pretty bleak numbers, and in a weird way it made him feel better, like he wasn't alone in having experienced something as gut-wrenchingly awful as the last few weeks had been. No wonder so many folks who had lived through the Great Depression vowed never to touch stocks again. He was beginning to sympathize with them.

He wondered if it was mere chance that the Great Depression had happened a little over a hundred years ago. Maybe human beings were doomed to repeat disasters in roughly one-hundred-year increments—just beyond their typical lifespans, and thus outside of their firsthand experience to prepare for in any practical way.

Or maybe he was just seriously drunk.

But what struck him—what rang true despite his impaired state—was that if it had happened before, it could happen again.

Ninety percent losses (or worse) were not off the table.

Twenty-five years (or worse) could elapse before markets bounced back again—if they ever did.

The situation he was in right now could be *worse* than the Great Depression.

"To the Greatest Depression," he toasted, downing another.

For one thing, it was all happening so much faster this time around. People back then had had *years* to adjust to the new reality of the Depression Era. That was why it was called an era, after all. Now, they were compressing into three weeks what had taken folks in the 1920's and 1930's three *years* to accomplish, if accomplish was the right word for it.

He was suddenly convinced things were only going to get worse. Much worse. There would be no recovery this time around. There would be no bounce-back. Yes, the stock market was resilient. Yes, it had bounced back from two world wars and even (eventually) a great depression. But this time things really *were* different.

For one thing, Wall Street itself might soon cease to exist. For all he knew, aliens might arrive at any moment and destroy the world—or at least the human beings living in it. If that wasn't cause enough for a worldwide depression, he didn't know what was.

The one certain thing was this: the markets *hated* uncertainty, and you couldn't get much more uncertain than what they were experiencing right now in 2041.

He downed another shot and noticed the bottle was empty. No problem, he had a bottle of tequila tucked away back there somewhere.

Last week they'd worried about gremlins popping out of eggs, and no one had known what to do about them. This week, miniature force fields were popping up all over the place, and guess what?—no one knew what to do about them. Next week, whatever disasters came, Royce was sure of one thing: no one would know what to do about them.

"Time to hit the panic button," he intoned to his empty shot glass just before passing out in front of his computer.

September 4 – Wall Street, New York

The next morning, drastically hung over and depressed, he came face to face with a grim reality: his old dreams were over. It was time to forget about stocks and start thinking about survival.

Because that was where things were heading now. Whether his investment accounts stood at one billion or one million or three hundred thousand didn't matter all that much. A world might be coming where 401(k) plans and investments didn't exist or were inaccessible, where people barely survived from day to day, and where guns and food mattered more than portfolios and profits.

He didn't have much time to prepare.

He didn't know exactly what he was going to do, but he knew his days of working as a financial broker were numbered.

He forced himself to shower and dress for work. It might not be the End of Days quite yet, but it was closing in on *his* end of days on Wall Street.

*****

When he showed up for work, multiple screens were tuned to the news and business channels, as always. Politicians and pundits were out in force on the morning talk shows, all busy explaining why disaster simply couldn't and wouldn't befall them in the days to come.

"The markets are being flooded with stimulus money even as we speak. Just watch: the economy is going to turn around, and it's going to turn around *fast*."

"Who cares about some tiny dome half a mile away from Wall Street. It's not like it's *doing* anything. It's just sitting there! People need to stop fretting about worst-case scenarios that are never going to happen."

"I have it on good authority the U.S. military is already actively engaged in destroying these domes. We have powerful weapons at our disposal, and once we bring them to bear, these domes will begin to fall like dominoes."

What Royce heard was: "Don't worry, stay calm, we have things under control."

What Royce thought to himself was: No they don't. Not by a longshot.

No one knew what they were doing. There *were* no experts when it came to how to respond to an alien invasion, if that was what this was (and he had come to suspect it was).

The only good thing the government had done so far was moving as many ovates out of the cities as they could. And they had almost succeeded: they had rid New York City and Washington D.C. of all known ovates. But still it hadn't been enough. And Royce suspected that was how things would continue to play out. Whatever humans did, it wouldn't be quite enough.

He worked methodically throughout the day, placing an endless succession of sell orders for his clients. Meanwhile, he was making his own plans in his head. Sometime this weekend he should buy a gun. He needed to do some research on that. He knew next to nothing about guns but thought he might need one in the coming days. And he should take a firearms training course so he didn't do something stupid like shoot himself in the foot. Liquor was high up on his list, too: there was no way he could face the end of the world without more liquor on hand.

He supposed food was important, too; he should probably stock up on groceries. Simple things like ramen noodles, chili, tuna fish, canned fruits and veggies…and an extra can opener, while he was at it. It wouldn't do to have canned goods in his cupboard and no way to open them. And water. Don't forget water. He should fill up his bathtub, just in case.

Basically, he should prepare for a siege.

A part of him was still tempted to hold onto his existing shares of stock. After all, the Federal Reserve had just announced it would slash interest rates to zero, pursue a policy of unlimited quantitative easing, and buy trillions of dollars worth of bonds. Meanwhile, Congress was busy passing an enormous stimulus package to put money directly into the hands of the people. You never knew, maybe it would be enough to calm the markets. If he waited a few more days, maybe things would get better.

Or then again, maybe they wouldn't. He decided then and there he should sell his shares and lock in seventy percent losses before things got even worse. Whatever money was left on the table he should take and turn into something useful going forward, like gold.

Such a course of action would have been unthinkable to him even a day ago. But now the blinders were off. He was done sugarcoating things: the world as he knew it was over.

*****

At the end of the trading day, he placed sell orders for his entire remaining portfolio, locking in losses of some seventy-five percent. It made him sick to his stomach but he did it anyway.

The proceeds were automatically deposited into his money market account. The question was, where to put it now? Where was a safe haven in times like these?

His first instinct, which came from the old him that thought like a stockbroker, was to put the money into U.S. Treasuries. After all, U.S. government bonds were considered just about the safest investment on the planet. But the new him couldn't help wondering if even *they* were safe. What if the U.S. government defaulted for the first and only time in its history? It didn't seem impossible.

On Capitol Hill they were running around like ants on a kicked-in anthill. All you had to do was turn on the nightly news to see just how nuts things were getting.

Last night the President had spoken comforting words to the nation and said he was calling in the military to destroy these domes once and for all. It was this last hope that kept the markets from tanking even further than they already had.

But Royce was becoming a full-blown pessimist about the domes and what humans could do to stop them.

In the end he decided to take most of his money and invest it in gold. Not gold certificates, not shares in a gold mine, but actual gold. His new mantra was, If you can't touch it, it's not real.

Of course, the old him knew that buying gold was just about the dumbest thing he could do at this point, because the price of gold had been bidden up so high. But the new him suspected that what sounded ridiculous today might seem like genius tomorrow.

If things kept getting worse in the coming months, as he suspected they would, then gold, jewels, cash, and bartered goods might be the only things left that still held any value.

September 7 – Jersey City, New Jersey

The weekend finally arrived, and Royce soon discovered he wasn't the only one who thought the end of the world was at hand.

Pistol Pete's was located on the outskirts of Jersey City, in a sketchy neighborhood Royce wouldn't have felt comfortable visiting after dark. The shop was packed full of people buying guns and ammo on a Saturday morning. Judging from their purchases, it looked like they thought Armageddon itself was fast approaching.

Royce knew next to nothing about guns, so he had to rely on the guy behind the counter to help him make a decision. "Aliens or humans?" the guy asked gruffly, and when Royce said humans, the guy showed him two types of handgun: a 9 mm and a .40-caliber. In the end, he went with the guy's suggestion: a Glock 19 semiautomatic pistol with 9 mm bullets and ten rounds, the maximum allowed per New Jersey state law.

"Good choice," the guy said. "Great for beginners. Small, lightweight, concealable (with the right permit), less recoil, and more repeat fires without a reload. Plus it's cheaper, and the ammo's cheaper too. Betcha didn't know the FBI phased out their .40-calibers for 9 mils because they're faster to shoot, more accurate, and more reliable."

"I didn't know that," said Royce, hefting the gun in his hand. "But whatever's good enough for the FBI is good enough for me."

He learned that gun laws in New Jersey were among the most restrictive in the country, so he wasn't able to walk out of the store with a gun that same day. First he'd have to acquire a state permit to purchase a handgun from the Chief of Police in Jersey City, which was typically a one- to two-month process. Royce thought life might get pretty crazy in the next month or two, so he also bought a stun gun and some pepper spray canisters at Pistol Pete's, since they didn't require permits.

He'd come to the reluctant conclusion that Greater New York was not the ideal place to call home if the world were falling apart: it was too crowded and too dependent on outside services to function well in a crisis. Once the supply chain that made city living possible began to break down, things could turn ugly fast. He and Aubrey (if he could convince her) needed to get out of the city altogether. In fact, what they really needed was to be *mobile*. That would let them go wherever it felt safest—and wherever the domes were not.

He called up Aubrey. "Hey, wanna go shopping tomorrow? I've got some big purchases in mind."

"Shoes?"

Royce laughed. "No, a little bigger than shoes."

September 8 – Jersey City, New Jersey

Aubrey showed up dressed in jeans and a white t-shirt, which was to say, nothing special, but somehow they looked special on her. "Are you ready for the shopping spree of all shopping sprees?" Royce asked.

"I was born ready."

They hadn't seen each other since their last date, so as they walked along, he caught her up on all that had been happening in his world: the fact that he was now a two hundred fifty thousandaire, that he was now invested in gold and cash instead of stocks, that he was in the process of buying a gun—

That was as far as he got.

"You bought a gun?" Aubrey asked disbelievingly.

"I'm working on buying one. First I've got to get the permit."

"That doesn't sound like you at all."

"I know. But things are going downhill fast and I want to be prepared. The next few months could get dicey."

"Well, aren't you the bundle of joy. Guns, gold, the end of the world—anything else I should be aware of?"

"Yes, actually, I was just getting to that. I don't think it's going to be safe to stay in the New York area for much longer."

"Jesus, Royce, you're *moving*?"

"Well, not exactly. It's more like I want to be *on the move.* I want to be mobile. And that means getting some wheels. I'm going vehicle and RV shopping."

"Wow. That's a lot to hit me with, Royce. I can't believe you're moving."

"Come with me. I'd love it. In fact I'm hoping for it."

Her expression softened somewhat but she shook her head. "I can't, Royce. I just can't. My family's here. Parents, grandparents, brother, sisters. If things get as bad as you say, they're going to need me. I can't go traipsing around the country in an RV and leave them to fend for themselves."

"I can see that."

"Plus there's my job. I love my job. *And* my apartment."

"Yeah."

"I love you too, Royce, I really do, but there's no way..."

"I know. I figured you'd say that. But I'm not leaving anytime soon. In fact I'm going to stick around as long as I can. I just want to start preparing for the future is all. Whatever I end up buying today, I'm going to store it outside the city. It'll be waiting for me—or us, if you should change your mind—when necessary, but not before."

"Kind of like an insurance policy."

"Exactly."

Royce stopped at the corner and stood there waiting. "What are we doing here?" Aubrey asked, looking around.

"Waiting for a bus."

"Boy, you really know how to treat a girl."

"The fare's on me. Here it comes now."

They headed west towards the oddly named Communipaw Avenue. The bus made some twenty stops along the way, so they had plenty of time to chat. "Our goal," Royce said, "is to visit a string of car dealerships along Highway 440."

"I gotta tell you, it's hard to get excited about shopping for your boyfriend's getaway vehicle."

"I'm trying to get away from the city, not you. There's a big difference."

"Is there? Me and the city are sort of a package deal."

"You may come to think differently in the coming months, Aubrey, that's all I can say. A lot of people will be trying to get out of here soon. I'm just trying to get a head start before everything's taken."

Aubrey nodded. "Okay, I can see that. So we're going shopping for your insurance policy."

"A very big insurance policy. First up is a four-wheel-drive to pull the RV. I want something big and powerful."

The bus dropped them off near the car dealerships. "Hey, there's an IHOP," said Royce. "This date just keeps getting better and better, doesn't it?"

"I'm already starting to miss you less than I thought I would."

They wandered around the lot looking at all the shiny, expensive merchandise for sale. "Have you ever shopped for a vehicle before?" Aubrey asked.

"Never. Who needs one in the city? But never fear: I've done my homework. I know what I want and roughly how much I should have to pay."

It only took half an hour for the salesman to talk Royce into buying what he already knew he wanted: a Dodge Ram 3500 heavy-duty pickup capable of towing a small kingdom if need be.

"But can you afford a brand new vehicle?" Aubrey whispered. "We just took the bus, for God's sake. It's like you're two different people. I can't figure you out."

"I had to pay *cash* for the bus. This is different; this is on credit. My plan is to buy everything I can on credit going forward, with the expectation that I might not have to pay all of it back in the end. I'll simply make the minimum payments and wait for the whole system of credit payments to come crashing down."

Aubrey shook her head. "I think you've really gone off the deep end, babe. Are you sure you've thought this through?"

"Worst-case scenario, I have to pay it all back, right? Best-case scenario, I get a brand-new truck and only make a portion of the payments."

"Whatever you say, hon. It's your money. And your credit rating. But I'm a little worried about you, and I'm only half kidding at this point."

An hour later Royce was the proud new owner of a Dodge pickup. He paid the minimum he could get away with up front, signed the loan for the longest length of time available (seven years, with no monthly payments for the first ninety days), and drove it off the lot.

"Yee-haw," Royce shouted. "This here is one happy redneck."

Aubrey couldn't help but laugh. "No redneck would ever say that, Royce, even I know that much. You're crazy, you know that? But I gotta say, I like this ride a whole lot better than I liked the bus."

"Hey, I almost forgot the IHOP." Royce made as if to make a U-turn.

"Don't you dare. You take me somewhere nice."

"Don't worry. I have something in mind."

They drove north half an hour, marveling at how easy it was to get from place to place with their own set of wheels. "Hey, this part *is* fun," said Aubrey. "I haven't been out of the city in ages."

"See? I told you. And the shopping spree has only just begun." Before long he pulled off at an upscale restaurant called Frasca Mediterranean Cuisine.

Over the course of the next hour, they had one of the best meals of their lives, all paid for on his credit card.

"Enjoy these things while they last," Royce said, waving his credit card in the air in front of her. "They're going the way of the dinosaur."

"You have truly flipped your lid, mister," said Aubrey, but she was smiling. After a meal like that, it was hard not to.

*****

They drove straight to RV World out in the boonies of northern New Jersey. There were hundreds of new and used models to choose from, but after popping into a dozen or so, one in particular caught their eye: a brand-new Wildcat thirty-foot fifth wheel.

"Look at this living room," said Aubrey. "It even has a faux fireplace. And the picture windows are huge. I always thought an RV would feel cramped, but with these slide-outs, it's positively roomy in here. This place is bigger than your studio apartment."

"And way nicer too."

Aubrey peeked into the bedroom. "Hey, there's even a king bed in here. And a full shower. Oh, I'm liking this one, hon."

"Let's get it."

Once again Royce put the absolute minimum down and signed papers for a long-term loan. He also paid for six months of RV storage with his credit card.

"We've got one more stop to make. I want to stock up the RV before we leave."

They drove their pickup to a local grocery store, where they filled a grocery cart to the brim with canned goods and nonperishable items, paying on credit and stowing it all in the back seat of the truck before returning for more. They made four runs all told. The store clerk looked at them like they were crazy by the time they'd made their fourth run. "That's a lot of creamed corn," she said flatly as she finished checking them out.

"You can never have too much creamed corn," Royce replied with a straight face, but out in the parking lot they burst out laughing.

"I don't think we can ever show our faces in there again," Aubrey said, wiping away a tear. She looked around at all the bags of chips, powdered dips, powdered potatoes, powdered milk, ramen noodles, pasta, oatmeal, dried beans, energy bars, nuts, chocolate, and cans, cans, cans and shook her head. The entire back of the pickup was filled to overflowing. "You've got enough stuff in here to feed a small army."

"Some of this could be useful for bartering in a pinch. All these spices, seasoning packets, and dried sauce packets could become valuable once grocery stores run out."

"They're already emptying out. I can't find half the stuff I'm looking for these days."

"Here, have a creamed corn on me."

Aubrey laughed. "Thanks but I'll take some chocolate instead."

JUMP 1

September 10, 2041

On September 10th the iridescent soap-bubble colors on the dome walls began to swirl and pulse with increasing intensity, as if to announce to anyone in the immediate vicinity that something big was about to happen. Then the domes "jumped," going from over there to over here in an instant. Just like that, each dome doubled in size to around 800 square feet—about the size of a small apartment. The jumps weren't simultaneous but they were close. Most occurred in the early morning hours, with the rest playing catchup by early afternoon.

When people looked closer, they discovered something new: a dome within a dome. The smaller force field was still there at the center, protecting the ovate, but now a bigger force field had materialized around it. If anything, the inner force field looked smaller than it had before, as if it had pulled in even closer to the ovate at its nucleus.

The stock market, which had stabilized and even crept higher due to the extraordinary stimulus packages announced in recent days, plummeted again and only stopped falling when the circuit breakers kicked in and the NYSE closed for good at 11:30 am. By then another twenty percent of market value had been lost. There seemed to be no floor to this seller's market other than zero.

Even as panic selling was happening on Wall Street, panic buying was happening on Main Street. People were hoarding food and supplies in a mad rush to stock up before it was too late. Grocers began doubling and tripling prices on whatever staples remained, but items continued to fly off the shelves.

Meanwhile, inflation was spiking in a big way. A gallon of gas suddenly cost ten dollars. That meant delivery costs were increasing astronomically. The prices of meat and vegetables and canned goods and a thousand other items began to skyrocket.

The Great Depression was starting to look like small potatoes compared to this.

7

September 10 – NBC Nightly News, New York

"Good evening, this is Cory Phillips coming to you live from NBC Nightly News headquarters in New York. Ten days after what is being called the hatch, we have a new and disturbing development. The force fields have "jumped," suddenly doubling in size all across the world and within a few hours of one another. Everywhere, markets are in turmoil, inflation is spiking, and uncertainty about the future has never been greater. The one question on everyone's mind is, Was this a one-time occurrence, or is this just the first of many such jumps?

"Unfortunately no one has the answer to that question, but we can already see the disastrous consequences of this first jump, both in terms of the tanking economy and the impact it's having on individual lives. Later on in this broadcast, we'll be reporting in-depth on the situation in major cities such as New York, Washington D.C., and Los Angeles, but for now we have a host of reporters standing by with the aim of giving viewers a taste of what folks are facing elsewhere in this country. Let's begin with this report from Yosemite National Park in California."

"Thanks Cory. This is Roosevelt Moody, and I'm standing here with the majestic Half Dome behind me as we grapple with the reality of a new kind of dome, one that is most unwelcome. It saddens me to have to report that there are no less than eleven domes within the pristine boundaries of this park, including one situated smack-dab in the middle of the Yosemite Valley. Since its doubling in size earlier this morning, the dome is unmissable no matter how hard you squint, and the glare it gives off at midday is nothing short of appalling.

"Meanwhile, wildfires sparked during the hatch continue to rage out of control in multiple parts of the park, including remote backcountry corridors that are virtually unreachable by firefighters. You can see the thick pall of smoke behind me, and it has been like that for over a week now. Cory?"

"Thanks Roosevelt. Next let's check in with Deedee Mitchell near Kearney, Nebraska."

"Cory, behind me you can see a stretch of I-80 near the Archway Monument in Nebraska. Viewers may recall that when the ovates first hatched ten days ago, two domes sprouted up in the breakdown lanes located just behind me. One of them encroached into the eastbound lane, and the other into the westbound lane, and unfortunately, those domes were all but invisible to vehicles traveling at eighty miles per hour. The result was two horrific multi-vehicle accidents immediately after the domes formed. Six tractor trailers and thirteen cars collided at high speed with the domes, or with other vehicles that had just hit the domes, causing twenty-seven deaths.

"Now, with this first 'jump,' as it's being called, only one lane of I-80 remains open in each direction. And this is no isolated incident, Cory: this is just one of dozens of highways that are now impeded or blocked by domes all across the country. In Los Angeles, a dome in the middle of I-5 is causing major headaches for commuters. And on I-70 near Glenwood Springs, the dome's increased size has completely obstructed the narrow canyon through which the highway passes, resulting in the permanent closure of the interstate at that chokepoint. That means drivers now have to make a detour of some three or four hours just to get to where they're going. Cory, back to you."

"Thanks Deedee. Now let's head to Roswell, New Mexico, where Roxanne Fuller is standing by. Roxanne?"

"Thanks Cory. We're here in Roswell because of a cult known as the Greeters, who *intentionally* allowed themselves to be trapped inside a dome earlier today. These Greeters believe they'll be the first to meet the aliens if they simply wait inside—which is why they came prepared with food, water, bedding, and, of course, plenty of alcohol and marijuana. They claim that we in the news business have got it all wrong—that the sudden appearance of these domes is a *good* thing, heralding the arrival of our alien saviors. And they want to be right here, at 'alien ground zero,' as they call it, when the extraterrestrials arrive.

"Earlier this afternoon the Greeters got their wish: they were swallowed up inside a dome. In this clip you can see people crowding around the dome as its walls begin to swirl and pulsate, being careful not to touch the walls, of course. Some were praying, others dancing, others looking like they were in a rapturous state. Many raised their arms to the heavens as the big moment approached, chanting, swaying, and calling out for the aliens to come. I personally witnessed several people standing immediately in the path of the new dome wall as it came down directly on top of them, and amazingly, it didn't harm a single hair on their heads. It could have cut them clean in half *vertically*, but it did not. These people were able to step in or out—apparently it was their choice—and most stepped *in*, which is either really brave or really stupid, Cory, depending on your point of view."

"I have my own opinion on that, Roxanne, but I'll keep it to myself. Thanks for that report, and let's hope those Greeters stay safe. Next let's hear from Mabel Willis, who's standing by in San Diego."

"Cory, I'm reporting from just outside the elephant enclosure at the San Diego Zoo, and as you can see, with this first jump, the dome immediately behind me now extends directly into the elephants' habitat. When the matriarch touched the force field with her trunk earlier this afternoon, she got quite the shock, enough so that she started a stampede in close quarters, nearly trampling one zoo employee to death. Those elephants still haven't settled down, and neither has the employee.

"Another dome now extends into the bonobo habitat, and if you want to talk about curious creatures, bonobos put humans to shame. They've already touched the force field dozens of times, and they screech like nobody's business each time they get shocked—but ten minutes later they're back to doing it again. Employees here are taking bets as to how long it will be before they learn to leave it alone.

"But on a more serious note, Cory, these domes pose a genuine threat to the animals in our care, both at this zoo and every other zoo around the world. What if an animal is in distress, or needs food or water, and zoo employees can't reach it? We can't explain to an animal the way we could to a person that all they need to do is walk through the dome wall. A Bengal tiger might choose to stay put and die before passing through that energy field. Cory, back to you."

"Thanks Mabel. Our next report comes from Buckner, Missouri."

"Cory, this is Russell Aguilar reporting to you from a stretch of the Union Pacific railroad near Buckner, where a freight train derailed earlier this afternoon when it struck a dome head-on. The locomotive exploded, killing both the conductor and engineer. The remaining cars careened off the track, piling up into the endless jumble you see behind me. More than two hundred freight cars with over four-hundred piggy-backed shipping containers hauling some ten thousand tons of material hit the dome at high speed. Similar accidents have been occurring all over the rail system since the domes first made their appearance. Rail transport has been halted across the country for the second time in ten days until the NTSB can—" [CLICK]

Longmont, Colorado

Will switched off the news and stared at his wife. "Things just keep getting better and better, don't they?"

"We should stop watching the news altogether," Cynthia said. "All it does is freak me out. That dome near our home expanded again this morning, and—"

Will waved her off. "It's barely bigger than our garage. And it's still a quarter mile away. I'm sure the authorities will take care of it before it becomes a real problem." He headed off to the kitchen to get a beer.

Cynthia hoped her husband was right, but sometimes in the middle of the night she awoke with panic attacks. *Dome syndrome,* they were calling it on the TV talk shows. She knew she was a worrier by nature, and her best way of dealing with worry was to *plan,* so over the past week she'd packed 'bug-out bags' just in case—the kind an intelligence operative might use in an emergency. She had six of them stored down in the basement, one for each family member: herself, Will, the three kids, and the dog. Woof was family too, after all.

Her other way of dealing with stress was to make lists. She stored those in her nightstand beneath a pile of nondescript papers, like an incriminating diary she didn't want anyone to read. But when Will was off at work, she would pull out the lists and add more notes to the bottom: reminders of things she should do, things she should bring, things her kids couldn't live without, things *she* couldn't live without….She was up to six pages by now.

Josh and Kaley broke into her reverie as they came charging down the stairs. "Not in the house," she called, but they were yelling so loudly they didn't hear her (or, more likely, chose not to). They tore through the living room, around the kitchen island twice (Kaley calling out "Hi Dad!" as she passed him by at the kitchen table), then into the dining room where Josh finally tackled her onto the carpet. Thump! Squeals of laughter from Kaley. "Gotcha!" Josh said.

Cynthia stood in the dining room entryway, hands on her hips, trying not to smile. "What are you two up to now?"

"Playing capture the alien," Kaley said happily. "Josh makes a great alien—he's so ugh-ly." That earned her more tickles, enough to send her into renewed paroxysms of squealing. "I thought *you* were the alien," Josh said. "You certainly *sound* like one." "I thought *you* were the alien," laughed Kaley, "and you were chasing *me*."

"Whoever's the alien, take it outside, *now,* before you break something." Cynthia pointed imperiously towards the door.

"Maybe *she's* the alien," Kaley whispered.

"I heard that," said Cynthia.

"I think you were supposed to," said Josh. "Fine, fine, we're going. Must—obey—overlord," he said to Kaley as they made their way out. She burst out laughing and started walking like an automaton.

"Dinner's in half an hour," Cynthia reminded them. "Where's Ashley?"

"Where do you think?" Kaley answered, rolling her eyes Ashley-style. "In her room, as always, talking with one of her *boy*friends." She said it with such disdain, Josh and Cynthia traded a little smile.

"Okay," Cynthia said. "Your overlord commands you to be back in half an hour. Make it so."

"That's Jean Luc Picard," said Josh, "not an overlord."

"Yeah, Mom," chided Kaley. "An overlord would say something different, like, "Resistance is futile."

"Resistance *is* futile if you're not back here in time for dinner."

Woof stopped chasing after the kids and came back inside, staring up at her and wagging his tail. He barked once, alarm clock that he was. It was time for his dinner, and he knew it. She poured dog food into his bowl and set it down.

Now, what to make for the rest of the family? She opened the fridge and stared inside, trying to figure out what to make with half her ingredients missing due to all the shortages at the store.

JUMP 2

September 20

On September 20th every dome around the world jumped for a second time, doubling in size, transforming from the size of an apartment to the size of a large house. Each had a diameter of some 60 feet, encapsulating about 3,000 square feet of land. Worldwide that only amounted to about 500 square miles all told—roughly the size of Los Angeles—but the fact that the "plots" were scattered all over the place made it annoying to humans, who weren't used to having anyone but themselves decide where things should or shouldn't go. Man, it seemed, no longer had complete dominion over the Earth: land was being set aside by others for their own arcane purposes.

With ten days having passed between the hatch and the first jump, and another ten days between the first jump and the second, it was becoming apparent the domes were synchronized in some fashion. Every ten days came another jump. It wasn't quite like clockwork, but it was close enough—which meant the world could begin to anticipate another "growth spurt" on or around September 30th.

This awareness galvanized people into action. Anyone anywhere near a jump zone began moving whatever possessions they could out of their homes just as fast as they could: furniture, clothes, scrapbooks, electronics, jewelry. Whole houses were emptied in frantic fashion in a matter of days. U-Hauls and moving vans became impossible to rent, and storage facilities deemed safe in terms of their location quadrupled their monthly rates and still had a waiting list a mile long.

Those who couldn't rent a storage unit had little choice but to impose on family and friends. They jammed their cherished belongings into other people's attics and garages, filled drive-ways to overflowing with overloaded vehicles, and crowded into guest bedrooms "just for the night" (the standard phrase). Nerves frayed to the breaking point as distant relatives pushed the boundaries of kinship like never before.

Life was changing fast, and people were just trying to keep up. The next jump already felt inevitable.

8

September 20 – Oval Office

"So how many push-pins do we need in that map of ours?" asked the President.

"Too many," replied Cohen. "We estimate something on the order of 298,000 domes here in the U.S."

The President sighed. "That's a whole lot of pins. Less than Gil's back-of-the-napkin estimate, but not by much."

"Yes sir. His estimate was annoyingly accurate." Lametti remained silent, but Cohen thought he looked smug.

"What's the global count?"

"We're far less certain about that. Our best guess is between four and five million."

"Jesus! That many!"

"The good news is, some are in the middle of nowhere: places like Antarctica, the Sahara, Siberia, the Eurasian Steppes, and the Outback."

"Did some poor schmuck actually go out there and count all of them?"

"No sir, these are statistical estimates based on satellite data."

The President paced for awhile without speaking. "Gil, you're awfully quiet. What do you make of all this?"

Lametti had been looking pensively out the window, but now he turned his attention towards the President.

"The more I think about it, Mark, the more I think this is a land grab, plain and simple. These domes—each time they double in size, they're gobbling up land. Maybe not all that much so far, but if they keep doubling in size the way they've been doing, things could get ugly fast."

"Ugly how?"

"Rioting in the streets ugly. I think we can guess at this point what the ultimate goal of these aliens must be."

"And what's that?"

Lametti shrugged. "The takeover of the planet."

"*All* of it?"

He shrugged again, palms open wide. "Who knows? Maybe. Or at least a sizable chunk of it."

The President shook his head and resumed pacing around the Oval Office, looking deeply perturbed. "So what can we do about it?"

"I'm not sure there's much we *can* do. But I'd say we need to get as aggressive as we can. Ramp up the military's involvement. Station troops outside each dome—or at least the ones inside our major cities. Call up the National Guard and station them in those same cities to keep the peace once things go crazy—and they *will* go crazy. And most important of all—bomb one of these domes to kingdom come to see if we can't destroy it once and for all."

"Kingdom come. I assume you mean nuclear."

"Yes. Honestly I can't think of a response that would be too extreme at this point. This is an invasion, pure and simple, and we need to treat it as one. Just because we can't *see* the enemy with our own eyes doesn't mean we're not under attack. We need to respond with maximum military force while we still can."

"Hear, hear," cried Bill Cohen.

"You'll get no argument from me," said the President. "General McMillan has been pushing for the same thing. Let's try bunker busters first, then we'll go nuclear."

White Sands Missile Range, New Mexico

Stealth Bomber pilot Lionel Lawson had never flown a mission quite like this one before. For one thing, the target was located right here in the US of A, and for another, the payload was massively heavy.

Two 30,000-pound GBU-57 massive ordnance penetrators—more commonly known as bunker busters—were stored in the B-2's bomb bay. The plane felt sluggish compared to what he was used to.

These bunker busters were right at the top of the Air Force's ordnance scale. They were six times heavier than any other deep-penetrating bunker buster and held the title of world's biggest non-nuclear bomb. Lawson thought if any type of conventional payload was going to destroy a dome, it would be this one.

Problem was, the Air Force only had a small stockpile of them. Each one cost nearly four million dollars to produce, and there weren't nearly enough to address the hundreds of thousands of targets in America alone. Then again, most of the domes were located in populated areas, so dropping a bunker buster on top of them probably wasn't in the cards anyway.

But if even one dome could be destroyed, it would prove an important point. It would mean the domes were vulnerable to human attack. So far no other military options had worked. It was time to bring out the *really* big guns.

Lawson's mission was to drop both bunker busters on a dome located way out in the middle of White Sands Missile Range in New Mexico. You couldn't ask for a more desirable target for a test of this sort. It was such a remote and restricted location that there were no concerns about collateral damage. The bunker busters were designed to penetrate hardened targets, or targets buried deep underground, delivering a high explosive payload. Based on what the military had seen so far, no target was more hardened than these domes.

Lawson was just about in range now. "Target acquired," he said into his headset. "Launching payload one." The bomb bay doors opened and the first bunker buster was released. Moments later the second followed. Both were precision-guided so there was no question of missing the target here.

Moments later the first bomb hit. The explosion was spectacular. Fast on its heels came the second, and the amount of dirt and debris cast into the air was so great that Lawson couldn't see a thing at the target sight.

He listened from his cockpit while mission control stared at their screens waiting for the smoke and debris to clear.

Eventually the smoke thinned out enough that they could see…nothing!

Nothing but a huge crater where the dome had been.

Success! Cheers went up from mission control. Lawson sighed with relief. Finally something had worked. The domes weren't indestructible after all, which meant they had a chance.

"Hang on. Mission Control here."

The voice sounded subdued.

"Due east of the target area. A quarter click away. It's the ovate, with the force field still surrounding it. We can see all of it—the whole sphere. Resting on top of the sands. Looks to be intact. Target not destroyed…only relocated."

Shit.

Situation Room, Washington D.C.

"So the bunker busters were a bust," sighed the President. He was sitting in the Situation Room in the basement of the White House monitoring the White Sands mission.

The usual suspects were with him in attendance, sitting around the conference table, cabinet members and military brass alike.

He'd just witnessed two bunker busters create an enormous and quite expensive hole in the ground. It had been enough to blow the ovate about a tenth of a mile away, which, given how heavy it was, was impressive. But follow-up reconnaissance had confirmed that the ovate with its surrounding force field remained intact, partially sunken now, like a golf ball sitting in a sand trap.

Bill Cohen swore. "We *have* to go nuclear on these suckers."

"Agreed," said the President. "If we were to do that, how exactly would we go about it?"

Cohen had his answer ready. "Use the same dome out at White Sands, or another one like it in some remote corner of the country. Plant a nuclear weapon just outside of it and wait for the dome to swallow it up on the next jump. Then, once the weapon is on the inside, detonate it and see what happens."

"Detonate it how? Remotely?"

Cohen shook his head. "The signal might not reach through the dome wall. Better to put a timer on the weapon and have someone set it off from the inside, then make their escape. We already know the dome is designed to let people out."

"Why not just bomb it from the outside and be done with it?"

"If we detonate it *inside* the force field," replied Cohen, "then the full force of the explosion will be directed onto the ovate itself. That gives us our best chance of destroying both the ovate and the force field."

The President nodded. "Okay, Bill, you're in charge. Make it happen."

September 25 – Nellis AFB, Las Vegas, Nevada

Truth be told, General McMillan hadn't felt this alive since the war in Afghanistan. Not that he would ever admit it to anyone, but he was glad for the invasion. "Peace in our time" was a pipedream, what with these alien domes scattered all over the place, and McMillan couldn't have been happier about it.

He had the perfect enemy to fight, too: a non-human one that every American agreed had to be stopped. Of course, he couldn't *see* that enemy, but he was sure as hell they were out there somewhere, watching all the fun from a distance. No doubt they were laughing their heads off (if they even had heads) as the humans ran around with their hair on fire trying to destroy the domes.

It was genius, really. If nothing else, the domes served as an enormous distraction. Who could think about an *actual* alien invasion when domes kept popping up everywhere across the face of the Earth? McMillan snorted: the planet had developed a bad case of acne and that was all anyone could think about.

As for himself, he felt quite sure these domes were the equivalent of advance bases. The enemy would use them as beachheads for their coming invasion. Once the domes got big enough, he expected to see aliens drop out of the skies and occupy them. Then the real fun would begin. He had always relished a good fight, and this one was gonna be a doozy.

But for now his mission was simple: get a nuclear bomb into a dome in the middle of the Nevada desert.

Piece of cake. The bombs were already out here at Nellis Air Force Base, just north of Las Vegas. Nellis was one of two Air Force nuclear weapons depots in the U.S. (the other being Kirtland in New Mexico). The nukes were stored in a remote section of the Nellis complex known as

Area 2, so all he had to do was pick one out from the existing stockpile and have it transported to the dome.

Technically speaking, it was experts from the 896th Munitions Squadron at Nellis who would be choosing which exact bomb to pick. They had all sorts of things to say about what type of nuclear device to use, how to transport it, what buttons not to push, blah blah blah. They liked to talk even more than he did.

Area 2 had more than eight hundred gravity bombs removed from retired B-52 bombers, plus another six hundred surplus cruise missile warheads, so they weren't exactly starved for choice. As far as McMillan was concerned, they were all the "right bombs," since they were all nuclear weapons. Whichever one they picked, it was going to make one helluva boom. And since the dome was still only the size of your average house, one thermonuclear device planted inside it should vaporize it, oh, about ten million times over.

In the end the experts selected the B83, one of the most powerful nuclear freefall weapons in the U.S. arsenal. With a maximum yield of 1.2 megatons, it was eighty times more powerful than the bomb dropped on Hiroshima. Frankly, McMillan was of the opinion that if *that* didn't work, they were shit out of luck.

The stockpile at Nellis contained fully operational bombs kept in cold storage that were available in minutes. They weren't connected to delivery systems, but that wasn't an issue in this case. All they had to do was load one up onto the back of a specially designed truck and ship it out. The Munitions Squadron took care of all the details, so all McMillan had to do was stand around and look important.

Normally the transport of a nuclear weapon would have required all sorts of special permits and licenses, but they were in a hurry and had the blessing of the President of the United States himself to speed things along, so they didn't have to wait for the middle of the night, or escort vehicles, or security details, or anything like that. They just up and went.

Which was how General McMillan liked it: down and dirty. This was his kind of mission, and he was having a ball.

JUMP 3

September 30

Right on schedule, the domes jumped for a third time. Most of the jumps happened in the wee hours of the night. Some unfortunate parents awoke to discover their children or pets had just been swallowed up by a dome, with themselves on one side and their loved ones on the other. Coaxing terrified children, let alone dogs or cats, to pass through an electric wall of energy spelled the end of sleep for the remainder of that night for any such family.

Each dome was now roughly the size of your average Walgreens and the height of a three-story building. Their alien soap-bubble appearance looked out of place no matter what their surroundings. Most considered them a pox on the face of the Earth, but a few artist-types found glimmers of beauty too surreal to ignore.

One photographer captured the Eiffel Tower at sunrise with one of its legs enclosed by a dome and its pinnacle soaring high above—an image that quickly went viral. Another image depicted the Great Pyramid of Giza dominating a dome in a way that seemed to suggest humans couldn't help but triumph in the long run. At the Gateway Arch in St. Louis, onlookers remarked on a dome that was "almost cute" as it nestled near one of the arch's two enormous legs. And at the Grand Canyon, spectators marveled at an ovate perched near the very edge of the canyon with its force field extending out over the abyss, forming a shimmering sphere in the air.

Each dome now encompassed a quarter acre of land. For those keeping track, that represented about 2,000 square miles of land now out of commission worldwide—roughly the size of Delaware. That was still a pittance compared to the Earth's total land mass of some 57 million square miles (not counting land under the oceans), but the domes were annoyingly spread out and took up more psychological space than they did actual space. They were like noxious weeds invading a well-tended garden that refused to be uprooted no matter how vigorously people pulled.

9

September 30 – Situation Room, Washington D.C.

"Yessir, the dome gobbled up that nuke just like we thought it would," General McMillan announced to the President. "You just say the word and we'll have ourselves one hell of a going-away party for that ovate out yonder."

The President was once again in the Situation Room in the basement of the White House. It was cramped and stuffy in there, and he always felt like he was too far away from the television monitors to see as clearly as he would have liked, but protocol demanded that he sit at the head of the conference table and pretend to be happy about it. "All right, General," he replied. "Let's get this show on the road. And let's hope for all our sakes the dome is destroyed this time around."

"One hundred percent with you there, Chief," McMillan said. "Hang on tight for a sec; I'm gonna tell 'em to get started."

As Bill Cohen had suspected, remote detonation wasn't an option, since a signal wouldn't carry through the dome wall. That meant one soldier had to stand just outside the force field with a signaling device that flashed green or red depending on whether the operation was a go or no-go. At present it was flashing red, as it would continue to do until the moment its operator got the word from General McMillan to proceed.

Inside the dome was another soldier whose job it was to watch for the green "go" signal, then set the timer for fifteen minutes and hightail it out of there like his life depended on it—which it did.

They all watched as the soldier outside the dome got the word from General McMillan. He fussed with the signaling device for a second, then held it above his head so the soldier on the inside could see the flashing green "go" signal.

The volunteer on the inside gave a thumbs up, set the timer, checked to make sure everything was set, then flipped the switch to start the countdown. He stared at the timer for several seconds to make sure it was counting down properly, then ran like hell, passing through the dome wall at a sprint and diving into the waiting Humvee.

The other soldier was already behind the wheel, and as soon as his comrade jumped in, they peeled out of there like actual aliens were chasing after them. They made a beeline due east across the Nevada Test Site. There were no formal roads in such a remote place, only dirt tracks in the scrub that hinted at a way to go, but before long they had put plenty of distance between themselves and the nuclear bomb that was counting its way down to zero. Eventually they disappeared out of the zoomed-out video and were presumed safe.

The cameras zoomed back in on the dome itself. Five minutes to go and counting.

For the President and his cabinet members and military advisors waiting inside the Situation Room, those were the longest five minutes of their lives. They sat there in complete silence, waiting to see what would happen.

General McMillan announced the one-minute mark, and they all sat up straighter in their chairs.

"Okay, commencing countdown," General McMillan said. "That mother-effer should go off in ten, nine, eight..."

Everyone leaned forward. The President squinted and wished for the big-screen TV in his living room.

"...seven, six, five..."

If this didn't work they were screwed. He had no more aces up his sleeve. This was it—their last hope of fighting back.

"...four, three, two..."

What on God's green earth was he going to tell the American people if this didn't work?

"...one..."

A blinding flash of light appeared on the screen.

Their eyes turned away involuntarily for a second, as if they might be blinded from a nuclear blast even as seen through the lens of a television camera. The screen remained dazzling white for several seconds, then fuzzy blackness slowly returned to the four corners of the screen and crept inwards, finally returning them to a picture that made sense.

But it didn't make sense. The dome was still there—down at the bottom of a brand-new crater, but still there. Above it rose a huge, roiling mushroom cloud, expanding even as they watched.

They all remained silent for a long time.

General McMillan sounded subdued when his voice finally came over the speaker. "Not in a million years did I see that coming."

"I think you speak for all of us, General," said the President heavily.

One of the most powerful nuclear weapons in the United States arsenal had just detonated *inside* a dome the size of a Walgreens and had done no discernible damage to it.

*****

President Mark Gardner prided himself on being calm in a crisis. He had served bravely in the war in Afghanistan, he had witnessed death and destruction with his own eyes, and he had been in tough spots before and had always risen to the occasion. But now, for the first time in his life, and certainly for the first time in his presidency, he felt real panic. Serious, overwhelming panic.

He was back in the Oval Office now, and the Oval Office was spinning. For some reason that struck him as funny—the Oval Office spinning—and it made him laugh out loud.

He realized he was having a full-blown panic attack and decided to lie down on the couch right in front of his Chief of Staff and Secretary of Defense.

Everyone was looking to him for leadership, and guess what? He had absolutely no idea what to say or do next.

What *could* he say? "Sorry, folks, we're in a bit of a pickle here. Seems the most powerful nukes in our arsenal are completely useless against this threat." He laughed again, much louder than he intended to.

"Can we get you anything, Mark?" Gil Lametti asked tentatively.

The President took several deep breaths and tried to calm himself. He sat up on the couch and tried to act normal, whatever normal looked like in times like these.

"What next?" he managed to croak out.

Lametti and Cohen both looked down at their feet. Clearly they were just as gobsmacked as he was.

"Gil?"

"Well, I don't know, Mark. I suppose we could try variations on a theme. Try exploding a bunker buster from *inside* a dome or dropping a nuclear bomb on the *outside*. Maybe see if our scientists have come up with any more bright ideas. Maybe something with magnets?"

We've tried those already," the President said with a frustrated wave of his hand.

"I know, I'm just grasping at straws at this point."

"That's okay, Gil," said the President, nodding and trying to be supportive. He took some more deep breaths and felt the panic subside to something more manageable. "And you're right. Hey, why not? Let's try out some bigger magnets. What do they call those things? Hallek Arrays?" he asked Bill Cohen.

"Halbach arrays, sir."

"Right. Let's try out some monster-sized ones. I mean, what the hell, what have we got to lose? Get our scientists on it right away."

Gil nodded and wrote it down in his notepad.

"Bill, what have you got?"

His Secretary of Defense looked flummoxed for the first time in his career. He didn't have a single military option to recommend that he thought would really work. Cohen finally shrugged and forced himself to speak. "There's nothing left, sir. We've blown our wad. We've tried everything realistic that I can think of."

"Everything?"

"Well...there are some newfangled DARPA weapons out there we could try. Futuristic stuff, but hell, half of them are still in the development stage, and the other half...well, they're powerful, but not as powerful as a nuclear weapon. And we've already tried that."

"Tell me about them anyway."

"Yes sir." Cohen thought for a moment. "Well, we could try using an electromagnetic rail gun. It's essentially a monster cannon that uses laser energy to fire projectiles at almost five thousand miles per hour. The projectiles can smash through concrete structures over a hundred miles away—but whether they'll work against a force field is anyone's guess."

"Okay, that sounds worth trying. Make a note of that, will you, Gil? What else have you got, Bill?"

"Well, there's MAHEM. That's another DARPA special. It stands for magneto hydrodynamic explosive munition. It uses a magnetic flux generator to fire a projectile—like molten metal—that can penetrate enemy armored vehicles. They're lethal on the battlefield, but I have no idea if they'll have any effect on a dome. Personally I doubt it, sir."

"Let's try it anyway. What else have you got?"

Cohen pondered for a minute. "Maybe an e-bomb?"

"What's that?"

"An electromagnetic pulse or EMP weapon. Essentially it's a high-powered pulse that can be used to knock out electronics by inducing a surge of electric current. A conventional EMP bomb generates a pretty intense pulse—but we have nuclear versions that can *really* wreak havoc."

"That sounds promising."

"It could be. The nuclear version produces some pretty incredible current and voltage surges—and the gamma radiation emitted from the blast ionizes the surrounding air, creating a secondary EMP."

"I like the sound of that," said the President. "Gil, write that one down. Anything else?"

Cohen thought for awhile. "Nothing else that I can think of."

The President nodded. "Okay. Every military option that we can come up with, let's throw it at those domes, and I mean *everything*. Meanwhile, I'm going to need to address the American people—and to be honest, I have no idea what to say." He turned towards Gil Lametti, his oldest and most trusted friend.

Lametti thought for a moment. "The truth," he said at last, spreading his hands. "Tell them the truth. They deserve that much, at least."

"Won't that create a panic?" Cohen asked.

"Isn't a panic already underway?" Lametti replied. "The truth may help calm people down, especially if we sprinkle in some half-truths about additional military options that are still on the table."

"Okay," said the President. "Okay, I like that. People already know the bunker busters and the nuke didn't work—the media will have taken care of that for us. But I'm still going to have to address the American people directly; they're going to want to hear it from me."

"Agreed," said Lametti. "And you may want to start preparing them for the fact that we may simply have no viable answer to this alien technology."

"What good would *that* do?" demanded Cohen. He sounded outraged at the very thought of admitting such a thing in public.

"Maybe none. But it might help prepare people for the inevitable. For the new reality that's coming."

"And what reality is that?" inquired Cohen.

"That we're going to be hosting guests from out of state soon," Lametti replied dryly."

"Hosting guests! Boy, that's a nice way of putting it. Welcome, aliens: mi casa es su casa."

"Look," said Lametti. "If aliens really *are* coming, and you're a bright-eyed optimist, then the best-case scenario is that we'll have to learn to share our planet with them. That's if we're lucky. Maybe they'll be like benevolent monarchs who will have our best interests at heart once they arrive. Think Frederick the Great, only greener."

"Monarchs," Cohen growled. "Despots, you mean."

"Tomato tomahto. Benevolent ones, anyway."

"Who will lord it over us in every possible way."

"Who may help us in ways we never could have imagined. They could be light-years ahead of us in medicine, for example. Maybe they'll show us how to cure cancer."

"That would be wonderful, of course," Cohen conceded, "but I *hate* the idea of kowtowing to anyone. I hate it to my very core."

"Hear, hear," said the President.

"I'm not saying we should *like* it," Lametti said. "I'm just saying we may have no choice."

"We could die fighting," Cohen pointed out.

"*If* we can even get to them. Once they're inside their domes, what can we *do*, exactly?"

They thought about that for awhile.

"We'll be on the outside looking in," Lametti continued. "They'll be on the inside looking out."

"Like some strange new apartheid," said the President. "Segregation taken to the extreme."

"If they were as friendly as you make them out to be," Cohen observed, "they wouldn't *need* domes. And they certainly wouldn't have put them right in the middle of our goddamn cities. They could have located them in remote places where they'd have done less damage."

"The domes weren't domes at the beginning," Lametti pointed out. "According to our scientists, they were seeds or spores that fell from the sky. *Randomly*. It doesn't sound like the aliens directed them to fall anywhere specific."

"Maybe they should have," replied Cohen. "If they're so advanced and all."

"You really think they might be friendly?" the President asked.

Lametti shrugged. "They might be. Consider this: if they really wanted to kill us outright, they could have just sent spores containing a tailored virus that would have exterminated us all in an instant. Instead, we have these domes, these force fields, which seems to suggest they're occupiers, not terminators."

Cohen grunted. "Occupiers is just a euphemism for invaders. For all we know, it's not apartheid or segregation they're after but slavery."

"What a terrible thought," murmured the President.

"It is," Lametti agreed. "And now we're on to the more pessimistic side of the equation. If you're cynical, then you can imagine other reasons why the aliens might be coming—and what they might do with us once they arrive."

"They might use us as slaves to work in their factories or mines for their own benefit," Cohen suggested. "Or to work in the fields to provide them with food."

"Or maybe we *are* the food," observed Lametti.

"Jesus," exclaimed the President.

Lametti shrugged. "That's the worst-case scenario I can come up with, Mark. Sorry, but we need to consider all the possibilities so we can prepare as best we can."

"How the hell can you prepare for something like *that*?" demanded the President.

"I don't know," replied Lametti. "Distribute cyanide pills, maybe?"

Cohen barked a laugh. "Razor blades would be cheaper."

"This conversation is turning far too bleak," said the President. "We're not committing mass suicide as a people. We're going to *fight* to the death, not give up to the death."

"Agreed," said Lametti. "I wasn't being wholly serious. Just a little gallows humor there."

"Frankly," said Cohen, "I'd rather be wiped off the face of the planet than become a food source."

"Me too," said Lametti."

"Me three," said the President.

All three sat there soberly, reflecting on their dismal prospects.

"Either way, optimist or pessimist, our days of having the Earth to ourselves as the sole dominant species appear to be numbered," said Lametti.

More silence as they digested that thought.

"Well, that sucks," said Bill Cohen finally.

The President laughed ruefully. "Don't it ever. I sure as hell can't tell the American people *that*."

"No, you can't," admitted Lametti. "I think I've talked myself out of it: you can't tell the American public the whole truth. No one wants to hear it—it's just too depressing. And I'm not sure what good it would do anyway."

"So what *do* I tell them?"

"That we're fighting like hell, and that we'll keep on fighting," declared Cohen. "That America never gives up."

"That sounds...presidential enough," said the President. "What do you think, Gil?"

"Sounds about right to me," said Lametti with a sigh. "And hell, who knows? I'm no fortune teller. Maybe I've got it all wrong. Maybe those domes *weren't* sent by aliens. Maybe they're just harmless barnacles floating through the vastness of space—barnacles that somehow managed to get stuck to the bottom of spaceship Earth. Maybe they'll detach and float away one day without our ever having to lift a finger."

"You don't really believe that, do you?" demanded Cohen.

Lametti shook his head. "No, I don't. But I'd *like* to. And as long as there's a possibility of no aliens, however remote, then that's a story we can tell to the American people without sending them into a panic. It's not a lie—not exactly. It *could* be true. It just probably isn't.

"Well, half truth is a politician's bread and butter," said the President, getting up to his feet. Lametti and Cohen stood up with him.

"I feel better already," the President said. "I can sell that idea. Maybe the domes are the worst of it. Maybe there *are* no aliens coming behind them. That would at least explain why it's so quiet up there, wouldn't it?"

"Too quiet by half," growled Cohen. "Not to rain on your parade, Mr. President, but I'm a military man, and whenever the enemy is *this* radio-silent, we know we're in for some serious trouble. Whatever they have up their sleeves, if they even *have* sleeves, I think a serious shitstorm is coming our way."

October 9 – Fort Bliss, Texas

"Well, Mr. President, I'm afraid I have some more crappy news to report," said General McMillan by way of video. "Those newfangled weapons of ours didn't work worth a damn."

The President blew out a long breath. "Strike three," he murmured. "And we're out."

The General chuckled wearily. "More like strike thirty, if you ask me."

"I'm not surprised, really," said the President. "After we dropped that second nuke and watched it fail, well... let's just say I didn't hold out much hope."

"Me neither, sir."

"Tell me what happened anyway, General. I'm curious."

"Well, we tried each one in turn, just like you asked. The Halbach array of magnets—those are the ones that augment the magnetic field on one side of the array while cancelling the field to near-zero on the other side—those were a complete bust."

"As expected."

"And the electromagnetic rail gun—well, sir, that was a treat to watch. I've never seen a projectile fired at those speeds before—but in the end it deflected off the dome wall just like them bullets did. Punched quite a hole in a nearby mountainside, though."

"Of course it did."

"Next up was MAHEM. That's the one that uses the magnetic flux generator to fire a molten metal projectile. It made a big fiery splash against the dome wall, but that was about it."

"And what about the e-bomb?"

"That was the one I had the most hope for."

"Me too. In fact, it was the only one I thought had real promise."

"Well, unfortunately, the nuclear EMP did a whole lot of nothin', other than wipe out a bunch of computer and electronic systems back at Fort Bliss. By the way, that was an accident, sir, one I take full responsibility for. We didn't think the pulse would reach that far. The test was performed in the middle of the test range, and yet it fried electronic systems all the way back at Fort Bliss, and even a few as far away as El Paso. That's some pretty powerful shit, sir, but it did absolutely nothin' to the dome. It didn't even piss it off."

"Sorry to hear that, General."

"No worries, sir. Luckily, we have backup systems in place at Fort Bliss. Things should be up and runnin' in no time. Leastways, that's what the techies tell me."

"Good."

"Now, the mayor in El Paso—that's another matter. He's none to pleased with me at the moment. Nor is the commander at Fort Bliss, when you get right down to it. Might be best if I were to find a new base to call home for awhile."

"Anywhere you like, General, you've earned it. And General—is there anything else you can think to try that we haven't already tried?"

"Not one damn thing, sir, not one damn thing. That's the cold hard truth."

The President nodded. "That's what I was afraid of, General."

JUMP 4

October 10

Jump Day was now a thing. It had entered into the general vernacular, like a host of other expressions that had suddenly popped into existence along with the domes themselves.

On this particular jump day, each dome instantly doubled in size to about 50,000 square feet—the size of your average supermarket—and was now the height of a five-story building. The domes continued to squash down in the vertical direction. Any dome architect worth his salt could tell you a squashed ellipsoid shape is ideal for creating a maximum amount of usable square footage on the ground without too much wasted space above—an efficient way to cover as much land as possible while using a minimal amount of energy.

Each dome now incorporated about one acre of space. It would have taken roughly a minute to walk from one end of a dome to the other in a straight line—with a slight detour, of course, around the radiantly glowing ovate at its center. The domes' total coverage worldwide was now estimated at 10,000 square miles, or roughly the size of Maryland.

With each jump offering another trackable data point, scientists were now able to predict with some degree of certainty not only when the domes would jump but also how much space they would occupy. That meant they could predict when the Wall

Street Dome would actually envelop Wall Street—and their prediction was unsettling, to say the least.

Four more jumps. Forty days. That was all it would take.

Which meant that, on or around November 19th, Wall Street would cease to exist as a functioning entity. Technically speaking, it would continue to exist inside a dome, but what good would that be to anyone? It would have no connectivity to the outside world. And if another jump were to occur after that, on or around November 29th, it would mark the end of New York's entire Financial District.

10

October 14 – NBC Nightly News, New York

CLICK: "...I spoke to several of the Greeters nearly a month after their ordeal, Cory, and here's what they had to say:"

"I couldn't breathe in there. I thought for sure I was going to die. So much for the aliens welcoming us."

"I was so worried about my boyfriend. I could see him lying in there, not moving, and there was nothing I could do. He had all his stuff with him—tent, sleeping bag, food and water—he never thought he'd need an oxygen mask!"

"At first I thought I was imagining it, you know? Like maybe I was claustrophobic. It was really tight quarters in there—no plumbing, no electricity. Man, things got grody fast! I only made it one night and then I was, like, Where's the toilets? Where's the lights? Then it started to stink to high heaven and I was outta there."

"I was one of the last ones out. Looking back, I'm amazed I made it three nights. I really wanted to be, like, the Last Greeter or something. But I swear to God it felt like the air was getting thinner each day. By the end it felt like I was on Mount Everest and couldn't get enough oxygen

into my lungs. I suddenly realized no one could rescue me even if they wanted to. Crawling out of there was the hardest thing I've ever done in my life. But you have to admit, it's a pretty effective deterrent when you think about it—no oxygen, I mean. If you were an alien, and you wanted to keep people out of the domes—I mean, like, from occupying them—then what better way than to lessen the amount of oxygen little by little? Not very friendly on their part, I suppose, but I guess they want to keep the domes for themselves, which is understandable."

"There you have it, Cory, from the mouths of the Greeters themselves. Obviously they didn't receive the kind of welcome they were hoping for, but at least they're still alive. This is Roxanne Fuller reporting live from—" [CLICK]

Goodland, Kansas

"Well, there's our answer," Ken Stubbs announced to his wife Marie as he turned off the news.

"Our answer to what?" asked Marie, who was busy knitting hats with earflaps for the grandkids at Christmas and only half-paying attention to whatever the news was saying. She found she was happier that way.

"Those—you know, *dead* zones—inside the six domes on our property. All the wheat is dead inside the original circle, as well as the two newer rings that came after it with each jump. That's despite getting plenty of sunshine and rain. I've *seen* it raining through the domes with my own eyes. But the stalks are all brown and crackly in there, and not a single thing is moving—not a gnat, not a fly, not a bug of any kind. But the *outer* ring, where the jump just occurred, is still healthy and full of life. I couldn't figure out why. Now I know why: it's because of a lack of oxygen once you get past a certain number of days."

Marie looked up from her knitting. "Say again?"

"A lack of oxygen," Ken repeated. "Didn't you hear on the news just now? After three or four days, all the oxygen runs out of the domes. That's why all the plants died."

Marie looked flummoxed for a moment. "I thought plants needed carbon dioxide to survive, not oxygen."

"Well, they need both. It's true they soak up carbon dioxide during the day, but at night the roots in the soil absorb oxygen."

"They do?"

Ken nodded. "Plants have active metabolisms, just like people. They *breathe*."

"How is it I'm a farmer's wife and didn't know that?"

"Well, *I* didn't know it until pretty far in," Ken admitted.

"But the roots are underground. How in the world do they get oxygen in the first place?"

"Well, there's no photosynthesis down there in the soil, so the roots, they get their oxygen from little pockets of air between the dirt particles in the soil."

"Really?"

"Yeah, you'd be surprised just how much empty space there is in soil. Earthworms are always churning up the dirt down there. I read about it in one of those agricultural magazines." Ken nodded and tried to remember exactly what he'd read. "Something about…let's see now…if you put a non-aquatic plant in waterlogged soil, then the roots will rot, and the plant will die, because the roots can't get enough oxygen."

"Huh."

"And you know what, Marie? That's bad news. That's really bad news for every single living thing inside every goddamned dome on this entire planet."

"You don't need to swear to make your point, dear."

"Well, I think I do, Marie—because it means that every plant, every flower, every tree, every insect—every living thing inside every single dome around the world is going to die in four or five days after the oxygen runs out."

"What about the animals?"

"Them too, unless they can get out in time."

"So the plants *and* the animals will all die inside a dome after four or five days?"

"That's what I'm telling you. Or leastways, that's what I'm *hearing*. And it fits with what I've seen in our own fields. Not only are the crops all dead—there's not a single living thing so big as a gnat inside those domes after the fourth or fifth day. Either they've flown the coop or they've crawled out—or else they've returned to the soil from whence they came."

"Well, that's just...*terrible,*" said Marie, looking suddenly distraught.

Ken nodded. "I'm liking these domes less and less with each passing day."

"I didn't know how much I disliked them until this very moment," said Marie.

Just wait until our entire farm disappears, Ken thought to himself dismally, but he didn't say it out loud.

October 15 – JPL, Pasadena, California

Some of the smartest people in the world were all confined together inside a dome that had already run out of air—and how smart was that?

Dr. Rachel Cavanaugh was one of them. She and her fellow scientists had been trying everything they could think of to get past the inner force field protecting the ovate, but without success. Now all that remained was to admit defeat and get out of there...and yet she couldn't quite bring herself to leave.

They'd been wearing portable oxygen tanks and breathing artificial air for some twenty-four hours now. Absolute exhaustion had set in. Her fellow scientists had been complaining of headaches and shortness of breath, and Rachel herself could feel a raging migraine coming on...but the thought of having to inform the President of the United States that they had made no progress whatsoever kept her in there, staring at that damned ovate with its protective shield as if she could unlock its secrets simply by glaring at it hard enough.

"Okay, let's get out of here," she said reluctantly, and she saw instant relief in her fellow scientists' eyes. They'd been ready to leave hours ago, but still Rachel had kept insisting they try one more test, one more permutation, one more option. There *had* to be a way in. It was like fiddling with a Japanese puzzle box: sooner or later your fingers would happen upon the right pattern or sequence of actions, and *voila,* it would open. But there were so many variables to try with this particular puzzle box—she could spend the rest of her life in here and never figure it out. Of course, the rest of her life might be less than an hour if she didn't get out of here soon.

"Doctor, are you coming?" she heard a concerned voice ask from behind her, but she shooed whoever it was away.

An indeterminate amount of time passed as she tried a few more tests, adding them to the long list of failures. Making a note in her notepad, she found her eyes were having trouble focusing and realized with sudden dread that if she were to lose consciousness in here, literally no one could save her.

She lurched towards the dome wall. "A few more days," she muttered to herself. "Then I can try again."

Because the domes would jump again. She felt certain of it.

October 19 – Jersey City, New Jersey

As soon as Royce received his permit in the mail, he made a return visit to Pistol Pete's and picked up his gun and ammo. He paid for them with cash (he had no other choice—Pistol Pete's would only accept cash now) and left the store feeling safer than he had in weeks.

The entire metropolitan area was in the throes of upheaval. Store shelves were bare most of the time, and as soon as they were restocked they were emptied again. There were reports of shootings over mundane disagreements like who should get the last bag of potato chips or the last container of powdered milk.

The sight of National Guard troops on every major street corner was both comforting and distressing. They kept the city safer than it would have been otherwise, but in their camouflage uniforms (which made them stand out rather than blend in here), they added a menacing presence to a city already on edge. Cradling their automatic weapons, they eyed each passerby with suspicion, which did little to calm frayed nerves.

New York's mayor, Shawn Santos, was threatening a city-wide curfew if "hooligans and troublemakers," as he called them, didn't stop looting and causing mayhem each night. Police in riot gear had become a nightly fixture, and they were now authorized to shoot rubber bullets in addition to using tear gas, pepper spray, and tasers to maintain control. The very idea of a curfew in The City That Never Sleeps was universally unpopular, and it was a step the mayor vowed not to take unless he absolutely had to. "But these people may force our hand," he warned.

As Royce made the short walk from the PATH stop at the World Trade Center to Wall Street each day, he passed more people begging in the streets than he had ever seen before, including entire families with young kids. He gave what he could to help them, and so did a lot of other New Yorkers, to their credit, but it did nothing to lessen the numbers of destitute from growing each day. From what he could gather, only a few had lost their homes as a direct result of a jump—most were out on the streets due to job loss or soaring inflation.

Meanwhile, the markets continued to unravel, reeling from the one-two punch of dome expansion and hyperinflation. Stocks were down more than ninety percent from their all-time high of only two months ago. That surpassed the worst losses of the Great Depression.

Royce personally knew of dozens of companies that continued to be profitable—grocery chains in particular were raking in cash as people stocked up on food and supplies at any price—but the companies' stock prices didn't reflect that anymore. It was as if faith in the financial underpinnings of the system itself had been shaken. No one trusted putting money into anything other than gold, government bonds, or FDIC-insured bank accounts—which, come to think of it, wasn't so different from his own logic.

The other day he'd popped into an REI with the thought of buying some survival gear, just in case the worst happened, but the store shelves had all been bare. Things like parkas and fleeces and tents had long since sold out in anticipation of a hard winter ahead with no guarantee of shelter. Everything else on his mental list was gone, too. Dried food: gone. Water bottles, purifiers, and sterilizing pens: gone. Camp stoves and sleeping bags and inflatable sleeping mats: gone. Backpacks: gone. Compasses and fishing poles and survival kits: gone. Most of it had been unavailable for weeks now, according to the lone salesperson still roaming the aisles. It looked like the store had been robbed at gunpoint it was so empty.

He'd wandered into a ShopRite immediately afterwards to see if he could do any better there, and he had quickly discovered that canned goods and bottled water were unavailable at any price. People were hoarding as many nonperishables as they could. Frozen dinners and simple-to-prepare meals were impossible to find. Just the other night, he'd had to resort to bartering for food with his neighbors—this piece of frozen chicken for that bag of frozen broccoli—in order to make dinner.

Meanwhile, restaurants were posting armed guards outside their entrances to keep their patrons safe. Of course, these same patrons were being fleeced in a different manner by the restaurants themselves, which were now charging quadruple the prices they had two months ago. Even fast food prices were getting out of hand. The same gyro that had cost him twelve dollars two months ago now cost him thirty—and they only accepted cash. An armed guard stood next to the joint, warily watching the line of customers for any trouble.

Just as he'd predicted, credit cards were no longer being accepted by most businesses. They were demanding cash up front before they'd cut your hair or do your nails or serve your meal. Everyone wanted their money *now*, not a month from now, which Royce thought was yet another indication of just how quickly things were unraveling.

To Royce it felt as if the millions of interconnected cogs that kept the city running day and night were slowly grinding to a halt. One look around his neighborhood was all it took to see just how fast things were deteriorating. Streets had become dicey at night, break-ins had become commonplace, and store owners had stopped replacing shattered plate-glass windows, boarding them up instead with wooden planks. Garbage was piling up in the streets because sanitation workers were on strike and had stopped making their usual rounds, claiming they were no longer receiving a living wage. As a result, the whole city was beginning to stink.

Things were falling apart fast, and the aliens hadn't even arrived yet!

And what did that spell for the city in the long run? To Royce's mind it spelled disaster, it spelled famine, it spelled death. The more he thought about it, the more it made sense for him and Aubrey to get out of the city *now* while they still could.

If only he could convince her to come with him.

JUMP 5

October 20

With Halloween fast approaching, every dome around the world transformed itself to roughly the size of a Walmart Supercenter. Each was now a tenth of a mile in diameter and the height of a ten-story building, encompassing about five acres of land. Worldwide that amounted to about 35,000 square miles of land—roughly the size of Indiana. That total would have been even higher if it hadn't been for a new phenomenon witnessed by countless observers: the merging of hundreds of thousands of domes.

According to eyewitnesses, two domes that happened to overlap during a jump would briefly merge into one larger dome with two ovates inside. But in a matter of seconds, one ovate would dim while the other glowed brighter, then the dimmed ovate would "implode" (there was no better word for it), vaporizing into nothingness. The implosion did no damage because the dimmed ovate was contained within its own miniature force field that winked out of existence at the same moment as the ovate itself. Immediately afterwards, the force field recentered on whichever ovate survived, in effect jumping a second time to keep the ovate at its center. The end result was a single dome the exact same size as every other dome around the world where two had stood before. Satellite counts indicated a reduction from around 4.5 million to 4 million domes on just this one jump alone.

How the ovates "decided" which got to survive and which did not was a mystery, but the leading theory was that the ovates had the equivalent of a pecking order built into them. Perhaps an algorithm in their "DNA" made the decision for them. Keen observers were quick to point out that the surviving ovate always seemed to be the one located closest to an urban population center—which didn't bode well for cities, if such were the case. If the aliens wanted to disrupt human society as much as possible, then preprogramming the ovates to selectively skew towards urban areas would certainly be a powerful way to do it.

11

October 21 – Longmont, Colorado

Rap rap rap.

Someone was insistently knocking on their front door. When Will answered it, he was surprised to find a policeman standing there. "Can I help you?" he asked.

"Sir, I'm here to inform you your home is in the jump zone," the policeman said. "You should be making plans, if you haven't already, to evacuate your home in the coming days. The domes are expected to jump again on October 30th. That's not this Wednesday but the next. You need to have yourself and your whole family out of here by then. Is that understood?"

Will stared at him speechlessly for several seconds before finally nodding. "Yes, I understand."

The policeman nodded back. "Sorry for the bad news."

Will watched as he headed for their next-door neighbor's home to deliver the same grim message. On the other side of the street he could see another policeman knocking on doors.

Cynthia, who was standing just behind him, remained silent as Will closed the door. He turned towards her, reluctant to meet her eyes. "Hon, I'm real sorry," he said. "I'm an ass. This whole time I've been so sure the dome wouldn't affect us—that the authorities would take care of it somehow before it became a real problem—and yet here it is affecting us in the biggest way possible. I feel like an idiot."

"You *are* an idiot," Cynthia said, but she said it gently. She'd been getting pretty pissed off at her husband over the past week what with his refusal to accept the inevitable, but her anger melted away at the look of despair in his eyes. "The good news is, the dome only just jumped, so we've got nine days to deal with things before it jumps again. That means we can prepare. Figure out where we're going to live. Clear out the house. Tell the kids."

"Jesus, tell the kids. Ashley's not going to like it."

"So what else is new?"

"I'm really sorry, hon—you were right all along."

"It's almost worth losing our home just to hear you say that. *Almost*."

Josh came pounding down the stairs. "Hey Mom, hey Dad, what's up?" Will and Cynthia looked at each other and were silent. That really got Josh's attention. "It's the dome, isn't it? I knew it. I'm not surprised."

"Oh really?"

"Yeah, it was bound to happen. Our teacher has been using the domes as examples in math class. They're following a geometric progression with a constant factor of two. There's no way our house wasn't going to get swallowed up soon."

Will looked at Cynthia with one of those adult looks that was all in the eyes. "Well, at least Josh is taking it well."

"Sure I am," said Josh. "It's just a house. I'm sure we'll find another."

"Well, aren't you Mr. Positive," said his mom. "I wish I could feel as calm about it."

"Think of it as an adventure," Josh said with his usual sunny optimism.

"Mmm. Well, since you're so smart, where do you think we should live?"

Josh had been about to make a beeline for the front door, but now he backtracked. "That's a good question. Dad still needs to be close to work, so we can't light out for the high country like I'd really like."

"The high country?" said his dad with an amused smile. "We're already in Colorado. How high do you want to go?"

"I don't know, some place like Crested Butte or Ouray. Or maybe even farther north like Wyoming or Montana. You know, really out there."

"Mmm, that does have some appeal," said Will, and he didn't sound like he was being facetious.

"But you need to be near work, and winter's nearly here, so that's out. Maybe Loveland or Hygiene. Not too many domes in those parts, and they're close by. Hey, maybe we could get a horse in Hygiene. That's horse country, you know."

"We're *not* getting a horse," said Will. "The last thing we need right now is more beings to take care of."

"Yeah, I guess you're right—but don't even think about getting rid of Woof."

"We'd never dream of it," said his mom. "Woof is family."

"He sure is. Aren't you, Woof?" Josh patted his head like he always did whenever the dog was within range. "Well, I've gotta go; I'm supposed to meet my friends over at Centennial Park and I've still gotta bike there. Bye Mom, bye Dad," he said as he dashed out the door.

"That kid is always in high gear," said Will.

"He sure is. His brain seems to be in high gear too. Maybe we should listen to him more often."

Will nodded. "I should listen to *you* more often, too."

"That's music to my ears. So—let's find a place to live in Loveland or Hygiene. If we don't find somewhere to rent soon, all the good places will be gone."

"All right," said Will, "I'll start looking on Airbnb. I haven't even begun to think about what we need to pack—and what we need to leave behind."

"I have," said Cynthia. "I've been making lists for weeks."

"Of course you have."

*****

"You've *got* to be kidding me," said Ashley. She was sitting on the couch with her sister Kaley. Her mom and dad had called a family meeting minus Josh, who was still out with his friends.

"We knew you wouldn't take it well," said her mom.

"Take it well? How am I supposed to take it? You're telling me I've gotta move out of the only house I've ever lived in since I was, like, *born*?"

"Yep, that's pretty much what we're telling you," said her dad. "We don't really have much choice in the matter."

"I knew these domes were gonna mess everything up," Ashley moaned with a depth of despair only teenagers could muster.

"Well, I think it's *great*," said Kaley with unbounded enthusiasm. She was bouncing up and down on the couch while still technically sitting. "I'm so *tired* of everything being the same all the time."

"There's that ennui again," said her mom.

"On what?" asked Kaley, confused.

"Ennui," repeated her mom. "E-N-N-U-I. Boredom."

"Not me, no ennui, not anymore. Thanks to the aliens, life is suddenly plenty interesting."

"You can't possibly be my sister," said Ashley.

"I am and there's nothing you can do about it," said Kaley, bouncing in place. "So when do we move?"

"Soon," said her dad. "In nine days or less. I'm glad you're excited about it."

"I am. Where to?"

"Maybe Loveland, maybe Hygiene, maybe Niwot. We're still looking for the right place."

"I can't wait," Kaley said. "Maybe we can live in a dome."

"Umm, no, that's not going to happen," said her mom. "I'm sure you've heard you can't breathe in those things for very long."

"You could if you had one of those scuba thingies. An oxygen tank or whatever."

"No you couldn't, dork," said Ashley. "That would only last for a few hours and then you'd be dead."

"*You'd* be dead. I'd just get another oxygen tank," said Kaley, still bouncing.

Ashley rolled her eyes and didn't bother to reply.

"Getting away from domes is the whole point of why we're moving, Kaley," said her dad.

"What's the point in *that*?"

"To be safe, you idiot!" yelled Ashley, despite her best efforts to stay silent.

"We should just stay here and let the dome swallow us up," said Kaley. "That'd be so *cool*."

Ashley shook her head.

"Well, we might be able to arrange that, Kaley," said her dad slowly, "if that's what you really want. I'll tell you what: we can stay behind, let the dome swallow us up, and then we can drive out through the dome wall with our last load of stuff. How does that sound?"

"That sounds *a-maz-ing!*" Kaley shouted.

"You've *got* to be kidding me," Cynthia said to Will with the most dead-eyed expression he'd ever seen from her—and that was saying a lot. "You are *not* staying in here with my daughter and letting a dome swallow her up. Besides, you heard what the policeman said."

"What's he going to do, arrest us?" Will asked, sounding genuinely surprised at her resistance to the idea. "Thousands of people have done it by now. It's safe. It's proven."

"What are you, a pharmaceutical commercial? It's an alien dome, for God's sake. There's nothing safe or proven about it. It's an unnecessary risk."

"*Mom,*" moaned Kaley.

"Jeez, Mom, just let them do it," Ashley said, sounding irritated. "You know they're gonna wear you down eventually."

Cynthia shook her head in frustration; so much for Will listening to her more often. But after stewing in silence for a few seconds, she gave in as she always did and said, "Fine, but I'm not happy about it, not happy at all."

Kaley jumped up and gave her a big hug, and there was no resisting that.

*****

One week left to pack. One week left to cherish the home they'd lived in since before Ashley was born. Cynthia spun around in a slow circle in the living room, her eyes taking in the fireplace where the stockings hung each Christmas, the kitchen where she'd been preparing meals for the past fourteen years, the dining room where they'd shared their meals as a family. She started to get teary-eyed; she couldn't help it. She'd thought this would be their forever home, and now she was being forced to leave it.

Looking out the window at her back yard, she saw Woof rolling around in the grass. Birds were drinking from the fountain. Two squirrels were attacking the bird feeders despite the protective cones that were supposedly guaranteed to keep them out.

She hated leaving it all behind.

They had a rental set up in Hygiene for one month. Just one month, and then what? What kind of life was it going to be from now on with no permanent home of their own and a family of five to take care of? Six, if you counted Woof.

The birds and squirrels were going to miss their food sources in the back yard, that was for sure. She wondered how they would adapt to the dome suddenly intruding on their space. Would they be smart enough to escape once the air started to run out? She hoped so. How many shocks would it take before they stopped trying to reenter? She pictured an innocent bird flying into one of the nearly invisible dome walls and cringed at the thought. Fried bird seemed like the most likely result. The cats would be happy anyway: plenty for them to eat.

Her thoughts were turning morbid, as they often did when she was alone in the house. The kids were at school (amazingly enough, despite all that was going on) and Will was at work, still soldiering away on some big accounting project. Meanwhile, a big part of her was still living in denial. Upstairs and in the basement, half-packed boxes were strewn everywhere, but on the main floor no boxes were visible at all. She wanted to keep the fantasy of normalcy alive as long as she possibly could.

She figured she had maybe three days left to pretend all was well in Longmont-land. Three more days to share breakfast with her kids at the kitchen table. Three more days to pull cereal boxes out of the cabinet, cut up a banana, get the milk out of the fridge, make some toast with butter and jam, call to her kids up the stairs, and watch them come running down (or trudging down in Ashley's case). Josh would be late, of course; that would be true no matter where they lived. But all the little rituals that made life such a pleasure for her would soon be gone. Eight-year-old

Kaley might love the idea of change, but middle-aged Cynthia hated it.

She felt especially sorry for Woof; he was so attached to his yard and his routines. He liked chasing the squirrels from the feeders and barking at the neighbors' dog through that hole in the fence. And then there was Ashley. She was moodier than ever these days, walking around with a permanent cloud over her head. Truth be told, Cynthia understood her attitude more than she did the keen excitement Josh and Kaley seemed to feel.

Will, meanwhile, had turned into a packing fiend. He threw stuff into boxes each night with an intensity that left her breathless just watching him. Everything *not* coming he tossed into the garage, vowing to have the ultimate garage sale before they left—but who was going to buy all that junk now that the domes were taking over everyone's lives? Each night around midnight he fell into bed in a near-coma of exhaustion, then he was up at five the next morning and off to work for another day. He told Cynthia he had to make as much money as he could right now because he wasn't sure how much longer his company would last.

Will had always been a good provider, but he was an accountant and not exactly suited to all this apocalyptic stuff. It was almost a cliché, wasn't it? Bean counters weren't the ones you wanted around at the end of the world. But so far he was handling himself surprisingly well. In truth, Cynthia was more worried about herself than she was about him. *She* was the one who kept having panic attacks out of nowhere. Like right now, for instance. Just thinking about panic attacks was sometimes enough to trigger one.

She sat in the middle of the living room floor, cross-legged, and tried to calm herself, focusing on her breathing. She felt her pulse begin to slow as she meditated on what really mattered to her most in this world.

Which was easy: family.

Everything else could get stripped away: the house, the yard, even the friends and neighbors. As long as she had her family she'd be okay. So that was what she'd focus on from now on: keeping her family together. Keeping her family safe.

October 29 – Hygiene, Colorado

"I *love* this place," said Kaley. "There's a barn with real hay and it smells like horses." She was standing at the front door with pieces of straw sticking out at odd angles from her tousled hair and clothing.

"What in the name of heaven have you been up to?" her mother demanded.

"Hay rolling," Kaley said matter-of-factly. "There's a tire swing, too, up in the barn loft. You can swing right out over the *whole barn*. Dad said he'd do it with us later."

"Did he now? Because that definitely does not sound safe." (Who was this man she'd married?)

"That's what makes it so exciting," said Kaley. She ran back outside, beelining towards a prairie dog hole with a prairie dog crouched in it. The prairie dog reared up on its hind legs, squeaked a startled warning, then disappeared down the hole. Cynthia watched her daughter peering down the hole on all fours and just shook her head.

Woof was whining and scratching at the kitchen door, wanting to get out and join Kaley in her prairie dog hunt, but Cynthia kept it firmly shut. But as Will strode in from the garage with another load of boxes from the car, Woof scampered past him through the half-open doorway. He ran straight towards Kaley, barking all the way. Cynthia shook her head again and decided to focus on the issue at hand. "What's this about a tire swing? " she demanded as Will strode by.

"Oh, she told you, did she?" Will laughed, stopping in his tracks. "I was going to wait to tell you until after it was all over so you wouldn't worry too much, but Kaley's not much for keeping secrets, is she?"

"A tire swing in the barn loft? That sounds dangerous, Will."

"I'll go first and make sure it's safe. If it can hold my weight, it can definitely hold Kaley's and Josh's."

"So Josh is in on this too?"

"Are you kidding me? It was his idea in the first place."

"Why am I not surprised."

"Look, as long as they hold on tight, they'll be fine. The tire swing wouldn't be there if it wasn't safe, right? And like I said, I'll go first."

"That's very comforting. I'll put that on your tombstone: 'He Went First.' I thought you were afraid of heights."

"I am. But it's important to the kids, so I'll just have to suck it up and get over it."

"Don't tell me Ashley is in on this too?"

"No way, not Ashley. Sorry but I've gotta put this load down—it's heavy." He headed upstairs to the master bedroom.

Cynthia looked around at the home they would be inhabiting for the next month. It was a peaceful farmhouse set out in the countryside, away from all domes, and it was costing them a small fortune. She could see horses grazing in nearby fields, bales of hay wrapped in white plastic, and mountains in the distance that were already turning white with snow. Cynthia shivered at the thought that winter was on its way.

Folks on the Front Range tended to think of Halloween as the dividing point between fall and winter. Snow was always a possibility on Halloween night. The kids' costumes were often layered atop thermals to keep them from freezing to death. But what with the craziness of the move, all thoughts of Halloween had flown right out of her head this year. There were no costumes and no candy. And besides, the closest home was a good quarter mile away, so neighborhood trick-or-treating was out of the question. She should really go to the store and buy them some candy—assuming the stores still had any left.

Their old home in Longmont (they were already calling it their old home) was mostly empty now except for the beds and the furniture, which they had decided to leave behind. Two bays of the three-car garage were piled high with junk, right up to the rafters. The yard sale idea had quickly gone out the window as time had run out.

Their Ford minivan still occupied the last bay of the garage, its entire back half filled to the brim with possessions. Will had promised Kaley they could make their great escape after the dome had enclosed their home, and she was making him stick to his promise with daily reminders of just how important it was to her. Of course, Josh, as soon as he'd heard about it, had wanted in too, so now all three were going.

Cynthia sighed. They were treating this whole thing as a lark instead of the catastrophe it was. Ashley, meanwhile, was sunk in a depression so deep nothing could shake her out of it.

Who knew, maybe Will, Josh, and Kaley had the right of it—why not think of it as an adventure? Given the state of the world these days, she supposed a tire swing in a barn loft was pretty low on the totem pole of things to be concerned about. She decided to lighten up on the kids, and on her husband, and let them have their fun.

Woof was barking up a storm and periodically sticking his entire snout down the prairie dog hole. Kaley was laughing and staking out another prairie dog hole in the immediate vicinity, hoping one would pop up. All Cynthia could think of was rabies and bubonic plague, but she held her tongue and didn't call out to them. She was going to try to turn over a new leaf and not worry so much. What good did it do anyway?

Ashley moped into the kitchen and sat down on a stool, looking utterly defeated.

"Hey, babe," her mom said, putting her arm around her shoulders. "How you holding up?"

"I hate this place. None of my friends are here."

"I know, sweetie, but they're only half an hour away. You can still see them at school."

"But there's nowhere to shop or hang out. I feel like I'm stuck in the middle of nowhere."

"You could always join your sister and hunt prairie dogs."

Silence. "Is there anything to eat?"

"No, I still have to go shopping. Wanna come with? We could check out the town of Hygiene on our way to Longmont."

"What town? There's, like, two old cafes and a post office." Ashley moped back out of the kitchen on her way to her bedroom, which was still piled high with unopened boxes.

Josh came in from the garage with a box that was sagging at the bottom and looked like it might fall apart at any moment. "Dad?" he called up the stairs. "Where do you want these books?"

"Up here," came the reply.

"Why don't you buy e-books like the rest of us?" Josh grumbled as he trudged up the stairs. "These are heavy."

"They're called novels, and stop complaining. Help me unpack, will you?"

"Okay, okay," Josh said. "But you promised you'd help me hook up my video game later, remember?"

Cynthia thought about all the work going into this one move and wished they'd been able to rent the place for a year. But the owner had been vehement: one month only. He wanted the place for himself after that (lucky bastard), which made sense since there were no domes anywhere in sight for miles.

Which meant they'd have to do this all over again somewhere else in another month.

Wasn't life grand?

JUMP 6

October 30

As the domes continued to jump and merge, the question on everyone's mind was: Exactly how many more jumps would there be? It was a question no one could answer, even though the answer was of the utmost importance. The domes were already a huge problem for human and animal alike, but five or six more jumps would be catastrophic—and beyond that, cataclysmic.

At least the domes were predictable in certain respects: scientists could now say with some certainty that if the domes kept jumping, doubling in diameter each time, they would follow a growth rate that looked something like this going forward:

Jump #	*Jump Day*	*Dome Diameter*	*Dome Area*
6	*30 Oct 2041*	*0.2 mi*	*< 0.1 sq mi*
7	*9 Nov 2041*	*0.4 mi*	*0.1 sq mi*
8	*19 Nov 2041*	*0.8 mi*	*0.5 sq mi*
9	*29 Nov 2041*	*1½ mi*	*2 sq mi*
10	*9 Dec 2041*	*3 mi*	*7 sq mi*
11	*19 Dec 2041*	*6 mi*	*28 sq mi*
12	*29 Dec 2041*	*12 mi*	*113 sq mi*
13	*8 Jan 2042*	*24 mi*	*452 sq mi*
14	*18 Jan 2042*	*48 mi*	*1,810 sq mi*

There was little point in calculating beyond the 18 January date. By then, based on scientists' calculations, most of the available land on Earth would be covered by domes. Human and animal alike would have little land left to live on and would have to survive as best they could in the interstices between domes. Billions would asphyxiate. Some small patches of habitable land and some remote islands would continue to support life, so humanity would avoid outright extinction, but that was rather small comfort for the rest of mankind. The hard truth of it was, most of the human race was facing a death sentence within the next three months if the domes didn't stop jumping.

Such news did little to help people sleep at night, but that didn't stop doomsday prophets, news anchors, and scientists alike from trumpeting doomsday scenarios to the heavens. They couldn't seem to help themselves.

A surprising number of people seemed fascinated by their own approaching death sentence. Some appeared almost greedy for it. It was a strange phenomenon akin to a death wish on a species-wide scale. There was much talk of mankind being a plague on the Earth and how the planet would be better off without us. But even those who could accept the end of humanity with equanimity had trouble accepting the end of all or nearly all terrestrial animal life.

Survivalists, meanwhile, decried what they saw as defeatist attitudes and made their own plans. They reckoned where the domes were most likely to leave gaps and hunkered down in those spots, preparing for all-out war with the aliens (and each other, no doubt). Others set off in boats or planes for the most remote islands they could find—much to the vexation of locals who already lived there. Such intruders rarely received a warm welcome, and some, it was said, disappeared under mysterious circumstances. A few uber-wealthy billionaires took the direct approach and purchased their own islands, complete with fresh-running water and fruit trees, as a sort of insurance policy against the end of the world. Who might or might not be invited onto these private island paradises was the subject of much speculation over the coming days and weeks on daytime talk shows.

Meanwhile, anger was boiling over at the aliens who were behind all this—but it was hard to vent anger at an invisible foe. The aliens felt unreal because they were unrevealed: faceless, nameless, amorphous somethings.

Our fellow humans, on the other hand, made for much easier targets. They were in our faces every day, and it seemed we didn't like each other all that much—at least not when we were being pushed—pushed out of our homes, pushed onto other people's lands, pushed to the very limits of poverty and hunger—maybe even pushed off a cliff with nowhere left to go.

12

October 30 – NBC Nightly News, New York

"Good evening, this is Cory Phillips. Thanks for being with us tonight. This is a historic night for all of us here at NBC News as it's our final broadcast from our studio headquarters at 30 Rockefeller Plaza. The dome outside the studio is expected to jump at any moment. The other two domes in Manhattan have already jumped. If our broadcast should suddenly cut out, you'll know why. But never fear: all of us here at the studio will be able to exit the dome safely, and our Chicago affiliate is standing by to pick up wherever we leave off. Tomorrow night I'll be coming to you live from our new headquarters at the NBC Tower in Chicago.

"Now let's get started with the news. We have a lot to cover tonight, as always seems to be the case on jump days. Let's begin with Jim McDonald in Manhattan. Jim?"

"Thanks Cory. I'm standing as close as I can get to the statue of the Charging Bull, the symbol of Wall Street, which was swallowed up earlier this afternoon when the Wall Street Dome jumped. The entombment of this symbol of financial optimism is a blow to the psyches of New Yorkers everywhere. The dome, now nearly a quarter-mile in diameter, stretches from the Charging Bull at its northern edge to Battery Park at its southern edge.

"Meanwhile, numerous skyscrapers along Broadway and State Street have become inaccessible since the jump. While their tops still tower over the dome, the question becomes how to access them, now that their ground floors have been cut off.

"Adding to the fun, Battery Tunnel is now closed, along with Bowling Green subway station. Subway lines aren't deep enough here in New York to escape the dome's—or rather I should say sphere's—current 200-foot depth. Electrical, gas, water, and sewer lines have also been cut off as a result of the sphere's recent expansion. Utility crews are working frantically to fix these problems, but as you can imagine, they're overwhelmed. Cory, back to you."

"What a mess. Thanks for that report, Jim. Now let's turn to Mindy McGuire, who's standing by just outside our studios."

"Thanks Cory. As you mentioned at the beginning of the broadcast, the jump is imminent for the Rockefeller Dome, and when it does jump, it's expected to have a major impact on Central Manhattan. At that point it will stretch from 50th Street north to 46th Street south, forming a circle that will include the western half of Rockefeller Center, which includes our own studios.

"The Rockefeller Center subway station has been closed in anticipation of the jump. Trains will continue to run uptown and downtown on either side of the station, but people will now have to get out and walk to the next subway station along the line if they want to continue onward. Taller buildings in the jump zone have already been cleared of occupants to avoid their getting trapped *above* the dome's ceiling, which would keep them from being able to exit the building, short of a helicopter ride from the roof. Cory?"

"Thanks Mindy. Next we have Kristen Howard in Central Park. Kristen, what can you tell us about the situation there?"

"Cory, when the Central Park Dome jumped earlier this afternoon, it cut off a tiny corner of the Metropolitan Museum of Art. Otherwise, the country's largest art museum is still safe for one more jump. But you can only imagine the frantic levels of activity that have been taking place here over the past several days.

"Specialized moving vans have been moving precious works of art out of The Met and taking them to—well, we don't know to where. We've tried interviewing museum curators to get a better handle on where all this fine art is going, but they're keeping mum about it—which makes sense when you consider the billions of dollars worth of irreplaceable art being transported even as we speak. Each moving van is flanked by armed security vehicles, and any attempt to follow them is strongly rebuffed. We should know: we tried. Cory, back to you."

"Thanks Kristen. Now let's turn our attention to the nation's capital, where the Capitol Dome has jumped to within spitting distance of the Capitol Building itself. For more on that, let's check in with our Washington correspondent, Stephanie Wilson."

"Thanks Cory. I'm standing near the Capitol Reflecting Pool, which, as you can see, was cut in two today when the dome jumped earlier this afternoon. The dome is now less than one hundred feet away from the western steps of the Capitol Building, and sena—"

[WHITE NOISE]

Oval Office, Washington D.C.

"So much for that broadcast," Gil Lametti sighed, turning off the TV in the Oval Office. "All four major broadcast networks were headquartered in New York City, but not any longer. Feels like the end of an era, doesn't it?"

The President grunted; he was busy signing documents at his desk.

"Mark, I've been thinking—"

"Never a good sign."

Lametti continued, undeterred. "These domes—they're like a string of hurricanes heading straight for us, one right after the other, each one increasing in size and strength."

"Uh-huh."

"Right now we're at Category 3, let's say, but coming up fast is a Cat 4, then a Cat 5, then a Cat 6."

"There is no Cat 6," said the President, still only half paying attention. "Five is the highest."

"Exactly. Now picture Categories 7, 8, and 9, striking not just *one* coastal city but every city in America all at once. Hundreds of millions of citizens, all affected at the exact same time."

The President stopped signing and looked up, troubled. "What an awful thought."

Lametti nodded. "Twenty million people live in Greater New York alone. Picture it: twenty million New Yorkers all displaced at once. All trying to get away from the city at the same time. It's like a disaster movie unreeling in slow motion. We can see it coming, and we can predict its outcome—but we can't stop it."

"What are you getting at? What do you think we should do?"

"Evacuate our biggest cities, starting with New York and L.A."

The President nearly knocked his chair over he stood up so fast. "*What?* Are you kidding me, Gil?"

Lametti put his hands up in a whoa motion. "In *stages,*" he said. "Neighborhood by neighborhood, depending on which neighborhoods are closest to the domes."

"Where are we going to put twenty million displaced New Yorkers, Gil?"

"That's exactly the question we should be asking ourselves, Mark. Because it's coming and we need to deal with it before it's too late."

"Twenty million New Yorkers," murmured the President. "Fifteen million Angelenos. Ten million Chicagoans. And that's just three of fifty metropolitan areas in the U.S. with populations over a million. There's no way FEMA can handle those kinds of numbers."

"I know," said Lametti. "We have an enormous problem on our hands. Or we will, assuming these domes keep jumping."

"Maybe they'll stop."

"Maybe that's wishful thinking."

"So out of the four hundred million or so people in the United States, how many, exactly, do you think are going to be displaced?"

Lametti shrugged. "It's anyone's guess at this point. Maybe a quarter? Maybe half? Who knows? But we'd better start planning for it now."

"Most will never go, even if we order it."

"You can use your bully pulpit to encourage them to evacuate while they still can. Better an orderly retreat than a chaotic one."

The President snorted. "*Retreat*. That's exactly what we're talking about here, a retreat from an unseen enemy."

"Well, the domes *are* advancing, and we can't stop them. What else would you call it?"

"So let me get this straight: you think we may have to evacuate something on the order of a hundred or two hundred *million* people nationwide? Where do you suggest we put them all?"

"In tent cities, for starters. We could begin setting those up immediately. And we could start identifying dome-free lands for laying out new cities from scratch."

"You've gotta be kidding me, Gil. You want to build *new cities* in the midst of the worst crisis our country has ever faced?"

"It's better than doing nothing, isn't it?"

The President shook his head and sighed. "I suppose." He got up from his desk and paced for a minute. "All right, Gil, go ahead and build your tent cities. And build your *actual* cities if you really think you can pull it off. But let me see the maps of where you plan to put them before you break ground."

"Fair enough. What about funding?"

The President gave a weary shrug. "What about it? Congress is a mess. They're too caught up with their precious Capitol Building being threatened to get any actual work done. I'm sure you know the dome jumped to within a hundred feet of it today."

Lametti nodded.

"Well, all they can do is make speeches about it—on the western steps, of course, as close as possible to the dome's edge. They're preening for the cameras like teenagers taking selfies near a cliff's edge. Ten more days—just ten more days—and the Capitol Building will be cut in half, and won't that be symbolic."

"A little too symbolic, if you ask me. So how should we proceed, Mark?"

The President thought for a moment. "I'll do what I always do nowadays: I'll issue an executive order and wait for Congress to scream bloody murder. We'll figure out the funding as we go along. Maybe the money we're saving on stationing troops overseas can be funneled into building tent cities—and real cities, too, assuming we can manage it. Hopefully Congress won't object too loudly."

"Oh, they'll object all right," said Lametti. "That's all they do these days. But they're so disorganized, they couldn't stop a dead bill in its tracks."

"Good point. Let's move forward then. What the hell, we're already hundreds of trillions of dollars in debt. What can a few extra trillion matter?"

"That's the spirit, Mark. I'll get right on it."

Longmont, Colorado

"This feels kinda creepy, waiting in the dark for a dome to swallow us up," Josh said.

He and Kaley and their dad were in their old house in Longmont, sitting together on the sectional sofa in the living room as the evening gloom deepened. The furniture was still in place, but there were no lamps, paintings, photos, knickknacks, or television to make things feel cozy. Echoes sounded in the foyer without the braided rug to soften things up, and the house felt too quiet by half without the tick of clocks, or the distant sound of music pounding from Aubrey's room, or Woof's barks, or other familiar sounds to which they'd all grown accustomed.

Earlier on, Josh had wandered up to his bedroom for a nostalgic look around. He had beaten a quick retreat—it didn't feel like *his* anymore, empty as it was. Could this really be where they'd called home for so many years?

Will turned on the flashlight for the umpteenth time to make sure it was still working, then turned it off again. "I agree, this is creepy. And the night before Halloween, no less. Are you two sure you want to go through with this?"

"Yeah," both kids said with limited enthusiasm. They both seemed bound by some pact they'd made in the past and couldn't get out of now.

"When's it supposed to jump?" Kaley asked.

"Well, that's the tricky part, Kaley. We don't really know. It could be any minute now, or it could be some time after midnight. The domes all jump within a twelve-hour window or thereabouts, but that leaves quite a bit of leeway."

"Good thing we brought our sleeping bags, then," Josh said with a yawn.

"Yeah," said Kaley. "Dad, if we're asleep, do you think we'll know when it jumps? Does it make a sound?"

"I have no idea, hon."

"I think it sizzles like bacon."

"As long as it doesn't sizzle *us*. Look, let's try and get some rest. There's not much else we can do. I'm guessing we'll know, somehow or other, when the jump happens."

They snuggled down in their sleeping bags and drifted off to sleep—only to come bolt upright in the middle of the night.

It was pitch-black in the living room, and they couldn't see a thing, but *something* had changed. The power had gone off, but it was more than just that. They all felt it: a sudden change in the air pressure or something.

Will turned on his flashlight. Everything looked normal enough. He got up.

"Dad, where are you going?" Kaley's voice sounded small.

"Just having a little look around, sweetie."

"I'll come too," said Josh, but Will motioned him to stay put.

Will peered into various rooms and finally cried "Aha!" from the den. He shone the flashlight around, revealing a dome wall that sliced the den neatly in half. The curvature of the dome made it apparent they were on the inside looking out. "Kids, come here; you should see this."

They got out of their sleeping bags, hugging themselves close to keep the cold at bay.

"*Wow*," said Kaley. "So this is what a dome looks like from the inside. Can I touch it?" She reached her hand out but her dad grabbed it.

"Me first, okay?" said Will. He stuck his hand out tentatively and passed it right through the dome wall. "Amazing! I don't feel a thing."

"Let me try!" Josh and Kaley both said at the same time, plunging their hands in too. Over the course of the next several minutes, the kids looked like they were doing the hokey pokey as they waggled various arm and leg parts in and out of the force field.

"I thought the hairs on my arm or the back of my neck would stand up at least," said Josh.

"Why would they?" demanded Kaley

"I don't know— I thought it would be like a lightning storm or something, when the static electricity builds up. You know, like when you rub a balloon against your hair or rub your feet on a carpet. Haven't you ever felt that, Kaley?"

"No, but I want to! How did I miss that?"

Josh shook his head. "This is so *weird*. How can it let us pass our hands right through from one direction and shock us to kingdom come from the other?"

"I don't know, Josh," his dad replied, "but there's a famous quote from Arthur C. Clarke—"

"Wait, I think I know that one. Something about a sufficiently advanced technology being indistinguishable from magic."

"That's right. I think that's what we're dealing with here. It's not magic: it's technology. It's just that we don't understand it. Not yet, anyway."

"That's for sure." Josh found himself fascinated with the force field. Suddenly he knew what he wanted to do with the rest of his life: he wanted to understand the dome's secrets—and, if possible, find a way through from the outside.

*****

"All right, kids, everyone buckled up?"

"Yep," both kids chimed in. They were sitting crammed together in the front seat because the back seat was stacked full of possessions.

Will hit the garage door button and nothing happened.

"Are we trapped?" Kaley's voice sounded small again.

"No, hon, there's a manual release. The dome wall must interfere with the house's electrical system, since the power grid is on the outside." He got out of the car, pulled the manual release, and pushed the garage door up. It rumbled open, much to Kaley's relief.

"All right, say goodbye, kids. We may never see this house again." He turned on the engine and began backing out of the driveway, but then he stopped and whistled at the view in his headlights. "Wow, would you look at that? The dome wall cuts right through our house. Jeez, it barely swallowed us up this time around. We almost could have had another ten days."

"I'm glad we didn't," said Kaley. "I like our new place."

"Yeah, well, don't get too used to it, Kaley. We only have it for a month."

"Yeah, but then it will be something even newer and cooler."

"Let's hope so." Will jumped out, closed the garage door out of old habit, then got back in and drove about two miles per hour along the street, searching for the far dome wall up ahead.

Mrs. Parker, one of their neighbors, was also inside the dome packing up her car in the middle of the night. Will stopped (it didn't take much) and rolled down the windows. "Hey Mary," he called out.

Mary Parker looked up and smiled. She was in her eighties and spry but looked a bit tired tonight. "Hey everyone," she said. "Quite the adventure we're having, isn't it?"

"You can say that again," said Will. "Hey, do you need any help, Mary? We'd be more than happy to help you pack up the car or move some boxes—whatever you need."

"That's sweet of you, Will, but I'm just about finished."

Will eyed what little was in her car. The open trunk only contained two boxes and a suitcase, and the back seat was empty except for her purse. "It doesn't look like you're bringing much."

Mrs. Parker laughed. "When you get to be my age, Will, you don't need much. I've got a few changes of clothing, plus my scrapbooks and photo albums. Those are my prized possessions. All the rest—well, it isn't that important to me anymore."

Will nodded. "I can see how that might be. So where are you headed?"

"Lawrence, Kansas. That's near Topeka. I've got family out that way. Kids, grandkids, great grandkids. They'll keep me busy—maybe a little too busy. They told me to just bring myself, so that's what I'm doing. Moving a house at my age just isn't in the cards."

"Seriously, we'd be glad to help. Anything at all."

Mrs. Parker shook her head. "Not necessary, Will, but thanks, that's kind of you. So where are you folks headed?"

"Up to Hygiene. We're renting a house up there for a month."

"The coolest house ever," broke in Kaley. "With a barn and a tire swing and prairie dogs."

"Wow," said Mary. "That does sound cool."

"After that," said Will, "we don't know."

"Well, you stay safe, and you stay together. Family's what's important in times like these."

"We know," Will said, smiling. "You take care, Mary."

"Bye Mrs. Parker," the kids called out. They waved, and Mrs. Parker waved back. At two miles per hour, they all waved for quite awhile.

"I wonder if we'll ever see her again," Josh mused.

"I doubt it," said Will. "Not unless we find ourselves near Topeka. It doesn't sound like she's planning on coming back."

The dome wall was visible up ahead. "There it is," Will said. "Are you two ready?" The two kids nodded as their dad made the slowest getaway in the history of getaways. He even braked halfway through it.

"Amazing!" he said. "Safe and sound, halfway in and halfway out of a dome wall." They all looked back to see the dome wall slicing through the back seat of their Ford minivan. "Crazy times we're living in, kids."

Will pulled forward and left the dome behind. "Just remember not to touch one of those things from the outside." He was going a full twenty miles per hour now, which felt downright reckless.

"We know, Dad," said Kaley. "We're not stupid."

"No, you're not. In fact I think you're two of the smartest and bravest kids in the whole wide world."

"You *have* to say that, you're our dad," Kaley replied. "Now if Josh would just move his big fat butt over!" She punched her brother in the arm and squirmed for more room as they made their way through the moonless Colorado night.

November 4 – Goodland, Kansas

A pond stood near one corner of Ken Stubbs' property. It wasn't much to look at, but it was home to darters and minnows and other small fish, as well as toads and frogs. The pond was ringed with sedges that played host to red-winged blackbirds, song sparrows, and other wetland birds and insects. The whole thing had been swallowed up in the last jump. Now, five days had passed, and Ken stood there looking in from the dome's edge.

What he saw made him sad. The surface of the water was covered with a thick scum of dead insects and bugs. Bulging out from the scum, like ghastly islands, were dead fish and frogs floating upside down. Two songbirds floated in the muck, heads down, wings spread wide as if in final flight. A duck floated lifeless on its side. Along the pond's edge were a surprising number of dead voles and mice. Why the birds hadn't flown out of the dome in time he had no idea. Maybe they hadn't been able to summon up the courage to fly through the force field, or maybe they hadn't even realized there was a problem until they suddenly keeled over from lack of oxygen.

Ken clambered aboard his ATV with difficulty—he'd been stress-eating of late, which wasn't helping his mobility any—and drove to the next dome on his property. There he stared morosely at a dense row of evergreen trees that had been swallowed up two jumps back. He had planted them ages ago to serve as a windbreak at the western edge of his property, but now they looked spindly and forlorn. Most of the needles had yellowed and fallen off, but a few clumps still clung stubbornly to the branches.

Just beyond the dome's edge, the row of trees continued as green and healthy as ever. The stark contrast left him feeling hollowed out inside. He had always been a good caretaker of his land—a *steward* was the word his father had always used—so to see so much damage being done to his family farm—to see a foreign invader take root on *his* land and mistreat it so—well, it nearly killed him. And right here in America no less, land of the free, or so their national anthem declared.

When the six domes had first appeared on his land, he had tried everything he could think of to destroy them. He'd used fertilizer to create an explosion near the base of one dome. He'd tried dousing another with sprays of potent chemicals. He'd fired bullets at a third and watched them ricochet off like bits of hail against a window pane. Finally, in desperation, he'd even run one of his biggest tractors on autopilot straight at one of the domes—but of course the tractor had merely crumpled into a wreck. That last attempt had been an act of sheer idiocy, of course, but by then he'd just about lost his mind anyway. Watching your life's work disappear before your eyes could do that to a fellow.

But all of those attempts were in the past—two whole months ago—a lifetime ago—when he'd still had some fight left in him. Now, he'd just about given up. The domes were unstoppable—he knew that now. Unless they stopped of their own accord, all that was left for him and Marie to do was to prepare for the unthinkable and begin looking for a new home somewhere else.

JUMP 7

November 9

There was nothing lucky about the number seven jump. Following the jump, each dome was nearly half a mile in diameter and some 300 feet tall. All told, the domes occupied more square miles than the state of Texas. In cities around the world, sanity levels dropped to all-time lows as basic supplies and services became unattainable to all except the ultra-rich. The one percent became the point-oh-one percent, and former one-percenters fumed as they watched their fortunes disappear forever.

New York's Financial District prepared to get jumped in ten days' time. The Wall Street Dome now stretched from just shy of Exchange Place—dangerously close to Wall Street—all the way south to South Ferry Station. Meanwhile the Rockefeller Dome had just taken another big bite out of the Big Apple. It now stretched from 7th to Madison and 52nd to 43rd. That meant all of Rockefeller Center and Radio City Music Hall had been devoured. Times Square was safe for one more jump, but that was about it. Further to the north, the Central Park Dome had just gobbled up the entirety of the Metropolitan Museum of Art, along with half of the Great Lawn.

In Washington D.C., the Capitol Building had just been cut in half. The irony was not lost on reporters, who joked that the divide between the two parties had never been greater. And just across the Potomac, the Pentagon—the world's second-largest office building—was only one jump away from the unthinkable. It was abuzz with activity day and night as personnel cleared out a seemingly endless supply of computers, office equipment, and file cabinets filled with classified information. "We're at DEFCON 1," one general was heard to exclaim, much to the delight of the media, which ran with DEFCON 1 as a description for just about everything having to do with the domes from that point forward.

13

November 19 – Brooklyn, New York

"We should go see the city one last time while we still can," Royce suggested to Aubrey as they ate their breakfast in her apartment. "How does a walking tour of Manhattan sound?"

Aubrey eyed him like he was crazy. "Dangerous is how it sounds." She took a bite of her cereal and made a face. They were eating it with powdered milk, but it was better than nothing.

Ten days had passed since the seventh jump, each one more difficult than the last. Now it was the morning of the eighth jump day. None of New York's domes had jumped as of yet, but they had already jumped in other parts of the world, so everyone was holding their breath and waiting for the inevitable. Royce, who had finally quit his job after the seventh jump, found himself with time on his hands for a change, so he was hanging out with Aubrey and thinking about ways to spend some quality time together before his planned departure in less than a week. "Aren't you the least bit curious?" he asked her now.

"About riots and muggings and shootings? Not particularly. I'll stay home and watch the coverage on TV, thanks very much."

"We're talking about the center of the universe flaming out. We may never get another chance to see Manhattan again with our own eyes. And besides, I've come prepared: I've got pepper spray *and* a stun gun. Both are legal in New York and New Jersey without a permit, if you can believe it. I would've brought my real gun too, but I could get arrested for that."

"Who are you all of a sudden, Rambo? Where'd you get so many weapons?"

"Pistol Pete's in Jersey City, your one-stop shop for physical deterrents of all kinds. It's now or never, babe: our last chance to see the great city of New York before its demise."

"I'm fine with never. Sorry, but count me out."

*****

A half hour later Royce was ready. "Hon, I'm heading out," he called through her bedroom door.

Aubrey opened the door and stood there in a tattered pair of jeans and a simple hoodie with her hair pulled back in a pony tail. She wore basic sneaks on her feet and had removed every last piece of jewelry. "If you're bound and determined to do this, then I'm going with you. Someone has to protect you from yourself."

"And that would be you?"

"That would be me. You'd probably end up stunning yourself."

"That does sound like something I might do."

"Not to mention you're leaving soon, and I miss you already."

"Come with me; then you won't have to miss me."

"We've been through this, Royce; you know I can't."

"Your whole family could come. The RV's big enough. It could be the ultimate road trip."

"Or the ultimate road disaster," Aubrey laughed. "There's, like, fifteen of us."

"That *would* be a lot for one bathroom, but we could stop at rest stops along the way. Come on, it would be much safer than staying here—you know that."

"Those diehard New Yorkers you read about in the papers all the time? That's my family."

"They can *still* be diehard New Yorkers, just in Virginia or Florida."

Aubrey shook her head. "They won't budge. Not until the sky comes crashing down."

"It just might."

"What about *your* family?" Aubrey asked.

Royce shrugged. "My dad's out in San Diego and we're not all that close, but he's fine. I talked with him just the other day. You know my mom passed away when I was in college, and I have no brothers or sisters, so you're all the family I've got. I might as well adopt *your* crazy family as my own, don't you think?"

Aubrey caressed his cheek. "We'll see. For now, let's go on this stupid walk of yours. If we make it back alive, then we'll talk."

"Deal."

Aubrey blew out a deep breath. "Well, here we go. Got your stun gun?"

"Of course I've got my stun gun. And my pepper spray."

It took them less than twenty minutes to walk from her apartment to the Brooklyn Bridge. Once they were on the promenade, which was elevated above traffic, they walked directly towards the Manhattan skyline in all its glory. Only a handful of pedestrians were walking along with them towards Manhattan, but a steady stream of people were coming the other way, many with shopping carts piled high with possessions. "That's a bit concerning," murmured

Royce. "But otherwise you'd hardly know anything was amiss. The domes are still hidden behind all those skyscrapers."

The Promenade deposited them close to City Hall Park, which, as it happened, was overflowing with people at the moment. Thousands were milling about or sitting wherever they could find a spot. A protest was happening on the steps of City Hall. They could hear a crowd chanting while holding up protest signs: HOMES FOR THE HOMELESS. HOMES NOT DOMES. SHAWN BE GONE—this last a reference to the Mayor of New York City, Shawn Santos.

"So that's what they're chanting," said Royce. "Shawn Be Gone, over and over again."

"They sound angry."

"The ones on the steps do. But most of these people are just sitting around looking lost. Maybe they've been pushed out by the domes—or are about to be pushed out."

"What's with all the shopping carts?"

Royce shrugged. "Most New Yorkers don't own cars, so I guess they're just loading whatever they can onto shopping carts as a way of keeping a few of their belongings."

"They're not all sleeping outside, are they? It's getting seriously cold at night."

Royce shook his head. "I hope not."

"I read somewhere the mayor was using convention centers and sporting venues as temporary shelters," Aubrey remarked. "I wonder why they don't go there."

"Maybe they're full already. Two million people call Manhattan home, but there are ten million in New York City and twenty million in the greater metropolitan area. That's a whole lot of people to house and feed."

"If this crowd were to turn ugly..."

"Don't even think about it. C'mon, let's go."

They headed south on Park Row until it merged into Broadway. As its name implied, Broadway was a wide avenue with ample sidewalks, but it felt overcrowded at the moment. Thousands of homeless occupied the sidewalks, sitting with their backs against whatever wall they could find, or in some cases resting on piles of blankets between parked cars. They didn't look like they were going anywhere anytime soon. Some were preparing meals on cook stoves right out on the streets. Others were scarfing down fast food from whatever joint they could find that was still open. Empty food wrappers, soda cups, and beer cans littered the pavement. Half the stores and businesses along Broadway appeared to have been boarded up and closed for good, the other half were charging exorbitant prices, but from what they could see, people must still be paying those prices with whatever life savings they had left.

Tiny St. Paul's Chapel was overrun with squatters who had clambered over the fence and claimed it as their own. The steps were jam-packed and the chapel doors locked tight. "That's the oldest surviving church in Manhattan," Royce noted, "but I don't think it's up to the task of helping this many people. It was built for a different age."

They continued walking south. No domes threatened this area yet, and a fair number of people were going about their normal business—or as normal as was possible under the circumstances. Men and women in business attire picked their way through crowds of displaced residents, stepping gingerly over arms and legs. Many forsook the sidewalks altogether and walked briskly out in the street, daring taxis and other vehicles to hit them. They seemed determined to carry on with business as usual, ignoring the obvious signs of misery all around them.

To their right they caught occasional glimpses of One World Trade Center, the tallest building in the Western Hemisphere. "That entire building will be inaccessible after the next jump," Royce remarked. "I mean, not today's jump—the one after that, if it happens."

The piles of trash turned into heaps the further south they ventured. The whole street reeked of garbage untended for too long. Boarded-up windows gave way to gaping black holes leading into derelict storefronts.

The skyscraper at One Liberty Plaza, with its imposing black façade, stood stolid and uncaring of the human misery strewn at its feet. Its entrance was being kept clear by a platoon of armed guards. All around the guards were masses of desperate-looking people who appeared ready to storm the gates if the right opportunity presented itself.

A long line of police stood sentry along the stretch of Broadway south of One Liberty Plaza. Aubrey noticed any number of shady characters loitering in nearby alleyways, apparently biding their time until nightfall. "I'm not loving this," she said.

"We should be okay as long as it's daylight. Look, plenty of pedestrians are still going about their business."

"And why are we doing this again?"

"Because this is our last chance to see Rome before the fall."

They crossed Liberty Street. "This is where the Wall Street Dome is expected to jump to later today," Royce said. "Liberty Street and everything south of here will be gone by morning: Wall Street, most of the Financial District, and what little is left of Downtown Manhattan."

Inside the jump zone things instantly felt different. "Can you feel it?" Aubrey asked. "The energy just changed."

Royce nodded, waggling his hands in eerie fashion. "You are now entering the twilight zone."

At Zucotti Park, every bench, table, and inch of pavement had been taken up by hordes of the destitute. Some had tents, others huddled under tarps or wrapped themselves in blankets. The omnipresent shopping carts and duffle bags of the dispossessed were strewn everywhere.

"See that bright red seventy-foot-tall sculpture?" Royce said, pointing. "That's called *Joie de Vivre*. I used to come here sometimes during my lunch breaks."

"I'm not feeling much joie de vivre at the moment."

At Trinity Church, squeezed between skyscrapers, more homeless haunted the premises. Even the small cemetery adjacent to the church was overrun with encampments. A squad of police stood by but made no effort to disperse those who had decided, for whatever reason, to call the cemetery home. "Creepy," Royce muttered.

"Don't these people know they're inside a jump zone?"

"Maybe they *want* to be inside. Maybe they're waiting to loot the place after dark."

"You're saying they're here to pick over the bones of Downtown Manhattan?"

Royce nodded.

Across from Trinity Church was Wall Street itself, packed with people, but most of these were in business attire. "Home sweet home," Royce said with a sigh.

Aubrey stared at the frantic hustle and bustle happening in front of her. The narrow confines of Wall Street were abuzz with activity. "It feels like we're the only two people standing still on this entire street. Didn't these people know a jump was coming? Why'd they wait till the last minute?"

Royce shrugged. "Human nature? I can tell you a lot of my fellow brokers have been in a state of denial for weeks. Not *here*. Not on Wall Street."

"I never thought you brokers were a very smart lot."

As if on cue, a man in a business suit carrying a load of boxes tripped on the curb, sending papers flying every which way. People skirted around him, looking annoyed, as he struggled to shovel papers back into the boxes.

All up and down the street they could hear people yelling back and forth, trying to communicate over the rumble of idling trucks.

"Not *that* truck, you idiot. *That* one."

"Where d'ya think it goes dumbass? With the rest of that crap over there."

Four brawny men staggered out of the gold-and-glass doors of the former Trump Building lugging an enormous mahogany desk that must have graced one of the penthouse suites. Grunting all the way, they hefted it into a moving van whose front half was already piled high with furniture and boxes.

Royce and Aubrey stood still amidst the chaos and watched in fascination as people rushed to do what they should have done weeks ago. "People are idiots," Aubrey announced as a kind of general verdict on the human race.

"You're just realizing this now?"

They resumed their walk, following alongside the New York Stock Exchange. "What do you suppose is going on in there?" Aubrey asked.

"Not much—they already cleared out. I read about it in *The Wall Street Journal*. The article was entitled 'NYSE to Know You.'"

Aubrey groaned. "You've been waiting to say that all morning, haven't you?"

Royce grinned. "Since last night, actually."

Straight ahead, near Exchange Place, they finally got their first glimpse of the Wall Street Dome glimmering in the sunlight. They walked straight up to it and watched the soap bubble colors slide up and down its surface.

"It's disturbingly pretty when seen up close," Aubrey said. "Too bad it's such a pain in the ass." She pretend-caressed the dome. "Hello dome. What are you doing here?"

"I don't think it can hear you."

"You never know: maybe it's tied into the mothership. If you can hear me, alien beings, please go elsewhere and leave us alone."

"Great job saving the planet, Aubrey. If it weren't for you, all would have been lost."

"Hey, just doing my part. How far does this dome extend?"

"All the way down to South Ferry Station. Battery Park is all gone, but they say you can still visit the Statue of Liberty viewpoint at its southernmost tip. But after today the dome's going to double in size again and extend right out into the water. A whole lot of expensive waterfront real estate is going to get gobbled up."

"Yikes. These domes are getting *big*."

"Each one already covers some sixty city blocks. Assuming they jump again today, it's going to be more like three hundred *acres*. I don't know how many city blocks that is, but it's a lot. In a city as dense as this, that's a whole lot of prime real estate going away for good."

"Don't I know it," said Aubrey the real estate agent.

They walked back towards Wall Street. A feeling of imminent doom hung over the district. The jump was coming—people could feel it—and the level of activity was only growing more frantic as the time drew closer. Employees moved boxes from hand to hand out of surrounding buildings and into waiting trucks, like old-fashioned fire brigades passing buckets of water. Trucks already loaded and ready to go blared their horns but remained stuck in traffic, unable to move because of other vehicles idling in front of them. A symphony of horns ensued, impossibly loud, as still more trucks joined in the chorus. A harried U-Haul driver dashed out of a building and started his truck, pulling onto the curb so the angry drivers behind him could pass.

A distant gunshot resounded through the skyscraper canyon that was Wall Street, but it was impossible to tell from which direction it had come. What might have been return fire, equally distant, stuttered then stopped.

Royce and Aubrey looked at each other. "Time to go," said Royce.

"You don't have to tell me twice."

*****

They retraced their steps, pausing for refreshment at a Shake Shack located right at the edge of the jump zone. As they splurged on hamburgers, fries, and chocolate shakes, they asked the manager if the dome was going to affect his business. "It's gonna be close," the manager said. "Depends on which side of Liberty Street the dome lands on."

At Fulton Street, they peered down the subway stairs and found them crowded with homeless to either side. The station was still open for trains heading uptown but not downtown. It spoke to the piecemeal nature of the subway system these days, where detours and workarounds were fast becoming the norm. To Royce it felt as if the great beating heart of New York City was on life support and fading fast.

They tiptoed down the stairs, picking their way carefully, and found the dimly lit subway platform even more densely packed with the destitute and homeless. The look and smell and feel of the place left something to be desired. They both felt relieved when the train finally came, taking them uptown towards Grand Central at 42nd Street. That subway stop stood just beyond the Rockefeller Dome's expected jump radius.

Royce consulted his phone as they rode along. "After today's jump, six of the major north-south avenues in Midtown Manhattan will be blocked: Park, Madison, Fifth, Sixth, Seventh, and Eighth Avenues. It'll be like someone plopped a mountain down right in the middle of Midtown Manhattan and forced everyone to funnel around it."

"Traffic's going to be a nightmare."

"Nearly every subway line will be affected too."

"People are going to have to remember how to walk again."

"My legs are already tired from the walking we've done so far, and that's *with* taking the subway between points. Manhattan's big once you have to start hoofing it on foot."

Aubrey nodded her agreement. "Without a workable transit system, the other four boroughs will be all but cut off from Manhattan."

"You're right. One more jump after this and there won't *be* a Midtown Manhattan. The only north-south avenues that will still be open at that point will be—let's see—" he consulted his phone—"FDR Drive and First Avenue to the east, and West Side Highway and Eleventh Avenue to the west."

"That's crazy."

"Yep. New York Crazy."

*****

They emerged from Grand Central subway and were surprised to discover a sea of people sitting not only on the pavement but on the avenue itself. "That's something you don't see every day," Aubrey observed. "People camped out in the middle of Park Avenue."

She asked one fellow sitting atop a throw pillow what was going on. "It's the dome," the guy said. "We're on one of the higher floors of that apartment complex over there. They won't let us back in until after the dome jumps, since the dome might block our way down the stairs or elevators. Guess they don't want a million people all calling the fire department at once for rescue. If the dome misses our building, they say we can go back up. Otherwise we're screwed."

"Wow, that sucks," said Aubrey.

"It does. Everything we own is up there."

They decided to make their way towards Times Square for one last look around. Long before they got there, they could hear a muted roar coming from up ahead. The streets became so congested they could barely move. "I guess we're not the only ones who thought of this," Aubrey said.

They inched forward, finally making their way onto the square itself. There they were greeted by what seemed like a million revelers all cheering at the top of their lungs, welcoming in…what? A new year? A new age? The arrival of the aliens? It didn't seem to matter. They were on Times Square for what might be the last celebration ever to take place here, and they all seemed to know it. They cheered like there was no tomorrow.

Royce and Aubrey grinned at each other and started cheering just as loudly as everyone else. It was crazy, infectious, and the release they all needed. Many wore party hats saying "2042" or glitzy glasses or colorful robes. "I guess we're celebrating New Year's Eve on November 19th," shouted Aubrey.

"Why not?" Royce shouted back. "Nothing else makes sense at this point. Why should New Year's be any different?"

"Happy New Year!" they shouted to each other and the world.

"Should ooold acquaintance beeeee forgot…" A huge swell gripped the crowd and took them along with it. They all belted out "For Auld Lang Syne" *a cappella* at the top of their lungs, and it was one of those moments where nothing and everything made sense at once. A huge cheer erupted from the crowd at the end of the song.

"I'll never forget this moment," Aubrey shouted, eyes sparkling with joy.

"Me either," Royce yelled back. He kissed her and she kissed him and it felt like the whole world disappeared for a moment.

It was at that moment that the dome jumped, encompassing them all. Its soap-bubble colors iridesced above their heads, and instead of crying out or lamenting, a huge roar erupted from the crowd and they hollered even louder than before as if something truly wonderful had happened.

Royce took a look at his watch. It was 2:23 pm on November 19th and they had just ushered in the strangest new year of all time.

*****

Throats raw, voices hoarse, emotions spent, they inched their way back out of Times Square, surrounded by throngs of happy well-wishers, and eventually reached 42nd Street. In time they reached the dome wall itself. It cut 42nd Street in half near Park Avenue. It looked like the apartment of the guy who had been sitting on the throw pillow was safe for one more jump.

Staring out at the world from inside the dome, they saw hundreds of people doing an approximation of the chicken dance as they stuck various appendages in and out of the dome wall. Royce and Aubrey joined in, laughing.

"This is ridiculous," said Aubrey, but she was smiling and her eyes were alight.

"It sure is."

She kissed him then, half in and half out of the dome wall, and whether some hidden current was running through them or they were just crazy-happy in love, either way it felt electric.

JUMP 8

November 19

By the eighth jump—dubbed the Times Square jump by some—each dome increased to approximately three quarters of a mile in diameter and some 400 feet tall. All told, the domes now occupied more square miles than the four biggest U.S. states combined—Alaska, Texas, California, and Montana.

As the domes continued to increase in size, clever New Yorkers were finding creative ways to use the top portions of skyscrapers even as their entryways became inaccessible. The one hundred tallest buildings in New York all stood taller than 600 feet (with sixteen taller than 1,000 feet), so a lot of prime real estate was available above the 400-foot mark, if only it could be accessed. One solution was hastily constructed stand-alone elevators that whisked riders upwards to a series of catwalks radiating outwards to surrounding skyscrapers. New entrances were carved into the exteriors of the skyscrapers, new power lines run along the catwalks, and each building's elevators modified to function only on the floors above the domes' reach. In such a fashion, diehard New Yorkers were able to continue living and working in the city despite the presence of the domes.

Younger New Yorkers were also finding creative ways to party despite the domes—or rather, because of them. "Oxygen Blasts" were the latest craze. Participants would wait inside a dome until the air ran out, then don lightweight scuba gear and break into the most fantastic places—billionaires' penthouses, Broadway theaters, even Radio City Music Hall—celebrating with their besties until their oxygen tanks ran low, at which point they would make a mad dash for the exits. It was said to be great fun, right up until the air ran out, at which point it became a little less fun.

But why should the young play it safe? They might all be dead in a few weeks anyway, so why not have a little fun along the way?

14

November 20 – Oval Office, Washington D.C.

"The Capitol Building looks like a snow globe," the President observed.

"Huh?" Lametti was busy scribbling in his notepad.

"The Capitol. With the dome enclosing it, it looks like one of those snow globes. You know, the kind you shake up and the snow comes falling down?"

"Lord knows the Capitol could use a good shakeup."

The President nodded but seemed to miss the joke. He seemed far away. "Of course it's snowing *inside* the dome, which makes it look even more like a snow globe. Funny how something as simple as snow can get through a dome wall but we can't."

"You, uh, you all right there, Mark? You seem a little distracted."

The President nodded. "The Declaration of Independence is in there too, inside the Library of Congress, or at least it was. Hopefully not anymore. The symbol of independence trapped forever inside a dome…too symbolic by half, don't you think?"

"Mark…"

"A big chunk of the Pentagon's gone, too, along with the Supreme Court, the Air and Space Museum, and the

National Mall. What a strange view that must be now, looking out from the Washington Monument."

"Mark, are you all right?"

The President seemed to shake himself awake. "Where were we, Gil?"

"We, uh, we were discussing which city should be our next seat of government."

"Right. And we agreed Baltimore was out, since it has its own dome to worry about. Didn't we settle on Philadelphia?"

"I think we did, but yours is the final word."

"Philadelphia was the first capital of our country, so it makes a certain sense, doesn't it?"

"And it's dome-free, that's the most important thing. You can't say that about many East Coast cities."

"No, you sure can't. Then Philadelphia it is." The President rubbed his hands together. "Well, that was easy. What's next?"

"We should discuss some of the specifics of the move," suggested Lametti. "The order in which the various branches of government should transfer, what buildings we're going to have to claim by eminent domain, which federal agencies are destined for which building, what..."

The President's thoughts drifted away again as he imagined the White House sitting inside a snow globe. He pictured a giant alien hand shaking it up and down and watching the snow fall, gentle as ashes.

"...and then we should really discuss the progress of the cities being built," he half-heard Lametti say. "They're coming along nicely, but there are a lot of particulars to consider..."

The President stared out the window at the dome that was slowly but surely encapsulating his city and wondered where it would all end.

JPL, Pasadena, California

"Rachel, we appreciate everything you've done for this organization during your tenure here as Director, but unfortunately we think it's time for a change."

Dr. Rachel Cavanaugh had only just emerged from the dome that had swallowed up her lab. It had been another marathon session of experiments while wearing portable oxygen tanks, but once again it had all led to failure—to the same frustrating inability to get past the inner shield that protected the ovate.

She still felt breathless from oxygen deprivation, and her head seemed to be pounding in sync with her heart. She hadn't showered since exiting the dome and was still wearing the same outfit she'd gone in with. She was a mess and she knew it—only to be asked to proceed immediately to the office of the president of Caltech.

Now she was having to process the news that she was being fired from her position as Director of JPL. She felt herself deflate like a balloon right in front of him.

"...feel like maybe you've lost some perspective when it comes to the domes," he was saying. "We think you could use a break, to be honest, Rachel. No one questions your dedication or your work ethic, believe me—you've worked harder than anyone to crack the secrets of these domes. But your actions of late have bordered on...well, on the obsessive, if you want the truth. Some of your colleagues have complained you're endangering them by keeping them inside the dome too long, and—"

"Who said that?" she heard herself mumble.

"Does it matter?" Caltech's president asked, spreading his arms wide. "The point is, it's time for a change, Rachel. Once you've had a chance to rest, we'll revisit all this and see if we can't find a right fit for you going forward. One where..."

She tuned out the rest of what he said, stood up when he was finished, accepted his condolences, and stumbled out of the office.

November 26 – Brooklyn, New York

Royce stood half-in and half-out of Aubrey's door as they said their goodbyes.

"I can't believe you're going," she murmured.

"I can't believe you're not coming with."

"My family."

"I know."

The two could practically talk in shorthand by now. Their eyes told the real story: they were both miserable.

"I'll call. A lot."

"I'll answer. A lot."

Royce kissed her, squeezed her hands, then headed out the door of her apartment. He couldn't help feeling like he was leaving her forever.

He had been convinced Aubrey would change her mind eventually and see the wisdom of going with him, with or without her family. But he couldn't very well force her to go, and he couldn't afford to stay put any longer in a city that was fast going to the dogs. Many stores had closed their doors altogether: it was simply too dangerous for them to remain open anymore, what with looters running rampant and people fighting over the last scraps. Who knew how much worse things could get, or how quickly?

The Wall Street Dome—the one that affected them the most—was preparing to gobble up everything south of City Hall in three days' time. That would be the ninth jump. By then the dome would extend halfway across the Hudson River to the west, and right up to the Manhattan side of the Brooklyn Bridge to the east. Royce's apartment in Jersey City would be swallowed up whole on the next jump—the tenth jump, assuming it happened, which Royce expected it would. He didn't believe the domes were done jumping yet.

He and Aubrey had done some back-of-the-napkin calculations together, and it looked like her Brooklyn apartment should be safe for two more jumps—the ninth and tenth—but after that all bets were off. Where would she go after that? Where would her family go? They had no plan worth calling a plan. They all lived near one another in the same Brooklyn neighborhood, so if one home went, they all would.

Royce didn't like leaving Aubrey behind, not one little bit, but what else could he do?

A voice in the back of his head said, You could stay. Come hell or high water you could stay. That's what you would do if you really loved her.

But another voice said, Wouldn't she come with me if she really loved me?

He took a circuitous route back to his Jersey City apartment, one that involved multiple transfers—par for the course these days. Eventually he reached his crappy little basement studio. He had already cleared the place out, all except for one last box containing a safe designed to be bolted down to an RV floor. Inside the safe was two-thirds of his remaining net worth: two hundred thousand dollars in gold coins, diamonds, and cash. The other third he had decided to leave right where it was, in his checking account. Even with the world falling apart, it turned out a debit card tied to a checking account was still useful—like letting him pay for the Uber ride he had just ordered.

When the Uber arrived, he locked the door of his studio apartment for the last time and clambered into the car, lugging the heavy box with him.

"You want that in the trunk?" the guy asked, eyeing the way the seat next to Royce sagged visibly under the weight of the box.

"No thanks," Royce said. There was no way he was putting a safe filled with two hundred thousand dollars in gold and cash in the trunk of an Uber—not these days.

Half an hour later he was at RV World. Huffing and puffing, he made his way to the RV, then he locked himself inside and got busy installing the safe. It took him three hours instead of the one hour the instructions claimed it would take, but in the end it was installed under a removable cabinet drawer in the kitchen, out of sight and as secure as he could make it.

He locked the RV, climbed into his Dodge Ram, and started the engine. If he was going reach his intended goal before nightfall, he'd better get moving. He'd mapped out a path that would take him west into the quieter parts of Pennsylvania before heading south into West Virginia. After that, his plan was simply to keep heading south until winter was a distant memory.

He should have felt excited, but instead all he could think about was Aubrey. He sat there with the engine idling for a good ten minutes. More than once he put the truck into gear, only to return it to park.

"*Dammit!*" He slammed his hand against the steering wheel.

Turned off the engine. Locked the Dodge Ram. Opened the RV. Packed some clothes and toiletries into a knapsack. Added packets of dehydrated food, bars of chocolate, and other goodies from his stash. Collected his gun and other deterrents. Double-locked the RV door. Walked to the bus stop and took the bus home. Took the same laborious series of transfers back to Brooklyn that he'd taken earlier that same morning. Knocked on the door.

When she answered he said, "I couldn't leave."

She threw her arms around him and said, "Thank God."

November 28 – Hygiene, Colorado

"Do we *really* have to move so soon?" Kaley asked.

"I'm afraid so, hon," said her mom. "I'm not happy about it either, believe me."

Their one-month lease was almost up in Hygiene, and it felt like they'd barely arrived. Tomorrow by noon they had to hit the road again.

"But can't we live in the barn or something?"

"No, sweetie, the gentleman who owns the place wants it for himself."

"Where are we gonna live, then?"

Cynthia was silent for a moment, looking over at Will. "That's a great question, Kaley. We're still figuring that one out."

Will spoke up. "We're going on a little road trip, honey. It's gonna be great."

Will had lost his job last week. The need for accountants just wasn't what it used to be, what with the complete meltdown of society happening all around them.

"A road trip?" exclaimed Kaley. "That sounds fun!"

"It will be," Will assured her. "We're going to head north and see where the road takes us. Maybe find a cabin in the woods somewhere."

"Wow. We'll be like nomads."

"We sure will, hon."

Ashley, who was sprawled out on a couch at the other end of the living room, rolled her eyes but remained silent. Her parents had already had "the talk" with her about the tough situation they were in and how she needed to be supportive—or at least not openly hostile.

Josh was playing a game called *DomeWrecker* on the TV. He was crushing it: domes were disintegrating left and right as his soldier sent withering blasts from his dome blaster and somersaulted into safety. Cynthia only wished it were so easy. The game was good fantasy escape material but hardly true to life. Josh had begged his mom and dad to leave the game station hooked up until the last possible moment, insisting dome blasting was good therapy. They had acquiesced, but Cynthia knew he was going to go through some serious game withdrawal tomorrow once they hit the road.

The owner, an elderly man, said he hated to kick them out but had no choice since he and his extended family were moving in. He was allowing them to leave a few dozen boxes of their possessions behind, tucked away in a corner of the barn. Will and Cynthia were grateful; finding suitable storage at this late date was pretty much impossible. They had taken turns calling every storage company in Colorado, Wyoming, and Nebraska and had come up empty; any place that was away from the domes was already full to capacity, with a waiting list a mile long.

They'd had to pare down their possessions drastically in order to fit them into two cars, along with their three kids and one dog. In fact they were down to mostly clothes, camping gear, an on-the-road kitchen box, and some food. Josh insisted on bringing his game station and said he would store it on his lap if necessary. Ashley said she couldn't live without her hair and makeup products and swore she would store those on *her* lap if she had to. Kaley, only half-seriously, insisted on bringing a prairie dog, but her mom convinced her Woof would get too excited with a live prairie dog in the car.

The cars were already packed. First thing tomorrow morning they'd be heading off for parts unknown. What parts those would be had been a major topic of conversation last night, after the kids had been put to bed (all except Josh, who played *DomeWrecker* in the living room until who-knew-what-hour).

Will was all for heading north to Wyoming or Montana where the population pressures would be less intense and the simple living options greater. "All we need is one small cabin," he kept saying. Cynthia wanted to head east towards family, which would have been fine with Will except their families lived all the way on the East Coast. "The East Coast is not where you want to be right now," he said with some reason. "Have you heard the stories coming out of there?"

"Yeah, but I've talked with my mom and dad and they say things are okay," Cynthia replied.

"For now, sure. But who knows what it'll look like in another month. Bethesda is way too close to D.C."

"What about your family?" Cynthia asked.

"Pittsburgh's no better. My mom and dad are getting out. In fact they were thinking of coming *our* way before our home got swallowed up. The whole East Coast is too congested. Look, why don't we try Wyoming or Montana for a month? If that doesn't pan out, then we'll head east."

Cynthia had acquiesced, contingent on no camping.

"No worries, the camping gear's for later," Will assured her. "It's too cold for camping this time of year anyway. For now, we'll find a cabin somewhere not listed on Airbnb."

All the places they'd found online had been exorbitant beyond belief, and with Will's job being gone, they couldn't afford to pay those prices anymore. Privately, Cynthia wasn't sure how much more luck they'd have finding a cabin offline than on, but she'd given in in the end, like she usually did.

Last week they'd emptied out their bank accounts, stuffing huge amounts of bills into wallets, purses, and hidden parts of their cars. Otherwise they were broke; even their retirement funds had been cleaned out. Supposedly, the ten percent penalty on early withdrawals still applied, but they had no intention of paying it. The IRS could hunt them down if they wanted.

Cynthia was in a place so far beyond scared that she felt calm in a numb sort of way. For the kids' sake, she told herself, she had to be strong. She had to stay positive. She couldn't freak out like she wanted to. But God did she want to.

Will, for his part, wasn't doing much better. The loss of his job had hit him hard. He was no longer the reliable provider for his family. Could he find an accounting job in Wyoming or Montana—or anywhere else for that matter? Things being what they were, accountants weren't exactly in high demand. But what else was he qualified to do? These were the dark thoughts that haunted his nights.

A wife three kids and a dog. A wife three kids and a dog. A wife three kids and a dog. This was the mantra that played over and over in his head each night. What in the hell was he going to do?

*****

At ten the next morning they piled into their two cars. Will was in the lead minivan, with Josh in the passenger seat. Kaley sat in the back with Woof and plenty of boxes for company. Cynthia followed in the car behind, with Ashley sitting beside her.

It was a straight shot north to Wyoming, or would have been if I-25 hadn't been clogged with cars and endless detours. The interstates weren't what they had once been. Domes randomly blocked most highways every fifty miles or so. Road construction crews had begun anticipating the next several jumps, so the detours on graded dirt roads circled further and further out of the way before rejoining I-25.

Getting past Fort Collins took them three hours instead of the usual forty-five minutes.

"This sucks," Ashley said as they sat in traffic.

"It most certainly does," Cynthia replied.

"Mom, what are we gonna do? We can't just drive around Wyoming looking for a random place to live. Dad's gone off the deep end."

"I know, hon. One day at a time. That's all we can do right now. We shouldn't have taken I-25, though; I've never seen it this backed up."

"It's jump day. Maybe that's why."

"Good point. Everyone's on the move right now, just like we are."

"Isn't Dad ever gonna stop? I really need to pee." Ashley was just about to call him when she saw his blinker. "Oh, thank God."

They got off at the exit just north of Fort Collins; after that, exits were few and far between until you reached Cheyenne. Pulling into a busy McDonald's, they clambered out of the cars. Ashley headed straight for the restroom.

"Josh, take Woof for a quick walk, will you?" his dad called out to him. "We'll order some food."

After Woof got his walk, Josh left him in the back seat and headed inside. Ashley was still waiting in line for the ladies room, doing a little dance of impatience. Meanwhile, Will and Cynthia were wincing at the prices for food enough to feed five. Everything had to be paid for in cash these days; even McDonald's wasn't accepting credit cards anymore.

Ten minutes later they were all sitting down and eating. "This isn't going so well," Josh observed around bites of his hamburger.

"No, it's not," said his dad. "But now that we're past Fort Collins, the going should get easier."

Half an hour later they hit the road again. They made better time than before but still had to detour around another dome on the way to Cheyenne. They were startled to see individuals, and sometimes whole families, walking south next to the highway.

"I hope they're not heading to Denver," Will said to Josh. There were stories about how bad things had gotten in Denver. It was the Wild West all over again, it was said, with gun battles commonplace over cars and possessions and scraps of food.

By the time they reached Cheyenne, another three hours had passed and it was starting to snow. Somehow it was already four o'clock in the afternoon.

Josh checked his phone. "There's a Motel 6 up ahead off the next exit. Maybe we should try that."

Will nodded wearily. They exited and pulled into the motel's parking lot. When they got out of their cars, they could see their breath.

"Jesus, it's freezing out!" yelped Ashley. She dove back into the car yelling, "Close the door!"

Kaley got Woof-walking duties this time around, while Will headed in to talk to the receptionist. She just shook her head when she saw him coming. "No vacancies," she said.

"Not at any price?"

"'Afraid not. There's more motels up at the next exit, though, where I-25 meets I-80. Maybe one of those will have some room."

Will nodded his thanks and headed back out. "Next exit," he called to everyone. But once they got there, all the motels showed no vacancy signs. Finally they found a Marriott with one room available, but at a nightly rate that knocked their socks off. "That's half of what we paid for a whole month in Hygiene," Cynthia whispered incredulously to Will.

Will just shook his head hopelessly and started laying out bills on the counter. "What else can we do, Cynthia? Our kids are waiting out there in the cars, and it's freezing."

"Will, wait. Let's think about this for a minute."

Will stuffed the bills back in his pocket, and they sat down on a bench in the lobby to talk.

"Will, we can't keep heading north. This isn't working."

"I know. It's hopeless."

"Maybe we could throw ourselves on the mercy of the owner in Hygiene and ask if we could spend just one night in his barn."

Will winced at the thought; he didn't like the idea of having to accept charity. "Maybe. Maybe we could pay him for one night."

Josh came in at a full gallop, rubbing his hands together. "Hey, what's up?" he asked his mom and dad.

"We're just trying to figure out what to do next," said Cynthia. "They have a room here, but it costs a small fortune."

"What about Woof?" Josh asked immediately.

"I was afraid to ask the desk clerk," muttered his dad under his breath. "I was thinking maybe we could sneak him in after dark."

"He'd freeze to death out there," Josh said.

Will shook his head. "I don't know what I was thinking. Heading north in late November—what a stupid idea. My brain must be turning to mush."

"We're not used to having to think about not having a place to stay for the night," said Cynthia gently. "You were picturing a nice cabin in the woods—not this."

"No, not this. But finding that cabin just driving around in the snow…it's not going to work, is it?"

"No, it's not. So what do we do now?"

Will just shook his head, looking miserable.

"It's jump day," Josh said, apropos of nothing.

"Yeah? " said his dad. "So?"

"So maybe we could camp outside the Longmont Dome and reclaim our home for a couple of nights. At least long enough to regroup."

Will's and Cynthia's eyes both lit up. "Hey, that's a brilliant idea, son," Will said warmly. "I knew there was a reason we brought you along."

"That way Woof would have a home too. And we could use some of that stuff you stored in the garage for heat. The fireplace is still working, isn't it?"

Will nodded. "I'm not looking forward to driving back in a snowstorm, but it's better than staying here. All that gas wasted!" He shook his head again. At sixteen dollars per gallon and rising, even a short trip was becoming a big deal.

"Don't think about that," soothed Cynthia. "Think about getting back home."

"And starting a fire," said Josh.

"Then we'd better hurry," said Will. "The domes are expected to jump later tonight. If we don't get a move on, we might miss it."

*****

The drive back took seven long hours in the snow. Both Will and Cynthia were shaking with fatigue by the end. But compared to the people trudging through the snow on foot next to the highway, they were among the lucky ones. Those people looked miserable beyond belief, with their heads down and their coats wrapped tightly around them.

"Why don't they drive?" asked Kaley.

"They must be out of money," said her dad. "Gas is super-expensive now, and if you don't have cash on hand, you're in big trouble. You can't buy stuff on credit like you used to."

"I feel bad for them," Kaley said.

"Me too, hon."

"Maybe we should give them a ride."

"Look around, Kaley; our car is filled to the brim, and so is Mom's. There'd be nowhere to put them."

When they finally pulled up to the Longmont Dome, they were immensely relieved to see it hadn't jumped yet. "Thank God," whispered Cynthia. "I'm beyond exhausted."

"Where are we going to sleep tonight?" Ashley asked, already knowing the answer.

"Right here in our cars, unfortunately."

"Couldn't we stay with friends?"

Cynthia shook her head. "It's nearly midnight, and we can't risk leaving the dome's edge or we might miss the jump altogether."

Ashley nodded resignedly.

"Our tank is on fumes. We'll need to turn the engine off to conserve what little fuel we have left. It's going to get cold in here, Ashley. Bundle up." She turned off the engine and called her husband on the phone.

"I'm on empty too," said Will. "What a waste of a trip. I see you've turned your engine off." His lights went dark too. "Maybe we can find a way to siphon off some gas from another car once we're inside."

"Maybe. As long as we don't get shot doing it."

JUMP 9

November 29

Thanksgiving fell late that year, on the 28th, but it was hardly a time of bounty for most Americans. The only things bountiful were the domes, which continued to prosper. The ninth jump increased each dome's diameter to 1½ miles—enough to obstruct the entrance to the Empire State Building and Carnegie Hall, among other landmarks. Walking from one end of a dome to the other was beginning to amount to a legitimate form of exercise, one that could take half an hour at a normal clip.

The bigger the domes got, the more often they overlapped and merged. As a result, the total number of domes worldwide had dropped dramatically over the past several jumps, from roughly 4 million to 1½ million; but even so, collectively they encompassed some 3 million square miles of land—larger than the continent of Australia.

By now, watching the nightly news had become something of an ordeal. Even simple human interest stories were grim, like the story of a baby trapped inside a dome with the distraught parents on the outside looking in. The newborn was too young to crawl out, there was no way to get in, and the dome wasn't expected to jump for another ten days. Everyone understood the baby would be dead by then, but no one could do anything about it. A story like that could mess you up for weeks just hearing about it.

15

November 29 – Longmont, Colorado

The dome jumped while Will and Cynthia and the kids were asleep in their cars. The next morning they found themselves on the inside looking out and felt nothing but relief.

Driving through the empty streets, past forlorn trees and dead grass, they parked in their driveway and wandered into their old home like zombies. The kids crashed on the couch, shivering and half-asleep, while Will went to the garage and broke an old crib into firewood. Tearing pages out of a book for kindling, he started a fire in the fireplace. Before long they were all removing extra layers of clothing.

Cynthia busied herself in the kitchen, making a simple breakfast from supplies they'd brought with them in the van. They enjoyed a simple meal, fed Woof, then brought their sleeping bags inside and crashed for several more hours. After lunch they finally started feeling more human again.

"We've got maybe three days in here before we have to leave," Will said. "After that it's going to get hard to breathe, or at least that's what they tell us. Hopefully our next trip won't be as big a disaster as this one was. That was my fault, and I'm sorry for it. The big question we have to answer now is, where to next?"

"South," Josh said immediately. "South is warmer."

"I agree with Josh," said Kaley.

"You *always* agree with Josh," Ashley scoffed with one of her patented eye rolls. "But in this case I agree: warmer is better. We learned that the hard way last night."

"At least we won't freeze to death heading south," said Will. But we should stay away from big cities like Denver and Colorado Springs on our way down. That means staying away from I-25 and finding less traveled roads south. What do you think, hon?"

"I'm willing to go south," said Cynthia, "but if that doesn't pan out, then we should head east towards family."

They all nodded in agreement. "South it is, then," said Will. "Maybe Texas, maybe Arizona, maybe New Mexico."

"Or old Mexico," said Kaley. "Sí señor."

"Or old Mexico," said her dad with a smile. "Assuming they let us past the border."

*****

That afternoon, Josh snuck out with his dad on what Will was calling a secret mission. "I'm not trying to teach you bad habits, son, but I think we're going to have to be a little less moral and a little more practical going forward in life. That means breaking a few rules now and again."

"Um, okay, Dad. What did you have in mind?"

"Nothing too terrible. Just a little breaking and entering. And a little stealing. And a little siphoning off of some gas."

"No murder?"

"Definitely not murder. But if we should happen to come across a gun, we should take it."

"Seriously?" Josh sounded shocked.

Will nodded. "In principle I'm against guns, but my principles are wearing a little thin these days."

"Maybe principles only work when the world works," said Josh. "The world's not working so great right now."

"That's very wise of you, son. Now just remember, what Mom doesn't know won't hurt her. No need for specifics when we get back. She might not be so thrilled, for instance, to learn that we broke into the Andersons' home, or Mrs. Parker's home."

"We're going to steal from our next-door neighbors?"

Will shrugged. "Maybe. I just so happen to have the keys to those two homes. Mrs. Parker and the Andersons gave them to us years ago so we could check up on things whenever they were away. It's what neighbors do for neighbors—or did, anyway."

"So now we're gonna use them to break in."

"*Is* it breaking in if you have a key? I'm not sure. We can always say we were just checking up on things."

"Wow, Dad, lying too. We're really hitting all the commandments today, aren't we?"

At the Andersons' home they found nothing; it was bare to the bone. But Mrs. Parker's home was another matter.

Will whistled. "Jackpot."

"We're not really going to steal from sweet old Mrs. Parker, are we, Dad?"

"Mary said she was moving to Topeka to be with her family, remember? I highly doubt she's ever coming back. A lot of this stuff will just go to waste or get stolen by someone else if we don't take it."

"You're seriously messing with my moral compass, Dad."

"We'll leave a note if it makes you feel any better, son. But we really need this stuff if we're going to survive the next few weeks." Will was busy opening kitchen cabinets. "Like these canned goods! You can't even buy this stuff anymore. Canned green beans. Diced tomatoes. Soups. Chilis. This is a gold mine right here." He peered into the pantry. "And looky here: snacks! Peanut butter, crackers, potato chips, chocolate—and more chocolate! Mrs. Parker must have a sweet tooth."

Josh just shook his head.

"I'm starting to think I should have brought Ashley along on this mission instead of you. She'd be rifling through Mrs. Parker's clothes and jewelry by now."

"Get real, Dad—Ashley would never be caught dead in anything Mrs. Parker would wear." Josh opened the door to the garage. "Hey, Mrs. Parker's car's still here! It must be her second one." They took a look at it. It was a Kia Sorento with almost no miles on it. "There's no way we can take that, is there, Dad?"

"Wow, I don't know, Josh. Stealing cars is a bit more than I had in mind."

"There's no way Mom is going to be okay with us stealing Mrs. Parker's car."

"Yeah, I suppose you're right. But we can at least siphon off some gas. That we really *do* need. And hey—" he held up two red plastic gas containers—"these are full, too."

Will got busy packing canned goods into an empty cardboard box he'd found in the garage. "Come on, son, help your father steal some stuff. Get a move on."

"Jesus, Dad," Josh said, but he headed to the garage and started looking for good stuff to steal.

In the end they really did leave a note at Mrs. Parker's before leaving with boxes of canned goods and snacks, and, most importantly, gasoline. After repeat visits to the Sorento and an abandoned car parked along the street, they managed to siphon off enough gas to refill both of their cars. They also refilled the two gas containers as backup.

"I'll never be able to look Mrs. Parker in the eye again," lamented Josh.

"You'll never have to, son. This is probably the last time we'll ever be inside this dome again. It's weird, isn't it? Being the only ones inside."

"At least that we know of. It's so big now, there could be other people in here and we wouldn't even know it. Maybe we just haven't crossed paths with them yet."

"Yeah, well, let's keep it that way. Crossing paths with people these days isn't always safe."

Cynthia poked her head out into the garage. "Hey, where'd you find all this great stuff?"

"Oh, um, in an empty house down the way," Josh said, pointing vaguely. "No one was there, so we took it."

"Great. I'm proud of you guys. Way to be survivors."

"We, um, siphoned off some gasoline too."

"Thank God. We needed it." She headed back into the kitchen, already shouting the good news to Ashley and Kaley.

Father and son looked at each other for a long moment. "So much for Mom being mad," Josh finally said.

"Yeah. Maybe we should've taken the Sorento."

*****

On their third evening, Kaley said she was having trouble breathing. As soon as she mentioned it, they all felt like they were having trouble breathing, and they knew their time in their old home was coming to an end.

"We'll leave first thing tomorrow," Will said. "To be honest, I'm surprised we made it this long, but maybe as the domes get bigger, it takes longer to dispel all the oxygen. In any case, we've gotten everything we came for and more."

He didn't mention to any of them that, on a later visit, he'd also taken some of Mrs. Parker's gold and silver jewelry and a wad of cash he'd found hidden in an old coffee canister on the top shelf. Josh was dealing with enough moral dilemmas without having to know about that too.

"Since there's no internet inside the dome," Will continued, "Josh and I dug up some old paper maps when we were rummaging through one of the houses the other day. It looks like there's a route out east on the Colorado plains that holds some promise. Route 71 south."

"Yeah," said Josh, "it passes right through a town called Last Chance. How cool is that?"

Will nodded. "Last Chance, then Limon, then another unusual place called Punkin Center."

"You must be making that up," said Cynthia.

"I'm not."

"Punkin Center?" cried Kaley. "I *have* to visit Punkin Center!"

"You will, if all goes according to plan. From there we can choose which direction we want to head next: towards the Texas Panhandle or towards New Mexico."

"What about old Mexico?" Kaley asked.

"Mexico is pretty far away, hon. For now, let's get excited about Punkin Center, okay?"

"And Last Chance," said Josh.

"Don't expect too much out of them," warned Cynthia. "Some of those eastern Colorado towns aren't much more than specks on a map. You may be disappointed when you see them in person."

"Your mom's right. They're probably not much more than road crossings."

"Will it be warm?" asked Ashley.

"Not at first," said Will, "not until we get further south."

"What about bathrooms?"

"Not in Last Chance or Punkin Center, but in Limon, yes, there will be bathrooms and fast food and gas. Otherwise we're going to have to rough it for a few days. Is that all right with you, Ashley?"

"Do I have a choice?"

"No, but it seemed like the polite thing to ask."

"Then I'm fine with it."

"There's our girl," said her mom. "We knew we could count on you." She squeezed her daughter's shoulders and almost managed to elicit a smile out of her.

*****

They all had a hard night's sleep and awoke feeling short of breath. It was time to go. The lack of electricity and plumbing was also beginning to weigh heavily on them. The cars were already packed, so they headed off first thing in the morning, saying goodbye forever to their old home for the second time.

This time around, Ashley rode with her dad in the car, while Josh and Kaley and Woof kept their mom company in the minivan. Snow was falling but the roads were clear. They risked taking I-76 east and found it mostly free of traffic. Twice they had to detour around domes, which were big enough now that you could see them coming for miles. At the town of Brush they left the interstate behind and headed south on Route 71. No domes blocked their way, and they found themselves in Last Chance before the morning was out.

Last Chance really was a crossing of two roads in the middle of nowhere. Other than a few modest homes and a line of telephone poles, there wasn't much to see. But that didn't stop Josh and Kaley from getting out of the car and standing in the middle of the intersection shouting "Last Chance!" at the top of their lungs as they danced around like idiots. Luckily there was no one around to see them.

Another forty-five minutes of driving brought them to Limon. They passed several domes along the way but none blocked the road. In Limon they found all the people. It was situated along I-70, and the interstate was packed with cars, trucks, motorcycles, and even bicycles. Hordes of people were on the move, heading both east and west. The traffic looked horrendous. To the east they could see a dome rising up and cars detouring off the highway at a slow crawl to get around it.

"Where do you think they're all going?" Kaley asked.

"Family, I'd guess," said Cynthia.

They stopped at a Subway in Limon and paid outrageous prices for five subs. Will used his coffee canister money to pay for it and quietly thanked Mrs. Parker for the meal. Woof stayed in the car and wolfed down tidbits of meat Kaley and Josh donated from their subs.

They waited for over an hour in a long line of cars to get gas, paying dearly for it. That cleared out the rest of Mrs. Parker's coffee canister money and then some.

Then they were back on the road again, heading south along Highway 71 into some of the emptiest country they'd ever seen. "Look, antelope!" Josh exclaimed at one point, and there they were, a small herd out on the plains with white rumps and small horns.

"Those are pronghorn," said Cynthia, slowing down for a look. "I haven't seen them in ages. You're looking at the fastest animal in the Western Hemisphere, kids—second-fastest in the world after the cheetah." As she accelerated again, it must have startled the pronghorns because they started running at full speed.

"They're keeping up with the car!" exclaimed Kaley.

And they did, too, for about ten seconds, before pulling up short.

Josh and Kaley launched into a raucous rendition of "Home on the Range," with their mom laughing and joining in by the end. After that the kids kept busy looking for more pronghorns and found them surprisingly often. How the antelope survived in such harsh conditions and with so little water was a mystery to all of them.

It seemed like the towns were spaced out every forty-five minutes or so. They reached Punkin Center by two in the afternoon, and once again Josh and Kaley jumped out in the middle of an empty intersection of two rural roads and called out "Punkin Center!" at the top of their lungs, dancing their crazy dance. Nothing was there: no gas station, no café, no general store, just a tiny sprinkling of homes.

"Can you imagine living somewhere this remote?" Will asked Ashley as Josh and Kaley piled back into the minivan.

"No way," Ashley snorted. "Just shoot me."

It was just an expression, of course, but Ashley's reference to shooting stirred up some concerns in Will that he'd been trying to bury but couldn't. His biggest fear was running into a group of armed bandits on the road. He and his family remained defenseless: he had no gun, not even a knife (other than a kitchen knife). Out here in the middle of nowhere, there would be no one to see, no one to hear, no one to help. They were completely on their own, and that thought scared him more than he cared to admit.

The fear of bandits was a legitimate concern these days, given the growing levels of desperation out there. Going without food or shelter could turn an otherwise law-abiding citizen into something he never would have been otherwise. A truly desperate man might be willing to kill a family for their cars, their cash, and their possessions. Will pushed his fears down deep, hoping and praying their path would stay safe exactly because they were so remote.

Over the next hour they drove through some of the most desolate countryside they'd ever seen. There were no buildings, no farms, just empty grassland and the long blacktop road running straight through it. Every five miles or so they saw a dome on one side of the road or the other, sometimes far off, sometimes close at hand. The domes had become as commonplace as wind turbines. Eastern Colorado was so flat you could see the domes coming for miles ahead, and the long drive was making it obvious just how many there were dotting the landscape.

Between Punkin Center and Ordway, they finally came across a dome that blocked the road directly. It stood smack-dab in the middle of the road, stretching for three quarters of a mile in each direction. The police (or someone) had put up hazard cones warning drivers of the danger up ahead, but they could see it with their own eyes long before they got there.

"Uh oh," said Will, slowing down then coming to a full stop. There were no cars or trucks visible in either direction.

"There, Dad," said Ashley, pointing to a rough dirt path making its way around the dome to the left. The simple barbed-wire fence that had once stood along the roadside had been mangled into nonexistence. Apparently vehicles had driven over it until it laid flat.

Unless they wanted to backtrack for miles and miles, it looked like they were going to have to do some off-roading to get around the dome.

"Okay, here we go," said Will, letting out a deep breath.

"Are you sure we can do this in a regular car, Dad?" asked Ashley.

"I'm not sure of anything, hon, but I guess we're about to find out."

He put on his signal to let Cynthia know what he was up to then pulled off the road. The car jounced like crazy but continued moving ahead, right over the mangled barbed-wire fence, under some low-hanging telephone poles, and into the wild sagebrush bordering the side of the road. "Never done this before," he said a little wildly to Ashley.

He looked in his rearview and saw Cynthia following at some distance behind. He wondered how much she was cursing him at this point, but there wasn't much else he could do but forge ahead. The car tires crunched over sagebrush and shortgrass. Four-wheel-drive vehicles and trucks had already marked out a shallow path of sorts, and Will did his best to follow in their tracks.

It was the bumpiest ride they'd ever experienced. One section was so full of ruts and bumps that Ashley gripped the edge of her seat like she was riding a bucking bronco. "Yee-haw," Will said under his breath. He kept his foot steady on the gas, afraid that if he let up, the car might get stuck in a deep rut and never get back out. In his rearview he could see Cynthia gripping the steering wheel with both hands and (he thought) cursing up a storm. At least he could see her mouth moving something fierce. The van rocked and rolled in his rearview.

The phone rang. "Don't pick up," said Will. They were about halfway around the dome now: there was no going back.

Up ahead, he could see the "road" dip out of sight. "That can't be good," he said, but he kept driving on towards it.

They came to what amounted to a deep ditch, a natural drainage of some sort. Over that ditch were a series of rough planks that someone (the police, or truckers, he had no idea who) had placed over it. "Oh, hell no," said Ashley. The phone rang again and Will knew that if he stopped at that moment, they would never let him go forward again, so he kept on going.

"Dad," said Ashley, "you can't be serious," but he kept on moving, the wheels of his car grabbing onto the tops of the planks, which rattled as he inched forward. The planks felt like they were rolling beneath the wheels of his car but he kept whispering to himself, "slow and steady, slow and steady," and the next thing he knew he was across to the other side.

"Phew," he said, glancing over at Ashley, who looked pale and disbelieving.

He looked behind him and saw Cynthia still on the far side of the planks, stopped dead in her tracks and looking for all the world like she might stay there forever. He pulled forward some more and finally picked up the phone.

"Yeah, hon?" he asked, all innocence. He had to hold the phone away from his ear for a good minute before she ran down.

Ashley shook her head and laughed. "You are in such deep shit, Dad."

He got out of the car, shut the door behind him, and walked back across the planks to the minivan, all the while holding the phone away from his ear. He knocked on her window and motioned for her to open the door.

"Okay, everyone out," he said with cheery bravado. "I've got this, guys. Come on, now, Cynthia."

And for once they listened. Out they came, first Josh and Kaley, then Woof in a happy bound, then, reluctantly and still swearing up a storm, Cynthia, but she got out of the driver's seat and made way for him. He could hardly believe it. He told them to walk across the plank bridge and they did that too.

He turned on the engine and calmly drove the minivan across the planks. Easy-peasy.

He got out and felt them eying him with something that might have been respect or might have been the wariness one shows to a crazy person.

"Off we go," he said.

He got back in the car and started the engine. "Jeez, Dad, when did you become such a badass?" Ashley asked.

It was the nicest thing she'd said to him in years.

*****

Badass or not, Will had rarely been more relieved in his life than when they hit pavement again and could continue on their way. In another half hour they reached the town of

La Junta. It was small but loomed large in comparison to Last Chance or Punkin Center. Here were motels and gas stations and a population of maybe ten thousand. More important was what was *not* here: domes.

Will and Cynthia had agreed on one rule above all others: no traveling after dark. Darkness came early this time of year. By four in the afternoon the light was already fading, so it looked like this was the end of their first day of travel. They topped off their tanks at a local gas station that was gloriously empty of people. They only had to add about a quarter tank to fill them, so the spectacularly high prices didn't faze them too badly. Then they began looking for a place to call home for the night. Before long they stumbled across a place called the Stagecoach Motel. The rates were exorbitant, but the front desk clerk said they took pets (for a fee, of course). They paid for a room with two beds and an extra cot and counted themselves lucky.

Dinner that evening was almost celebratory. They found a Taco Bell and laughed over the prices for a simple taco. Even Cynthia was in fine spirits now that the plank crossing was in the past. Ashley and Kaley finally found something they could agree on, which was that their dad had gone completely bonkers. They laughed together (miracle of miracles) about what they were calling the plank adventure, and even Cynthia nudged Will at one point and said, "You did good, hon."

"Aw, shucks," he said, squeezing her hand. "'Tweren't nothin'. Any accountant woulda done the same."

*****

The next morning they sat in their motel room sharing plastic-wrapped danishes and coffee in styrofoam cups, courtesy of the Stagecoach Inn. They had a big decision to make. To the southwest was Route 350 towards New Mexico. To the southeast was a slightly more complicated route towards Texas. Which way to go?

Ashley found an app called DomeDoc that identified all the domes in each state. Route 350 between La Junta and Trinidad was clear, but several of the likely routes into Texas had domes standing in the way. Meanwhile, Josh announced that Google Maps also showed the location of all known domes. The two teenagers put their heads together and mapped out a plan that had them heading southwest along Route 350 to I-25 into New Mexico.

"Ugh, not I-25 again," said Cynthia. She still had bad memories of their foray north into Wyoming on I-25.

"But look, Mom, no domes the entire way," Ashley said.

"There's a town in New Mexico called Truth or Consequences," said Josh. "Maybe we could go there. You know, continue our quest for towns with unusual names."

"Truth or Consequences?" exclaimed Kaley. "No way! That's its name? We *have* to go there."

"As long as it's not as small as Last Chance or Punkin Center," said Will.

Josh looked it up. "Nope, it's a town of about eight thousand."

"And there are no domes anywhere nearby," added Ashley.

"They have a Motel 6 and about ten other motels I can see," said Josh. "It's about seven or eight hours from here."

Will and Cynthia looked at each other. "Truth or Consequences it is, then," said Cynthia. "As long as there are no domes, I'm happy."

*****

They drove all day, with most of their route following the I-25 corridor. Traffic was heavy but not unbearable. Many of the cars on the road were packed to the brim with belongings, like their own. People were moving en masse to wherever the domes were not. The urge to escape their presence was the overriding force behind the mass migration happening all across America, and presumably the rest of the world as well. Whoever arrived first at a domeless town had the best chance of finding a new home before they were all taken.

They paused midday in Las Vegas—not the glitzy city in Nevada but the tiny town in New Mexico. They all agreed they could call Las Vegas home if Truth or Consequences didn't pan out. It had a collection of Victorian homes from its long-ago days as a railroad town, and there were no domes anywhere in sight—now the top priority on everyone's list. These days, beachfront properties had nothing on no-dome homes.

Once again they went through the ritual of waiting in line for gas and paying a small fortune for the privilege of filling up. They ate simple sandwiches Cynthia had prepared before their journey.

Another three hours brought them to the outskirts of Albuquerque. Here again they saw people walking on foot along the highway, carrying their meager possessions on their backs or pushing them in shopping carts. As they entered the city proper, the elevated highway rose up on pillars, with protective concrete barriers to either side. Clearly the highway wasn't designed with foot traffic in mind, so the sight of so many people trudging along in the breakdown lane was disconcerting.

I-25 cut right through the heart of the city. Below them they could see masses of people on the move, some on foot, others in cars loaded down with belongings. Mattresses were strapped to car roofs, open trunks were piled high with possessions, and truck beds were heaped to overflowing with furniture and baggage. Albuquerque was cursed with no less than three domes (merged down from five originally), so people were busy clearing out.

Traffic was stop-and-go the whole way through the city. Up ahead it came to a sudden halt, a sea of brake lights all turning red at once. Some kind of disturbance was happening up ahead. Will, who was in the middle lane, looked in his rearview mirror and saw Cynthia at the wheel of the van behind him. He shrugged and she shrugged back. He could see the concern evident on her face even through the rearview.

Four or five car lengths up ahead, Will could see people on foot streaming onto the highway itself. He could hear yelling and cursing. He rolled down his window, and the next thing he knew he heard a gunshot.

"Jesus," he said. He rolled his window back up and said, "Ashley, stay low."

Further up ahead he could see the stop-and-go congestion ease as cars beyond the trouble spot sped away. But the four cars directly ahead of him remained unmoving, trapped in place by a line of angry people standing in the middle of the highway with guns in their hands.

Another gunshot. Will watched in horror as, four car lengths ahead, a driver and passenger were forcibly thrown from their car by two armed men. The men were dressed in military fatigues and looked wild with desperation. They held their guns at the ready as they got into the car and gunned the engine. The tires squealed as they took off.

The stunned couple lay on the pavement. They were older and didn't appear to be shot, just in shock. No one got out to help them for fear of getting shot themselves. The couple crawled towards the breakdown lane in obvious distress.

Other armed men still blocked traffic. They were waving guns and seemed to be encouraged by the success of the first two. They yelled at the people in the first row of cars to get out and threatened to shoot them if they didn't.

A beefy man in a pickup truck ahead and to the right of Will suddenly leaned out of his driver's side window and shot at the men up ahead. One man went down with a cry. Another man shot back.

Now bullets were zinging in both directions and Will and Ashley were caught in the crossfire. They both scrunched down in their seats and watched in horror as a gun battle took place right in front of them—then all around them as even more desperate people on foot started shooting from the breakdown lanes. Will took a quick peek in his rearview mirror and caught Cynthia and Josh diving for cover in the back seat of the van. It looked like Cynthia had turned the engine off first. He prayed their doors were locked—his certainly were.

The beefy man in the pickup truck cried out as he took a hit. His front windshield shattered as more bullets came his way. He continued firing back until a bullet caught him in the head.

People in other cars were now firing back too. The amount of concealed weaponry in America these days was on full display in Albuquerque. Men and women alike were leaning out of their car windows and firing with grimaces on their faces, some shouting at the top of their lungs, others grimly silent. Will saw a matronly woman in the passenger seat of a car catty-corner to his own go down with a shot through the chest.

The men up front weren't backing down. If anything, more seemed to be joining their ranks from the breakdown lane. They were desperate and ready for a fight to the death if necessary: anything for a car filled with possessions.

A bullet zinged into Will's front windshield and left a radiating bullseye of shattered glass. Ashley screamed and scrunched down even lower.

Suddenly a new development: an SUV at the front line of the confrontation suddenly gunned its engine and tore forward, straight into the group of men holding up traffic. Two men screamed and went down as the SUV ran right over them.

It was like a lightbulb went off for the other people at the front of the line. They had a weapon better than any gun: they had their vehicles. More engines revved and the unthinkable happened as a whole row of cars drove straight over the people in front of them, mowing them down like so many bowling pins.

Some of the armed men managed to dive out of the way in time. As soon as they regained their footing, they shouted in incoherent rage and randomly started shooting at vehicles from the side of the highway. People shot back from their windows, picking them off one by one.

The cars in front of them surged forward, tires squealing, and the last of the armed men still standing in the middle of the highway scattered to safety.

Will found himself stuck in the middle lane behind a car that wasn't moving; maybe the driver had been hit, or maybe he or she was simply too stunned to move. The right lane was already blocked by the beefy man in the pickup who was now dead. Gunmen were already swarming around his vehicle and pulling him out of the driver's seat.

Two men with guns crouching in the right breakdown lane spotted the stalled car in the middle lane and started to approach, eyes greedy with anticipation. Will realized three more armed men by the side of the road were eyeing his own car and muttering between themselves. They began making their approach.

Meanwhile, cars were gunning past him in the left lane, horns blaring. Will cursed, blared his own horn, and pulled savagely into the left lane. He sideswiped another car already there but didn't dare stop. Both cars raced forward, sharing the same lane as if they were in a demolition derby and no longer cared about the state of their vehicles. Will's left headlight was mangled and the whole left side of his bumper hanging off, but that hardly mattered at the moment: what mattered was getting out of there.

He hit the gas pedal and felt the car jounce over a large bump in the road (he could guess what that was) and then another—and then he was past the worst of the trouble and racing forward a hundred yards or so before swerving hard to the left and pulling into the left breakdown lane. He slammed on the brakes. Cars flew past him, horns blaring.

He looked in his rearview and willed his wife to get moving.

The van was still stopped. He couldn't see Cynthia in the driver's seat. She must still be in the back, hunkered down and hiding from the bullets.

Will cursed and was about to open the car door and run back to the van. It was a suicide mission but what else could he do? He opened the door.

"Dad, don't leave me!" Ashley cried unbelievingly, and at the same time he saw Josh—Josh, who was all of ten years of age and had never driven a vehicle before—clamber into the driver's seat.

The stopped van was like honeycomb to a bear, impossible to resist. Men with guns were weaving their way through moving traffic to get to it. Cars flashed by, creating their own lanes, horns blaring, and still the men came on. Will was muttering, "Come on, Josh, come on." He saw the front headlights illuminate, which meant Josh had managed to get the car started.

Josh shifted the van out of park and pushed down on the accelerator. The van jerked forward as he rode the gas pedal and the brake at the same time. It jerked again another foot. Men were reaching for the door handle, finding it locked, and yelling and waving their guns in the kid's face, but he kept on jerking forward in starts and stops until he reached the stalled car in front of him. One of the men shot his gun into the air and screamed at Josh to get out; he looked ready to shoot Josh the next second if he didn't.

Just as his dad had done earlier, Josh suddenly rocketed into the lane to his left, sending the men around him spinning. One guy on the passenger side clung to the door handle for a second before letting go with a cry.

Josh ignored the sudden blare of horns as the cars already in that lane protested in the only way they could—but they screeched to a halt and let him in since the van was bigger than they were—and moments later he was past the worst of the chaos.

The men who had been approaching the van—the ones who were still alive anyway—shifted their interest to another stalled car. Will watched in his rearview as a woman, apparently dead, was tossed from the driver's seat onto the highway and several men climbed in.

He didn't wait to see any more. He forced his way back onto the highway, right behind the van Josh was driving. Apparently the bashed-in driver's side of his car gave people pause, because a whole lane of cars came screeching to a halt to let him in. Will could see the guy swearing up a storm and blaring his horn behind him but he didn't care.

Josh was driving twenty miles per hour in the left passing lane, so cars were now honking incessantly and tearing around him on the right. Will watched as the men who had just hijacked the car passed him on the right; he caught a glimpse of them laughing and high-fiving as they tore ahead and were lost to sight.

Josh suddenly swerved into the lane to his right with no signal. Will stayed right behind him, flashing his signal to provide cover of a sort. More blaring horns—but now that the immediate danger was past, cars slowed to let them in.

Will kept his turn signal on and kept moving steadily to the right until both cars reached the breakdown lane.

Will jerked to a stop and was out of the car and knocking on the van window in seconds. Ashley got out too. Josh opened the driver's side door and got out shakily.

Will took his son by the shoulders to steady him. "Where's Mom? Is she okay?"

"She's in the back. I think she got shot, Dad." His face was streaked with tears.

"Jesus," Will said.

"She's not moving, Dad."

"Okay, hold tight, Josh. Get back in the van—on the passenger side. Ashley, you've driven before; get in the driver's seat." Ashley looked stunned but didn't argue; the only driving she had ever done was around an empty parking lot in Longmont.

Will took a quick look around at his surroundings. They were well past the chokepoint by now, but there were still plenty of folks on foot in the breakdown lane who looked desperate enough to try their luck if an easy opportunity presented itself. Even though nothing bad was happening at the moment, Will knew how fast that could change.

He raced around to the van's passenger side and opened the sliding door. Clambering inside, he closed the door behind him. He heard the doors lock. Good job, Ashley.

Cynthia was sprawled across the floor of the van. Kaley was crying inconsolably and hugging Woof, who was whimpering. He turned his wife over and saw she was bleeding profusely from a wound to the upper chest. A pool of blood had already soaked into the van's carpeted floor. She was unconscious. He cursed and took off his shirt, pressing it into the wound, applying as much pressure as he could. He hoped it would be enough to stanch the bleeding.

He put his finger to her neck and could feel a faint pulse. "We need to get to a hospital fast," he called to Ashley. "Hold on, I'll drive. You get back here and stay with Mom."

Ashley clambered between the two front seats and into the back, crouching next to him. "Keep holding pressure right here," he told her. Then he clambered forward, climbing into the driver's seat and starting the engine.

"What about the other car?" Ashley asked.

"Leave it," Will said, knowing it was a death sentence for the car and all its possessions, including the cash tucked away in various nooks and crannies. It wouldn't last a minute out here with so many people milling around. At this point an abandoned car was like a wounded animal on the savanna.

He pulled out into traffic and tore ahead. "Josh, look for the nearest hospital on your phone. *Josh*." Josh had a dazed look on his face but he startled into action at his dad's request.

A minute later he said, "There's a hospital up ahead, Dad. Presbyterian Hospital. Take the next exit."

"Come on, come on," Will said impatiently to the slow-moving traffic up ahead. He veered into the right breakdown lane and blared his horn. People with shopping carts barely got out of the way in time as he careened down it. Angry men shook their fists at him, gesturing and shouting, but what else could he do? His wife had a gunshot wound and he wasn't about to let her die because of a traffic jam.

He could see police cars and ambulances racing past in the other direction, sirens blaring, towards the craziness they had just left behind. He merged into the exit lane for Central Ave. "What next?" he asked Josh.

"Straight ahead, through this next intersection, then left onto Central Ave."

Will could have cursed as he saw a sea of red brake lights up ahead—they had reached a red light. "Jesus, this is taking too long," he muttered. "Ashley, how's Mom?"

"Your shirt's soaked through and she's really, really pale. She's still unconscious." Will could hear Ashley patting her mom's cheeks and crying, "Mom? Mom?"

"Okay, hang tight, we're moving again." The traffic inched forward through what must have been a major intersection, then the traffic eased up as they got past the red light. Will shot ahead all the way to the front of the line at the next red light. He was at Central Avenue. He didn't wait for the light to change. Blaring his horn repeatedly he entered the intersection and turned left. It sounded like a million horns all blared back at him at once but they screeched to a halt and he darted through.

He passed beneath the highway overpass and in another block saw the sign for Presbyterian Hospital. The red "Emergency" sign on top had never looked so good. His tires screeched as he pulled up in front of it. Jumping out of the van, he threw open the sliding door and called out to anyone who could hear, "Help! My wife's been shot!"

A nurse got there first and called for a stretcher. In a matter of seconds they were hustling Cynthia into the emergency room.

Will realized he was shirtless and freezing. He quickly dug out a shirt from the back of the van and threw it on, then he locked the door with Woof inside and ran into the hospital. His three kids were already inside.

They were told to wait in the emergency room lobby. By the time Will got there, Cynthia was already out of sight. A nurse asked if she could get them anything and Will croaked out, "Water." The nurse came back with a paper cup of water and told him she or another nurse would be back with word shortly. Will's hands shook so badly he could barely drink.

"Is Mom going to be okay?" Kaley sniffled.

"I think so, hon," Will said, hugging her tight.

"She was really bleeding. I didn't know what to do. Woof was barking and going crazy and—." Kaley looked like she might hyperventilate.

"It's okay, hon." He squeezed her tight. "Your mom's in good hands now."

The next hour felt interminable. Finally a doctor came out, mask pulled down on her chin. "She's going to be all right," she said.

Will felt his head swirl with relief. He didn't faint but he felt dizzy enough he thought he might. All three kids blew out air as if they had been holding their collective breath for the past hour.

"She lost a lot of blood, so it's good you got her here when you did. Great job stanching the wound—you may have saved her life with that. She's getting a blood transfusion even as we speak. The bullet is out. She'll be in some pain over the next few weeks, so I'll prescribe some pain medication for her."

"Is she conscious yet?" Will asked. "Can we see her?"

"Not yet. Let's give the anesthesia some time to wear off. How did this happen, if you don't mind my asking?"

Will described the horrific scene a couple of miles back on I-25.

The doctor shook her head. "You kids must have been terrified." All three nodded.

"Most people don't know this, but Albuquerque ranks among the highest in the nation for gun violence and auto theft. We—" She cut off as she heard sirens approaching from outside. "Looks like more are coming in," she said. "Sorry, gotta go."

*****

"So much for our other car," was the first thing Cynthia said when they were finally permitted to see her. "There goes half our money."

"As long as you're okay, that's what matters," Will replied, caressing her hair. "That car was pretty banged up anyway."

"Was it ever!" exclaimed Josh. "The front bumper was nearly torn off."

"Not just the bumper—the whole front driver's side was bashed in," said Ashley. "And don't forget the bullet hole in the windshield." She actually laughed.

"How did you get hit?" Will asked Cynthia.

"I have no idea. I dove for the back seat, and the next thing I knew, I felt a stab and something wet on my chest. I looked down and realized I'd been shot—and then I just sort of... blanked out. I guess I must have fainted when I saw all that blood. *My* blood."

"Well, you lived to tell the tale."

"You're not getting rid of me that easily. A little gun battle's not enough to stop me."

"That's the spirit."

"Hey kids, that was even scarier than the plank adventure, wasn't it?" their mom said, sounding sleepy all of a sudden.

They all hugged her gently, then let her rest.

JUMP 10

December 9

On the tenth jump day, each dome jumped to 3 miles in diameter and nearly a thousand feet in height. With something on the order of a million mergers worldwide continuing to skew the domes towards urban areas, it was becoming easier to talk about the major cities that didn't have domes than the ones that did.

To the short list of domeless American cities that always seemed to begin with Philadelphia, one could also add (in alphabetical order): Austin, Cleveland, Colorado Springs, El Paso, Jacksonville, Kansas City, Miami, Milwaukee, San Jose, Seattle, Tampa, and Tucson. However, these 'safe cities' were facing some of the same problems as Philadelphia: exactly because they were safe, people were flocking to them in droves. And none were remotely prepared to handle the extraordinary influx of people coming their way.

In Colorado Springs, for example, millions of Denverites drove an hour south to try and start over again. But not surprisingly, millions of extra homes were not to be found in Colorado Springs, so impromptu tent cities sprang up all around the city. Then winter hit, and food and water ran scarce, and authorities became completely overwhelmed: they had no idea what to do with so many extra people. Inevitably, those camped on the outskirts of the city—cold, hungry, and armed as often as not—finally got fed up and decided to take what they couldn't get otherwise. They stormed the city proper and stole food, supplies, medicines, and even lodgings by force. The result? An absolute explosion in crime.

Some refugees naturally became frustrated with the situation in Colorado Springs and decided to head further south to the next obvious choice: Tucson.

Maybe a little too obvious: Tucson became even more overrun than Colorado Springs. Everyone from Phoenix had already fled there, followed by slews of people from points north. Reporters who had seen Tucson's tent city with their own eyes said the word "sprawling" didn't begin to do it justice, and the gunfights over water rights alone were said to be legendary.

16

December 9 – NBC Nightly News, Philadelphia

"Breaking news tonight: the nation descends into chaos as the domes jump for the tenth time, claiming more land than the United States, Mexico, and Central America combined.

"I'm Cory Phillips reporting to you live from our third headquarters in six weeks, this time from the Comcast Technology Center in Philadelphia. Like so many others in America, we've been forced to migrate yet again, this time because of the expansion of the dome in downtown Chicago late last night. Philadelphia appears to be a more promising home for us going forward, as it's the only major city in the Northeast that remains dome-free.

Tonight's special report focuses on three linchpin cities here in the Northeast: Washington D.C., Philadelphia, and New York. All three are facing extraordinary challenges. Let's begin in Washington, where Stephanie Wilson is standing by. Stephanie?"

"Cory, I'm standing on the steps of the Lincoln Memorial, and the view from here is nothing short of surreal. From this vantage point, you can see the Capitol Dome rising up in commanding fashion just beyond the Reflecting Pool. Since its jump, the Capitol Dome has become a true behemoth, incorporating some eight square miles of federal real estate. The dome's eastern perimeter can't even be seen from here, as it stretches well past the Capitol Building to Lincoln Park.

"Just beyond the Reflecting Pool is the Washington Monument, which, as you can see, is completely domed. The Capitol Dome is currently about 1,000 feet tall, while the Washington Monument, the tallest obelisk in the world, stands at 555 feet. The White House, situated just to the north of the Washington Monument, is also domed. This aerial footage shows America's most famous house at the moment it was swallowed up.

"You may notice people moving around *inside* the dome. Those are military personnel. They're escorting anyone out who doesn't have an official reason to be inside, with the hopes of avoiding the ransacking and destruction that have occurred in so many other cities. Authorities are trying to preserve as much of downtown D.C. as possible, in the hopes of a return of the federal government someday in the future.

"The aerial footage makes clear just how close the second dome, known as the Pentagon Dome, is to the Capitol Dome. The two are kissing cousins, as it were, not quite touching at the Potomac River. In fact, if we swing our camera around, you can see that the Pentagon Dome has literally swallowed up the Lincoln Memorial directly behind me, so as I stand here on the Memorial's steps, it's like I'm perched on a narrow isthmus of land between two domes.

"In case you were wondering, Cory, those sounds you're hearing in the background are gunshots. It's December 9th, only twelve days from the shortest day of the year, so it's a grim time to be in D.C. with no roof over your head or food in your belly. Fires are burning out of control in undomed parts of the city to the north and west of the White House, and there is no one left to put them out.

"While D.C. is still technically the nation's capital, what's left of it feels more like a war zone than a capital. I wouldn't be standing where I am right now if it weren't for the military, which is still defending this narrow corridor between the two domes. The statue of Lincoln now overlooks a mostly defeated city. You could call this spot Lincoln's Last Stand and it wouldn't be too far off the mark."

"Stephanie, I hope you and your crew have plans to get out of there; it doesn't look safe to stay put much longer."

"Indeed it's not, Cory. We have a helicopter standing by to evacuate us to Alexandria as soon as we wrap up."

"Incredible. Like Saigon at the end of the Vietnam War, but right here in our nation's capital. Thanks, Stephanie, and please stay safe. Next we take you *inside* the Capitol Dome with Kristin Hines. Kristin?"

"Thanks Cory. Earlier today we received special permission for a skeleton crew to remain inside the dome to bring you these never-before-seen images. I'm standing outside the dome now so that I can broadcast, but this first video was taken about an hour ago from inside. Dusk was descending as we stood on the White House lawn shortly after the dome had jumped. It was eerily quiet, and a sense of abandonment pervaded the place. No lights were on in the windows, the fountain was off, and the building was dark instead of floodlit. We all know how Washington *should* look at night, but instead our nation's capital feels like a vacant movie set.

"We actually managed to capture the moment—right here—when the dome jumped earlier this afternoon. At that point we had our cameras pointed towards the Capitol Building, and as you can see, the dome wall simply vanishes from in front of us. For one wild moment we thought the dome had gone away entirely—but it had only jumped to a further distance. Curiously, that meant that the Capitol Building, which before had been inaccessible, suddenly became accessible again, so we were able to walk over and stand on the Capitol Steps one last time. Which raises an interesting point, Cory: until the domes stop jumping, this kind of walk down memory lane remains possible in places all over the country. Just something to keep in mind for any future inside editions."

"Great idea, Kristin, thanks. Now let's turn our attention to Philadelphia, the new seat of power in this country, where Salvador Massey is standing by. Salvador?"

"Cory, I'm standing in the bustling heart of Philadelphia, known as Center City, with its mix of skyscrapers and historic sites, including the Liberty Bell and Independence Hall. Over this past week, numerous buildings in Center City have been claimed by the federal government by virtue of eminent domain. This preemptive action took nearly all Philadelphians by surprise. The government promises compensation, but in these strange times, the word of the federal government doesn't count for as much as it once did, so you can only imagine the amount of discord now present in the City of Brotherly Love.

"The Mayor of Philadelphia, Myron Delgado, has vehemently protested what he calls 'this invading army'—and he's not referring to aliens in this case but to our own federal government. For its part, the government counters that it has to set up shop *somewhere*, and Philadelphia is by far the best option. They say they don't have time to build a new capital in the midst of this crisis— which may be true, Cory, but the fact that the President brought along the military to enforce his will has done little to win him local support. Philadelphians point to the irony of *not* being displaced by a dome, only to be displaced by the federal government instead. Cory, back to you."

"Salvador, if I may, I'm also familiar with the challenges being faced in Philadelphia, since our own Comcast Technology Center is located here. Some of our viewers may not be aware that this is the tallest skyscraper in the United States outside of Manhattan or Chicago. Just last week, Comcast executives were approached by, let's just call them military advisors, and were told to vacate the top ten floors immediately. The former occupants, including a Four Seasons Hotel and a high-end restaurant, were summarily booted out.

"The topmost floor—the penthouse suite, you might call it—is now the home of the Philadelphia Oval Office. That whole floor has been extensively renovated, and in record time. One part of it now resembles the Oval Office in Washington D.C.—at least as long as the drapes are shut. Other parts of that same floor are now devoted to the Cabinet Room, Situation Room, Chief of Staff's office, and so on. The next floor down provides additional space for the executive branch, along with the residential portion of the White House. The eight floors below *that* all serve as space for Congress, providing working quarters for the House and Senate. An entire suite of elevators has been set aside to service these top ten floors exclusively, much to the frustration of others in the building."

"That's exactly right, Cory, and that's only the tip of the iceberg. Many of Philadelphia's other skyscrapers have been claimed, in whole or in part, by the Department of Defense, the FBI, the CIA, the NSA, the Supreme Court, and a seemingly endless number of government departments like Agriculture, Commerce, and Homeland Security, to name just a few. That's a whole lot of federal workers descending on one city at one time—some would say like locusts. Cory, back to you."

"Thanks Salvador. Let's wrap things up in New York City. For more on developments there, we turn to Jim McDonald."

"Thanks Cory. Yesterday two domes—the Central Park Dome and the Rockefeller Dome—momentarily merged into one huge dome covering most of Midtown and Upper Manhattan. An instant later, the Rockefeller Dome blinked out of existence and the Central Park Dome survived. That means Midtown Manhattan has made a surprise comeback, however short-lived. Why the Central Park Dome survived and the Rockefeller Dome did not is a mystery—but then again, Central Park is called Central Park for a reason: it's about as central as you can get in Manhattan.

"In any case, Manhattan is only two-and-a-quarter miles wide at its widest point, so the Central Park Dome's jump to three miles in diameter means all of Central Park and everything on both sides of it—including the Upper East Side and Upper West Side—has been swallowed up. You can't drive around it or get past it via any form of public transport, because the dome extends right out into the water on both sides. Meanwhile, all of Downtown Manhattan has been swallowed up by the Wall Street Dome, along with Brooklyn Heights and parts of Jersey City.

"One World Trade Center, at 1,776 feet, is one of only sixteen skyscrapers still sticking up above the 1,000-foot-tall dome, but there's no practical way to access it anymore, unless one happens to fly in by helicopter. Which begs the question: even if you *could* reach the upper floors, what good would it do you? It's not like you can pop down for a bite to eat at your favorite restaurant. You'd be stuck on the top floors of an 'island skyscraper' with no electricity or running water.

"So to summarize, Cory, as things stand now, everything north of Central Park is undomed, along with a strip of Midtown Manhattan stretching for some three miles from 55th Street to Spring Street. Spring Street marks the Wall Street Dome's northernmost limit at present."

"And what are conditions like on the ground at this point, Jim?"

"Pretty awful, Cory. The huge influx of people pushed out of their homes and into surrounding neighborhoods has created a host of new problems—and a terrible spike in violence. The 'nouveau needy,' as they're being called, have no shelter, no food, and no potable water. Even bathrooms have become difficult to come by for the hordes of displaced suddenly turned loose into the streets like abandoned animals.

"That has created a nightmare scenario for the police, who are trying to keep a handle on the situation. Some displaced individuals are forcing their way into people's homes and ejecting them at gunpoint, stealing whatever food, money, and possessions they have. Others who are unwilling to resort to violence are literally starving on the streets of New York. Meanwhile, mobs have gotten so out of hand in certain neighborhoods that the police refuse to go there anymore without military backup. Armed skirmishes have broken out across all five boroughs. As soon as one riot is quelled, another pops up somewhere else. It's like trying to play whack-a-mole with an entire city."

"Jim, are those alarm bells going off behind you?"

"Those are building alarms, Cory, and they've been going off for hours now. I'm reporting to you from the Bronx, which is the only borough without a dome to its name—but that doesn't mean it's safe. If we pan around a little, you can see broken glass littering the sidewalks. Shop windows have been smashed and numerous shops looted. Over here we have an actual pool of blood, and in the alleyway to my right, an actual dead body thrown into a dumpster that we suspect goes along with that blood. All we can see is a shoe sticking out, but that's enough. No one from homicide has shown up to investigate, even though we called it in an hour ago. Our crew is fortunate to have an armed security detail protecting us as we make this report, but your average New Yorker isn't afforded the same level of protection."

"I understand you have some video clips you'd like to share with us, Jim. "

"That's right, Cory. This first one shows a liquor store being looted by what appears to be an organized crime syndicate. Crews head in and out, loading product onto trucks, before the building is torched. Smoke can be seen billowing out of its smashed-in doors and windows. This kind of theft and wanton destruction has become all too commonplace across all five boroughs.

"In this video of a Macy's being looted, mobs push through barricades set up by the police and storm through, braving tear gas and rubber bullets in their frenzy to get whatever goods they can to barter for food or lodging.

"Each night the city spirals into worsening levels of violence. As the police try to maintain order, they're pelted with bricks, bottles, rocks, or worse, so they respond by launching pepper balls, tear gas canisters, and flash-bang grenades to disperse the crowds. In this video, mobs can be seen rocking a SWAT van and setting it ablaze with the officers still inside. Fortunately the four officers escape with their lives, as you can see in this highlighted clip, tumbling out of the van and forming what amounts to a phalanx with guns pointed in all directions as they back out of the area.

"Moments later, another police vehicle arrives, lights flashing, as the officers try to intervene. Watch as the mob surges forward with clubs and crowbars and batters the police vehicle with such force that it begins to back up. Officers can be seen shooting through the half-open windows, trying to force the crowd back. The police themselves barely manage to escape becoming the mob's next target.

"You've heard of mean streets, Cory: well, these are some of the meanest streets I've ever seen. It feels like we're descending through the various levels of Dante's inferno to see just how far down we can go. Whatever the supposed aliens may do to us in the future, it could hardly be much worse than what we're doing to ourselves right now."

"Jim, there are no words. Can you leave our viewers with any good news at all?"

"Only that remarkable acts of kindness have occurred amidst all the cruelty and destruction, Cory. Families with children have been rescued by strangers and granted shelter. The elderly and starving have been ushered into homes and given food. Women confronted by gangs have been shepherded out of harm's way by other women, often at great risk to themselves. And children separated from their parents have been reunited thanks to the gallant efforts of good samaritans. These heartwarming stories stand in stark contrast to the tragic ones and offer us a glimmer of hope in troubled times."

"Indeed they do, Jim. Thanks for that report. Our coverage will continue after these messages."

17

December 10 – Goodland, Kansas

Ken Stubbs' worst fears had come true. Three months after watching the first ovate hatch, he found himself standing outside a single enormous dome looking in at where his farm used to be—or still was, technically speaking, but he couldn't reach it anymore. His family's ancestral home was gone, along with his barns, his farm equipment, and his whole way of life.

He and Marie were safe, thank goodness, and so were the animals, but what were they going to do now? They had no income without their land and what it could produce. At present they were living off the good graces of their neighbors, who had offered them the second bedroom in their own home, along with temporary holding pens for the animals. Without their kindness, he didn't know where they'd be right now. Probably out on the streets, wandering around like so many other lost souls. He was grateful beyond measure to his neighbors, but it also made him squirm to have to rely on their charity when he had always made it a point to rely on himself and himself alone. He had never had to beg a day in his life.

Earlier that morning he'd heard Marie weeping in the bedroom as he'd approached the door and had been about to come in—and he'd turned around and walked right back the other way into the living room. He'd had no idea what to say to her. It felt like the knot in his stomach kept twisting tighter and tighter each day, and he felt closer to despair than he ever had before in his life.

Now he stared moodily at the dome in front of him. Its outer edge stood less than a quarter mile away from his neighbor's home. At least it was one dome now instead of six, but that was small comfort. Either way the result was the same: he'd been pushed off his own land.

He and Marie had been standing on their neighbor's front porch yesterday morning when it had happened. The six separate domes had all merged into one, all in a split second too fast for the mind to fathom. For a few seconds afterwards, the single merged dome had stood there in front of them, massively huge—on the order of ten *miles* in diameter, as best they could guess—and then, *pop, pop, pop, pop, pop,* five of the six ovates had imploded and the dome had shrunk down to three miles in diameter, just like every other dome in the world. The surviving ovate—the one at the very center of his farm—had glowed brighter with each *pop*. It was like watching a weird sort of magic trick on a grand scale.

Now the dome glimmered in the late afternoon sunlight. At certain hours of the day, near sunrise and sunset, it almost looked pretty, but at other times—near noon, for instance, when the sun beat straight down upon it—it could turn glaringly ugly.

Would it expand again? That was the unspoken question on everyone's mind. If it did, then their neighbor's farm would be swallowed up in less than ten days' time, and then where would they be?

Where would any of them be?

18

December 11 – Truth or Consequences, New Mexico

The small town of Truth or Consequences sat about three hours south of Albuquerque. Blessed with an abundance of hot springs and a cool desert climate, it was situated just far enough off the main highway that it hadn't been overrun with refugees yet.

Josh had read to them from a Wikipedia entry about how the town had gotten its name. Apparently some fellow named Ralph Edwards, who had hosted a popular quiz show called Truth or Consequences, had announced he would air the program on its tenth anniversary from the first town that was willing to rename itself after the show. The tiny town of Hot Springs had obliged, officially changing its name in 1950. Edwards had broadcast his program from there the very next evening, just as he had promised—and he had kept visiting the town for the next fifty years.

They all agreed that was a pretty cool origin story and decided to call Truth or Consequences home for the foreseeable future. That first week, they stayed at a no-frills motel, bartering their extra containers of gasoline, along with gas siphoned off from their van and a boxful of Mrs. Parker's canned goods, in exchange for a cramped room. While Cynthia recuperated from her gunshot wound, Will went in search of more permanent lodgings.

"And you're absolutely sure there are no domes anywhere in the area?" Will asked the apartment manager for the second time.

"I'm sure," said the manager with a chuckle.

"You've been lucky. You should see the rest of the country."

"I do—every night on TV, and I don't like what I see."

"So...about payment."

"Yeah, about that," said the manager.

"I'm a little short on cash."

"That *is* a problem. Without money up front, it's a no-go, amigo. And it has to be cash, not credit."

"Of course it does. Look, can you at least hold the place for one day? I'm going to go see what I can pawn off."

"No can do, amigo. Sorry, but whoever pays first, stays first. Nothing personal."

"All right, then, I'll be back as soon as I can." Will got into the van and drove to the center of town. He'd passed a pawn shop earlier that morning and had an idea. Some of Mrs. Parker's rings looked to him like they might be made of real gold and real diamonds. Maybe, just maybe...

He tried to look nonchalant as he entered the pawn shop. He had no idea what the rings were worth and no idea how to bargain effectively with a pawn shop owner. In the end he simply handed over the first ring and asked, "What can you give me for this?"

The pawn shop owner looked it over, examining it under a magnifying gizmo of some kind, then weighed it and announced a number that was much higher than Will had been expecting. "Really?" he said, unable to hide his surprise.

"Really," said the pawn shop owner. "That's solid gold you've got right there, my friend. You can't get much more valuable than gold right now. Lucky for you I'm an honest fella—most folks who choose to live in a town called Truth or Consequences are—because you seem just a little wet behind the ears. But I'll treat you fair if you treat me fair, that's my motto."

"I certainly will. Um, can you pay me in cash?"

"Of *course* I can pay you in cash," he chortled. "Who would take credit these days? You'd *really* have to be wet behind the ears to settle for that." He counted off a roll of bills and handed them to Will, who stuffed them into his pocket. "Now, what else you got?"

Will handed him the next ring, with roughly the same delightful results. Another roll of bills came rolling his way—and suddenly he had enough to pay the first month's rent *and* the security deposit.

"My gosh, thanks," Will gushed, all pretenses of playing it cool gone. "You've really saved my bacon." But he knew in truth it was really Mrs. Parker who had saved his bacon. Mrs. Parker who, it turned out, was rich not only in canned goods and chocolates but also gold and jewels. Who had left her entire home intact for some unexplained reason, just waiting for him. Thank you, Mrs. Parker, he said for the hundredth time. He sold one more of her rings, this one a diamond, and suddenly had enough spending money to pay for groceries too.

He raced back and peeled off a roll of bills to the apartment manager, who seemed surprised to see him back so soon. "I hope that ain't drug money," the manager said doubtfully.

"No, sir. Do I look like a drug dealer to you? I'm actually an accountant." A part of him wanted to add, "These are just the ill-gotten gains from the jewelry I stole from my neighbor's house," but he wisely remained silent.

"An accountant, huh?" said the apartment manager. "That's interesting. You lookin' for work?"

"You hiring?" asked Will, taken by surprise for the second time in ten minutes.

"Not me," said the manager. "But I know a guy who is. You want me to give him a call? He's a U-Haul dealer here in town. Says he's never been busier. Seems like everyone's movin' somewhere these days. He can barely keep track of it all. He's been lookin' for someone like you to help him with his books, and maybe help out at the front desk. If you're interested, that is."

"You bet I am," said Will enthusiastically. It was quite a step down from his corporate accounting days, but who cared? It was work, and it would help pay the bills.

When he got back to the motel room, he told his family the good news. "We can move in today."

"And they take pets?" Josh asked.

"Of course they do. We wouldn't stay anywhere Woof wasn't welcome. Woof is family, after all."

"I'm so relieved, Will," Cynthia said.

"And look at this—" Will waved a handful of bills in the air. "We have money to pay for groceries too."

"Where'd you get all that?" Cynthia asked, amazed.

"I have my ways," Will said mysteriously. Josh was eyeing him sideways but he ignored it.

"And I saved the best for last: it looks like I might have found a job." Exclamations of joy followed that announcement. He filled them in on what the apartment manager had told him. "I have an interview tomorrow. So I guess things are looking up, aren't they?"

"They sure are," Cynthia replied. She looked around for something to knock on. "But let's not jinx it."

19

December 18 – Brooklyn, New York

Aubrey peeked out the window of her darkened third-floor apartment. The power was out again, but it hardly mattered—they were keeping the lights off anyway to avoid unwanted attention. "Brooklyn crazies are the worst kind of crazy," she muttered.

"Aren't they ever," said Royce.

The eleventh jump was expected to come some time after midnight. It was projected to swallow up a big chunk of Brooklyn, and Brooklynites, it appeared, were none too happy about it. A sort of continuous roar came from down below as the mob protested the end of life as they knew it. They howled their anger, drank themselves into a stupor, broke bottles against brick walls, smashed sledgehammers into doors, shot off guns (hopefully into the air, but who knew), hurled rocks and bricks into glass windows, trashed the park, and generally created such mayhem that Royce and Aubrey feared for their lives. They didn't want to say it out loud—they were each being brave for the other—but they were scared.

Aubrey took another peek out the window. "I feel like a cat trapped in a tree by a pack of coyotes."

Royce nodded uneasily as the cacophony down below was punctuated with shrill screams and bursts of gunfire. It was so dark outside they could barely see. All they could make out was a seething mass of shadowy shapes in the street down below.

"What if they try to burn down the building?" Aubrey asked.

Royce winced at the thought. "Does brownstone burn?"

"I don't think so—not from the outside. But if they got into one of the ground-floor units, then all of that wood and furniture…"

"It won't come to that. And even if it did, you've got a fire escape, right?"

Aubrey nodded. "Out back. It leads to an alley behind the building."

"Well, then, we'll use that if we have to. We should pack a bag just in case. Just the stuff we can't live without."

"Like my shoes?"

"Exactly. Only the necessities."

"I've already packed. Didn't you see my bag in the bedroom?"

"That's it? I'm amazed."

"Well, I can't very well ask you to be my pack mule *and* my champion."

"I haven't saved you yet," Royce pointed out.

"But you're *here,*" Aubrey said, as if that settled the matter.

They were both quiet for a minute, which only made the incoherent shouts and gunfire more noticeable. "We're sitting here in the dark imagining worst-case scenarios," said Royce, "but maybe this mob will just loot the neighborhood and move on. I don't think they'll go so far as to, you know, burn people alive."

"God, I hope not. I really don't want to go that way."

"You're not going *any* way, Aubrey. We're going to get out of this, I promise."

"But how? I mean, just look out the window. They've gone berserk."

"We'll just—." An explosion shook the building hard enough to make the plates rattle inside the kitchen cabinets. Royce jumped up from the couch. "What the hell was that? It sounded like a gas explosion." Peering out the window, he saw flames licking out of a building halfway up the block. "Jesus."

Aubrey started pacing around her apartment like a caged animal. Stutters of gunfire reached their ears from down below, as if a pitched battle were going on between opposing forces. The screams rose in intensity as people dove for cover. They could see shadowy shapes fleeing en masse into the park. A space emptied out in the middle of the tree-lined avenue below them, where flashes of solitary gunfire mingled with the staccato of automatic weaponry.

"Holy hell, it's like a full-blown war down there," Royce muttered. "And the dome hasn't even jumped yet."

"They're saying the two domes—the Wall Street Dome and the Central Park Dome—won't quite merge this time around."

Royce nodded. "The Wall Street Dome is the one we have to worry about here in Brooklyn."

They were both silent for a time as Aubrey continued pacing around the couch. "You were right," she said at last. "We should have left sooner."

"Do you think your family would finally go now?"

Aubrey laughed hollowly, gesturing towards the window. "Yeah, I think this might just convince them! They're stubborn but not that stubborn. Besides, what choice do they have? We're going to be *inside* a dome after tonight, assuming it jumps."

"That'd be good news in my—" They both flinched as something hit the window hard but didn't break it.

"Yikes. Anyway, I was saying the dome jumping tonight would be good news in my opinion."

"Why?"

"Because it will force change. People will act differently after the jump. All those people down there won't have any choice in three days' time: they'll *have* to get out if they want to keep breathing."

"Yeah, but that's true for us, too. We can't just hold our breath."

"But we can wait until the worst of the crowds clear out. *We* have a warm bed to sleep in at night: *they* don't. And we have at least some food and water: they don't, unless they can steal it. Once they've done whatever looting they're going to do, they'll probably move on. Then we can gather your family and move out as a group. At least that's the best I can come up with at the moment."

Aubrey was nodding. She had stopped pacing and looked a little calmer. Even the gunfire had subsided for the moment. "That's a good plan, or at least the start of one. So what should we be doing right now?"

Royce thought for a moment. "I'd say call your parents while we still have cell phone reception and tell them what we're thinking. Tell them we should meet up once it's safe."

"*After* the dome jumps," clarified Aubrey. "*After* the crowds have thinned out."

"Right. In a day or two. Right now it would be crazy to go out there. Make sure they understand that."

Aubrey nodded. "Okay, I'll call. Hopefully I can get through." She paused for a moment, hand hovering over the phone. "You know there are like fifteen of them, right?"

"The more the merrier," Royce said gamely.

"Hello, Dad?" he heard Aubrey say, then her voice disappeared into the bedroom.

Royce tried to think things through, but his mind felt sluggish from lack of sleep. How in the world were they going to get all fifteen of her family members, along with themselves, to safety? He'd met some of Aubrey's relatives and they weren't exactly fitness fanatics. Would they be able to hike all the way out to the boonies of northern New Jersey where the RV was parked? That was a long way to walk. And *how* could they walk, with both the Brooklyn Bridge and Manhattan Bridge being blocked by a dome?

Were the ferries still running? They were on an island, after all—a big island, Long Island—but an island nonetheless. A quick search online yielded nothing useful. The ferry website *said* they were running, but that post was from three days ago when things were still semi-normal in Brooklyn. How accurate would it be now? And with such a mass of humanity all trying to take the ferries at once, how dangerous would it be to even approach a ferry terminal? He pictured crazed hordes all trying to get off the island at once, ferry boats overloaded to the tipping point.

"Dad, put Mom on," he heard Aubrey say with exasperation. Could her dad still be resisting leaving? It didn't seem possible.

Back to the question at hand: How were they going to get off Long Island and reach the mainland safely? They couldn't exactly swim across the Hudson, not with freezing-cold water and fifteen family members in tow. He pictured her grandma and grandpa trying to dog-paddle their way across the Hudson and dismissed the idea immediately. Maybe they could hire a boat. It would cost a small fortune, but it could work if the family pooled their resources—and managed not to get robbed along the way.

Once they reached the mainland...But he didn't want to think that far ahead. One thing at a time, he told himself. The first thing was to survive the riots, let the dome jump, then wait for the crowds to thin out and find a way across the water. He could figure the rest out as they went along. They'd have to do a lot of improvising if they were all going to make it out alive. His gun might well spell the difference between survival and death in the coming days. He tried to steel himself to the thought of actually using it.

Aubrey came out of the bedroom holding her hand over the phone. "Mom says we should meet them at their place. Most of the family is already there. She says we have a better chance of making it their way than they do ours."

"Good point. Remind me, which floor is their apartment on?"

"The third, like mine."

"That should be safe enough. Okay, tell her we'll meet them there once the crowds disperse."

Aubrey headed back into the bedroom saying, "Okay, Mom, that should work," before her voice faded away again.

In the meantime they were in for a long night. The gunfire had started back up again, mixed with occasional wails and hoarse shouts of anger. He heard hard thudding on the doors down below and braced for the worst—a sudden invasion of crazies into their isolated world—but then it passed.

Aubrey came back in; apparently she hadn't heard the thudding, which was a good thing. "Okay, we're all set. Mom said they'll wait for us as long as they can, until the morning of the third day if they have to. She liked your idea of waiting until the crowds thin out, but she's worried if we wait too long we won't have enough oxygen to get out of the dome in time. It's gonna be six miles in diameter after the jump tonight—assuming it jumps tonight—so they want to give themselves plenty of time to, you know, find an exit. So what's next?"

"Nothing's next," said Royce. "We lay low for the next night or two, that's it. And we try to stay out of trouble."

"Out of trouble. I'm not very good at that." She approached him slowly.

Royce sensed a change in mood. "No?"

In one swift motion she pulled off her top. "Help me forget all this, Royce."

"I think I can help with that."

Aubrey straddled him on the couch. "Two whole nights with nothing to do. How will we pass the time?"

"Backgammon?"

"Mmm, maybe...or maybe a little strip poker. See, I've already lost the first hand. You're on a roll—you can't lose." She kissed him passionately.

"No, I can't," he mumbled around her kisses while unhooking her lacy black bra from the back. "Look at that, you just lost again."

A crash reverberated from below, followed by a bang that sounded like a cannon, but other than a startled jump they hardly lost a beat. "I thought tonight was gonna suck," Royce said as his shirt came off, "but suddenly I'm feeling a lot better about it."

JUMP 11

December 19

Here's a little geometry refresher for those of us who have been out of school for awhile and may have forgotten:

As the diameter of a circle doubles,
its area increases four times

Thus, when the domes jumped for the eleventh time, each dome's diameter doubled from 3 to 6 miles while its area quadrupled from 7½ to 30 square miles. As a result, the collective domes worldwide now encompassed some 9 million square miles of land—roughly the size of North America.

By now the domes were well beyond the nuisance stage. They were fast becoming an existential threat.

20

December 19 – Brooklyn, New York

When the dome jumped, Royce and Aubrey were both fast asleep, but a huge caterwauling that sounded like ten thousand cats all yowling at once warned them something dramatic had just happened. They startled awake.

Their clothes were strewn across the floor, and they themselves were strewn across the bed in a delicious heap. Their lovemaking last night had been wild, as if they were trying to out-frenzy the frenzied masses below. Maybe it was the fear or the adrenaline kicking in, but whatever it was, it was on a whole new level. Royce found himself thinking he was glad he'd come back, however things turned out. This was where he belonged: with Aubrey by his side.

They crept to the window and peered out, but they couldn't make out much in the darkness. It was December 19th, just shy of the longest night of the year. It certainly *felt* like the longest night of the year, as if the darkness itself were uncoiling like a snake and stretching out to its fullest length.

Bonfires were visible in Fort Greene Park. Shadowy shapes were cavorting around them. Other shapes appeared to be fleeing, but fleeing *what* they couldn't say.

People were out there gesticulating, shouting, screaming, shooting. Even through the closed window on the third floor, the noises they were hearing sounded brutish. Mass hysteria seemed to have set in.

Aubrey checked her phone. "No signal."

"So we're cut off from the world. Now it's just us and a couple million crazies all stuck together on an island."

"How romantic."

"I doubt I'll be able to get back to sleep tonight," Royce said with a yawn and a stretch.

"Who said anything about sleep?" Aubrey pounced him again, and the noises faded away for awhile.

*****

When he awoke the next morning, it was full daylight and the sun was shining—through a dome, mind you—but shining nonetheless. He looked over at Aubrey: she even slept pretty. He resisted the urge to wake her and climbed out of bed, padding over to the window in his bare feet.

The multitudes sounded less feverish out there. *Were* there still multitudes? Royce peered out the window and saw...

Dozens of dead bodies strewn along the street in both directions. Some of the bodies were contorted at unnatural angles, angles that made him want to look away instantly. The street was still clogged with people, but they were quieter now. Hundreds were shuffling past the bodies in what appeared to be a death march as they hugged themselves against the cold. They picked their way around the bodies the way one might edge around a prickly shrub.

Each body was like an island in a sea of people. Royce winced when he saw just how many of them wore police or National Guard uniforms; they must have been among the first to go down. No doubt some of the pitched battles they'd heard last night had been between the police and

National Guard on one side and gangs on the other. One glance was enough to tell him which side had won.

To his dismay, he realized several of the bodies were still twitching. That was even worse in a way. He couldn't hear their moans through the third-floor window, but he could imagine them in his head. In the distance he could see a small band of good samaritans moving from body to body, checking for signs of life, then going on to the next. He could see their puffs of breath as they worked, a sign of just how cold it was this morning. The living were being carried on improvised stretchers towards the park for medical attention—or whatever passed for medical attention inside a war zone inside a dome. Royce saw others carrying dead bodies to a different part of the park. The bodies were being laid out in neat rows, like cars in a parking lot.

Elsewhere in the park, Royce could see men and women who had passed the point of exhaustion and had simply given up: they lay crumpled in heaps in the park, arms folded over their heads, tattered clothes wrapped around their bodies, as if they were already dead and waiting to be buried.

The street itself looked as if it had been hit by a tornado. Stately trees had been mutilated, debris and broken glass littered the pavement, and one or two buildings further down the block continued to belch black smoke. The remains of mangled doors and splintered window frames blocked sections of the sidewalk. Royce couldn't see the first-floor units directly below him, but he could imagine their sorry state.

Every parked car lining the one-way street below him had had its windows smashed and its interiors vandalized. The park itself had gaps in its greenery like missing teeth. Burnt tree limbs were strewn about on the grass, some of them still smoking. At least one bonfire must have burnt out of control because he could see trees still on fire in the distance. Seeing all this made Royce realize just how fortunate they'd been to be on the third floor, away from the worst of the mayhem.

Meanwhile, the marathon of the half-dead continued down below. Most appeared ready to faint from a combination of exhaustion, cold, and hunger. They shambled along, heads down, moving towards some unseen goal with dogged determination. Some carried duffels or listlessly dragged suitcases behind them containing the last of their possessions. Others had abandoned their suitcases altogether, too tired to pull them any longer. Most of these had been jimmied open by strangers in the hope of finding treasures within, but for the most part the contents looked pathetic more than prizeworthy: trampled undergarments, odd socks, random toiletries, tchotchkes that held meaning only for the owners—all strewn about for everyone to see.

He wondered why they were all moving *towards* Manhattan instead of away from it—and then it dawned on him: when the Wall Street Dome jumped last night, it 'reopened' the Brooklyn Bridge! Now they and the bridge were all inside the expanded dome together. That meant they could cross back into Manhattan on foot—and then to the mainland itself via the Holland Tunnel or some other means. It seemed so obvious in hindsight that he felt like a fool for not realizing it sooner. Of *course* the Brooklyn Bridge would be open again. They didn't need a boat: they could simply *walk* off the island.

So that explained why all the people were heading towards Manhattan. Well, not *all* the people. A few were working their way upstream, against the crowd, cradling crowbars or weapons. They dominated the residential side of the street and forced people to scramble out of their way. People gave them a wide berth—even wider than they did the dead bodies.

Here were the predators, the ones who craved chaos the way most craved peace. Royce felt sure these were the ones who were behind the worst of the violence last night, and he sensed they had no intention of leaving until the last of the air had run out and they had done their worst.

Even as he watched, he saw one predator, loitering on a sidewalk with what looked like a bloody mallet in his hand, reach out and grab things he wanted from persons passing by—a purse, a duffel bag, a wedding band—and invariably they let him have it. After last night, they knew that to resist was to die.

Another, a heavily muscled fellow with tattoos running up and down his arms and a thick gold chain dangling from his neck, happened to glance up, as if he sensed he was being watched from above. He stared straight into Royce's eyes through Aubrey's third-floor window, then raised his gun and mimicked shooting him.

Royce recoiled from the window as if he *had* been shot. That didn't look like the kind of fellow you could reason with about how we should all just get along. The world, he realized, was getting seriously ugly out there. He wondered how ugly *he* would have to get in order to bring Aubrey and her whole family through this nightmare experience unharmed.

Aubrey joined him at the window, looking deliciously disheveled. Her hair was mussed and she radiated a spirit of well-being—until she looked out the window.

"Ugh. How awful."

"Don't look too close. It's not pleasant."

"Are those *dead bodies*?"

"Uh-huh."

"Jesus. Some of them are police. And National Guard. And women and children. And all those people, they're just...stepping around them like they're not there."

Royce said nothing: there was nothing to say.

After a long pause: "Well, at least the worst of the rioting has stopped." Her look of well-being was long gone.

Royce nodded. "Maybe everyone's too exhausted or hoarse to shout any longer. By the way, I think all these people are heading back over the Brooklyn Bridge. It should be open again, now that the dome has jumped."

Aubrey's eyes lit up. "That's right! Why didn't we think of that last night?"

"I guess we had other things on our minds."

"I guess we did." She shook her head. "All those poor people. I wish we could do something for them."

Royce was silent for a moment. "Maybe we can."

Ten minutes later, they brought food and bottled water down from their apartment in boxes, watching them disappear so fast that whatever criminal elements were around didn't have time to react. No doubt most of the baddies were sleeping off their debauchery from last night anyway. Fervent thanks and calls of "bless you" reached their ears as the food and water vanished, followed by hard eyes and frustrated looks from those who had just missed out. Some looked hungry enough to eat Royce and Aubrey themselves if they weren't careful.

Heading over to the park, they asked if they could help and were put on burial detail. At least that was what the organizers were calling it, even though there were no actual graves being dug. Instead they were simply tasked with removing bodies from the street and lining them up in the park. The first ten minutes were the worst, then they got used to it—or if not used to it, at least able to endure it without retching.

It took about an hour for them and other volunteers to clear the surrounding streets of bodies. By then the park looked like an outdoor morgue. The poor souls who were still clinging to life were already being ministered to by doctors and nurses, so once their work with the bodies was done, they were sent home with thanks. They returned to their apartment and scrubbed off the stench of death, then tried to rest and forget about what had just happened.

*****

"Did we leave any food behind for ourselves?" Royce asked later on.

Aubrey rummaged through her cabinets and came up with two cans of Hormel Chili. "How about this?" she asked, waving the cans in the air like trophies. While she heated the chili up on a portable gas stove meant for camping, Royce set the table and placed a bottle of hot sauce between them.

"Fine dining at its best," he said.

"Did I mention I have a bottle of red wine stashed away?"

"Did I mention you make everything perfect?"

Within minutes their feast was finished. They poured generous glasses of wine and lounged on their favorite couch for what might be the last time. Aubrey lit some candles as they prepared for what they hoped would be a quieter evening than the last.

In the end, she didn't light just *some* candles, she lit her entire remaining supply, until the apartment looked like it belonged in a romance special where the bachelor makes an over-the-top gesture to his beloved. All that was missing were rose petals leading to the bathtub.

Looking impossibly lovely in the soft light, Aubrey turned to him as she lit the last candle and asked with an innocent smile, "Backgammon?"

"Definitely backgammon."

*****

Early the next morning Royce peered out the window once again. Last night *had* been quieter; they'd still heard plenty of unpleasant noises from down below, but nothing like the mass hysteria of the night before. He'd kept his gun close at hand on the nightstand, just in case, but had never needed it. Perhaps their location on the third floor was just inconvenient enough to deter most criminals, given the easy pickings on the first and second floors. All of Brooklyn was at their disposal, so why trudge up an extra flight of stairs if you didn't have to?

What Royce saw this morning was a reduced stream of people heading towards Manhattan. Most appeared weary beyond reckoning. A few with perkier steps looked like they'd spent the night in their own apartment and were now joining the throngs of escapees intent on exiting the dome before the air ran out.

There were still the predators to worry about, of course, lying in wait to pounce on any outliers. They certainly had their pick of prey this morning. They grabbed items off people as they stumbled by, brazenly unconcerned about the consequences. No police were left to stop them, and their ample supply of weaponry and willingness to use them were hard to argue with.

Royce watched as one young fellow tried to remonstrate with one of the criminals and got cold-cocked for his troubles. He went down in a heap. Royce flinched at the sight. Then his heart leapt into his throat and he cried out involuntarily as he watched the same criminal casually drag the guy's girlfriend off by the arm. The rest of the crowd kept their eyes averted and heads down despite the young woman's pleas.

Royce shook his head in disgust and considered rushing down the stairs to help—but he knew he'd end up dead for his troubles, and then Aubrey would be left all alone to fend for herself. He couldn't risk that. He felt sick to his stomach but turned away from the window. Apparently he wasn't so different from all those other people averting their eyes.

He didn't tell Aubrey what he'd seen that morning when she joined him at the kitchen table. Instead he said, "I think we should head over to your mom's and dad's just as soon as we can. If we wait too much longer, the streets may clear out altogether, and that wouldn't be good. There are some unsavory types out there, and I wouldn't want to meet them on a lonely street."

Aubrey nodded. "Makes sense: safety in numbers and all that. Plus, if we get there today, it gives us a little more cushion before the air runs out."

"Air *is* important."

"It's settled then; we leave later this morning."

*****

Royce insisted on using the most beat-up duffel bags they could find. After what he'd just witnessed, he wasn't about to flaunt any Louis Vuitton luggage for the predators to see. In the end, he found two ratty duffels buried in the back of the closet. "Those are from my college days," Aubrey confessed. "I should have thrown them out years ago."

"I'm glad you didn't: they're perfect."

The last hour was a flurry of activity. Aubrey couldn't bear to leave her apartment behind messy, so they made the bed, emptied the fridge, and piled bags of trash next to the door. "You do realize we're not coming back, don't you?" asked Royce.

Aubrey nodded. "It's *because* we're leaving it for good that I want to leave it clean. That way I'll always remember it that way."

"That actually makes a weird kind of Aubrey-sense."

"Aubrey-sense, huh? You're treading on thin ice there, mister."

While Aubrey was putting the finishing touches on her packing, Royce searched through her jewelry drawer one last time, looking for anything barter-worthy she might have overlooked. Deep down in the pile of jewelry he found one contender.

Aubrey gasped when he showed it to her. "I can't believe I missed that! That's my grandma's wedding ring. I mean, my other grandma, on my dad's side—she passed away years ago. She wanted me to have it when I got married."

"Then we should keep it safe, shouldn't we?" Royce pocketed the ring, giving her a significant look that didn't escape her. She was savvy that way.

They packed their smartphones and a few changes of clothing and some toiletries—enough to get them through the next few days—and that was all they had room for. The jewelry and whatever cash Aubrey had lying around got stuffed deep down into the bottom of each bag.

"I'm really going to miss this place," Royce said. "I think I've had some of the most fun of my life on that couch of yours."

"If you've had any more fun anywhere else, I don't want to know about it."

"I promise you that would be impossible."

"My shoes!" Aubrey lamented. "Can't we bring at least a few of them?"

"Not unless they can walk themselves."

"Bye shoes, bye wardrobe. I'll miss you!"

"Bye bed, bye couch! I'll miss you most of all."

*****

They locked up behind them and descended the stairs. The sad state of the apartments on the second floor gave them pause. Royce had his gun and other deterrents in his jacket pockets, ready to use if necessary—but he hoped he wouldn't need them. They were only walking a short distance to her parents' apartment today, not all the way to Manhattan or the mainland. As they reached the entrance, a blast of cold air hit them. "Jeez, it's freezing out today. Are you ready for this?" he asked.

"Ready," she said with a determined look on her face, pulling her cap down lower on her forehead as if she were preparing to head out on a mission.

"Then let's get going."

They hurried down the front stairs. The main doors were missing, ripped off their hinges and tossed into some nearby bushes. The first-floor windows were missing too, and every apartment on that floor had been ransacked. After descending to street level, Royce immediately steered them across the street and towards the park, away from the buildings where the worst of the predators lurked.

They skirted the park and turned onto Dekalb Avenue, joining throngs of people moving towards the Brooklyn Bridge. It seemed like all of Long Island was emptying out in the same direction, like water pouring down a drain. Royce hoped their endpoint wasn't the equivalent of a sewer.

At first they kept their eyes fixed straight ahead, trying to avoid any interaction with the people around them, but eventually Royce realized there was little to fear: these weren't the predators, they were the prey. Some had babies in their arms, bundled up against the cold. Others had kids beside them. The parents' faces were suffused with fear, the kids' with tears. The kids seemed dazed, walking on autopilot or in many cases being carried by their parents.

He found himself walking next to an older man with cracked eyeglasses and what might once have been a nice suit. The man was shivering and hugging himself against the cold. Royce nudged him to get his attention. "Hey, you heading to the Brooklyn Bridge?"

The man seemed startled out of a reverie. He coughed and said with a hoarse voice, "Of course. We all are." His coat was torn and his hair a mess and his face haggard and unwashed, but somehow the cracked glasses gave him a professorial look. "They're promising food and water at the bridge."

"Who's they?"

"I don't know. Someone in charge, maybe the military. But I haven't eaten in three days, so if someone says food, I'm there."

"Three days? That's a long time."

The man nodded.

Royce rummaged in his pockets and came out with a small candy bar, the kind you hand out to kids on Halloween. "Here," he said, handing it to him.

The man's eyes opened wide. He tore it open and scarfed it down in one bite before someone else could take it from him. He practically moaned with delight. Once he had finished he said hoarsely, "My God, that was good. Thanks." Then in a near whisper, "But I wouldn't let anyone else know you've got food in your pockets. Some folks would literally kill for a candy bar right now."

"These folks seem safe enough," Royce replied.

The older man looked around and grunted. "Maybe so, but there are others..."

"Yeah, I know the ones you're talking about. Were you outside the other night?"

"I was," the man replied grimly.

"We saw some of it from our apartment window. It looked—it *sounded*—awful."

It was. Beyond awful," the man said in his hoarse voice, eyes welling up behind the cracked glasses. "I've never seen anything like it, and I never hope to again. Half the folks had just been kicked out of their homes by thugs, the other half were just trying to get out before the dome jumped.

That's what I was trying to do—then things went nuts. Gunfire, stabbings, beatings..." He stopped and just shook his head.

"What happened to your glasses?"

"A punch happened to them. Some guy punched me in the face and stole my bag. I lost all the cash I had left, plus my laptop, my phone, and my last bits of food."

They shuffled forward, forced to walk at the sluggish pace of the crowd. "You couldn't find food anywhere else?"

The man's laugh was strangled. "Scraps. Scraps from trash bins. We were like rats rooting through garbage, but most of it was already picked over. We would've eaten the rats themselves if we could've caught them. I drank from a puddle in an alleyway; I don't even know where that water came from, but I drank from it anyway."

"Yikes."

"That's what real thirst will do to you."

They walked a bit further in silence. "So how'd you hear about the food at the bridge?" Royce asked.

The man shrugged. "Word of mouth. Like you and me talking now. The guy next to me, he says, 'Hey, did you hear? They got food at the bridge.' And I say, 'What bridge?' And he says, 'The *Brooklyn* Bridge: it's open again.' So I think to myself, that's where I'm heading." He walked a few more paces in silence, then whispered hoarsely, "God, I was getting seriously dizzy before that candy bar. I think you just saved my life."

"It was just a candy bar. Not even a big one."

The man shrugged again, gave him a final nod of thanks, then continued on towards the nirvana of food awaiting him up ahead.

"Did you catch all that?" Royce asked.

Aubrey nodded. "Promises of food and water."

It took them three times longer than usual to reach her parents' home. People were shuffling along so slowly, it felt like they were in line at an amusement park. Finally they reached the turnoff for her parents' apartment and broke off from the crowd, turning left onto quieter Portland Avenue. Her parents' apartment was in a three-story brownstone halfway down the street. A short set of stairs led up to the entryway door. Aubrey had a key for the door but didn't need it—the door was torn off its hinges.

"Uh-oh," she said.

They hurried up two flights of stairs. The ground-floor apartments had all been broken into and looted. Whatever had happened to their occupants, they were long gone. On the second floor they saw a mix of intact and demolished doorways. Maybe the criminals had begun to lose steam by that point. On the third floor they found all the doors intact. "Thank God," Aubrey breathed.

She knocked and heard her Dad yell, "Don't answer it!"

An eye at the peephole, a gasp, and then "Aubrey!" as the door opened wide. "We weren't expecting you yet!" Her mom hugged her so hard Aubrey grunted. "And who is this strapping young fellow?"

"*Mom,*" Aubrey said. "You already know Royce."

"Of course I do, I'm just kidding, Royce. Thanks for keeping my daughter safe. These are dangerous times for anyone to be out walking alone."

"My pleasure, Mrs. Powell."

"Call me Trish—I told you that last time, remember?" she said with a fierce expression. She had iron-gray hair and stern features offset by a warm smile that reached all the way up to her eyes.

"Okay, Trish, I'll try to remember this time." He and Aubrey had been dating for well over a year now, but Royce had only met her parents once or twice before.

"Is that Aubrey?" a gruff male voice asked.

"Dad," Aubrey said, getting another big bear hug. "You remember Royce, don't you?"

"Of course I do. Hello there, Royce," he said, shaking hands. He had a bushy mustache and bushy eyebrows and a handsome, wrinkled face. It took Royce a moment to remember his first name: Tony. Trish and Tony. "Strange times we're living in, aren't they?"

"They sure are."

"Come on into the living room and meet the rest of the gang." Tony led the way, limping.

"Dad," Aubrey exclaimed, "why are you limping?"

"It's nothing," he said, waving off her concern.

"*Dad*. What happened?"

He seemed loathe to answer. "Just a little encounter with some troublemakers at the door the other night."

"They tried to storm the apartment," Trish said by way of interpretation.

"Storm the apartment," scoffed Tony. "They *knocked* was all."

"If that was a knock, then I'm the Pope."

He mock-bowed to her. "Your Holiness."

"They practically beat down the door until your father opened it for them, brandishing that ridiculous pistol of his. Someone took a swipe at his leg with a crowbar, and that's when your father nearly shot the guy's head off."

"You're kidding," said Aubrey.

"There's the bullet hole to prove it," Trish said, pointing across the hallway.

"That's a pretty big bullet hole," Royce observed. "What kind of gun do you have?"

"A Magnum revolver," Tony whispered with mock confidentiality. "Forty-four caliber. I call it my Clint Special. Just the sight of it scares most people away. Not these fellas, though: they needed a bit more convincing. So I sent a shot over their bow, so to speak."

"I'd love to see it." Royce started pulling out his own collection of deterrents, and before long the two of them were huddled over in a corner of the living room comparing notes.

Aubrey, meanwhile, entered the living room with her mom and was enveloped in a conga line of hugs.

"And who's this?" Aubrey asked at the sight of a newborn baby she'd never met before.

"We're calling her Dominique," said her cousin Dana. "Get it? Dome? Dominique?"

"I've got it now," laughed Aubrey, "and I'll never forget it. Well, hello there, Dominique. When did you arrive?"

"About two weeks ago," said Dana. They had the 'D' thing going like Trish and Tony had the 'T' thing going; Dana's husband's name was Daniel.

"Well aren't you just the cutest thing," Aubrey said, tickling Dominique into a smile.

"Who's that?" came a papery voice from one of the bedrooms. "Is that who I think it is?"

"Grandma," cried Aubrey, rushing over to give her a gentle hug. It had to be gentle, because she was so small and bent with age she looked like a white-haired hobbit.

"Hello, little peanut," she said, which was funny coming from her.

"It's so good to see you, Grandma. And here's Grandpa too! You're all here. Are we the last ones to arrive, then?"

"You are," said her mother. "Fashionably late, as always."

"Don't you listen to her," said her grandpa with obvious delight at seeing his youngest granddaughter. He was a thin rail of a man who didn't look like he had an ounce of fat left on him. A wisp of wind might blow him away. Even his voice felt like it might disappear if you didn't listen carefully. "You're the star of the show, Aubrey: you're supposed to make a grand entrance."

Aubrey struck a diva-like pose and everyone laughed.

"If it weren't for what's going on outside," said her mother, "this would be a wonderful reunion, wouldn't it? I can't remember the last time we were all together."

"I can," said Dana. "It was back on the Fourth of July, before the domes. I remember because I was four months pregnant. Nothing like being pregnant to help you keep track of time."

"Isn't that the truth," laughed Trish. "Why, I remember when I was pregnant with Aubrey—"

"Not that story again," Aubrey moaned.

"Well then, let's just say I'm the only one in the family who can say they survived a ten-month pregnancy and leave it at that."

"I was worth the wait," said Aubrey, striking an even sillier diva pose. "Wasn't I, mother?" she said with some of her mother's own fierceness.

"Yes you were, dear."

"The Fourth of July," said Royce from the far corner. He and Tony were apparently done comparing weaponry for the time being. "That's when this whole mess began."

"Say what?" asked Trish.

"That's when the domes first arrived in seed form, according to the scientists—back around the Fourth of July. I guess you could say they fertilized the Earth at that point, and here we are today with a whole lot of big fat dome babies no one wants."

"Big fat dome babies," said Trish. "That's the strangest thing I've ever heard anyone say, Royce, and I love you for it. You just keep plotting over there in your corner with Tony."

Royce laughed along with everyone else. "It's just—I can't believe it was such a short time ago. Less than six months, and look where the world is now. Unbelievable."

"Those babies have grown up fast," said Grandpa in his reedy voice. "They're as big as North America if you put 'em all together. Bigger than Russia."

"That's one big baby," said Trish.

Aubrey's two older sisters, Christy and Beth, smuggled Aubrey into one of the bedrooms for a private chat. Judging from the amount of giggling going on in there, Royce guessed he might be a topic of conversation. Christy and Beth were both married, and they seemed to think it was Aubrey's turn next.

Aubrey's mom and dad motioned for him to come to the kitchen table for a little chat of their own. Trish got right to the point. "I'm worried about my parents—Aubrey's grandparents," she said. "You've seen them: they can't walk five or six miles in a day, if that's what it's going to take to get them out of the dome and off the island."

"Do they have wheelchairs? We could push them."

"Grandma has one, thank goodness," said Tony, "but Grandpa doesn't and insists he can walk himself. But he might slow us down quite a bit."

"What do you propose, then?"

"We could leave today; that would give us more time."

Royce looked out the window; it was already getting towards dark. "I don't know...Nighttime is when all the crazies come out."

They both nodded as if they'd already come to the same conclusion. "Or we could leave first thing tomorrow morning," said Trish.

"I like that idea a lot better."

Tony and Trish both nodded again. "All right, then, next question: where do we go from here?"

Royce related to them what they'd learned during their walk. "It sounds like we can just walk across the Brooklyn Bridge. After that, I'm not sure what to expect, but if nothing else, the Holland Tunnel might offer a way across. Or better yet, there may be people at the bridge who can help us. If they have food and water, they may also have transport."

"That's a comforting thought," said Trish, "but I'm afraid to count on it too much."

"Well, if it comes to it, we can always carry your father on our backs. He can't weigh all that much from the looks of him. I'd be happy to take a turn, and I'm sure I'm not the only one."

"That's kind of you, Royce," Tony said. "You're a good man. If we all take turns, I'm sure we can find a way to make it work." He patted Royce on the shoulder and started to stand up, anticipating Trish's next words.

"Now, you boys get out of the kitchen and let me cook," she commanded. "I'm preparing a last supper of sorts, and no, I don't need any help from the likes of you. Now shoo."

An hour later they were all enjoying a fine feast, so rich and plentiful that Royce almost felt guilty, given how many people were starving down below, but it didn't stop him from having seconds. It might be the last good meal he had for some time.

There were too many of them to fit around the dining room table, so they spread out into the living room and kitchen, sitting randomly on couches and chairs and even the floor. They were a happy, rowdy lot, the Powells, and Royce was glad to be a part of them. There really were fifteen of them, just like Aubrey said—sixteen if you counted the baby. Besides her grandparents and parents, he counted their son Patrick (the eldest), along with his wife Angela and their four-year-old daughter Sara; Christy (Aubrey's oldest sister) and her husband Nick; Beth (the middle sister) and her husband Stuart; Aunt Rita and Uncle Joe; and finally, Cousin Dana and her husband Daniel and their newborn Dominique.

He counted six men besides himself who looked like they could hold their own in a fight: Aubrey's dad Tony, brother Patrick, brothers-in-law Nick and Stuart, Uncle Joe, and cousin Daniel. That was a pretty good crew; he hoped it would be enough to dissuade any hoodlums from messing with them during their escape from Brooklyn. Nick and Stuart in particular looked like firefighter types who could handle themselves in a fight—and might even welcome one. As for the rest, Aubrey's older brother Patrick was calm and serious—and seriously obese. Uncle Joe was beefy and boisterous and laughed like a backfiring pickup truck. Cousin Daniel was as thin as a strand of uncooked spaghetti and the only quiet one in the bunch.

Aubrey joined him halfway through the meal; she sounded a little hoarse from all the talking she'd been doing with the members of her extended family. "Everything okay?" she asked.

"Everything's fine," Royce assured her. "I had a nice chat with your mom and dad earlier, and it sounds like we'll be heading for the bridge first thing tomorrow."

"Good. That means one more evening at the old homestead before all this goes away forever."

The whole Powell clan finished their packing immediately after dinner, under strict orders from Tony and Trish, then went to bed early in anticipation of an early wakeup call. Some of the younger members of the clan, including Royce and Aubrey, were relegated to couches or air mattresses or sleeping bags on the floor, as there simply weren't enough beds to go around.

*****

The morning dawned drizzly and cold inside the dome. "I guess the aliens welcome all sorts of weather," Aubrey muttered as she looked out the window, stretching herself awake.

They were up by five and ready to go by seven—even Aunt Rita and Uncle Joe, the sleepiest outliers in the group. They chowed down on a quick breakfast—nothing like the feast from the night before, but enough to nourish them. Then they said their goodbyes to their family home, locked the door behind them for old time's sake, and headed downstairs. Brother-in-law Stuart carried Grandma down the three flights of stairs like it was nothing, while brother-in-law Nick brought the folded wheelchair. Tony guided Grandpa down the stairs one careful step at a time.

At that early hour of the morning, and on that quiet side street, there were no predators waiting to jump them, but Royce kept his hand near his gun just the same, especially for that first minute as they all stood together on the steps getting their bearings. The missing front door was the first thing Grandpa and Grandma noticed. "When did that happen?" Grandpa asked in his reedy voice.

"Two nights ago," Trish replied.

"Isn't someone going to fix it?"

Trish shook her head. "I doubt it, Pops."

Stuart carried Grandma down the outside steps and settled her into her wheelchair, and then they were on their way. They headed north along Portland before turning left onto Dekalb and right onto Flatbush. Now all they had to do was walk straight along Flatbush until the turn for Tillary Street and Brooklyn Bridge Boulevard.

It was cold, but not as bitterly cold as it had been the past two days. They huddled together near the center of the wide avenue. One or two vehicles passed them along the way, but most people were on foot.

The walk to the Brooklyn Bridge normally would have taken Royce and Aubrey less than half an hour, but with Grandma and Grandpa accompanying them, Royce could see it was going to take a lot longer than that. Grandpa's steps were slow and careful, and Grandma's wheelchair skewed to the left like an errant shopping cart. Tony was already huffing and puffing from trying to keep it straight.

The streets were emptier than they had been the day before; you could walk normally instead of shuffling along. But Royce felt like they were too exposed at the pace they were going—like wounded prey animals separated from the herd. Unfortunately they made for easy targets for any predators out there.

After fifteen minutes of slow progress, they reached a stretch of Flatbush that felt dodgy. Devil's Tattoos and Red Cat Lounge stood on one side of the street, and a boarded-up fish and chips shop and a graffitied pizza joint stood on the other. Construction scaffolding covered both sides of the sidewalk just beyond. Small groups huddled together for safety as they hurried down the middle of the street, keeping their heads down. Most tried to keep as far away from the buildings as they could. Royce found himself wishing his group could walk a little faster. Their slow pace was just asking for trouble.

As if to prove his point, a soft voice said from behind them, "Yo, bro', where ya headin'?"

Royce and the entire Powell clan turned around and saw two men standing in front of a boarded-up bar called Vinnie's. Some of the boards had been ripped away, and the two men appeared to have emerged from within its dark confines. They were smiling thin smiles that looked anything but friendly. Each cradled a semi-automatic weapon (banned in the state of New York, but obviously these guys didn't care). They were heavily muscled and heavily tattooed and had shaved heads. Royce thought they looked like skinheads on steroids.

One guy's mouth was scarred into a permanent sneer. He was apparently the spokesman for the two. "Yo, I asked ya, where ya headin'?"

"To the bridge, obviously," Aubrey's father Tony replied for the group.

"Without payin' a toll? You hear that, Ronnie?"

Royce could see other groups coming up from behind, but they quickly detoured to a side street and went around to avoid the confrontation. He could hardly blame them.

"That's, like, highway robbery," the sneering guy said.

"It sure is," his pal Ronnie replied. "There are penalties for things like that." He was eyeing Aubrey in a way Royce didn't like.

"Ya gotta pay the toll," Permanent Sneer said.

"Okay," Tony said. "So whaddaya want?"

"That bag you got on your shoulder, for starters."

Tony shrugged and tossed him the bag. "Hope you like old-guy clothes."

"We're just gettin' started, old man. This is a *serious* toll. One bag a clothes ain't gonna cover it."

"Uh-uh," said his partner. "Not even close." He was still eyeing Aubrey.

"Toss *all* your bags over here," Permanent Sneer said. "We'll take what we're owed."

They tossed their bags over. With two semi-automatics trained on them, there wasn't much else they could do.

Permanent Sneer started rummaging through the bags while Ronnie kept his weapon trained on them. "There ain't jack shit in here," Permanent Sneer complained. "Just old clothes and crap. Where's the good stuff?" he demanded, looking up at them.

The good stuff was in fact under the wheelchair cushion beneath Grandma's butt, but they weren't about to tell him that.

"That's all we got," said Tony. "Hey, whaddaya want from us? We're just tryin' to get outta here like everyone else. Give us a break, why don't you?"

"You mouthin' off to me?" Permanent Sneer swung his rifle around and pointed it straight at Tony, looking ready to shoot him on the spot.

"I've got the good stuff," Royce said, holding his hands up in the air—anything to get the gun off Tony. Permanent Sneer spun around and pointed his weapon at Royce instead.

At the same time Ronnie, the other thug, sauntered over and grabbed Aubrey's arm. "This is all the toll I want right here," he said with a leer.

Permanent Sneer glanced over at Aubrey with an appreciative eye, then grabbed Royce with one hand while holding the rifle steady with the other.

At that moment Aubrey clawed at Ronnie's cheek. The guy screamed and yelled "Bitch!" and took a swing at her all at once. Aubrey shied away from his oncoming fist, but before it could connect, Tony drew his Clint Special from its holster and fired it at Ronnie. The guy cried out as a bullet took him in the arm. He let go of Aubrey and clutched at his arm instead.

Permanent Sneer wheeled around to shoot Tony, but at the same instant Royce reached into his jacket pocket and came out with the stun gun. He jabbed it at Permanent Sneer's neck and watched the guy go down. He laid there like a puddle of water.

"Shit," Ronnie cried, panicking now. He tried to raise his weapon with his other arm, but Tony wasted no time putting a bullet through his heart.

"No one threatens my daughter," he growled at Ronnie, staring down at the guy's twitching body. He came over to where Permanent Sneer was lying, and before anyone could say or do anything, he raised his gun and shot him. "That oughta cover your fucking toll," Tony snarled.

"Jesus, Dad!" cried Aubrey. "He was already down."

"Now he'll stay down. I don't want him following us. I've seen guys like this before, and they're nothing but trouble."

Royce looked around. All eyes were on them now, that was for sure. He bent down and picked up Permanent Sneer's semi-automatic rifle, and Tony did the same with Ronnie's.

More predators were emerging from their hideouts at the sound of gunshots, curious as to what was going on. "Holy shit, they shot 'em!" one of them yelled disbelievingly. He started to raise his gun, but Tony shot him before he could bring it to bear.

Tony obviously knew his way around a gun. "Anyone else?" he asked.

"Jesus, Rambo," hissed his wife Trish, "you're gonna get us all killed if you don't stop shooting people."

But the other predators who'd popped their heads out to see what was going on seemed to decide it wasn't worth the trouble—at least not with two semi-automatics trained on them.

"Ah, screw it," one of them said. "It's too early in the morning for this shit. Those two were assholes anyway."

"Woke me up from a good night's sleep," grumbled another. They disappeared back into their hideouts.

Aubrey grabbed onto Royce and didn't let go. "Is that it, then, or are they coming back?"

"Let's not wait to find out," Royce said. "Hey Tony, what say we get out of here?"

Tony was eyeing the boarded-up shops as if he half-hoped there might be some movement in there. "Right," he said gruffly after a moment. "Let's get going. Nice job with that stun gun, by the way, Royce. That sneering fella woulda shot me for sure."

"No problem," said Royce. "Just remind me never to get on the wrong side of an argument with you."

"Don't mess with my daughter and you'll be just fine."

"Don't worry, I won't."

"I know you won't. Now, why don't you go ahead and take point? You lead and I'll hang back, just to make sure none of those hoodlums crawls back out of the woodwork and tries to follow us."

"God help them if they do."

Hurriedly they stuffed their clothing and meager possessions back into their bags. "Okay, let's move out," Royce said. "Isn't that what they say in the military, Tony?"

"That's exactly what they say. And here I thought you were a stockbroker."

"I was," said Royce. "Once upon a time."

*****

They got maybe ten paces before a shot rang out from one of the boarded-up shops behind them. Tony went down with a bullet in his back. "Shit," Tony said. He tried to crawl forward but didn't get far.

"Dad!" Aubrey cried. She and Trish and the entire Powell clan came running back, heedless of the danger. Royce, who was on point when the shot rang out, was among the last to get back.

Nick and Stuart, the two strapping sons-in-law, tried to pick Tony up and drag him out of there. Tony groaned and looked like he might pass out.

"Patrick, pick up that rifle," Nick huffed, pointing with his chin at the semi-automatic Tony had just dropped. "Give us some cover."

Heavy-set Patrick bent down to pick it up and promptly got shot for his troubles. He spun around in a pirouette like a kid overacting his death scene and toppled to the ground.

His wife Angela and his daughter Sara both screamed and ran towards him. Angela went down in another quick burst of gunfire, and four-year-old Sara was left standing on her own, confused, turning in a circle, and bawling her head off.

"Shit!" several of the Powells yelled at once.

"Down!" Royce cried, dragging Aubrey down to the pavement with him. "Get down!"

Multiple guns fired from the boarded-up shops near Vinnie's, mowing down half of the Powells who were still standing before they could react. Royce saw Nick and Stuart both go down, along with the already injured Tony. Aunt Rita and Uncle Joe both went down, too, their bodies riddled with bullets.

Aubrey's oldest sister Christy was still standing; she was uninjured but looked stunned into immobility. Finally she surged into motion, grabbing her niece Sara and diving for the pavement.

Grandpa, God help him, bent down and tried to pick up the same semi-automatic Patrick had just gotten shot over and took a slew of bullets in the chest. The bullets nearly blew him back ten feet before he fell.

Grandma had been left in her wheelchair several yards behind the rest of the group unattended. She gave a little cry and tottered to her feet and began making her way towards her fallen husband one slow step at a time.

Cousin Daniel dragged his wife Dana and their baby Dominique down to the ground and lay over them both, protecting them with his body as best he could, but he was so thin he didn't offer much in the way of protection.

Trish was standing next to Tony, wringing her hands and crying. "Stay here," Royce whispered to Aubrey and crawled over to Trish, pulling her down by force. "Get down, get down!" he hissed at her. If Trish heard him she didn't respond; she was too busy mourning her husband, but at least she stayed down.

Christy and Beth, with their niece Sara in tow, were both crawling towards their shot husbands.

Royce positioned himself flat on the pavement and aimed his semi-automatic in the general direction of Vinnie's and let loose with several shots. He heard a cry from within and continued shooting.

"Get them out of here!" he yelled over at Aubrey.

Aubrey started tugging on people's shirts, trying to get them to leave, but most were too shell-shocked to move.

Someone from the hideouts returned fire at Royce. He felt specks of asphalt strike his face. He rolled once, twice, three times to the right, away from the rest of the group, hoping to draw fire away from them. Then he returned fire. Whether he hit anything he didn't know; he heard no screams this time, but he kept on firing in periodic bursts to keep their attention on him and away from the rest of the group. He was rewarded with another scream and knew he had just connected with someone inside.

Jesus, he was in an active gun battle with who knew how many gangsters inside a bar called Vinnie's in downtown Brooklyn. This didn't look good at all.

Grandma was caressing her husband's forehead and speaking softly to him when a bullet struck her in the forehead and she toppled over almost gently atop her husband. Shit! Why would anyone shoot her? She couldn't hurt a fly.

Royce pressed down on the trigger again and heard the semi-automatic click on empty.

The other semi-automatic was near Trish, who was still mourning her dead husband and eldest son. "Trish!" he called. "The rifle!"

She was oblivious. He pulled out his handgun and started firing with it.

Another burst of weapons fire from Vinnie's had him rolling for cover even further to the right. Either the thugs in there weren't very good shots or he was just lucky, because none of the bullets hit him. He felt several whiz by over his head, though, so he kept as low as he could.

Aubrey was finally having some luck getting her family members to move. She half-tugged her two sisters away towards safety. Nick was still alive somehow and was dragging himself along with them as best he could. It looked like Stuart, the other brother-in-law, wouldn't be going anywhere ever again.

Daniel, meanwhile, was pulling Dana away, urging his wife to stay low to the ground. Dana clutched her newborn and guarded her from any stray bullets with her own body. They half-crawled, half-stumbled away from the boarded-up shops.

Another round of bullets pinged too close for comfort. Royce got up in a half crouch and made a mad dash towards the other semi-automatic. Weapons fire followed him the whole way, as if he were a duck target in a fairground shooting contest.

He dove towards the gun, grabbed it, and took cover behind the already dead Patrick, whose obese form shuddered with repeated shots.

Jesus, what was he doing? How had he gotten himself into this mess?

He positioned himself behind Patrick's body and began firing in steady spurts at Vinnie's and the surrounding buildings. Looking behind him, he saw that the remaining members of the family were moving further out of the line of fire. Christy and Beth were struggling to keep Nick on his feet. Trish had picked up her granddaughter Sara and was finally moving on her own. Maybe having a granddaughter to protect was giving her a renewed sense of purpose.

Aubrey, meanwhile, was much too close to the gunfire for Royce's liking. He'd hoped to see her at the head of the little group making its escape, but instead she was keeping low and checking on each family member to make sure they were dead. Jesus, Aubrey; he admired and feared for her at the same time.

He turned forward again and began laying down heavy fire to make sure she stayed safe. He heard another cry from the hideouts and felt nothing but satisfaction. They could all die in there as far as he was concerned at this point. If he'd had a grenade, he would have tossed it in at them.

He turned around again and saw Aubrey crawling away on all fours as fast as she could. He laid down another heavy round of fire and then began backing up himself. Poor Patrick's body was a riddled mess at this point, but in an odd way he had saved Royce's life, taking the deluge of bullets intended for him.

At the wheelchair, he had just enough presence of mind to grab the bag of valuables tucked under the cushions. Then he upended the wheelchair and used it as a shield as he backed up behind it.

Bullets pinged off the wheelchair and thudded into the seat. Jesus. Why didn't they just give up already?

One of the bullets made it through the wheelchair and clipped him in the arm. "Shit!" He sent another barrage of bullets at his tormenters and continued backing away.

He could feel his arm bleeding and see the blood soaking down the left sleeve of his shirt.

He made a run for it then, abandoning the wheelchair and just hauling ass as fast as he could in the other direction.

He heard a whoop from behind and realized what was about to happen. His pursuers were leaving their hideouts to chase him down and finish him off. They weren't about to let him get away now.

But he wouldn't give them the pleasure. In fact he might have a little surprise in store for them if they came out into the open. He heard rather than saw the first bullets whiz past his ear and dove to the pavement, ignoring the pain in his arm, flipping over immediately and taking aim at his pursuers.

He laid down a steady stream of bullets and watched his pursuers fall to the ground one by one.

He got up and ran again, then dropped and looked behind him. He had almost caught up to Aubrey, who was trailing the group and urging them forward from behind.

His pursuers appeared to be down to one or two diehards. The rest were either dead or injured or had given up the chase. Frankly he didn't know why they were chasing him at all at this point—it wasn't like he was a Rockefeller, heir to a fortune—he was just a broke stockbroker trying to get out of Brooklyn. But sometimes these things took on a life of their own once they got started, and some battles were fought for no other reason than pure bloodlust.

He aimed at one of his two pursuers and heard a *click* and realized he was out of ammunition.

Shit. Did *they* know that?

He pulled out his handgun and reloaded it, feeling the steady drip-drip-drip of blood through his shirt and onto the asphalt.

"Are you okay, Royce?" he heard from just behind him.

Double-shit. Aubrey.

"Fine," he hissed. "Now get out of here!"

She was keeping low but didn't leave. "Here, take this," she said, pushing something towards him.

It was her dad's Clint Special.

Bless you, Aubrey. The Clint Special was a lot more formidable than his handgun.

"Thanks! Now get out of here!" He thought he heard her crawling away but didn't look back to check. Instead he aimed with the Clint Special and pulled the trigger—and watched as one of his two pursuers—the one who had decided he was out of ammunition and was charging at him full-on like a maniac on PCP—crumpled to the ground as a bullet tore through his chest.

One down, one to go.

Royce actually crawled *towards* the guy he'd just shot, intending to use him as cover.

A moment later he had his last pursuer dead in his sights. The thug, seeing what had happened to his comrade and realizing Royce wasn't the sitting duck he'd believed him to be, thought better of it and ran the other way. Royce had never felt more tempted to pull the trigger; he could have shot the guy in the back. He certainly deserved it after what he and his comrades had done, but he resisted the urge and watched him scuttle away.

Good riddance.

He felt the bloodlust drain from him. Then he remembered that actual blood was draining from him.

He began to shiver with a combination of shock and cold.

Aubrey was back at his side. She never listened to him, and he loved her for it.

"Here, let me help you." She rummaged through her duffel and found a scarf to serve as an impromptu tourniquet. Wrapping the scarf around his arm and over the wound, she tied it as tight as she could until he grunted in pain. "Tight enough?" she asked.

"Yeah, plenty tight." He was feeling more than a little lightheaded.

"Let's go then," Aubrey said.

He wasn't about to disagree. He let himself be led.

She pulled him away from a scene of carnage that had to have happened to someone else, not him. Tony and half the Powell clan couldn't possibly be dead.

“I think I’m in shock,” he said aloud.

“I think we all are,” Aubrey replied. He looked over and saw she was crying, not just a few tears but a storm of them. Her family: the family she had stayed behind for. Now half of them were gone and the other half…well, who knew?

He stumbled along beside Aubrey until they caught up to what remained of their diminished group. Despite his injury, he found himself counting like the stockbroker he was. One, two, three, four….He counted eight altogether besides himself and Aubrey.

Trish, who was comforting her granddaughter Sara.

Christy and Beth, struggling to hold up the injured Nick between them, who looked like a dead man walking. Both sisters had tears streaming down their faces.

Dana, Daniel, and Dominique, all three alive and well.

And that was it. The rest: gone.

Left for dead in Brooklyn amidst a torrent of gunfire.

JUMP 12

December 29

Worst. Christmas. Ever. That was the general consensus. For many the holiday passed without their realizing it was happening at all; they were too busy trying to survive to celebrate. For those who did commemorate the day, their observations were subdued, befitting a funeral more than a birth. It was the unholy birth of the domes that was on everyone's minds these days.

In many ways, the twelfth jump marked the beginning of the end. Each dome now had a diameter of some 12 miles and a height of over half a mile. All told they encompassed some 17 million square miles of land worldwide—nearly thirty percent of the total landmass of Earth, or roughly the size of Asia including the Middle East.

Four hours of walking at a steady clip would get you from one side of a dome to the other, assuming you encountered no major obstacles along the way. If you were elderly, infirm, weak from hunger, or otherwise unfit and found yourself stuck in the middle of a dome with no vehicle, your chances of ushering in the new year were beginning to look a little grim. What amounted to a manageable hike for the young and healthy could equate to a death sentence for the old and infirm.

"Happy New Year," if it was said at all, was said sarcastically to usher in the year 2042.

21

December 29 – Oval Office, Philadelphia

The President slammed the report down on his desk. "This says tens of thousands died last week because they ran out of air! How is that possible? I thought we were supposed to be prepared for this!"

Gil Lametti regarded the President with a pained expression. "A lot of people underestimated just how long it would take to get out of the domes. Some locked themselves inside their apartments, trying to avoid all the chaos, and never came out. Others were too old or lame or sick or otherwise unfit to walk the distance it took to escape on limited air. Others were so busy looting or causing trouble, they were miles away from a dome wall when the oxygen ran out."

"But this says some died even though they made it to the evacuation points, where there were shuttle buses, for God's sake!"

"There weren't enough shuttles, Mark. *Millions* were trying to escape all at once, just as we feared. The buses kept making the journey back and forth as long as they could, but after the third night, the drivers started suffering from hypoxia. They started swerving off the roads and crashing. Bridges and tunnels got blocked, which made it impossible for other buses to get by, and after that it was pretty much every man for himself. Some made it, others didn't."

The President remained silent, stewing internally. "Where were the police in all this?" he demanded. "Where were the National Guard?"

Lametti's expression turned even more pained. "Half of them never made it out alive."

The President just stared at him in disbelief.

"The plan was for them to work in pairs to keep the streets safe in each neighborhood—you know, help the people along who were trying to escape. They were supposed to go door-to-door to make sure everyone got out... but things didn't go as planned."

The President snorted.

"Most of them died fighting their own citizens, and that was never their mission."

"How awful. What's become of us as a people that something as awful as this could happen?"

Lametti shook his head; he had no answer for that. "All I can tell you is that once the buses stopped coming, things went downhill fast. They say the last buses left with dozens clinging to them for dear life. Other buses were mobbed by people on foot desperate to get on."

"My God."

"All hell broke loose after the last shuttle left and no more came to replace it. The officials who thought they still had time to get people out suddenly realized they couldn't get *themselves* out. Some officers fled in their patrol cars and to hell with everyone else; others stayed behind to the bitter end trying to help as many as they could. There were heroes in there, Mark, I can tell you that much."

The President fumed in silence. "*I'm* responsible for those deaths, Gil," he said at last. "The buck stops here: that's what Harry Truman used to say, and he was right."

"Be reasonable, Mark. You can't put all of this on yourself. I'm at least as much to blame as you are—probably more so. Lincoln himself couldn't have anticipated all the... all the *shit* that has gone down these past four months. I doubt even he could have done much better."

"I can't agree with you there, Gil. The truth is, the American people deserved better, and I just wasn't up to the task."

"Well, who was? Take a look around and show me any leader anywhere in the world who's been up to the task. This is a global catastrophe, Mark, and it's *not your fault*. Every other leader is struggling with the exact same shit you're dealing with."

"Struggling with shit: that sounds about right. And I'm the one stuck holding the shovel."

"Look, you didn't sign up for an alien invasion, Mark—none of us did. You signed up to lead your people, and that's what you've been doing. No one could ask more of you than that."

"Oh no? Tell that to the dead police, the dead military, and the dead women and children. Tell that to the ones who aren't dead but wish they were—starving or homeless or grieving or dying. I have no idea how to help them."

"You're building homes for them, Mark. You're building roads to get them there. You're mobilizing food banks so they don't starve to death. You're setting up evacuation points so they can get out of the domes in time."

"Yeah, and look how well that turned out."

"If people had stayed calm instead of running amok, who knows? Maybe things would have turned out better. In any case, we'll learn from our mistakes and get it right the next time."

"There won't *be* a next time, Gil. This is it: the domes just jumped for the twelfth time. The two domes in Manhattan just merged into one. What *was* the Central Park Dome is now the Manhattan Dome—a single dome covering all of Manhattan and then some! And the D.C. Dome just swallowed up what little was left of our nation's capital. As for the rest of the country—well, it's a mess, let's just leave it at that. I can feel it, Gil: our nation is disintegrating around us. I'm not even sure there will *be* a Union in another month."

"Mark—"

The President raised his hand. "Don't worry, Gil, I'm not going to say that out loud to anyone else, but I've *got* to say it to someone, and that someone is you."

Lametti nodded soberly. "Well, as long as we're being honest with each other, I'm worried about that too. But what else can we do that we're not already doing?"

The President shook his head. "I don't know, Gil, I don't know...but I *hate* that it might happen on my watch. How can the United States stay united when these damn domes keep dividing it all up into pieces? 'A house divided against itself cannot stand.' Those were Lincoln's words, and now they've taken on a literal meaning."

Lametti sighed. "I suppose the best we can do is fight like Lincoln fought to hold the Union together. No one ever accused him of not trying hard enough. Hopefully the same can be said of us someday. If we go down, we go down fighting."

The President walked over to his Chief of Staff and clapped him on the shoulder. "That's exactly what I'm afraid of, Gil—that in the end, unlike Lincoln, we really *will* go down fighting."

22

December 30 – Wantage, New Jersey

One week had passed since their escape from Brooklyn, and none of them as yet had any idea what to say to each other. Their grief was still too fresh to talk about.

Christmas was an awful affair with no cheer whatsoever. Royce and the remaining Powell clan spent it inside the chain-link parking lot at RV World trying to forget recent events. The bottles of booze stored in the RV both helped and hurt: they dulled the pain but didn't make it go away, and each morning they awoke groggy and depressed.

Beth, the sister closest in age to Aubrey—the one who had lost her husband Stuart in the gun battle—was in the worst shape; she slept in the RV's top bunk all day long and barely ate.

Four-year-old Sara, who'd lost both her parents in the same battle, wasn't doing much better, but her grandmom was showering her with so much love and attention that she was starting to come around. Trish herself had returned to the land of the living with a vengeance; she was fiercely protective of her entire clan and most especially of her granddaughter.

As for the injured Nick, he seemed to be out of the woods physically, but privately he told Royce he blamed himself for Patrick's death. "I asked him to pick up that rifle. If I hadn't, he might still be alive."

"Nonsense. You and Stuart were heroes rushing in like that."

Nick blew out a sigh. "Sometimes, when Trish looks at me, I think she blames me for her son's death."

"Look, Nick, we're all grieving right now and trying to process what happened. It's only been a week; give it some time."

Nick had spent four hours in the Red Cross triage tent at the Brooklyn Bridge. He had been in there so long, all of them had feared the worst; but lo and behold, he had emerged, limping but alive. He had suffered two gunshot wounds, one to the leg and one to the upper torso, and yet somehow he had managed to survive. His wife Christy had literally moaned with relief when she saw him.

The medical staff had pulled Royce into the triage tent too, but he had only been in there a short time. A nurse had examined his arm, told him brusquely that the wound wasn't life-threatening (apparently the bullet had passed straight through), and applied an antiseptic that stung so fiercely it had nearly shocked him out of his shock. Then she had sewed him back up with nothing more than a local anesthetic, slapped some fresh bandages on, handed him two Tylenol and some antibiotics, and told him to move along to make room for the next patient.

After Nick had gotten out, all ten of them had limped their way past a seemingly endless food and water line to a shuttle bus at the halfway point of the Brooklyn Bridge. The bus had taken them through the Holland Tunnel, dropping them off right at the edge of the dome itself—to none other than Royce's old stomping grounds, Jersey City.

Since Royce had last seen it, Jersey City had become a sprawling refugee camp. Most of the city, including his crappy old studio apartment, was now domed, but its western margins were still undomed. Lincoln Park, once a pleasant green space, was now an endless field of FEMA tents. The tents covered not just the park itself but also the adjacent Skyway Golf Course, a nearby dog run, a collection of baseball and soccer fields, and even the Holy Name Cemetery. Even the parking lots and some of the lesser used side streets had become encampments. The once-green grass of the park had been trampled into mud, and conditions inside the refugee camp looked anything but sanitary.

After exiting the dome, they had stood in a long line adjacent to Lincoln Park, waiting to purchase insanely expensive bus tickets. Three different buses and a long, cold walk in the dark had finally gotten them to RV World. By then they were utterly spent, both physically and emotionally. They'd entered the RV and crashed on whatever flat surface they could find.

One week later, they were still parked in the same spot at RV World and trying to come to grips with their new reality. The social dynamics of having ten emotionally raw people in such tight quarters was a challenge for all of them. Maybe Trish really *was* upset with Nick for getting her son killed, or maybe it was all in Nick's head. Who could say besides Trish herself? They certainly couldn't talk about it yet.

One thing *not* in Nick's head: Beth. She clearly resented Nick for living while her own husband, Stuart, lay dead and unburied on a Brooklyn street. She tried her best to hide it but couldn't. Christy walked on eggshells around her younger sister, not sure what to say or do. She wanted to celebrate Nick's recovery, but obviously it put Beth off, so instead she kept silent.

Meanwhile, Dana and Daniel were keeping mostly to themselves as they cared for their newborn infant. They strove to be as invisible as possible but couldn't quite manage it in such cramped quarters. Whenever the baby cried—and Dominique cried a lot—they looked like they wanted to fade into the woodwork. They whispered a lot, and Royce half-expected them to peel off from the awkward group dynamic any day now and venture off on their own.

Aubrey, for her part, was stuck in the middle of it all, trying to comfort her mom, trying to comfort her sisters, trying to comfort her niece, and so busy comforting everyone else that she sometimes forgot to comfort herself. She still had her own grief to work through.

The Powells had agreed with muted enthusiasm to Royce's suggestion of Charlottesville, Virginia as a destination. At least it was free of domes, and they had to go *somewhere.* Aubrey had been there before and had liked it, so why not? They certainly couldn't stay forever inside a fenced parking lot at RV World.

*****

Once upon a time, the drive to Charlottesville would have taken six hours, but that was in bygone days when American travel was easy and highways safe. They stayed on back roads, as far from major cities as possible. Domes were visible all along their route, sometimes on one side of the road and sometimes on the other. At twelve miles in diameter and over half a mile in height, they were hard to miss at this point. Topping one hill, they were greeted with a panoramic view of the surrounding countryside and counted no less than four domes spread out below them. One of them stood right in the middle of the road they were on. The detour around it took longer than the rest of the day's journey combined.

The next day's drive took them into Maryland and West Virginia along I-81, which was mostly dome-free, but the traffic was murder nonetheless. It felt like the entire Northeast was migrating somewhere—*anywhere.* Those without a vehicle, or who could no longer afford the gas, trudged alongside the highway on foot, heading south towards warmer climes. Some sat by the roadside looking exhausted and miserable. Others tried to hitch a ride, but few drivers trusted strangers these days: a stranger might kick you out of your own vehicle and steal your possessions.

As they turned off the highway for Charlottesville, the traffic lessened and so did the numbers of people on foot. Most everyone seemed to be heading further south—perhaps all the way south to Florida, recently dubbed the Milagro State because of the relatively small number of domes along its coast.

Royce and Aubrey took the dwindling numbers of people as a good sign. After the craziness of New York City, the less crowds the better, as far as they were concerned. They paid in advance for one week at an RV park on the outskirts of Charlottesville and counted themselves lucky.

23

December 31 – Pasadena, California

At the other end of the country, Dr. Rachel Cavanaugh was busy packing up her possessions in the South Arroyo neighborhood of Pasadena. She didn't have much choice: the JPL Dome had jumped on the 29th, swallowing up her home. Ironically enough, it was the exact same dome she and her colleagues had transported (in ovate form) to JPL some four months ago to study in depth. Now the dome had gotten its revenge, devouring not just her workplace but also her residence.

The loss of her job stung far worse than the loss of her home. Her work was everything to her. Before the arrival of the ovates, she had been involved in what she believed was crucial work focused on extending humanity's understanding of the cosmos—but now the cosmos had come to them. The instant the domes appeared, all other projects ground to a halt as the race to understand these strange new artifacts began. How could exploring distant stars and planets ever compete with investigating alien artifacts right here on Earth?

No period of her career had ever been more fulfilling or more frustrating to Rachel than the past four months. To this day she was convinced her team could have figured out the alien technology if given enough time. Perhaps the aliens suspected as much and had designed the domes to expand as rapidly as they had as a way of guaranteeing the humans didn't have time to play technological catch-up. Certainly the inner force field protecting the ovate itself was a stroke of genius on their part: it kept humans from meddling with the ovates from inside the domes and figuring out their secrets.

The JPL Dome in particular had become her obsession—her white whale. Even as she packed, she was thinking about it, wondering what kind of specialized harpoon might bring it down. Of course her packing suffered as a result; she had a lot of mismatched outfits thrown into her suitcase. As for valuables, she hadn't even begun to think about those, and it was already closing in on midnight. But she consoled herself with the thought that she still had until tomorrow afternoon before the oxygen would begin to run out. If she pulled an all-nighter, she should be fine.

She was so lost in thought as she busied herself packing that she didn't hear the front door open. The latch made a little *click*. She hadn't bothered locking it because she'd been making trips to and from the half-packed car in her driveway.

Suddenly she looked up from her packing. What was that? It sounded like voices. In *her* living room.

Maybe it was the couple next door, here to ask for some packing tape. Just to be on the safe side, she rummaged through her purse and found a canister of pepper spray. Palming it, she put her finger on the trigger.

"Hello?" she called down.

The voices downstairs abruptly stopped—

Then feet came pounding up the stairs.

Three beefy men stood in the doorway of her bedroom, staring in at her like *she* was the intruder. "Um, can I help you?"

"Yeah you can," one of them snarled. "You can get the hell out of here before we throw you out."

She was quite sure she'd never seen any of them before. The guy who'd just ordered her out of her own home had gold teeth. What was that called? A grill? Grillz? Something like that.

"Now hold on a minute, fellas—" Rachel started to say, but all three moved towards her menacingly, and Rachel found herself backing up until she ran into her own bed and couldn't back up anymore.

"Okay, I'm going, I'm—"

But apparently she hadn't moved fast enough for their liking, because the guy with the gold teeth grabbed her by the shoulders and began marching her towards the stairs. In response she sprayed him right in the face. He went down on his knees howling in pain and rubbing at his eyes.

"Shit! Bitch!" he screamed.

She spun around and sprayed wildly at the other two as they grabbed for her.

"Shit!" they both cried, but they must not have gotten as full a dose as the first guy because they kept coming at her. One tore the canister out of her hands and seized her roughly by the wrists, pinning her hands in front of her. The other snatched at her legs but couldn't get a good grip because she kept kicking at him. Both were squinting and tearing up like crazy from the pepper spray, but that didn't stop them from wrestling with her. Out of the corner of her eye, she saw the guy with the gold teeth still down on his knees swearing up a storm.

The one grabbing for her legs suddenly changed course and punched her in the stomach. *Hard.*

She found herself gasping for one long breath that wouldn't come. "Wait—" she tried to say. But the guy grabbed her by the legs, and this time she was doubled over in too much pain to stop him. He and his buddy hauled her over to the stairs like a sack of flour.

She felt herself go airborne in sickening somersault fashion.

Her head hit the steps and she blanked out for a second, then she came back to reality in a flash as she tumbled down the stairs. A sharp pain seared through her left knee, then her neck, then—worst of all—her head again.

24

January 1, 2042 – Goodland, Kansas

"Wish we could ask you to join us, but it's our daughter's home up in Nebraska," their neighbor Earl said with gruff embarrassment to Ken and Marie. "They got kids, lots of 'em. There's just no room. You understand."

"Course we do," Ken and Marie said together. Then Marie: "We're just so grateful for all you and Sally have done for us this past month. Bless you, bless you both. We're just so sorry to see your own home suffer the same fate as ours."

They were standing on their neighbor's porch, *inside* the dome now, which, like every other dome around the world, had grown to twelve miles in diameter and covered 120 square miles of land. The dome was kicking all of them out whether they liked it or not. If Earl felt any resentment towards them about "their" dome having infringed on his property, he didn't let on about it.

As Earl headed off to pack for his new life in Nebraska, Ken and Marie looked at each other. "Well, what now?" Marie asked.

"Pack up the truck, I guess," Ken said. "Set the animals free. Let 'em fend for themselves as best they can."

"Most of them will die without our help."

"What else can we do? We can't bring 'em with us in the truck."

"What about us? What are we gonna do?"

"I've no idea," Ken said. "No idea at all."

*****

They packed their suitcases and a few remaining belongings into the truck. Sally surprised them with a shopping bag full of candy bars and beef jerky as they prepared to head out. Marie clutched her in her arms with tears in her eyes as they said their goodbyes. They'd been neighbors for over forty years, and they knew it was unlikely they'd ever see each other again.

It was a cold, snowy afternoon when they headed out. They couldn't resist swinging by their own snow-covered fields and visiting their own homestead one last time before passing through the dome wall and leaving it behind forever. The two of them had decided to head east towards Kansas City in the hopes of finding food and some kind of employment there. Kansas City was supposed to be dome-free, from what they'd heard, and any place without a dome was good enough for them.

Back roads brought them to I-70, then they headed east along the highway. At first they congratulated themselves on their choice of direction because the highway heading west was an absolute mess. They lost count of how many miles the traffic jam must have stretched in that direction.

"Would you look at that," Ken exclaimed in amazement. "There's no end to it."

But to their dismay, they discovered the same mess waiting for them up ahead. Near Grinnell, they hit the traffic jam of all traffic jams and realized they had some serious troubles of their own. The cars weren't just moving slowly—they weren't moving at all. As more cars and trucks came to a stop behind them, they found themselves sandwiched inside a parking lot of epic proportions. Horns blared, people cursed, but it made not a lick of difference because no one could go anywhere.

After two hours of waiting in an absolute standstill, they decided to follow the lead of a few other drivers in pickup trucks and four-wheel-drives who were heading off onto the grassy verge at the side of the highway. Just getting to the verge was no small feat, because every lane plus the paved shoulder was crammed with cars, but the verge itself was manageable—if you happened to have the right kind of vehicle for it, which they did.

They jounced and bounced their way forward across the grass for several miles, actually laughing at the absurdity of it, until they reached a bridge that crossed the highway. The bridge created an impassable barrier where the verge disappeared into guardrail and concrete.

That didn't stop some of the drivers ahead of them: they plowed over a mangled stretch of fence, forged into the snowy fields to the right of the highway, then headed straight up and over the bridge's grassy embankment and out of sight.

"If they can do it, so can we," said Ken.

"Go for it," said Marie. "How bad could it be?"

Pretty bad, as it turned out.

Their pickup's all-season tires weren't quite up to the task; they crabbed sideways up the embankment. Another vehicle trying to negotiate the same slope with even less success skidded into them sidewise. Marie gave a little whoop of surprise as her passenger side door dented in towards her.

They crested the top of the embankment and had little choice but to keep going because the same out-of-control vehicle that had already hit them once was crabbing sidewise right up behind them, horn blaring wildly.

They crossed the narrow exit road, which, in the split second he had to look, Ken saw was littered with stopped vehicles, and slid down the other side of the embankment only half in control. Ken worked the steering wheel like a pro and made it safely down the other side—only to slide into a heap of other vehicles at the bottom of the embankment. He hit the brakes but they did no good whatsoever at such a sharp angle over snow-covered grass.

They slid sideways into the next vehicle in line at the bottom of the embankment, coming to rest at right angles to the highway. The wildly out-of-control vehicle behind them finished the tableau when it collided into them from the other side. Marie gave another whoop of surprise, followed by a cry of pain as the passenger-side door crumpled into her shoulder.

"Are you all right?" Ken asked urgently. Marie nodded but winced in pain.

If they hadn't been stuck before, they were stuck now.

Ken had a weird instant of connection with the drivers on either side of him—the one he had crashed into and the one who had crashed into him. Both looked at him with an apologetic look that Ken returned in kind. There was nothing any of them could have done to avoid the disaster that had just played out. It was what you got for driving up and down a grassy embankment in the snow.

They were wedged in tightly, and as more four-wheel-drives came tilting over the embankment and slid into the ones that were already there, their quarters became even more cramped. They would be lucky if they could exit their vehicle at all, the way things were going. Marie's side was already crumpled beyond hope. Ken tried his door and found it wedged so tightly against the car next to him that he couldn't budge it.

Great. Just great.

The pickup's engine was still running, and it was so cold outside that he left it running for the heat.

He leaned over as best he could and examined Marie's right shoulder. It was badly bruised and bleeding but didn't appear to be dislocated, thank goodness. Marie insisted she was fine. "I'll just sit here for awhile and say a little prayer," she said. "Don't you worry about me."

Waiting for the police to arrive proved hopeless.

Hours later the engine conked out, plumb out of gas, and they remained tucked in tight inside their vehicular prison.

Ken finally managed to kick out the front windshield with the heel of his boot. It was surprisingly difficult to do and left him feeling worn out, as if he'd just finished a long stretch of work out in the fields.

Just getting Marie out of the pickup's front windshield with her tender shoulder was no easy matter. They clambered through and crawled over the hood, Ken dragging the shopping bag full of snacks behind him—but before he realized what was happening, most of the candy bars and beef jerky fell out of the bag and disappeared between the vehicles, instantly irretrievable.

Dammit!

Abandoning their truck, they retrieved their luggage and dragged it along behind them across the snowy field. That lasted all of five minutes before they realized they'd collapse with exhaustion if they didn't leave most of their stuff behind.

Throwing on as many layers as they could, they stuffed the few remaining items of food they had into their pockets, then headed off on foot along the highway. Thousands of others were doing the same as it became apparent the traffic jam was never going to end.

Night fell like a hammer blow. It started to snow again. Then the wind started to whistle, and what had felt cold before felt downright balmy compared to the true cold of a Kansas winter night.

They struggled forward like the thousands of others around them. They were somewhere past Grinnell but before Grainfield, names no one but local Kansans would know—and even they didn't know them well because they were nothing but tiny farming hamlets.

They picked their way past dead hulks of vehicles on the highway. The whole of I-70 was filled with cars and trucks and big rigs that would never move again. The vehicles were half-buried in the snow and looked like relics from the past.

"Where are we going?" Marie asked, shivering.

"I wish I knew," Ken replied. "What a miserable night."

At last they did what they saw other people doing and started checking car doors, looking for an abandoned vehicle in which they could take shelter. It was Marie who finally found an unlocked Honda Civic buried deep in the snow in the middle of the highway. They clambered in, both shivering, locked the doors, and huddled together for warmth. Ken tried the glove box and the visors and everywhere else he could think of to look but found no car keys.

"At least we're out of the wind," Marie whispered. Their teeth chattered and they could see their breath, but in time their body heat started to make a difference. The windows turned foggy and the world outside fell away as they drifted off into an uneasy sleep.

Ken dreamed of an endless stream of candy bars slipping through his fingers no matter how hard he tried to hold onto them.

25

January 1 – Pasadena, California

When Rachel's eyelids fluttered open, the three men were long gone and so was her car. She could see the spot where it had been parked through the front door, which had been left wide open. Her blouses and undergarments were strewn across the yard like so much debris after a hurricane. Her suitcase gaped open on the lawn with nothing left inside.

She saw all this—the empty driveway where her car should have been, her favorite blouses trampled into the grass—from a weird ninety-degree angle. She was lying in a heap at the bottom of the stairs.

She tried to get up and yowled with pain. Her head felt like jello and her left knee wouldn't support her weight.

She dropped back down in a puddle of despair and didn't move for awhile.

What time was it, anyway?

She saw light slanting in from the front door.

Slowly, Rachel untangled herself from herself and reached a sitting position on the stairs. Her brain felt like it was sloshing around inside her skull, and she kept blinking to avoid seeing double. Clearly she had suffered a concussion at the very least.

Amazingly her glasses were still intact. She wished she could say the same for her body.

She stood up, gingerly testing her left knee, and found she couldn't put any weight on it at all without wincing. Her knee had ballooned up to nearly twice its normal size. She was no doctor (well, she was, actually), but she didn't think that was a good sign.

Rachel sat back down and stared at her watch for a long time until the digital display came into focus. Up in the top right-hand corner was a tiny number "1."

She tried to piece things together. The dome had jumped on December 29th around 2 pm, she was sure of that much. She'd been busy packing on the 31st—New Year's Eve—when she'd taken her little tumble down the stairs around midnight, with the help of her new friends. She vaguely remembered coming to in a groggy sort of way in the middle of the night before going back to sleep because it simply hurt too much to stay awake. If the "1" on her watch was correct, then it meant the oxygen could run out at any time after 2 pm on this, the third day since the jump.

Her watch showed 3 pm.

Not good; not good at all.

No car, no working knee, and a head that felt like jello.

As soon as she realized the air could be running out—as soon as that thought entered her mind—it felt like she couldn't breathe.

It came to her that she'd be lucky to survive the next few hours. Her white whale seemed intent on killing her.

She tried to think. How big was the dome at this point? It had to be twelve miles in diameter by now. She knew the dome's center was at JPL, which was about five miles to the north, so if she headed *south* for a mile or so, she might be able to reach its southern edge in time. *Might* being the operable word.

First things first: she had to improvise a crutch. She hobbled over to the closet, head sloshing around like a swimming pool on a cruise ship during a storm at sea, and took a look around. The best she could come up with was a golf club from her abortive attempt at picking up a new hobby. She drew the three wood out of the golf bag, tossed away the head cover, and used the head as a handle. It was more like a cane than a crutch, but it would have to do.

She began hobbling down the driveway in an attempt to walk her way out of the dome, but she only made it as far as the end of the driveway before realizing it was hopeless. Her knee kept screaming at her to stop. She backtracked up the driveway. Who knew knees could scream?

Inside the garage was her bike. Maybe she could *coast* out of the dome. She punched in the code for the garage. Nothing. It took her nearly a minute with her doubled vision to make sure she hit the right keys the second time—and still nothing.

Shit. The power was off.

The white whale snickered at her.

Rachel limp-hopped through the front door, then into the garage, head protesting with each hop. At least the criminals hadn't stolen her bike. It made her wonder what they *had* stolen. But she hardly cared at this point; having only a few hours to live had a way of focusing your mind on the things that really mattered.

Could she ride with her bum leg? She guessed she was about to find out.

She pulled the manual release and somehow managed to push the garage door up and open. It felt like an Olympic-level event for concussives. She literally had to sit down on the pavement afterwards to rest.

Then it was limp-hop, limp-hop, limp-hop over to the bike.

She swore the air felt as thin as a sheet of paper.

With great effort she managed to straddle the bike.

This could go really well or really poorly.

Tentatively she pushed off with her good leg and let the bike gain some momentum down the driveway. The pedals had straps, so she was able to put her right foot into the strap and leave her left foot dangling.

There was really no decision to be made at that point: she *had* to go downhill because she could barely pedal with one functional leg. Since *downhill* was to the east, she went east, waiting and watching for her chance to turn south—the direction she really wanted to go.

Rachel could sense the dome far above her head and could actually see the dome's wall curving downward about a mile south of her. Turning her head to look in that direction made her realize just how stiff her neck was on top of everything else. But at least she was heading east on California Boulevard, and that was a start. The boulevard had the good graces to stay flat, which meant her one-legged peddling could be kept to a minimum. It was also enormously helpful to her head that the ride over the pavement was as smooth as, well, pavement.

The bike wheels clicked with comforting familiarity as she let gravity do the work. Her path took her towards Huntington Hospital. Maybe she should pop in for a check-up. Ha! But who was she kidding? No one would be there at this late date. *She* wouldn't be here at this late date, if she'd had any choice in the matter.

At last she found a road heading south that was flat and held promise. Pasadena Avenue. Perfect.

She turned as carefully as she could—maybe a little too carefully, because she lost momentum, and her bum leg couldn't compensate like it should have, and her front wheel started wobbling like crazy, and the next thing she knew she lost control and crashed.

Excruciating blinding pain.

And deep rumbling laughter from below. Or above. She couldn't tell which.

*****

The sunlight had faded and she was shivering with what felt like ague by the time she regained consciousness. She looked at her watch, or tried to, but the numbers kept swimming in front of her eyes like a kaleidoscope. After a full minute of staring, she was pretty sure it still said "1" for the date—thank God—but now it was after 5 pm. Which meant it had been three days plus another three hours since the jump.

Why wasn't she dead yet?

Maybe because, as the domes got bigger with each jump, it took a little longer to expel all the oxygen. Which was a good thing if you happened to be Dr. Rachel Cavanaugh and found yourself stuck inside a dome on what was now the beginning of the fourth day and counting.

Did the air seem even thinner now? Oh yes indeed it did. Her lungs were having to work hard now just to take a breath. She was on Everest time, 28,000 feet and climbing.

Her bike was still in good shape—her crash had been about as gentle as a crash could be—but even the thought of trying to ride it again made her nauseous. She couldn't afford a third concussion: another fall, no matter how gentle, would kill her.

She looked around at her surroundings and realized she was less than a block away from Huntington Hospital. Two tan towers rose up ahead of her, connected by an elevated pedestrian walkway. A sudden thought came to her, and she began crawling towards the two towers. Her left knee howled in protest, but she gritted her teeth and ignored it.

She crept on all fours—well, all threes, actually—all the way to the emergency room entrance between the two towers. As she'd expected, no one was there. All of Pasadena had emptied out long since. But *someone* had been here since the jump: the front door was smashed to smithereens. She could see a baseball bat leaning next to the shattered door.

Glass shards littered the entryway like confetti. She crawled over them as carefully as she could, but slivers stuck into her palms and knees anyway; it seemed like a small annoyance compared to everything else that was going wrong with her. The fact that her burning lungs were starting to outweigh all of her other injuries combined was definitely cause for concern.

Probably a drug addict had bashed in the doors, she decided with hazy logic as she crept through the entrance. That would make sense. Speaking of drugs, she could go for some painkillers right about now. Anything to numb the pain before the end, because the end was definitely coming.

Someone had told her once that it wasn't one mistake that did you in, but rather a series of two or three mistakes compounded. Neglecting to lock her front door and getting tossed down the stairs like a human hackysack had been mistake number one. Trying to ride a bike with a concussion and a bum leg had been mistake number two. Crawling into an abandoned hospital as oxygen deprivation set in was beginning to look like mistake number three, the fatal one.

But *some* part of Rachel's brain must still be trying to function. She had thought of *something* earlier on, just outside the hospital, but what had it been? She lay in the Emergency Room lobby staring up at the ceiling, trying to remember.

Where was she? She felt herself fade in and out of consciousness. The white whale was pulling her down deeper.

She swam towards the surface by sheer force of will. No! She wasn't ready to give up yet.

And that was when it hit her: *Oxygen!* There were canisters of oxygen in hospitals.

Now all she had to do was find one in time.

*****

She needed to find a respiratory ward. Those usually had oxygen. She crawled towards the elevators, forced herself to her feet (or rather foot), and stared at the signage until it went from double to single print. There it was: Pulmonary / Respiratory Services: East Tower, 3rd floor.

Climbing the stairs felt impossible in her current condition, so she jabbed at the elevator "Up" button instead. To her surprise, the elevator dinged and opened; it must still be working on emergency generator power. She hobbled in and stabbed at the circular button with the "3" on it. It looked like "33" to her eyes. She sank back down onto the floor.

Ding! Third floor!

The doors opened. She crawled out, the doors closing on her bum knee before she could get clear. Yowling in pain, she found yet another reason to crave some painkillers. Dragging her way forward on hands and one knee, she made it past the elevator monster that was trying to kill her.

The next few…what? minutes? hours?...passed in a delirium of half-dreams and visions of oxygen plums dancing in her head. She awoke and slept, awoke and slept, and whenever she awoke she crawled as far as she could towards the respiratory ward before blacking out again. After an indeterminate length of time, she reached the nurses' station and dug through the top two drawers of the desk until she found a set of keys.

Dragging herself around the respiratory ward, she searched in vain for a utility room with even one oxygen canister. The fact that she had to reach up and try to put a key into a lock with double vision and about ten different keys from which to choose just about killed her, but she kept at it. Who knew she had such a strong will to live? She hadn't known it herself until now.

At last her determination paid off. She unlatched a door and discovered what felt like the equivalent of King Tut's tomb: an entire utility room full of compressed canisters of oxygen!

One canister was already in a portable cart, all set to go. In a near paroxysm of joy she fit the cannula to her nostrils and opened the cylinder valve to full.

Pure bliss.

She had died and gone to heaven. Or rather, she had *not* died and gone to heaven.

She set the tank to maximum air flow and still wished for more. The canister was meant to supplement breathing, not replace breathable air altogether—but after the oxygen deprivation she'd just been through, even a reduced flow of air felt like a miracle.

Her eyes roamed the room, taking in dozens of oxygen canisters—and this time it wasn't the double vision talking, they were really there—two storage racks filled with E cylinders. She figured each canister would provide her with about five hours of oxygen at maximum flow (something she knew from her time spent inside airless domes of late). The fact that her brain was trying to calculate just how long those canisters would last was an encouraging sign. It meant that, concussion or no, her cognitive abilities were still functioning.

She felt the white whale receding into the depths, biding its time. It wasn't done with her yet. But then again, she wasn't done with it, either.

*****

The next six days were the strangest of her life. She was stuck on the third floor of an empty hospital inside an empty city inside an empty dome, knowing she was the only person alive for miles around. There was no one else to talk to, so she talked to the white whale and it talked back.

Over time, she found crutches and wheelchairs and bandages and pain meds, so it turned out there were worse places in which to be stuck than a hospital. Percocet to the rescue!

The bottle's warning label read, "Percocet should only be taken in the manner prescribed by your doctor." Well, *she* was a doctor—a doctor of astrophysics, but hey, why split hairs? No other doctor inside this mausoleum of a hospital was going to contradict her, so she went ahead and prescribed herself a full dose. It made her loopy, but loopy was good—loopy was a big step up from dead. The worst of the pain went away, and even the white whale seemed to enjoy it.

She lived a strange half-life for the next several days, tied to oxygen canisters for life support and never quite feeling like she had enough air to breathe. She changed out the nasal cannula for a mask and still couldn't get enough. If she fell asleep and the canister ran out, she jerked awake, clawing at her throat for air. It was like the worst case of sleep apnea ever recorded in history. She always kept another canister within easy reach, ready to go—her cold metal security blanket.

At night the hospital glowed with red emergency lighting. She slept as much as she could through those red hours, praying she would wake again the next morning. On what she guessed was the third night, the red lights suddenly flickered out. The hospital's backup generator must have died, leaving her in total darkness.

She panicked: she couldn't see a thing! Even with the oxygen mask on, she gasped for breath out of raw, uncontrollable fear. She had no flashlight, no way to see! When the oxygen canister finally ran out in the middle of the night, as she knew it would, she was able, with trembling fingers, to exchange one canister for another by feel alone.

When morning arrived and the first meager light of day trickled in through the windows, her first order of business was tracking down a flashlight. She ended up collecting three of them from different nurses' stations, determined never to be so blind and helpless again.

With the generator off, the building became even more tomblike. She despaired of ever getting out. Maybe she was dead already and just didn't know it.

Her double vision improved after a few days, although she still felt seriously concussed. Her bum knee was even less cooperative: it remained swelled to nearly double its usual size, and she found she could put no weight on it at all without grimacing in pain. At first she used a collapsible wheelchair to get around the third floor, cradling an oxygen canister in her lap like a giant baby. Then she began using a rolling oxygen cart as a kind of crutch and found that that worked better. Each day she made several short trips around the third floor for water and bathroom breaks. The glug-glug-glug of the water cooler made a strange music to her ears as it filled the empty plastic bottles she'd managed to dig out of the recycling bin.

Food was her only other necessity. She used one of her empty oxygen canisters to smash the glass of a vending machine on the third floor and subsisted on chips, candy bars, and peanut M&Ms.

After six days and nights of this bizarre existence, she found herself down to her last five canisters of oxygen, with only one day left until the next jump (assuming there was one). Would five canisters be enough? It was going to be close.

It dawned on her that she might be the only person alive who had ever survived ten whole days inside a dome. If she were lucky and the dome jumped again, then oxygen in the form of good old-fashioned breathable air should come flooding back in, kickstarting the whole process over again. If she were unlucky and the dome *didn't* jump, then she was in serious trouble. She could *try* to hop down three flights of emergency stairs with a concussed head while dragging a portable oxygen canister behind her, but it didn't sound easy, and then she would have to pray the canister lasted long enough for her to make it to the southern edge of the dome.

The Percocet kept her feeling more relaxed than she would have otherwise. Of *course* she would get out of this little scrape. Of *course* she would live. She curled up beside her oxygen canister lover and drifted off to sleep for another endless night.

JUMP 13

January 8, 2042

Unlucky number thirteen lived up to its reputation. The thirteenth jump had catastrophic effects worldwide, resulting in the displacement or death of untold billions.

The total number of merged domes worldwide now stood at roughly 60,000. Each dome was some 24 miles in diameter and over 1 mile tall, encompassing an incredible 484 square miles of land.

On a planet with roughly 57 million square miles of land all told (not counting land under the oceans), the as yet unseen aliens now controlled 29 million square miles of it, as compared to the humans' 28 million square miles—which meant the aliens now had what might be called a controlling interest in Earth.

Did they intend to take over the whole planet or only half of it? The domes already "owned" nearly 51% of Earth's total land mass—the very definition of a hostile takeover in corporate terms. Was it possible these aliens were applying this same sort of logic to the planet as a whole?

26

January 8, 2042 – Oval Office, Philadelphia

The President's face was drained of all color. "These numbers can't be correct. They just can't." He looked like he might be sick.

Bill Cohen, his Secretary of Defense, stared at him solemnly. "I'm afraid they are, sir."

"Twenty million! You're saying twenty million Americans lost their lives this past week—and that was *before* today's jump?"

"That's our best estimate. Some died inside the domes, but the vast majority died *outside* of them this time around—from exposure to freezing temperatures, illness, starvation, violence, and a myriad other causes."

"Good Lord. And how many more are projected to die after *today's* jump?"

"We're reluctant to put a number on it, sir."

"Just give me your best estimate. I know you have one, Bill."

Cohen struggled to meet the President's eyes. "We estimate another eighty million. Additional deaths. Here in America."

"Eighty—. On top of the twenty million from before. You're telling me a quarter of the population of America could be dead in a matter of days."

"Yes, sir—assuming *any* of us survive. If the domes jump again ten days from now, all bets are off. Only survivalists may make it after that. These estimates assume no more jumps after the one that happened earlier today. Otherwise…"

"Jesus." The President buried his face in his hands and remained silent for a long time. "What are we talking about worldwide?" he mumbled through his fingers.

"On the order of two or three billion, if we had to hazard a guess, but there's no real way of knowing."

The President shook his head, looking impossibly weary. "All right, Bill, thanks." He waved him out.

"I'm sorry, sir."

"Not your fault, Bill."

As Bill headed out the door, the President sat down on the couch, or rather collapsed onto it, and closed his eyes. He sat there for a long time trying to forget what he'd just heard. "Shit," he whispered. "*Shit.*"

For once he was alone and no one tried to talk him out of his depression, which ran deeper than anyone suspected. He poured himself a stiff drink and downed it in one gulp.

"I'm in a fake Oval Office in a skyscraper in downtown Philadelphia," he said out loud to no one. "Nothing about this is real."

No one contradicted him.

"I think I may be fake, too. A cardboard cutout of a President."

If Gil Lametti were here, he'd tell him to buck up, not take all those deaths so personally, maybe even grow a pair. Actually, what Gil would say was, "Jesus, Mark, don't wig out on me!" But Lametti wasn't here. He was meeting with some congressional committee about something or other. Whatever it was, it didn't matter much anymore as far as Mark Gardner, fiftieth President of the United States, was concerned.

Last year, after a botched rescue mission *he* had ordered, in which five U.S. Marines had died, he'd had to look each family member in the eyes in turn and tell them how sorry he was. Now, he tried multiplying those five Marines by four million to arrive at the twenty million Americans now presumed dead, but it was an impossible feat—he couldn't even begin to wrap his mind around it.

He'd dreamt about those Marines the very same night after their deaths. They'd stared at him from the same contorted positions in which they'd died, inside the wreckage of their crashed helicopter. They hadn't looked accusatory, just sad. He wondered if he'd dream of twenty million sets of eyes staring down at him tonight. Would they look accusatory, or just sad?

He thought of a fragment of a poem by William Butler Yeats he'd had to memorize back in his college days. He spoke it aloud now to an empty Oval Office situated inside the tallest skyscraper in Philadelphia.

> *"Things fall apart; the centre cannot hold;*
> *Mere anarchy is loosed upon the world,*
> *The blood-dimmed tide is loosed, and everywhere*
> *The ceremony of innocence is drowned;*
> *The best lack all conviction, while the worst*
> *Are full of passionate intensity."*

Funny how he could still remember those lines after all these years. "The centre cannot hold," he said to himself again. He poured himself another, downing it in one go, then cut himself off. Two was enough for now. He had a press conference in fifteen minutes, and it wouldn't do for him to show up drunk—or for the White House press corps to know he was an actual human being who could be just as depressed as any other person in this world. They didn't want to know that, and he didn't want to tell them.

27

January 8 – Pasadena, California

Rachel didn't need an announcement over the hospital's loudspeaker to know when the dome jumped: she could feel the whoosh of air rushing in. Her ears actually popped! She tore off the oxygen mask and took her first deep breath in a week.

Talk about your simple pleasures!

She wasted no time saying goodbye to the hospital; she was more than ready to go. Stuffed in her two jacket pockets were a prescription bottle of Percocet and enough bags of peanut M&Ms to keep herself fed for a week. Her last half-full canister of oxygen she left behind; it was too awkward to carry down the stairs, and she shouldn't need it anyway going forward. Her plan was to get out of the dome and get out fast.

With the elevator no longer functioning, she had to limp down the emergency stairs one slow step at a time until she reached the lobby. Then she claimed one of the wheelchairs waiting near the hospital entrance and wheeled herself out of there like a lunatic escaping an insane asylum. She knew the hospital had saved her life, but that didn't make her any more fond of it.

No more half-breaths for her! She gulped the air, savoring it as if it were the nectar of the gods (and maybe it was).

Out on the street, she noticed the palm trees were missing their fronds. They looked like rows of pillars from a forgotten temple of old. The grass had turned a sickly brown. A week without oxygen would do that, she guessed.

She returned to the spot where her bicycle had crashed. It was still laying there (of course it was, since no one else was in here to mess with it), but she ignored it and continued wheeling herself down Pasadena Avenue in her wheelchair. Eventually she cut over on Bellefontaine to Fair Oaks and continued south. She was amazed at how fast she could go, now that she had actual air to breathe.

She followed Fair Oaks for a good mile. The avenue was broad, with two lanes each way and a red-brick median down the middle. Palms and southern magnolias grew alongside the road—usually a beautiful sight, but all dead now. The whole area looked dead, in fact. Restaurants were shuttered, businesses boarded up, parking lots vacant.

"The Apoc l pse is here," one sign with several of its letters missing read outside a restaurant, and she half believed it. A car had crashed head-on into a telephone pole adjacent to the sign, as if to bear witness to the fact. The dead occupants were still inside; Rachel could tell that much from a glance.

She saw no living persons in Pasadena but plenty of dead ones. They were scattered about randomly—a lone body here in the middle of a parking lot, another one there with his back propped up against the façade of an urban sweat lodge. One woman rested against the bole of a tree as if she were taking a nap, but the crow cawing on top of her head seemed to suggest otherwise. An older couple sat in rocking chairs on their front porch, heads canted towards one another; maybe they'd made a suicide pact and drunk poisoned lemonade together on the count of three. Two children in flowered dresses lay facedown on a brown lawn, unmoving. If they were playing at being dead, they were doing a really good job of it. A dog also appeared to be playing dead next to them.

More bodies of people and pets were visible on the side streets she passed, but she had no desire to look any closer. She pictured her own body lying prone next to her bicycle after the crash and knew just how close she'd come to being one of them.

The further south she went, the more crashes she saw. Drivers must have been trying to escape the dome when they went into hypoxic shock. One Buick was buried deep inside a Winchell's Donut House. Other crashes were far less spectacular, amounting to little more than fender-benders, but their occupants had fared no better for all that. They sat inside with their mouths agape as if they couldn't believe their fate. A few had managed to open their front doors and were draped across the seats or curled up on the pavement below, but that was about as far as they had gotten. She could picture them gasping for air, clutching at their throats, opening their doors in a last-ditch attempt to find more oxygen, but she knew better than anyone how doomed those attempts were.

Eventually Fair Oaks became so jammed with vehicles she could no longer proceed in her wheelchair. Some trucks had smashed violently into the cars ahead of them, as if their drivers had tried to force their way through the traffic jam. The pushed cars sat askew or even sideways to the road. Nearly every vehicle was vacant. Many had their front doors open, as if their owners had made a mad dash for the exits and hadn't bothered closing them. Rachel guessed that that was exactly what had happened; the dome wall from before today's jump must have been just up ahead.

Curiosity got the better of her: she hobbled forward on foot as best she could, picking her way through the press of vehicles and using them as impromptu crutches along the way. Eventually she came to the spot where the dome wall must have stood earlier this morning, before the jump. The line of demarcation was as visible as if it had been marked out with chalk—except in this case the "chalk" was piles of dead bodies. The bodies as a whole made a bend that mirrored where the dome wall itself had stood.

Just up ahead, maybe twenty feet or so, she could see another pile of bodies bending the *other* way. These bodies curved away from her, as if they were mirroring a second dome that had stood close to the first but hadn't quite merged.

Eventually she pieced it all together: before today's jump, two domes must have stood close together but not quite touching—no doubt the Glendale Dome and the JPL Dome. All the dead she was seeing must have gotten squeezed into a narrow corridor between the two domes. No doubt they had come rushing out of each dome in an absolute panic as the air had run out. The sheer crush of humanity must have resulted in a terrible chokepoint. Most of them had probably been electrocuted on the spot as they got shoved back against the very dome wall from which they had just emerged.

She took in the awful prospect. Just to her right was a yellow sign announcing "Dead End"—literally true now, as the side street in question was strewn with dead bodies. No doubt it had been a pleasant enough side street back in the day, with neat homes and tidy lawns, but now it looked like an apocalyptic nightmare. Most of the homes had been burnt to the ground, and the trees that had stood in front of them appeared to have been chopped down for firewood. A pall of smoke hung in the air. Bodies were strewn everywhere, drooped over the railings of half-burnt porches, curled up in fetal positions on sidewalks, sprawled face-down atop trampled lawns. Her nose twitched. The whole place stank to high heaven—although heaven had nothing to do with it. This was the work of some devil from down below.

On some of the lawns she spied piles of bones stacked near impromptu fire pits. In one pit she could see a cat's tail, but no cat, protruding from a fire ring. Other remains near other fire pits looked distressingly like dogs. She saw one or two scorched dog collars with no dogs inside and decided she'd seen enough for one day. Unbidden, a picture formed in her mind of survivors at their wits' end, reduced to eating cats and dogs and squirrels and rats in order to stave off starvation.

At least the crows were happy: hundreds were hopping about the area. Rachel didn't want to look too closely at what they were doing, nor did she want to focus too much on the feral dogs and cats helping themselves to the same bounty. She could hardly blame the poor creatures: turnabout was fair play.

It suddenly became crystal clear to her that she should stop heading south. South meant heading deeper into the chaos that was once L.A. Desperate urban survivalists were not the sort of people she wanted to be running into just now. She'd headed south mostly on autopilot, because that was where the nearest dome wall had been when she'd been trying to escape a week ago—but that logic no longer applied. *North* was the way to go, away from L.A. and towards the Angeles National Forest.

Another thought dawned on her quite suddenly: when the two domes had merged earlier this morning, only *one* of them would have survived. The Glendale Dome, most likely, since Glendale had a higher population than Pasadena and was closer to L.A. If so, the JPL Dome—her white whale—was no more.

Of course, the Glendale Dome would have a diameter of some twenty-four *miles* by now—so it would be big enough to encompass both her old home and lab even from its center in Glendale. She did some quick mental calculations and estimated the north end of the dome wall must be some *eighteen miles* from where she now stood.

There was no way she was going to wheel herself eighteen miles, much of it uphill, in a wheelchair. Clearly she needed a car.

Luckily for her, she had plenty to choose from—a whole traffic jam's worth of them. All she had to do was find one near the back of the pack, preferably one without a dead body inside. With so many air-deprived people having made a last-minute dash for the dome wall, Rachel felt sure she'd find any number of cars with the keys still inside.

She hobbled back the way she had come and dropped into her wheelchair with a sigh. As she sat there catching her breath, she noticed a few intruders already sniffing around some of the local homes and businesses. So—some of them *had* survived, and now they found themselves inside the jump zone—probably the same ones who'd been willing to eat rats. She wanted nothing to do with them, nor they with her.

Wheeling herself towards the back of the traffic jam, she reached the last few cars and began peering inside. All were empty.

In the end she chose a Lexus RX with the key fob still inside and an almost full tank of gas. Hey, why not travel in style at the end of the world?

She pushed the start button. The Lexus hummed to life, and for the first time in a long while, Rachel smiled.

Eighteen miles in a wheelchair might have been a big deal, but eighteen miles in a Lexus was nothing but a joyride. She had to weave around a few dead bodies lying in the road, but other than that the drive through Pasadena was a breeze.

She decided to stop at her old homestead first. She needed clothes and whatever valuables might have been left behind by the intruders after they'd finished ransacking the place. The good news was, she knew something they did not: there was a stash of cash and other valuables tucked away inside a safe in the basement, concealed behind a pile of flattened moving boxes. No intruder ever would have thought to look there, which was exactly why she had hidden the safe in that spot in the first place. She would need those valuables going forward if she was going to survive the next few weeks.

Pulling into her driveway—home sweet home—she hobbled down to the basement one slow step at a time and found the safe intact. She carried it upstairs even more slowly, placing it inside the trunk of the Lexus and making sure to lock the vehicle this time around. Then she packed a suitcase full of clothes and toiletries up in her bedroom. Otherwise there wasn't much to bother with, except a small collection of gold and silver jewelry hidden away in a shoebox in her closet where the intruders hadn't thought to look. They had made a mess of everything else in the house, but who cared? She wasn't planning on coming back anyway.

*****

On her way out of town, she passed her former laboratory at JPL. Being the curious scientist she was and always would be, she couldn't resist popping in for a final look around. Limping over to the lab door, she tried her electronic badge and found it didn't work, but her physical key did. Once inside, she hobbled over to where the ovate had been—and found nothing but ash and the remains of a scorched metal truss. The ovate was gone, reduced to a thick pile of dust on the floor.

So—her white whale really *was* gone. She rejoiced for reasons of her own, even though she knew there were plenty of other white whales out there to worry about—

including the one whose belly she happened to be in right now. That thought catapulted her into action. She hurried as fast as her bum leg would carry her back to the car and peeled out of the parking lot.

Before long she came to a junction and had a decision to make. To the northwest was undomed Santa Clarita, considered a safe haven, but she suspected it would be mobbed with people by now. To the northeast was the Angeles Crest Highway, a thin snake of a road that climbed into the San Gabriel Mountains for some sixty-five miles before depositing you more or less in the middle of absolute nowhere. Her gut instincts told her to go that way—away from people—and so she did.

After several minutes of twisting and turning along the winding roads, she saw what she had been expecting to see for some time now: the shimmering wall of a dome.

"Hallelujah!" she breathed. She drove through the dome wall—out of the belly of the beast—at seventy miles per hour, just for the hell of it, whooping all the way.

28

January 11 – Dorrance, Kansas

Ken Stubbs' beer belly was long gone. Looking down, he could barely recognize himself anymore—he could even see his own feet. Normally that would have been a good thing (his doctor would have been so proud), except in this case he'd lost the weight because he and Marie were starving.

He'd gone from fat to gaunt, and Marie, who had been thin to begin with, looked downright emaciated. Kansas, it turned out, wasn't America's breadbasket after all, at least not in the depths of winter when you were on foot with nowhere to go.

They might have been able to eat raw corn or wheat from the fields at a different time of year. They could have soaked the wheat grains in water long enough to make them chewable and digestible—but there was nothing growing at this time of year. The only crop was snow.

He thought of the animals they'd freed and wished for two of his horses back. If wishes were horses....On horseback they could have made it to Kansas City by now. Plus, you could eat a horse, if worse came to worst. The only thing cars were good for at this point was temporary shelter at night—and without gas there was no heat to warm them up, only the slim protection of the exterior to shield them from the worst of the elements.

They moved east, always east, during the day, past an endless cavalcade of vehicles frozen in place as if by a spell. The town of Salina was somewhere up ahead, but who knew how far? It wasn't much of a city, but it was better than nothing.

They averaged eight or nine miles per day, picking their way through a minefield of cars and semis and—increasingly—dead bodies. Maybe they could have done better if Marie had been in better health, but her shoulder continued to bother her, and her toes were frostbitten, and her heels covered in blisters. She wasn't used to walking long distances, and her shoes were the wrong sort for hiking anyway. She'd assumed she'd be arriving by pickup truck in Kansas City a few hours after they'd left, not trudging through the snow along the highway margins day after day like vagabonds.

They were shivering and coughing and half-lame to boot, and their food was all gone. Ken kept dreaming about those candy bars that had slipped through his fingers. He'd never been one to have recurring nightmares, but seeing that food fall out of the bag and between the cars had stuck with him somehow. The hungrier he got, the more he dreamt about it.

The snow served them as water now. Food was whatever crumbs they could get from others out of charity. They had literally nothing left to their name—and they were just two among thousands in the same awful predicament.

On the eighth day, they had come to Hays and had stayed the night in a Walmart Supercenter near the edge of town. The Walmart had been swept clean of all merchandise. It was like sleeping in an airport hangar it was so empty—except for all the people, that is. It was stocked with plenty of those, hundreds upon hundreds of them, all coughing and starving and sick. They'd slept in the aisles where shopping carts had once held sway.

Hays itself had been raided by so many other footsore travelers before them that nothing remained except the empty husks of old buildings. They'd passed a McDonald's, an Applebee's, and an Old Chicago Pizza—just the names were enough to make them drool—but one glance told them all they needed to know: these establishments had long since given up the ghost.

Pushing on past Hays, they'd hoped to find more civilization in Russell, but two days later their hopes had been dashed yet again. The detour off the highway just to get to Russell had been grueling enough, but to find it deserted was even worse.

Where was everyone? Where was FEMA? Where were the Red Cross and the Salvation Army and Feeding America and dozens of other charitable organizations? It felt to him like the people of Kansas had been abandoned to their fate and good riddance. One part of his mind told him that was unfair—that the entire country was one big Kansas right now, and that the scope of the disaster was so huge that no organization could cover it or be everywhere at once—but to have walked nearly a hundred miles and seen not one refugee camp or homeless shelter was hard to accept. On the other hand, he had to admit that they were in the middle of absolute nowhere right now, and that it would have been next to impossible for any charitable organization to have gotten here, given the atrocious conditions of the interstate.

He'd never realized before just how *big* Kansas was until he'd had to cross it on foot. He'd never thought of Kansas City as being all that far away from Goodland—just four hundred miles or so!—but *walking* that distance was a whole different matter than driving it. They might as well have been trying to walk to the Moon.

Marie mumbled psalms to herself as she shuffled forward on the eleventh day of their seemingly endless journey. She rubbed her bruised shoulder over and over again like a talisman. Ken propped her up whenever she stumbled, which was more and more often lately.

He quietly cursed—not God, but himself, for all the stupid mistakes he'd made. Why hadn't he brought more food? (Because he'd thought they'd be in Kansas City on the same day they'd set out, a voice said inside his head.) Why hadn't he gone north or south instead of east? (Because there was even *less* civilization in those directions, the voice said.) And why had he dropped those damned candy bars? (Because he was an idiot, the voice admitted.)

He figured they had maybe two or three days left before they simply keeled over and died from exhaustion by the side of the road. They'd have plenty of company, that was for sure. But he hoped against hope they'd make it to Salina before then.

As if to demonstrate just how bad things had gotten, Marie suddenly toppled sideways without warning and lay flat on her back in the breakdown lane. The snow turned red near her head where she'd hit the pavement on the way down. Ken was instantly by her side, calling her name and patting her on the cheek to try and revive her. "Marie, Marie!" he said. "Marie." He listened for breath sounds and heard none, tried to feel for a pulse and felt none.

He wept by the side of the road when she didn't open her eyes.

She was gone.

He carried her into the snow-covered field by the side of the road and laid her down, then laid himself down beside her, encircled her in his arms, and slept. Or tried to sleep. His emotions were too overwrought for that.

Instead, his mind wandered in a million different directions, finally settling on that tiny mouse that had saved him all those months ago. That mouse had shown him the way out of the dome when it was still barely the size of a yurt. No doubt the little fella was dead by now, suffocated by the dome when it ran out of air after one of its many jumps. That didn't sound like such a bad fate to Ken anymore as he lay there shivering beside his wife. He was tired of the struggle, tired of the cold, tired of the constant deprivation and hunger. Sleep was about the only thing that sounded good to him anymore.

Eventually he did drift off to sleep. He dreamt of candy bars as usual, except this time he caught one as it floated down like manna from heaven. He grabbed it in his hand and devoured it in three bites. Another appeared and he devoured it, too, and then another. Suddenly things didn't seem so bad anymore.

His wife woke up and he said, "Have a bite," and she did. Marie smiled her lovely smile and said, "That tastes good," and he nodded and held her hand and looked up to the heavens as candy bars drifted down like snow all around them.

The cold was brutal that night. He never woke from his dream and didn't mind at all.

29

January 12 – Truth or Consequences, New Mexico

Will's U-Haul job only lasted three weeks, then the flow of people who could afford U-Hauls slowed to a trickle before grinding to an abrupt halt. Moving one's possessions had suddenly become something only the ultra-wealthy did. These days, if you got out of a city alive, you were doing well, and if you had a car filled with luggage and a few cardboard boxes, you were thriving.

Fortunately Will was able to pick up work at a farm co-operative on the outskirts of town. Food deliveries from the outside had become so unreliable that the townspeople had decided to grow their own crops and fend for themselves. Will's job was to keep the books that showed who grew what, whose parcels were whose, which vegetables were bartered for which, and a hundred other small accounting tasks.

To supplement his meager salary, Cynthia worked out in the fields themselves growing winter vegetables. Her hands turned raw and blistered at first, then callused as she became used to the work. She hoed and weeded by hand, waiting impatiently to see the results of her labor. Her "salary" was a share of the grains and vegetables that would eventually be harvested.

More and more people were finding agriculture was where the jobs were at these days. Anyone with gardening experience was considered valuable and put to work. Even those without a green thumb could do grunt work and earn enough to avoid starvation. The town had tractors and harvesters and such, but gas had become too precious for such mundane tasks. Human muscle was cheaper, and plenty of people were desperate for work.

The town was fortunate to be situated near Elephant Butte Reservoir, a dammed section of the Rio Grande River, so water supply wasn't an issue, but getting it where it needed to be in the newly tilled fields surrounding town was a major undertaking. Laying irrigation pipe was an ongoing project, one that Cynthia and her fellow laborers pitched in to help with each day.

The other big employer in town was security. An extensive concrete wall topped with razor wire was being erected around the town center. Hundreds of laborers were working on various parts of the wall at once. Towers were being built at regular intervals where sharpshooters could stand watch. The four entrances to town, one at each cardinal point of the compass, were to be barred each night, with no one getting in or out after dusk. Once it was finished, the townspeople would effectively be living inside an armed compound, but at least they would be safe.

All roads leading into and out of town had already been heavily barricaded, with armed guards authorized to shoot if people tried to force their way past. The guards let individuals and families in on a case-by-case basis, especially if they happened to possess valuable skills like construction work or nursing, but anyone who waved a gun or blustered too much was turned away. A bullet whizzing by the ear seemed to work wonders.

A much bigger problem was the roving gangs of armed marauders who were growing more brazen by the day.

They had already successfully raided the town on several occasions. Invariably these raids came from the direction of I-25. The marauders would barrel towards town in heavy-duty pickup trucks, firing wildly as they drew nearer, forcing people to scatter, then loot stores and houses before making their getaway.

In response to these ongoing raids, the town council finally decided to bulldoze the two closest I-25 highway exits into oblivion. Once the exit lanes had been reduced to rubble, vehicular traffic from I-25 came to a sudden halt, and foot traffic reduced to a trickle. Anyone still finding their way into town tended to come via Highway 51 to the east, and that back road was heavily patrolled.

The council's final security decision was its most controversial: they decided to raze those parts of town closest to I-25 to keep them from becoming bases for roving bands of criminals. No amount of pleading from local residents with homes in those parts was enough to sway town leaders. The displaced were granted more humble quarters inside the walled parts of town, and if they didn't like it, they could leave. None left: they knew what awaited them on the outside if they did.

In such a fashion, Truth or Consequences sealed itself off from the outside world and became a kingdom unto itself. It was a feudal castle in modern times, offering protection in return for what amounted to serfdom for the majority of its inhabitants. But there wasn't a single occupant in town who didn't consider himself or herself lucky to be a serf in this modern age of the domes.

30

January 13 – Charlottesville, Virginia

"I *love* this place," Royce exclaimed. He was standing on the porch of a rambling three-bedroom ranch on the outskirts of Charlottesville. "I still can't believe you found it so quickly."

Aubrey shrugged. "It was simple, really. The house was in foreclosure after the couple that lived here died." (She didn't have to say *how* they died—that went without saying these days.) "Then it went to auction. All I did was submit the winning bid at firesale prices. Not many people are buying homes these days—at least not ones located inside a potential jump zone."

"Cowards."

"We have *you* to thank, of course—that gold of yours keeps going up in value. Less than half of it was enough for the bank to say yes. We got this place for a song." Aubrey stared out at the view from their porch with a look of deep satisfaction on her face.

They remained silent for a time, savoring the sunset. "Moving in certainly was a breeze," Royce said eventually.

"One of the unexpected benefits of having no belongings. I *do* miss my shoes, though."

"You make them sound like your children."

"They are...or were. I miss them every time I walk into one of those empty walk-in closets. But on the plus side, the house is big enough for all of us—and you were even able to build a crib for Dominique. Who knew you could be so handy?"

"Hey, I'm handy." Royce let his hands roam a bit to show just how handy he could be.

Aubrey laughed and slapped at his arms. "Hey, mister! My mom might see." But she snuggled in closer. "It's getting cold fast, isn't it?"

"Yeah, the sun's almost down. But it sure is pretty."

"It sure is. I have to say, I'm taking to this country living thing better than I thought I would."

"Not bad for a Brooklyn girl." Royce hugged her tight, keeping the cold at bay. "The rest of the world may be going to hell in a handbasket, but here we are, safe and sound in our little sanctuary."

Aubrey nodded but didn't say anything more. She didn't need to. They were both thinking the same thing: that one more jump would be enough to make this sanctuary uninhabitable. And somehow that put a damper on the excitement they otherwise might have felt at owning their first home.

JUMP...

January 18, 2042

Jump or no jump? This was the day that would determine the fate of the world. Half of the Earth's landmass was already under the control of others not human. Was the other half about to be wrested from human control?

Despair ran deep, and suicides ran rampant, but even at this late date no aliens had shown themselves. But then again, why should they? Why show up in the midst of a crisis? If all this was the equivalent of a mass extermination—the sort of thing one might do to an infestation of bugs—then why not let the place air out a bit before coming down to occupy it?

On the other hand, why have force fields at all if one's sole intent was to exterminate anything and everything in sight? Force fields seemed to suggest some sort of human presence on the outside—hostile, perhaps, but unable to reach those on the inside, like mosquitoes on the outside of a cold pane of glass.

31

January 18 – NBC Nightly News, Philadelphia

"Breaking news tonight: the President of the United States is dead. We repeat: Mark Gardner, fiftieth President of the United States, has died.

"The President took his own life late last night. Initial reports indicate he killed himself in the Oval Office with his own gun, at his own desk, in the middle of the night when most were sound asleep. Secret Service personnel instantly rushed to the scene, but the President was already dead. Despite being in mourning, the First Lady has already begun moving out of what is being called the Philadelphia White House in order to make room for its new occupants.

"Former Vice President Patricia Talbert was sworn in as fifty-first President of the United States earlier this morning. She is seen here taking the Oath of Office, with her husband looking on. President Talbert hails from Florida, an important swing state, which is why many believe she was on the ticket with President Gardner to begin with. Never a part of the former President's inner circle, she remains something of a mystery to most Americans as she assumes the presidency. Her remarks immediately after taking the Oath of Office were brief, so let's have a listen."

"I have always been proud to serve with President Gardner. I believe he was a great man and a great President, but the burdens of office lay heavy on him, and in the end, unfortunately, they simply became too much to bear. He presided over this country in a time of unprecedented crisis. Sadly, and perhaps inevitably, many perished under his watch, which is a terrible burden to bear for any President. It burdens *me*, I can tell you, and so I humbly ask for your prayers going forward, and I swear to you that I will do my best to faithfully execute the office of President of the United States. God bless this great nation and make it whole again."

"That was President Talbert in her initial remarks to the nation, shortly after taking the Oath of Office. She will surely have her hands full in the coming days. For more on how President Talbert intends to respond to the challenges ahead, we turn to Stephanie Wilson in Philadelphia. Stephanie?"

"Cory, I think it's fair to say that no president has ever come into office facing greater challenges than President Talbert does at this moment. First and foremost, there are the domes themselves. Each already incorporates nearly 500 square miles of land, but that would increase to nearly 2,000 square miles with another jump, leaving practically no habitable land for us humans. Whatever existence might continue after that would be hardscrabble at best. America as a united entity would almost certainly cease to exist, replaced by isolated enclaves of survivors.

"But let's assume the domes *don't* jump. Let's assume we're all saved, if that's the right word for it. Then President Talbert really has her work cut out for her, because Americans have never faced challenges greater than they do right now, ranging from homelessness and starvation to freezing temperatures and violence. Meanwhile, our highway system, our power grid, our water and sewer systems, our communication systems, our food production and distribution systems, and our financial systems have all been deeply and perhaps irrevocably broken.

"The President's first few weeks in office—if she is permitted to have them at all—may amount to little more than triage. Realistically speaking, all she can do is to try and keep as many people alive as possible. She has already promised to continue President Gardner's efforts to set up food pantries and temporary shelters outside each metropolitan dome. Those efforts have already saved millions of lives, and yet millions more have been lost due to poor planning or miscommunication.

"Most notably, people escaping the domes exit from every possible direction, which means many never find the refugee camps to begin with. Aid stations are forced to relocate after each jump. Cell phones and wifi signals don't work inside the domes, and physical signposts pointing people in the right direction become obsolete after each jump. Even once people escape and have reception again, they sometimes find they have to navigate around a dome with a circumference of some eighty miles. They're often too far away to reach a food pantry or refugee camp, unless they happen to have a vehicle with enough gas to get them there, not to mention a road going in the right direction.

"The other huge problem, of course, is crime. President Talbert has already vowed to increase military and police presence at refugee camps—but how? President Gardner already stationed as many troops as were available, but still they aren't enough. Less than two million active-duty troops currently serve in the U.S. Armed Forces—half of one percent of the overall population. That means the military is stretched too thin to meet all of the demands being put upon it. Cory, back to you."

"Thanks Stephanie. Next we turn to Jim McDonald, who is reporting to us from just outside the Manhattan Dome. Jim, what can you tell us?"

"Cory, as you can see behind me, New York City is completely enclosed within the shimmering walls of a single merged dome centered on Central Park. It encompasses not just Manhattan but also most of the Bronx, Brooklyn, Queens, and Staten Island. Even a sizable chunk of Newark, New Jersey has been swallowed up inside this one mammoth dome, which now stretches some twenty-four miles in diameter. The dome's height of over one mile means that even the tallest of skyscrapers is now dwarfed by comparison. And that's *before* today's potential jump. If that should happen, then the doomsday prophets can finally say I told you so.

"But even if we're lucky enough to survive the next few days, it's frankly impossible to overstate the extent of this catastrophe. We're essentially looking at a ghost city here, Cory. The buildings may still be present, but the people are long gone. And that's true not just for New York City but for almost every other major metropolitan area in the world.

"In truth, we can't even begin to get an accurate count on the number of American dead. The military's best estimates put the number at between fifty and a hundred *million*. To put that into perspective, if you were to add up every American death from every war ever fought, you would arrive at a number well below two million—so there is simply no precedent for anything like this before in American history.

"Meanwhile, our economy is in a shambles. Unemployment is so high that the Bureau of Labor Statistics has simply stopped reporting on it. In fact, the Bureau of Labor Statistics itself is down to just a handful of people, so if you can call a handful of people a bureau, then I suppose it still exists. The same is true for many other agencies and departments of the federal government: they are shells of their former selves. All nonessential functions have been shut down or reduced to a token presence. Those who have long dreamed of a leaner federal government are finally getting their wish.

"As for the markets, nearly all stocks are now penny stocks. Untold trillions of dollars have evaporated into thin air, and many exchanges around the world have simply ceased to exist. What many financial experts said could never happen—a total financial meltdown on a global scale—has happened. An incredible number of corporations have gone bankrupt, and the rest are on the ropes. I think it would be fair to describe the current financial situation as apocalyptic."

"Is there a risk of the U.S. government defaulting, Jim?"

"Not really, Cory. While it's true the debt load has never been higher, a federal default is unlikely because the U.S. government owns the printing presses. In effect, it can always print more money. So the real concern isn't default—it's hyperinflation. The more money that's printed, the less each dollar is worth, and you can already see that happening across the country as inflation spirals out of control. Gasoline now costs a national average of nearly fifty dollars a gallon at the pump, assuming you can get it at all, and the proverbial loaf of bread costs nearly twenty times what it did four months ago. If the government keeps printing money, we could see what happened to the Venezuelan dollar back in the 2020's happen to the U.S. dollar in the 2040's. Venezuela saw inflation of nearly 10,000 percent in just one year in 2019—and from 2016 to 2019, their overall inflation rate increased nearly 54 *million* percent."

"God forbid such a thing should happen here, Jim. So how are people surviving if they have no jobs, and no money, and prices are spiraling out of control?"

"The short answer is, they're barely surviving at all, Cory. Things are *disjointed* in America. A fortunate few continue to muddle along, living and working in communities that, by sheer chance, happen to be located far from any domes. The rest have fallen on what might euphemistically be called hard times. They did nothing to deserve their fate: they simply happened to live in the wrong place at the wrong time.

"Most of the displaced now live in refugee camps, with a government-supplied tent and what amounts to subsistence food rations to keep them alive. A black market exists in nearly every refugee camp where you can get more and better food—*if* you have something to trade for it. It's essentially a barter system: this loaf of bread for that raincoat—that sort of thing. Unfortunately, many have nothing left to trade other than their own bodies and have turned to prostitution as the only way in which to feed their families. Crime in every possible form is rampant in these camps."

"How awful. Has word of the President's demise reached these refugee camps, Jim? And if so, how has it affected them?"

"No doubt they've heard of it, Cory, but most are so focused on their own survival at this point that, to be frank, the President's death is low on their list of concerns. They've become desensitized to bad news unless it affects them directly."

Surely other parts of the world are faring better than we are here in America, Jim."

"Unfortunately, that's not the case, Cory. The whole world seems to be in a collective freefall."

"All right, Jim, thanks. To our faithful viewers, please stay safe, and please tune in tomorrow, assuming there *is* a tomorrow. This is Cory Phillips saying good night and God bless."

32

January 18 – Oval Office, Philadelphia

Half a bottle of Lagavulin single malt scotch sat on the coffee table between Gil Lametti and Bill Cohen. Both of their whisky glasses were full at the moment but wouldn't be for long. To their left was the Oval Office desk, still cordoned off with yellow tape until the Secret Service and forensics teams could finish up their investigation. The office was empty otherwise, except for themselves. Both men looked hollow-eyed.

"I knew he was depressed, but not *that* depressed," Gil Lametti said. "If I had, I would have done something."

"Like what?" Bill Cohen asked.

"I don't know. I could have taken his gun away."

"I'm sure the President of the United States would have loved that," Cohen said dryly.

"I could have talked him down, then."

"He wasn't standing on a ledge, he was sitting at his own desk. And it's called the Resolute Desk for a reason. I doubt you could have said or done anything to talk him out of it."

Lametti nodded, downed his drink, grimaced, and poured another. "Do you think we'll know if the dome jumps from in here?"

"I have no idea. I'm not sure I want to know." Cohen drank and repoured. "When is she expected to get here?"

"Any minute now. Better drink while we still can; I hear she's a teetotaler." They both followed his advice and drank again.

"Actually, I'm not sure about this," Lametti said after a minute.

"What's that?"

"Meeting President Talbert for the first time drunk out of our gourds."

"She's gonna fire us anyway. What difference does it make? Plus, it's the end of the world. It's our patriotic duty to get drunk."

"If you say so. I don't think she's gonna like seeing yellow caution tape around her desk, either."

"Can you blame her?"

They heard the click of heels in the hallway, then the door opened and President Talbert walked in. She surveyed the room with a practiced air, took in the Lagavulin sitting between the two men (who were now standing out of respect), and without a word sat down in the chair facing them. "Sit," she urged them.

"Madam President," they both murmured and sat back down on the couch.

"You two have had a rough day," President Talbert said. "I'm sorry for your loss."

"Thank you Madam President," they both said in unison.

"But we don't have time to mourn, do we, so please bring me up to speed."

"Aren't you going to bring in your own advisors, ma'am?" Lametti asked.

"I may eventually, but there's no time for that now. The whole world could go poof in another hour, so there's not much point in changing up the furniture, is there? Or the décor, as it were, which includes you two; you practically live here full-time, from what I understand." She eyed the quarter-full bottle of Lagavulin and their loosened ties with skepticism.

Lametti sat up a bit straighter and straightened his tie while he was at it. "Sorry, Madam President," he said. "We're both a little beaten up after what happened last night."

"You have every right to be. Now, tell me what's what."

"No jumps that we know of anywhere in the world so far—that's the big news, Madam President. Another few hours and we should be in the clear."

"That's great news, isn't it, boys?"

They both nodded.

"Normally I would say we should hope for the best and prepare for the worst, but the worst is so bad in this case that there's no point in preparing for it. So—we may as well go ahead and plan for the best, right?"

"Right, Ma'am."

"Which is to say, let's assume we'll all be alive tomorrow, and outside the dome walls rather than inside them, like Jonah in the belly of the whale."

"That seems like a good thing to plan for, Madam President," Lametti said.

"Then let's roll up our sleeves, boys," President Talbert said, "because we have a lot of work to do between what's left of today and tomorrow."

She glanced over at the Resolute Desk with an irritated expression. "And can one of you get me a pair of scissors? That yellow tape has simply got to go. The Secret Service can arrest me if they want."

33

January - May 2042

Ten days after what was being called No Jump, the dome walls changed, shifting from their usual iridescent soap-bubble appearance to a glassier look.

The following day the walls turned pink, as if they were reflecting the hues of sunset—except it was midday. The walls continued to redden throughout the day, as if they were developing a bad case of sunburn. It was still possible to see through them, but it was like looking through a red haze.

On the third day, objects inside the dome began to catch fire. Underbrush and anything made of paper went up first, followed by gas explosions that rocked entire city blocks. Wooden buildings and trees burned like kindling, and there was no one left inside to put them out. Forests trapped inside the domes fell victim to raging wildfires that blazed so fiercely, scientists began to wonder if the air inside was somehow oxygen-enriched instead of oxygen-poor.

Black smoke billowed up from all the burning trees and structures, wafting towards the domes' ceilings—but instead of exiting as it would have before, the smoke lingered there, swirling and blackening, growing thicker and thicker until drones and helicopters could no longer report on what was going on inside. It was as if each dome had a black stormcloud towering overhead stretching for some twenty-four miles in all directions.

Scientists speculated that the domes must have entered a new phase, one in which the oxygen *hadn't* been eliminated; otherwise the fires wouldn't have been burning at all. The domes had become, in effect, giant convection ovens—ones left on for too long, until the roasts inside had blackened beyond all reckoning.

By the fourth day, whirlwinds were forming inside the domes, whipping the tongues of flame into something that seemed almost living. The skyscrapers in New York City caught fire, and the entire skyline burned.

Spectators who witnessed it firsthand never forgot it, especially when the Empire State Building tottered, then came crashing down like a giant tree felled by an ax. Even more gut-wrenching was the 1,776-foot-tall One World Trade Center, which stood taller than any other building in New York City and was invested with more emotional weight than any other skyscraper in America. Its demise was nothing short of spectacular. Meanwhile, the Brooklyn Bridge caught fire, burned brilliantly for about an hour, then tumbled into the East River. Lady Liberty, who was on her own little island, held out longer than most, but finally she, too, toppled over in a smoldering heap into New York Bay. Her torch was lit with actual flames as she fell, along with her upraised arm and crown.

By the fifth day, every landmark that had ever been associated with New York City had vanished behind a thick pall of smoke. Reporters could no longer see within to report on what was happening. The show was over; a black curtain had come down over the stage, and the rest of the tragedy played out behind the scenes.

What happened in the Manhattan Dome happened everywhere else around the world at essentially the same time. Architectural wonders went up in smoke inside every dome across the planet. Much of the cultural heritage of the world disappeared overnight. Whole cities, massive cities—Mexico City, São Paolo, Istanbul, Mumbai, Tokyo, Shanghai, London, Paris—burned to the ground. Cities built of metal and steel lasted the longest, but they were no match for the incinerators the domes had become.

By the sixth day, underbrush *outside* the dome walls began to smoke and catch fire. People couldn't get within a hundred feet of a dome without feeling like they were standing in front of an open furnace. Firefighters tried to put the fires out but to no avail. Some homeowners whose homes stood just beyond the walls—who had thanked the heavens just days before for their apparent salvation—now cursed providence as their homes burned to the ground.

By the seventh day, the dome walls were encircled by rings of fire on the outside, a pale mimicry of what was occurring on the inside. Each dome was like a blazing sun surrounded by a corona of light and heat. Humans had no choice but to back away and let things burn.

So it was that the domes continued to wreak havoc even after the final jump day. Predator and prey alike fled from burning forests and stood trembling out in the open, not knowing where to run or where to hide. Refugee camps stationed just outside the domes were abandoned in such haste that many of the government-supplied tents that had served as shelters of last resort went up in smoke. The sick and injured were rushed away on makeshift pallets as the flames engulfed first aid stations and field hospitals alike. The loss of life was small compared to what had come before, but the losses to property continued to mount, and that was no small thing in the midst of a cold winter.

A pall of black smoke from all the peripheral fires rose to the heavens and hid what little sun remained in early February. The world turned colder, even as the domes themselves continued to burn like bonfires. But scientists were quick to point out that if the noxious fumes inside all sixty thousand domes had been allowed to escape into the atmosphere at once, things could have been far worse. A nuclear winter of sorts might have set in, with smoke-filled skies blocking the sun for years to come.

By the eighth day, the heat from the domes finally began to dissipate. The rings of fire around each dome burned themselves out, leaving behind rings of scorched earth. The dome walls themselves faded from scarlet to red.

By the ninth day, the walls softened from dull red to pink.

By the tenth day, they returned to their glassy look, and people could approach them again without getting sunburnt themselves.

For the next ten days and beyond, the smoke continued to swirl around inside the inverted ash trays the domes had become. People being people, they were deeply curious to know what was going on inside those domes, but of course the domes didn't oblige. They hadn't been obliging since the very beginning, so why should they start now?

The curtains remained closed for a long time to come.

34

May 2042 – Oval Office, Philadelphia

President Talbert stared out of her Oval Office window during a rare moment of solitude. Since the Oval Office was on the top floor of the tallest skyscraper in Philadelphia, the view looked nothing like it had back in D.C. She actually preferred this view because it was so expansive. It gave her the sense of floating above the world, making decisions from on high—like a god, if she were being honest, because that was what it felt like being President sometimes.

But what no one ever told you was what a pain in the tush it could be being a god. Nothing but trouble, trouble, trouble. For one thing, her power to effect real change was surprisingly small. Sure, she made decisions that could affect millions, but those decisions were implemented by others, and somewhere between the ordering and the doing a lot of the good got lost. For another thing, her fellow gods (or demigods, anyway) in the House and Senate continually battled amongst themselves and with her, apparently determined to make sure she never got anything meaningful done.

No, the Greeks had the right of it: the gods were a contentious lot who thought better of themselves than they deserved.

From her perch on high, she could see one distant dome to the northwest. It was still opaque, as it had been for months now. It looked like a tick latched onto the skin of the Earth. She imagined it sucking out the Earth's lifeblood, day after day, until it became engorged and bloated. It was a parasite that didn't belong here, and she longed to pluck it off.

If she had been a real god, she could have done just that; but alas, she was a mere mortal playing at being god, and that was the difference. Mortals wished where gods acted.

Now the aliens...*they* might be gods. They spoke and it was so. "Ticks shall descend upon the Earth and suck the lifeblood out of it." And behold, it came to pass. To her, the aliens' invasion plans seemed as immutable as the Ten Commandments themselves.

That was the fundamental problem: she was up against gods.

Gods, she suspected, couldn't be defeated outright, only deflected from their path. They needed to be tricked out of their inheritance, the way Jacob had tricked his father out of the blessing meant for his brother Esau.

But it was hard to trick a god. The only thing it was easy to do was bow down and worship a god.

Was that what these aliens wanted? Their subservience and obedience? After taking half the Earth without even bothering to show up, did they think themselves so invincible that humans would bow down before them and say, "Command me, oh lord?" Well, they didn't know humans very well if they thought that.

Humans were a troublesome lot: they might swear fealty to you with one hand while holding a dagger behind their backs with the other. Patricia's own career in politics had taught her that much. She knew just how devious humans could be when it suited their purposes—and that was a characteristic that might stand the humans in good stead once the aliens arrived.

Personally, she had little doubt the aliens *would* arrive, but it would be in their own sweet time. Everything about this invasion suggested a calculated approach: not rushed, not exposed, not risky. It was all being done step by step in an orderly, systematic fashion: first the invisible seeds, then the immovable ovates, then the impregnable domes, then the relentless jumps every ten days like clockwork.

Each dome was exactly the same size as all the rest. Each dome proceeded in lockstep with all the others, like well-trained soldiers—synchronized, efficient, precise. Whatever was happening inside the domes at present, she guessed it was the final step in the meticulously thought-out process that was meant to precede the aliens' long-awaited arrival.

To her mind, the only thing that seemed disorderly about the invasion was its genesis: the seeds appeared to have fallen randomly, and that bothered her, because everything else spoke of strict adherence to a plan. But perhaps, if the scientists were correct, with some fifty *million* seeds having fallen from the skies, the probabilities themselves spoke of order on a grand scale, their sheer numbers guaranteeing the outcome the aliens desired.

Flip a coin once and the result can go either way. Flip a coin a million times (or fifty million times) and the results become highly predictable. And if the coin is even slightly weighted to fall one way rather than the other—say, onto urban areas more than rural ones—then, the results can seem downright predetermined.

So perhaps there *was* order in the invasion's genesis after all, even though the seeds' distribution seemed random from the perspective of someone on the ground.

President Talbert reckoned these careful, deliberate aliens wouldn't know what to do with true mayhem and disorder. If the aliens *had* been watching over the past few months, she wondered if they felt any dismay at just how chaotic and troublesome their soon-to-be-subjects could be.

Could humans be troublesome enough to drive them right off the planet? She certainly hoped so. She needed to believe these aliens could be defeated—or if not defeated, *deflected*.

Let them lay their tick eggs on some other world.

35

June 2042

It took four full months for the domes to clear of smoke. When they finally did, and people could look inside for the first time, what they saw took their breath away...because there was literally nothing to see.

Not a single structure was left standing. All that remained was a thick coating of ash covering the floor of each dome. It looked like black volcanic ash that had been laid down after a major eruption.

Whether some kind of disintegrating acid had been added to the smoke-filled air during those four months was an open question. No scientist could get inside to take an air sample, but it seemed the aliens must have done *something* to break down any remaining structures and level them over the course of the intervening months. Stone and steel wouldn't have disappeared so completely otherwise. As it was, no trees, no vegetation, no buildings, no ruins, no debris of any kind survived—just flat, fallow ground stretching for twenty-four miles in all directions inside each dome.

New York City had been reduced to ashes, along with nearly every other major city and monument in the world. All of it was now incorporated within the three to six feet of ash that lay at the base of each dome. Spectacular natural wonders had also been reduced to nondescript dust. The Yosemite Valley looked like a slash-and-burn field. Yellowstone, when seen from above, was now pockmarked with circular dead zones. Outside the dome walls, all looked as magnificent as ever, but inside, every distinctive land feature had vanished altogether.

One can be just as surprised by what is not there as what is. Not seeing the New York skyline where it was supposed to be was just as jarring for most people as seeing an alien dome for the first time. Many were shaken to the core because it meant there was no going home now, not ever. Hometowns had been obliterated, leaving former residents feeling untethered from reality. Piles of rubble, at least, would have signified *something* had stood there once upon a time, but even the rubble was gone.

From the Amazon to China to Yosemite to New York, the terrain had been bludgeoned into submission. One half of the Earth's surface now looked as barren as the surface of the moon, pulverized into lunar-like dust. The aliens had somehow managed to achieve uniformity across sixty thousand domes spread across the entire surface of the Earth.

They'd also managed to piss off every single human being on the planet.

*****

On June 5th, 2042, the glassy surface of the domes gave way to the familiar soap-bubble look the world had grown to know and hate so much. However, for the first time, not just water but *air* was flowing regularly through the dome walls. This immediately became apparent as huge amounts of ash inside the domes began to disperse into the world at large.

Winds whipped through the domes, tossing the ash out into the world in blinding dust storms. In other places, heavy rains turned the ash into viscous mud that oozed out of the dome walls and into nearby towns and cities, creating a disgusting mess. In still others, tornadoes tore through, flinging stupendous amounts of ash into the atmosphere and spewing it for miles.

Besides natural weather events, the domes otherwise remained empty and unchanging, simply taking up space that could no longer be used by human or animal. At least there were no new jumps to worry about; the only real annoyance was the "moondust" that blew everywhere and did no one any good.

People in refugee camps slowly began to regain their footing. Now that the camps could stay put, it was easier to truck in food and supplies. Skeletal survivors of what some were calling the second holocaust started to put on weight and look almost human again. Many of these unfortunates had been forced to fend for themselves in the so-called dead zones on the far sides of domes—barren expanses remote from any food or water. Those who hadn't died outright had come stumbling into the camps looking like famished wretches straight out of a concentration camp.

After a horrific stretch in which one third of the human race was estimated to have died, things started to settle down and reach a new equilibrium. The worst of the violence was quelled, some semblance of law and order was restored, state and local governments showed hopeful signs of life, and supplies began to trickle into their intended destinations. Here and there, cooperation replaced hostility, and the better half of human nature began to reassert itself. Some optimists even claimed compassion and empathy were making a comeback.

Meanwhile, pessimists had their own take on things. They suggested humans had been beaten down on purpose so they would be too weak and distracted by their own problems to mount any kind of meaningful resistance to an invasion—which meant one was coming any day now.

The world held its collective breath as July 4th approached—the one-year anniversary of the first arrival of the seeds on Earth.

36

July 2042

Independence Day celebrations were subdued or nonexistent that year, except in the nation's new capital, Philadelphia, where an attempt at patriotic pride was mounted. The fireworks went off as scheduled, but after the horrors of the past few months, it felt like there wasn't much to celebrate.

July 4th passed without incident, and the human race heaved a collective sigh of relief. Perhaps the aliens weren't coming after all. Perhaps there *were* no aliens. Perhaps the domes would magically disappear on their own any day now. *Poof!*

Or perhaps not. On July 5th, exactly one year to the day since the seeds had first settled onto the planet, the city-ships arrived in the skies above Earth.

They appeared with virtually no warning. Trackers at U.S. Space Force, along with a handful of professional and amateur astronomers, had noted an occlusion of the star known as Ross 154 in the direction of the constellation Sagittarius a few hours before their arrival—but by the time the intelligence was confirmed, and the news broadcast around the world, the ships had already arrived. The lack of advance warning meant people were caught off guard by the fleet's arrival, even though they had been dreading it for months. The long-feared invasion was finally upon them, and people were surprised at just how surprised they were.

Ross 154, they all soon learned through constantly repeated newscasts, was a red dwarf flare star with a mean time between major flares of about two days. It stood 9.69 light years away from Earth, making it one of our closer neighbors. Whether the ships had come from some unknown planet orbiting Ross 154, or from some other more distant point in that same general direction, was impossible to say. Since the Galactic Center itself was located in the direction of Sagittarius, any number of stars or planets could have been the starting point for the aliens' voyage to Earth.

Most astronomers had been training their telescopes in directions other than Ross 154, which was considered an improbable candidate for the mounting of an invasion, since it was a flare star unlikely to support life. But improbable or not, here came the invading fleet!

*****

Just as the people of Earth were most in need of real-time information, many of the world's communication systems went down. The vast armada of ships entering Earth's orbit wreaked havoc on the delicate constellations of satellites encircling the planet. Hundreds of manmade satellites crashed into the alien fleet's protective shields, disintegrating into dust.

In the space of a few seconds, GPS systems went down, soldiers were cut off from command, pilots lost contact with air traffic control and had to fly blind, and satellite-based weather systems vanished. Even internet and telecom systems stopped functioning reliably as the GPS constellation they depended on for accurate time signal data disappeared.

Astronauts aboard the International Space Station came dangerously close to splattering like bugs against a windshield as the alien fleet entered low Earth orbit. The astronauts got one hell of a closeup view before miraculously missing the fleet altogether. Their exclamations of astonishment at what they saw were a precursor to the reactions of most humans on the planet over the course of the next hour.

Before long the city-ships became visible to the naked eye. As they continued their descent towards Earth, it became apparent just how enormous they were. Each was roughly ten miles in diameter—massive enough to cast a shadow that blocked the sun, just as depicted in scores of alien invasion movies. Then, too, when seen from below, the ships really did look like the prototypical flying saucers depicted in countless films. They were circular in shape and porcelain in appearance, a creamy off-white that looked like alabaster but was obviously durable enough to weather the rigors of an interstellar voyage. All told there were some sixty thousand ships—nearly one per dome—yet another indication of the aliens' precise and meticulous natures.

The ships enveloped the planet, hovering overhead until all were in place, as if to show off their invincibility before simultaneously beginning a slow and deliberate descent towards Earth.

It was at this moment that Russia launched its first missiles, followed by China and the U.S. All told, hundreds of missiles targeted the ships, but the ships were shielded with the same force field technology as used by the domes. The missiles splashed harmlessly against their shields, accomplishing nothing except to serve as an impromptu fireworks display for the people craning their necks upwards in awe.

The ships, for their part, didn't even bother firing back, nor did they pause in their descent. If anything spoke of the aliens' utter disregard for human weaponry, it was this.

Each ship descended towards a specific dome, as if it had been preassigned, settling towards Earth as gently as a mother laying her newborn in a crib. No propulsion or deceleration system was apparent; whatever slowed their descent was as incomprehensible as the domes themselves.

Meanwhile, every human being on the planet who was anywhere near a dome stopped whatever they were doing and stared upwards in silent wonder. Those who were indoors came rushing out, irresistibly drawn by the chance to see something truly once-in-a-lifetime.

For the briefest of seconds, each ship seemed to alight atop its chosen dome before passing through. The force fields did nothing to stop them. And why should they? They were built to protect these very ships! What humans had banged their collective heads against for months was inconsequential to the actual owners of the technology—which explained why they now owned half the planet, much to the dismay of its original inhabitants.

*****

At the exact center of each ship's flat underside was a concave chamber designed to fit over the ovate. As the ships settled to the ground, they nestled over the ovates like mother hens brooding over their eggs. Unfortunately for humans everywhere, this had no effect whatsoever on the ovates' ability to power the force fields, which remained as intact as ever.

The ships came to rest flush against the flat surface that had been prepared for them. In some instances, they straddled a major river bed, such as the Hudson or the Mississippi, in which case the river continued to flow directly beneath the ship. Less consequential rivers were forced to divert around the enormous obstacle suddenly blocking their path—much to the dismay of local communities, which now had flooding to add to their long list of woes.

As the ships touched down, huge clouds of ash and dust boiled out from below. The ash swept towards the onlookers gathered in mute wonderment just beyond the dome walls—a fine welcome from the aliens upon their arrival. People coughed and turned away as the ash clouds roiled over them.

Despite their enormous size, each city-ship was surrounded by some seven miles of open space in every direction—a generous buffer that made it all but impossible for humans on the ground to observe them. Nevertheless, as soon as the ash clouds dispersed, binoculars and telescopes were trained on them in fascination. At the same time, drones, reconnaissance aircraft, helicopter news crews, and any remaining spy satellites up in the heavens vied for a closer look. Everyone wanted to know what the ships looked like and who, exactly, might be on board.

The first thing everyone noticed was that the ships were anything but flat on top. Instead, they were covered from one end to the other with what could only be described as cities—strange alien cities, but cities nonetheless. Unlike the undersides, which were as smooth as pizza stones, the superstructures teemed with domes, spheres, and towers of every type and description.

One enormous domed structure stood at the very center of each city. Clearly this dome must serve as the beating heart of each city. Encircling it were four tall towers—spiraling helixes the color of alabaster, one at each of the city's cardinal points. Each tower had a colorful spire on top—yellow, red, blue, green—but what these colors might mean was anyone's guess. Spreading out beyond the towers were thousands of smaller spheres—individual dwellings, most likely. Everything about the architecture was curvilinear: curving dome walls, spiraling towers, circular portals, rounded windows, sinuous walkways.

It was instantly apparent to all who saw them that the aliens didn't need to *build* cities: they had brought them along with them. Prefab alien cities made perfect sense now that they were here staring people in the face, but no one had predicted them beforehand.

Since the hull of each ship was about fifty feet tall, the alien cities themselves were perched some fifty feet above the ground. This arrangement allowed the aliens to look down upon their newly acquired domains, like lords of the manor atop their castle walls, while humans had to look up from below like vassals of old.

Not that any lords or ladies were visible at the moment. Every portal and window remained closed, and so they remained for the rest of the day. No matter how many times people refreshed their news feeds, impatiently waiting for their first glimpse of an alien, they were left unsatisfied. They really should have known better by now: the aliens were nothing if not masters at disappointing people.

When night fell, the dome at the center of each alabaster city illuminated, as if a million flickering candles had all been lit at once. An ethereal glow radiated outwards, climbing floor by floor up to the tops of each helix tower, then extending outwards to the furthest spherical dwellings at the rim. People gasped at the sight, and all the cameras and video equipment came back out. For a fleeting moment, it was hard not to appreciate the beauty of the alien cities. But that beauty hid an ugly truth: the unleashing of genocide upon an entire planet, and that was something too awful to conceal behind soft lighting.

*****

Another day passed, and another, and still the aliens refused to show themselves. For all people knew, they might look like walking ferns or amorphous blobs. The desire to see an alien up close was intense beyond all reckoning.

News helicopters buzzed overhead like flies over a tempting dessert covered under glass. Each network was intent on grabbing that first sensational image that would blanket the airwaves from one end of the Earth to the other.

But the aliens remained decidedly uncooperative. For the rest of that week and into the next, they stayed locked up inside their alien cities, intent on their alien ceremonies, or their alien sports, or their alien sex, or whatever it was they were doing in there. Perhaps they just got a kick out of making the earthlings wait.

After prolonged days of this sort of thing, most humans finally got fed up and went back to their own lives. Which, of course, was when the first alien showed itself.

Actually, two aliens. Two friends? Two lovers out for a stroll on their new planet? A little walk around the dusty block?

A portal irised open like a camera lens, and out they came, on a summer's evening, strolling around what looked like a high observation deck encircling one of the spiraling towers. This particular sighting happened at the Topeka Dome. Similar sightings occurred elsewhere over the course of the next several days, but this was the first—the Big One—filmed from above by one of the circling helicopters and broadcast to millions around the world.

First impressions: they were bipedal and humanoid. Beanpole tall—eight feet at least—with bodies as spindly as spiders' legs, and elongated heads that seemed a bit too big for their bodies. They had two eyes and a mouth right where they were supposed to be, but only slits for noses. They were hairless and alabaster-white like their ships, and they were cloaked in what looked like white silk.

Their bodies were segmented like a wasp's, with impossibly thin "waists" that seemed to pivot all the way around in disconcerting fashion. One of the aliens swiveled around to talk to the other behind him/her/it as they walked along. It was impossible to tell their sexes, if that was even a thing for them. They seemed to be breathing the air just fine through their slit nostrils.

One of the aliens was more animated than the other, raising its hands in the air repeatedly as it talked. It was a tad shorter than the other, although still quite tall by human standards. Its companion had big hands and big feet and looked ungainly, like a giant adolescent still growing into its body. It appeared subdued or possibly lost in thought.

The animated one finished speaking, and the two stood there for a minute on the observation deck of their city-ship staring up at the heavens. What were they looking at? The helicopters? The drones? The color of the sky itself? A missing city-ship late coming to the party?

The two companions looked at each other for a long moment in silence, then reentered the portal. It spiraled shut behind them like a closing lens.

They had been outside for all of two minutes, but that was enough to feed the media frenzy for a week.

What they talked about was the subject of endless speculation. Memes poured forth that very same night. One imagined a wife berating her husband: "You forgot the camping gear? How could you forget the camping gear! I reminded you like a thousand times!" Another envisioned an alien priest accompanied by his acolyte: "Bless this earth, bless this sky, bless this dust mote floating by." Another depicted an enthusiastic tourist gesturing up at the sky: "It's blue, Muriel! Blue! Just like the brochures said!" Another pictured a world-weary traveler: "Halfway across the galaxy for some peace and quiet, and this is what we get: paparazzi! Paparazzi everywhere!"

In truth, humans didn't have the faintest idea what had been said, no matter how many times they watched and rewatched the video, analyzed it, dissected it, laughed at it. The only thing everyone could agree on was that the aliens had shown no interest whatsoever in the humans whose planet they now occupied.

Which was a little strange, wasn't it? Wouldn't *we* be just as fascinating to them as they were to us? Wouldn't *we* be the aliens from their point of view? How could they not want to come a little closer and have a look?

What was *wrong* with them?

*****

One frequent talking point was the strange coincidence of events that had brought the aliens to Earth exactly one calendar year after the seeds had fallen. What was *that* all about?

Why would an alien race care about Earth calendar years? And why would they go to so much trouble to land on July 5th, the exact same date scientists said the seeds had fallen? It beggared belief that it was mere coincidence.

It *must* have been planned, said most people. One year to the day? It had to have been formulated to happen that way by a species intent on…what? Temporal order? Chronological symmetry?

Ridiculous! said a vocal minority. It had to have been sheer chance. The aliens would have used their *own* calendar year, not ours, if they had wanted to lay out events in neat chronological order.

Not necessarily, countered the majority. It's not all that different from what international travelers do when they set their watches ahead to their destination's time zone. These aliens are simply synchronizing with our Earth years ahead of time, as it were, in order to avoid the ultimate case of jet lag.

That's absurd! said the minority. What kind of crazy OCD aliens are we talking about here, anyway? Why should they care so much about chronological symmetry? That's insane!

It's not insane, it's *alien*. You *do* know what alien means, don't you?

And so the arguments went, around and around. But since the minority had no compelling alternate explanation for why the seeds landed on July 5, 2041 and the ships landed on July 5, 2042, they usually fell back on name-calling at some point and left to find others who already agreed with them.

37

August 2042

On August 5th, one month to the day after their arrival, the aliens posted their first message to the world. They posted it on X, as if that were the most natural thing in the world for any alien to do. It read:

WE ARE THE PHANTS.
WE COME IN PEACE.
WE MEAN YOU NO HARM.
WE ARE SUBLIME THINKERS.
DO NOT DISTURB.

Oval Office, Philadelphia

"Like *hell* they come in peace!" cried President Talbert, slamming her hand down on the Resolute Desk. "And what do they mean no harm? They've harmed us plenty! Worse than any war or plague or natural disaster in our recorded history! Did they think we wouldn't *notice*? How can they say something like that?"

Gil Lametti was silent for a moment, reading the message over and over again. "'We come in peace.' 'We mean you no harm.' Those sound like the kind of trite phrases you'd expect to hear from a B movie about an alien invasion. I wonder if they've been studying our TV programming. Maybe that's what they've been holed up doing over the past month."

"They sound insufferable," said the President. "Where do they get off saying 'Do Not Disturb' after invading *our* planet? And what's all this nonsense about being sublime thinkers? Did they really say that? Are we sure this isn't a hoax?"

"It's for real," said Lametti. "It's been traced back to one of the domes."

"And it's gone out to the whole world?"

Lametti nodded. "In different languages, no less."

"Well, they may as well have told us to shove it."

"Haven't they been telling us that for months now?"

President Talbert read the message over again. "What do you make of the sublime thinkers part?"

"It reminds me of one of those bad translations from Japanese into English," Lametti said eventually. "You know, like when a non-native speaker looks up words in a dictionary and picks the ones that sound right, but they aren't quite right? Like 'Slip Carefully' or 'The Male Sex Toilet.' 'Sublime Thinkers' sounds a bit like that."

"But what are they getting at, even allowing for the bad translation?"

Lametti shook his head. "They sound arrogant, no matter how you slice it. Saying you're a sublime thinker is like saying you're super-smart or amazingly deep, and neither is something a human would say about himself, not unless he wanted to get laughed out of the room."

"I agree. They're arrogant."

"So it would appear, based on what they've chosen to put in their very first transmission to us. Maybe they're brainiacs. Maybe they pride themselves on just how smart they are compared to all the other species they've met. And

I'm guessing we're not the first species they've met, given how disinterested they seem to be in us."

"I hate them already, and I haven't even met them yet."

"Well, we may not have to worry about meeting them any time soon. If one thing's clear, it's that they don't want to be disturbed."

"Just hearing that makes me want to disturb them. Maybe we should set up amplifiers outside their domes and blast heavy metal music at them."

"That could be an interesting experiment—but let's let the Russians or Chinese try it first."

"Good thinking."

"Phants," said Lametti thoughtfully. "Spelled with a PH. That's odd, isn't it? Why not an F? Well, at least we know what to call them now."

"I wonder what it means."

"Probably 'Sublime Thinkers' in Phant."

President Talbert chortled. "They don't look like much physically, do they? Ungainly, I'd call them. If only we could get past those force fields of theirs, I'll bet we could take them in a fair fight."

"I doubt they'll ever give us the chance," Lametti responded. They may never come out of those domes of theirs. 'Do Not Disturb' makes it sound like they've got some serious thinking to do."

"About what?"

"Who knows? Contemplating their navels? If they even have navels."

"Well, they certainly don't have noses," sniffed President Talbert. "And those wasp waists—ugh!"

"At least they're humanoid after a fashion. They could have looked like spiders. Or blobfish."

"What's a blobfish?"

"It's ugly—look it up sometime." Lametti sat silent for a minute then shook his head. "You'd think after an interstellar voyage, they'd want to get out and stretch their legs a bit. You know, get the lay of the land. Go for a walk. Do anything *but* stay put and think."

"'Do Not Disturb.' That really fries my bacon. There's got to be *some* way we can contact them."

Lametti shrugged. "We could try messaging them back, but I doubt they'd read it. They made it pretty clear they don't want to be bothered. In fact, they set their reply settings to 'none,' which is like saying 'Do Not Disturb' in another way. It sounds like they only want the communication to be one-way."

"Sounds like them, all right." President Talbert stared at her phone for a moment before tossing it aside in disgust. "They already have more followers than anyone on X, including me."

"What? Just since this morning?"

Talbert nodded. "Crazy, huh?"

"Crazy is putting it mildly."

Truth or Consequences, New Mexico

"Did you hear?" Josh asked Kaley. He was practically exploding with excitement. Woof was at his heels looking equally excited.

"Hear what?" Kaley asked.

"They made contact."

"Who made—*ohh! They* made contact."

"Yep."

"What did they say?"

"You'll never believe it. They called themselves sublime thinkers."

"No *way*."

"And they told us not to disturb them."

"Get *out*."

"But they say they mean us no harm."

"Isn't it a little late for that?"

"It sure is. They call themselves Phants." Josh showed her his screen so she could read the message for herself.

"Weird. Phants. Sounds like elephants and ants: Phants. They don't *look* like elephants or ants though, do they?"

"Not really," said Josh. "Well, maybe a little like ants with those tiny waists of theirs. But they've got the opposite of elephant trunks—they've practically got no noses at all."

"That's what we should call them: No-noses."

"Yeah. Or Jabbars," laughed Josh.

"Huh?"

"Because they're so tall. You know, like Kareem Abdul-Jabbar?"

"*Who*?"

"Forget it. Anyway, they seem kind of annoying, don't you think? Calling themselves sublime and all?"

"What's sublime mean, exactly?"

Josh looked it up. "Of such excellence, grandeur, or beauty as to inspire great admiration or awe."

"Like Woof." Kaley gave Woof a warm hug. "But Woof would never say that about himself, would you, Woof? They sound kinda stuck-up if you ask me."

"I'll say. But their technology's sublime, there's no denying that. I still can't get over that landing." Josh fiddled with his phone for a minute, and then they were both watching a sped-up video of the ships—thousands of them—appearing from above, spreading out across the skies in formation, then landing in synchrony. "I could watch that a hundred times."

"It looks like a lot of people already have," said Kaley. "Look how many hits that video's gotten. These aliens are *rock stars.*"

"Reclusive rock stars. They've barely shown themselves over the past month."

"Too bad. I was really hoping to get to meet an alien."

"So you'd still want one of them to live with us, even after all they've done?"

Kaley thought about that for a moment. "Nah. I blame them for getting Mom shot, and a whole lotta other people killed."

Josh nodded. "Yeah, me too. They're definitely not making many friends down here, are they?"

"Ashley might like them. They sound as stuck-up as she is."

"Hey, be nice. Ashley's trying."

"I'm just saying, she thinks *she's* sublime, they think *they're* sublime..."

Josh gave his younger sister a disapproving look, but he couldn't keep the twinkle out of his eye. He pulled up a picture of the two aliens standing atop their ship and stared at it, with Kaley looking over his shoulder.

"They look so *weird*," Kaley said. "I can't believe we have actual aliens living right here on our planet with us. And not just *any* aliens: sublime ones."

"Sublime my eye. They're sublimely full of themselves is what I think. We need to take them down a peg or two."

"And how are we gonna do that? We're just kids."

"I don't know," said Josh. "I guess I've got some of my own sublime thinking to do. But what I *want* is to give them a taste of their own medicine. I want them to regret ever coming to this planet in the first place."

"They will once you get done with them," Kaley said with the absolute conviction of a younger sister for her older brother.

San Gabriel Mountains, California

Dr. Rachel Cavanaugh was one of the few people in the world who didn't despise the aliens for calling themselves sublime thinkers. She envied them instead for a culture in which sublime thinking was celebrated. Sublime thinking was underrated in her opinion.

Not wanting to be disturbed made perfect sense to her, too. Anyone who had ever tried to calculate how to land a rover safely on Mars would understand how interruptions could be fatal to success. Deep thought required deep concentration.

But having seen what she'd seen over the past several months—piles of dead bodies, traffic jam cemeteries, whole cities obliterated—she took strong exception to the alien claim that they came in peace. They came in anything but peace. Even if they didn't *mean* to harm humans in some abstract theoretical sense, they'd harmed humans plenty in the practical sense. The enormous death toll—human and animal alike—spoke volumes in that regard. The aliens could try to wash their hands of it, but their hands were bloody beyond the scope of the worst human tyrant—and that was saying something.

For now, Rachel was content to live in a cabin she'd found for rent in the tiny town of Wrightwood, which was located at the end of the Angeles Crest Highway deep in the San Gabriel Mountains. It was about as far away as one could get from the world and its problems these days. In exchange for teaching math to kids in the local school, she got a weekly food stipend. After classes, she'd pour herself a glass of wine (while there was still wine to be had), pull out her notebooks from her JPL days, and pore over them looking for answers.

There was still so much she didn't understand about the domes. So much to *obsess* over, in the words of her former boss. She didn't mind staying hidden away in her cabin for the time being, thinking her own private thoughts, with her own metaphorical "Do Not Disturb" sign on the door.

38

September 2042 – Charlottesville, Virginia

"So I was thinking: we should do something about these aliens of ours," Royce said one day as they sat outside rocking on their front porch.

Aubrey laughed—she couldn't help it. "What is there to do, Royce? They *won*. They came, they saw, they conquered. Just like invaders are supposed to do."

"Yeah, but what are the *invaded* supposed to do?"

"Lie down and take it?"

"*Resist*. Fight back. Scratch and bite and claw if they have to. Like you did in New York when that asshole grabbed you."

Aubrey rocked in silence for a time, recalling the worst day of her life. "So you want to scratch and bite, is that it?"

"And claw too. I want to fight back. And I think you do, too."

"Oh? And how do you figure that?"

Royce just stared at her. "C'mon, Aubrey. I've seen you staring up at the ceiling at night, trying to cope with what happened that awful day. Tell me you wouldn't want to avenge their deaths if you could."

"Of *course* I would, Royce, but it's *hopeless*." Aubrey began ticking off on her fingers. "Half of our land is gone, most of our cities are obliterated, our entire economy is in shambles, and we're second on the totem pole of our own planet. How can we possibly succeed against them?"

"That's not even the half of it." Royce started ticking off on his own fingers. "We have no idea how to destroy a dome or get inside one, the aliens have us licked when it comes to technology, our weapons are useless against them, and everything that *should* have been tried *has* been tried. The aliens clearly think we're beneath their notice."

"Wow, way to make your point, Royce," Aubrey said, rocking furiously all of a sudden. "You've really sold me on this whole resistance idea of yours."

"Now hang on. I have a plan, and I think it's a good one."

Aubrey stopped rocking just as suddenly. "You're kidding. *You* have a plan. For defeating the aliens. The federal government and the U.S. military and renowned scientists from around the world haven't been able to do it, but you have a plan."

Royce nodded.

"Okay, then, let's hear it."

"We offer ourselves up as adoring servants to the Phants."

"You're kidding me. *That's* your plan?"

"That's my plan. I'm betting that eventually—*eventually*—these Phants will bring certain vetted people into the domes to do their dirty work for them. You know, house cleaning, laundry, trash removal, janitorial duties, that sort of stuff. These 'sublime thinkers' certainly aren't going to do that sort of drudge work for themselves, are they? *That's* how we get inside. And once we're inside, we keep our eyes open, and we smuggle out whatever information we can to take down the domes."

"They could have robots for all that," Aubrey pointed out. "They may not need us at all."

"That's possible," Royce conceded. "But if they *do* need us for anything, we'll be ready. We could even learn a little Phant to make ourselves more useful to them. Maybe even play-act at being...you know...a bit worshipful of them."

"Ugh. I hate that idea."

"Of course you do. You're not supposed to *like* it."

"Doting servants. I don't think I could pull that off."

"Not even if it was our ticket in?"

Aubrey rocked in silence for a time. From inside the house, she could hear Dominique squalling, as she usually did right before naptime, and Sara giggling as she played a game of go fish with her grandma. "The Phants won't even talk to us at this point, Royce. I hate to say it, but your plan seems kinda iffy to me. It's based on a whole lot of assumptions, for one thing."

"I agree. I'd be worried if you *didn't* think it was iffy. I'd give it maybe a five percent chance of success at best. But even a one percent chance would be worth it given the stakes, don't you think?"

"Mmm, maybe."

"But all of that's way in the future anyway. All I want to do for now is recruit people to the cause." Royce leaned in closer. "So here's what I propose: we leave the house behind for your family and hit the road in our RV."

"Okay, I like the sound of that so far."

"We get the lay of the land, get a feel for just how bad things are in different parts of the country, then begin to organize a resistance."

"Like the Rebel Alliance."

"Go ahead, have your fun, but I'm serious."

"Well, you know how crazy this all sounds, don't you, Royce? The whole idea of organizing a resistance to an alien invasion from an RV is just bonkers."

"Of course it is."

"Besides, we don't know the first thing about organizing a resistance."

"Not a thing."

"And who's gonna listen to us anyway?"

"Maybe no one."

"But you want to try anyway."

"I do. I mean, what have we got to lose? I'm not going back to selling stocks, and you're not going back to selling real estate, and we can't just sit here rocking in these chairs for the rest of our lives. We're too young for that."

"Speak for yourself. I *like* rocking in these chairs."

"Sure, for now, but we both know it's gonna get old before too long. So why not do something useful with our lives? We're both good at persuading people, and we both know how to network and build trust. So let's make a beginning. If nothing else, we can harass the Phants into regretting they ever came here. Nip at their heels, annoy hell out of them, cause trouble at every turn...."

"We *are* good at causing trouble."

"Right? And if we get organized now, while the Phants are still busy ignoring us, then we can be ready to exploit any weaknesses we may find down the road."

"If they *have* any weaknesses."

Royce shrugged. "Only time will tell. But if they *do*, it's scientists we'll need to recruit most of all."

"Why scientists?"

"To set up a...a brain trust of sorts."

"A what?"

"A group of experts from a wide range of fields who can learn to read and understand Phant. Scientists, engineers, physicists, mathematicians, biologists, and the like. Because if we ever *do* manage to smuggle out meaningful data, we're going to need people on the outside who can read and comprehend it."

"And you want to do all this without the Phants knowing what we're up to?"

"Well, they're not exactly engaged with us at the moment, are they?" Royce pointed out. "They're hidden away in their domes thinking their sublime thoughts. From what I can tell, they've shown no interest in us whatsoever."

"That's true."

"Which means we have a free hand for the time being. We should take advantage of it and start recruiting people to the cause. Because if we ever do manage to steal their secrets and get a handle on their technology, then it's only a matter of time until we take them down."

Aubrey laughed. "You make it sound so easy."

"Not easy, but *possible.* If we can disrupt those domes of theirs, we have a fighting chance of kicking them off this planet."

Aubrey rocked in silence for a time.

Royce eventually spoke into the silence. "So, what do you think?"

Aubrey looked at him with a flat expression. "I think you're batshit crazy is what I think. But I'm tempted anyway, probably because I'm batshit crazy too."

Royce took her hands in his. "Is that a yes? I think it's a yes."

"Wow, you really are a recruiter." Aubrey let the silence stretch a little longer. "But yes. I'm with you."

"Really?"

"Really. Like you said, we can't just sit around here doing nothing for the rest of our lives while the world goes to hell in a handbasket. At least your plan involves traveling around the country in our RV, and I like the sound of that."

"Well, what do you know? My first recruit!" Royce leaned over and kissed her with such gusto she nearly fell off her rocker.

"You'd better not kiss all your new recruits that way, mister."

"Only you. Only my first."

"Then, God help me, I'm in."

Royce literally cheered, jumping up from his rocker with such enthusiasm that it kept rocking on its own.

"Now all we need is a slogan or a...a rallying cry or something for our new resistance movement. Something like...'Kick the Bastards Out.' No, that's stupid—sounds like we're talking about Congress."

Aubrey thought for a moment. "How about 'Earth or Bust'?"

"Hey, not bad! I like it! We could make it into a bumper sticker and put it on the back of our RV."

Aubrey got up too and started pacing around the deck, looking more enthused than she had in weeks. "You do realize this is insane, don't you?"

Royce laughed. "Of course! But here's the thing, Aubrey. *They* have somewhere else to go. *We* don't. That means we'll fight harder than they will. And we'll never give up. Not even if it takes a lifetime, or several lifetimes."

Aubrey laughed. "Let's just commit to one lifetime for now, what do you say?"

"I say Earth or Bust, baby—Earth or Bust!"

The End

The trilogy continues in Book 2: The Occupation

For reasons unknown even to himself, Robert Charlton loves to read and write about end-of-the-world scenarios and cataclysmic events that he would never in a million years want to experience for himself. The actual Robert lives peacefully in Boulder, Colorado and loves to hike and travel the world with his wife. Following the "Write What You Fear" school of thought, he has depicted a financial collapse in this novel that has no bearing whatsoever on the real world (he hopes). He begs you not to sell your index funds for gold coins and mattress money. To learn more about this fascinating study in contradictions, visit www.wherewebe.com.

Made in United States
Troutdale, OR
07/06/2024